False Flag

The Union Chronicles - Book 3

Abraham L. Thornton

©Abraham Thornton 2014. Except as provided by the Copyright Act no part of this publication may be reproduced, stored in a retrieval system or transmitted in any form or by any means without the prior written permission of the author.

Acknowledgements

As always, my first thanks goes to my lovely wife, Stacee. She puts up with the time I spend sequestered in my office, in addition to all of the hours I put in at my day job and my side gig as a firearms instructor. And once again, my thanks also goes out to my sister, Hailey, for her editorial input.

Thanks also goes yet again to the friends and family who have encouraged this little hobby of mine. You know who you are.

Finally, thanks to you, dear reader, for taking the time to support an amateur. Self-publishing has removed the roadblocks that separate content-producers from content-consumers, but this comes at a price: a lot of the material out there just isn't that good. Thanks for taking a chance on an unknown guy with a laptop, an internet connection, and a tale to tell. I hope you've enjoyed *The Union Chronicles* as much as I have.

Prologue

After weeks in space, all Roland Kendrick wanted to do was get his feet back on solid ground, and at this point, it didn't matter much to him where. He wasn't going home — after disappearing from his job what seemed like forever ago, showing back up at the precinct probably wasn't an option.

It seemed like forever, but how long had it actually been? Five months, maybe six? Was that all? Kendrick sipped his coffee and frowned. Six months was still too long. He would have been evicted from his apartment already, his meager personal belongings sold in order to pay his outstanding rent. He'd put in for a week's sick time when everything went down, but that had long since run its course, and the department had no way to get ahold of him, because he'd left his tablet and commlink in his apartment.

Along with the body of Sean Matroos, Kendrick reminded himself once again. He didn't really need reminded; the visage of his friend sitting at Kendrick's kitchen table, throat slit, blood pooling on the kitchen floor, had disturbed his sleep every night since he'd found the body.

2   *The Union Chronicles*

Strangely enough, the dead body in the kitchen was probably the least of Kendrick's problems. He was sure that had been cleaned up by the people who did it in the first place. Naval Intelligence Officer Matroos was almost certainly now listed as the unfortunate victim of a "training accident" in the official records, and the kitchen had no doubt been scrubbed clean by the time the landlord came to collect Kendrick's belongings.

The oddity of it all struck him. The murder, intrigue, gunfights, getting shot and nearly dying in a hotel bathroom, hijacking a Union naval vessel – now that it was all over, the fallout he was dealing with was so··· mundane. Certainly, the problems were real – he was jobless and homeless, after all, but after what he'd been through, the aftermath was annoyingly anticlimactic. Maybe that's why the action movies always ended while the wreckage was still smoldering···

An announcement over the orbital station's public address system snapped him back to the present. His starliner was boarding; in a few hours he would be cruising toward the Neirin system and a half-brother he hadn't seen in more than a decade. Wallis was nearly fifteen years Roland's junior – the product of his father's second marriage – and he'd left Teorann at eighteen to find his own way in the world. He had shown up ten years ago to attend their father's funeral, and the impression Roland had gotten was one of a brilliant but introverted eccentric. Roland hadn't even thought about tracking his brother down, and had been surprised when he had received a comm message from the younger man a few weeks ago, asking him to visit, if he had the time. *All I've got now is*

False Flag   3

time, Roland remembered thinking to himself as he composed the message telling Wallis that he would be there in a week or two.

As he headed toward his starliner's mooring, Kendrick noticed several uniformed Planetary Union Marshal's Service deputies at the gangway. They had set up a portable facial recognition scanner, and were using it to inspect every passenger boarding the vessel. Such a sight would be commonplace within the Union's borders — the facial recognition scanners were everywhere — but putting one up at the gate in a station outside of the Union was a bold move.

It also made Kendrick extremely nervous. Technically, he'd never been identified as a criminal, and Vice Marshal Delmont had guaranteed that his record would remain unblemished, but walking through the scanner onto the gangway would put that to the test.

Fuck it, Kendrick said to himself as he tossed the empty coffee cup into a receptacle and headed through the scanner onto the ship's gangway. His fears that an alarm would sound and he'd be hauled off to some desolate prison planet were unnecessary; he made his way through the scanner and aboard the ship without incident. The starliner was massive: Neirin was a major hub for tech development, and travel to and from the system was always busy. It was one of the only things Kendrick knew about the system; he'd never been there, and he wasn't particularly interested in tech developments. Wallis, however, was a brilliant physicist and communications engineer, which made the small system ideal for him.

Although it was massive, the starliner was showing its age. The fixtures and fittings looked dated, and the air had a stale, processed quality to it that Kendrick found slightly reminiscent of his tour of duty on the *UPN Kimball* more than three decades ago. No doubt this vessel was at least as aged as the old naval ship - and likely even older.

After boarding, Kendrick found a porter on the main deck. "What's with the goon squad at the gangway?" he asked, nodding toward the embarkation door.

The porter shrugged. "Word going around is that they're looking for political dissidents. Apparently there's quite a bit of separatist sentiment brewing in a few border systems, and they're worried about outside mercs and rabble-rousers coming in to stir the pot."

"You don't seem particularly concerned."

"Because it's probably bullshit," the porter replied. "They've got nothing better to do, so they hassle us. God forbid a Union government employee would get laid off and have to get a real job."

Kendrick laughed politely, and then made his way to his cramped cabin and settled in. It was a two week voyage to Neirin, and he figured he might as well make himself as comfortable as possible. In pursuit of that end, he raided the small minibar for a bottle of cheap whiskey and collapsed into the cabin's lone chair. Soon he was fast asleep.

***

It was close to midnight local time when Kendrick walked out of the shuttle terminal and onto the bustling streets of Luka, Neirin's most populous city. The summer air was sticky with humidity, and there were indications that a rainstorm had passed through recently, although

False Flag 5

the skies appeared to be clear.

The street Kendrick found himself on reminded him of his home city of Cyfalaf. Carbon composite skyscrapers stretched into the black night sky, and garish signs advertised bars, dance clubs, and restaurants. Even at this late hour, the sidewalks were crowded with pedestrians, and cars sped by on the maglev roadway.

Kendrick hailed a cab at a roadside terminal and fed the address of his brother's apartment building into the dash-mounted keypad. Moments later, the cab sped off towards its destination. Roland pulled his tablet from his pocket and keyed in Wallis Aeron's comm address, but received no answer.

Ten minutes later, the cab pulled up to an upscale apartment building. Kendrick paid the fare, got out, and went to the building's door. Locked. There was a terminal next to the door, which Kendrick assumed would allow him to call his brother to let him in. He keyed in the appropriate commands, but there was no response. Kendrick was checking the locking mechanism on the door, trying to figure out if there was a way to get past it, when a voice called out from behind him.

"Police! Down on your knees!"

Kendrick wanted to explain that he was there to visit his brother. He wanted to explain that he was a police officer, or at least used to be. Unfortunately, he could do none of those things. Apparently, the officer behind him had decided not to wait for compliance, and had instead hit him with an immobilizer. Now, not only could he not explain, but he couldn't even comply with the order – he was frozen in place. The device, which had been fired from a launcher slung under the responding officer's autorifle, attached itself to his back, and was using targeted high-frequency electronic pulses to short-circuit his nervous system. The device allowed his autonomic system to function, meaning he could still breathe and see, and his heart was still pumping, but all higher-order actions were gone. As Kendrick stood there, immobilized, the officer, clad in black tactical response gear, including a helmet that completely obscured his (or her) face, slipped electronic restraints onto his wrists. He then keyed something into his wrist-mounted tablet and Kendrick once again found himself able to move, although his joints were stiff, and he was still unable to speak.

He was led to a waiting cruiser at the curb. Once he was seated in the car, the immobilizer again rendered him motionless.

This was no surprise to Kendrick – he'd used similar equipment when he was a patrol officer, and had seen it used countless times when tactical teams executed warrants for his cases. He'd even been exposed to it during training. All cadets had been subjected to every non-lethal pacification tool at their disposal, so that they would have a better understanding of how they would affect suspects. In those days, the electronics had been a little less focused, and Kendrick had actually shit himself the first time he'd been hit with one. The programming had quickly been modified to allow the suspect to maintain control of their more base biological functions.

After placing Kendrick in the vehicle, the officer returned to the apartment building. The officer used his ident card to override the lock, and he and his partner went inside. They were gone for what seemed like hours, although Kendrick knew it wasn't – by the time they returned to the street, it was still dark – morning was still a few hours away.

Kendrick sat in immobilized silence while the two officers stood near the front door. Given the angle at

False Flag 7

which the vehicle was parked, and the fact that Kendrick couldn't turn his head, he could only see them out of his peripheral vision, and as they moved about, they would occasionally disappear from view completely. It was an unbelievably unnerving experience.

As he sat in the car, he wondered what was going on. He hadn't been at the door long enough for a nervous tenant to have called the cops on him, which meant that they had been headed to the building before Kendrick even showed up. *Talk about being in the wrong place at the wrong time*, Kendrick mused to himself. Eventually, the officers returned to the vehicle and pulled away from the house.

***

"Your employer thought you were dead. More than two decades of service, then you call in sick and disappear into the void."

The lieutenant, a mousy-looking man named Jennings, dropped a tablet on the table in front of Kendrick, which at a glance revealed the former detective's employment jacket, including a notation that he had failed to report for duty. His discharge was listed as "voluntary termination," the designation used when someone walked off the job without cause or notice. It was a depressing, and completely inadequate, closing remark both for Kendrick's career and for the real explanation behind his disappearance, but there was nothing to be done about it at this point.

The immobilizer had been removed when Kendrick had been dropped off in the interview room, and the shackles had been taken off when his Cyfalaf PD ident card had been presented. He was now more or less comfortable,

8   *The Union Chronicles*

but although he wasn't shackled like a suspect, it was obvious that he was not being allowed to leave just yet, either.

Kendrick moved his gaze from the tablet screen to the lieutenant. The man was a decade his junior, with a bearing that pegged him as a bureaucrat rather than a beat cop turned administrator. His piece said, Jennings gazed at Kendrick, arms crossed.

"I'm sorry; I didn't hear a question," Kendrick said. "Were you looking for a response?"

The former detective's relaxed response seemed to irritate the lieutenant, something that Kendrick had anticipated, and now relished with a sense of irony. He had been on the other side of the table hundreds of times, and now he wondered how often he had been the asshole, instead of the guy in his current place.

"As a matter of fact, I'd like to know where you were," Jennings replied haughtily. "A man with your service record doesn't just up and disappear without some kind of explanation."

"I went out for a joyride," Kendrick replied nonchalantly. "Hadn't been off-world for quite a while, and decided it had been long enough." After a pause, he continued, "You know, when I was in the Navy, I was told that space gets in your blood, and that every man who has been into the black will return. I guess it just took longer for me than most people." Kendrick decided that he'd done enough explaining. "So, are you going to tell me what in the hell is going on? Why am I being detained?"

Jennings sneered. "Why don't you tell me? After all, you were there before we were." The lieutenant was clearly getting frustrated by Kendrick's lack of fear. Most people, when tossed into an interrogation room, would do anything to get out. Kendrick, however, seemed right at

False Flag   9

home, which was in fact the case.

"It's like I told the officer earlier," Kendrick responded, "I went to visit my brother, and when I got there, the door was locked. I was trying to figure out how to get in, and then your guy popped me."

"I'm not buying it," Jennings said, regaining his composure. "You disappear six months ago, go completely dark, and then you just happen to show up at your half-brother's house at the same time as he goes missing?"

"Wallis is missing?" Kendrick asked with genuine shock.

"As if you didn't know," Jennings said. "Why don't you just tell me where he is?"

"How in the hell would I know?" Kendrick asked. "Your officers found me locked *out* of his apartment building, remember? You're really telling me that he's missing?"

Kendrick could see the conflict in Jennings' eyes. Sure, he could be lying, but if he wasn't, then the lieutenant was wasting precious time on a dead end. Kendrick knew the feeling well, but given the lieutenant's attitude, he couldn't feel sorry for the smug bastard.

"So you really expect me to believe that all of this is just a bizarre coincidence?" Jennings said.

"What can I say? Shit happens," Kendrick replied with a shrug. "If you'd seen half of what I've seen, nothing in the Universe would surprise you."

"So how'd you spend the last six weeks? Recruiting a crew to snatch your brother?"

Kendrick had had enough of being railroaded. "I was in Fuckyouistan. You don't have shit on me." With that, he stood up.

"You aren't going anywhere," Jennings said threateningly.

"Then arrest me," Kendrick shot back. It was a

dangerous play. Jennings could hold him illegally – it happened all the time. But Kendrick figured Jennings for the sort who would play it straight. He was an asshole, but he was an ambitious asshole, and there just wasn't much to gain here. It was obvious that Kendrick wasn't responsible for his brother's disappearance, and Jennings knew nothing would stick. If nothing else, the cab company's data footage from the taxi he'd taken to Wallis' apartment building would show that he had arrived after the call came in.

It was the right play. "Mr. Kendrick, I'm going to release you," Jennings said in an attempt to save face, "but I'll need you to remain on-planet in the event that I need to bring you back in for further questions."

"Whatever," Kendrick replied. "If you need me, I'll be at Wallis' place, trying to figure out what happened. You might want to give it a try yourself."

***

The apartment hadn't even been barricaded when Kendrick returned. It didn't really matter in any case; there was nothing there to disrupt. Kendrick had gone through the entire apartment and had found nothing of interest. The only thing out of place was the door to the den, which had apparently been locked and secured. It appeared that the responding officers had used a laser torch to get through the door, which now swung loosely on its hinges, a section missing where the lock had been reduced to slag. The room itself was full of gear that Kendrick couldn't even name, let alone operate, but it was devoid of clues. Kendrick couldn't figure it out: he assumed that Wallis had barricaded himself in this room, but it had still been sealed when the cops got there, and Wallis was gone. *How the*

False Flag   11

hell did he get out? And where did he go? Kendrick asked himself.

"Roland?" The sound of his name nearly made Kendrick jump out of his skin. Out of instinct, his hand went to his hip, reaching for a weapon that wasn't there. Finding the place where a Gauss pistol used to sit empty, he turned to face the voice unarmed. A haggard looking Wallis Aeron was in the doorway to the den.

"Wallis? What the hell? Where have you been?" Kendrick was even more confused now than he had been when he thought his brother had disappeared from a locked room.

"I was in my panic room," Aeron said, as though that was all the explanation that was needed. "But what are you doing here?"

"You invited me, remember?" Kendrick replied.

"Oh, right," Wallis said. "Has it been two weeks already?"

"No, Wallis; it's been three. It took longer than I thought to get here."

"Sorry, I guess I lost track of time. Working on something big."

Kendrick wanted to ask what it was, and if it may have something to do with the attempted break-in, but there was a more pressing issue. "Why didn't you come out when the cops were here?"

"As soon as I called them, the guys trying to break in bugged out," Aeron replied. "Someone tipped them off, which means I can't trust the cops. I probably can't trust anyone, really."

"Then why did you come out for me?"

Aeron paused for a moment. "Good point," he finally responded. "Perhaps I should have thought this through a little more. I assumed that our genetic relationship would

12   *The Union Chronicles*

come into play, but I'm not exactly sure why."

"Wallis?"

"Yes, Roland?"

"You are fucking weird."

"I've been told that, but I'm not clear as to why you felt that profanity was necessary to express your incredulousness."

***

"So let me get this straight," Kendrick said an hour later, sitting in Aeron's workroom, "You've figured out a way to communicate instantaneously between any two points in the Universe?"

"More than just communicate – I can transfer any digital data. Anything your commlink or tablet can transmit, I can send from here to anywhere else like it was in the next room. Better, actually, since there are no bandwidth concerns."

"And naturally, there are people who would like to steal that kind of tech."

"Naturally."

"How bad is this, potentially?" Kendrick was getting an uneasy feeling. "Who would be after this?"

"Foreign governments, megacorps – our government. There's a pretty big list, really. It's revolutionary, and potentially priceless."

"And to get it, all you have to do is take it from a weirdo holed up by himself in an apartment."

"I've been very careful about secrecy and security," Aeron retorted, for the first time expressing something approaching human emotion.

"Clearly not careful enough," Kendrick shot back. "So what do we do?"

False Flag   13

"Well, I have two prototype units and my files. We need to get them somewhere safe."

"I don't think we should risk trying to get off-planet until we've got some help. If powerful people are involved, getting spaceside without getting popped will be nearly impossible. We need some outside assistance." Kendrick smiled. "Fortunately, I know some people who have experience with this kind of thing."

The Union Chronicles

Chapter One

Volya Frye came out of the last bend struggling for breath. His legs were screaming for more oxygen, but the combined efforts of his respiratory and circulatory systems couldn't seem to get it there fast enough. In the distance, a short kilometer and a half away, he could see his house through the gap that the path he was on cut through the treeline.

"Don't tell me you're worn out already," his wife taunted from beside him.

Frye wanted to offer a witty retort, but that would have been suicide. Any respiratory effort not directed at his primary goal of staying upright was out of the question. Instead, he simply did his best to keep up.

It wasn't fair, he told himself. Alainn had been in much better physical shape when they met, and while he'd made great strides during the six months that they'd been home, he just wasn't there yet. Nevertheless, completing a ten-kilometer run would have been unthinkable only a few months ago, and now it was survivable.

Even though the run had been grueling, he relished both the exercise and the opportunity to be outside. Preparations were currently underway in orbit for their ship, the *Seguir*, to depart. For a few weeks, he and Alainn would be confined to the small craft while they made their way to Neirin and their friend Roland Kendrick. While the bridge of a ship would always be like a second home to him, he was getting used to being able to spend time outdoors, and the thought of a lengthy voyage left him conflicted. With the house in sight, Frye felt a second wind kick in, and he pushed himself a little harder, determined to finish strong. Next to him, his wife noticed the small change in pace. Smiling, she easily matched it, sticking by his side on the dirt trail.

Home, Frye thought to himself as he pushed forward. It was still a strange concept – for nearly his entire adult life, his domicile had been whatever ship he was working on or in command of. He had lived on his parents' farm into his early twenties, only leaving it after his their untimely deaths. Since then, he had been more or less a nomad, living and working on several interstellar craft. The house he had bought with Alainn shortly after their wedding was the first planetside home he had ever called his own.

The house itself was beautiful, but it was the location that had him sold. Located at the edge of Lake Mairsile, the house was situated on nearly 200 hectares of undeveloped forest – other than the house and gardens, the rough running path that they were currently on was the most man-made thing on it.

Alainn had paid for it all, of course; when he had met her he was in possession of nothing more than the shirt on his back, and even that had technically been stolen. She, on the other hand, was wealthy in her own right, and the daughter of a wealthy corporate security specialist. Yet their income disparity was never an issue; as soon as they

False Flag 17

had become husband and wife, everything she owned had become his, and nothing else had ever been said on the matter. It was yet one more thing that made her an amazing woman - and him the luckiest man in the Universe, at least by his own estimate.

Frye's reverie took his mind off of his burning lungs, and before he knew it, the house was a hundred meters in front of him. He slowed to a walk, sweat pouring off of his scalp, his t-shirt soaked.

He went through the deck door to the bedroom, grabbing the towel he had left on the bed and wiping the sweat from his hair and brow. Alainn followed him in and headed straight for the bathroom. A moment later he heard the shower turn on.

Frye was about to follow her in when a chime from the house's central computer indicated an incoming call. Damn, Frye thought to himself, grabbing his commlink off of the nightstand and slipping it into his ear.

"Volya," he answered.

"Hey, brother," a familiar voice on the other end responded, "got a second?"

Frye grinned. He didn't feel like telling his former navigator why it wasn't an ideal time.

"Sure, Wolf; what's up?"

***

Twenty-five thousand kilometers above Volya Frye, Wolfgang Hartmann was overseeing the conversion of Frye's ship, the *Veritas*, from a run-of-the-mill hydrogen fusion-powered, VASIMIR-propelled interstellar vessel to the same Casimir powered system that ran the *Seguir*.

The Union Chronicles

"Is everything going OK with the conversion?" Frye asked.

"There was an issue fabricating the silver plates for the generator, but we're back on track. I'm actually calling to let you know we'll be testing the drive this afternoon. If all goes well, we'll be ready to depart a day or two after that."

"That's good news. What happened with the plates?"

"They were fabbed, but the final scan showed some impurities," Hartmann replied. "I'm not sure of the details, but the manufacturer had to re-run them. It was a minor bump in the road; we'll still be ready on time."

"OK, Wolf. Is that all? Not having second thoughts about heading back into the fray, are you?"

"We're getting paid, right?"

Frye smiled, although he knew his friend couldn't see it. "Yeah, Roland says his brother is loaded. He's got a half-dozen tech patents and makes a small fortune in royalties. Even better – he doesn't care about the money. He lives in a small apartment and keeps to himself."

"A true eccentric," Hartmann mused. "I'll bet he's a pain in the ass."

"For what he's offering, it'll be worth it. Glad to see that the prospect of cold, hard cash has helped you overcome your 'I'm never going back to the Union' vow."

The remark was delivered off-hand, but to Hartmann, it was like a knife twisting in a wound he knew would never quite heal. Frye took note of the silence at the other end of the commlink. "I'm sorry, Wolf; I didn't mean to –"

Before Frye could finish, however, Hartmann cut him

False Flag   19

off. "No, you're right, Volya. You risked your life to bring our enemies to justice, and I chickened out. It's something I'll have to live with for the rest of my life."

There was another pause. "Look, Wolf, I understand why you did what you did. You had a shot at freedom, and you took it. I don't blame you. In fact, if you had been with us, you wouldn't have been able to take care of Imogen when she needed you. Besides, with you around, I'd have never had a shot with Alainn."

"Yeah, given the choice between the two of us, the ladies will pick me every time," Hartmann said good-naturedly, quickly returning to his normal, gruff self.

Frye decided to let Hartmann have his delusion and changed the subject. "We're good on the pilot, right?"

"Yeah," Hartmann replied. "I've got a freelancer who has done some work for Regis. He's not as good as you, but he comes highly recommended."

"He understands the risks?" Frye asked.

"Oh, he understands," Hartmann replied, "And he can't wait to ship out."

This gave Frye some pause. People who were eager to throw themselves into the fray tended to be less than stable.

Hartmann picked up on his friend's hesitation. "Don't worry, Volya; he's solid. I'm sure he'll be happy to explain his enthusiasm when you meet him."

"Can he do anything other than fly?"

"He's been working with Riker nonstop since I found him. Crash course – same as you and I got."

"Tell Riker whatever they're doing, double it for the

next couple of days until we sail."

"Damn, Volya, when did you become such a hardass?"

"When people started trying to kill me on a regular basis."

***

Cosmocor specialized in advanced propulsion systems, and as a result, they operated a massive and extremely advanced orbital station some twenty-five thousand kilometers over Volya and Alainn's home planet. The station included moorings for a dozen vessels, and one of those slots was currently occupied by the *Seguir*. The *Veritas* was currently undergoing a retrofit in the large hangar bay five floors down. Frye had gone down to see the progress, and had been overwhelmed by the facility.

Due to the stresses caused by lifting an object from a planetary surface into space, interstellar craft were always constructed in orbit, and in Frye's extensive experience, none were designed for atmospheric operation. A craft large enough to comfortably travel between star systems was simply too massive to use as a transport to a planetary surface. For one thing, the ion propulsion systems used in interstellar travel did not generate enough instantaneous thrust to reach escape velocity, meaning a secondary propulsion system would be required. Furthermore, the amount of fuel required for a vessel of that size to land and take off would be cost-prohibitive. Interstellar craft were made to travel between stars, and short-range shuttles provided the terrestrial connection. It was as simple as that.

As a result, interstellar craft were assembled in specially-designed moorings by shipbuilders wearing EVA

False Flag   21

suits and by robots. A tremendous amount of engineering had gone into making it possible to conduct shipbuilding activities in the vacuum of space.

Cosmocor had taken a different approach. At great initial expense, they had completely enclosed two construction docks at the far southern axis of the station. The docks were kept at standard temperature and pressure, so no suits were required. Engineers and technicians could work alongside their robotic counterparts in simple coveralls. The investment had been considerable – staggering, really, but there were no issues with EVA-induced fatigue, meaning that the shipbuilding crews could work twice as many hours in a day, and since the surroundings were far more conducive to the task at hand, ships could be constructed in significantly less time.

"If you're looking at the big picture, the payback is actually a no-brainer," Regis Quinn said as he concluded the explanation to a clearly overwhelmed Volya Frye. The Cosmocor CEO had personally taken the pilot on a tour of the facility so that he could see the progress that was being made on the *Veritas*.

It may have been a no-brainer to Quinn, but Frye could certainly understand why no one else had attempted it. It was by far the most ambitious building Frye had ever seen: the main floor was easily big enough to house two medium-sized starcraft: the *Veritas* was currently the only ship in the hangar, and it was dwarfed completely by its surroundings.

In another fit of brilliance, the gravity in the hangar was designed to be scalable. While the rest of the station was maintained at standard gravity, by using the same adjustable gravity-well technology that propelled the *Seguir* and the *Marco Polo*, the gravity in the hangar could be set anywhere from zero-g to standard. Currently, the gravity was off, and as Frye watched, a pair of technicians effortlessly guided components of the new drive system into place aboard Frye's vessel using nothing more than their bare hands and the compressed air jets on their belt-mounted booster packs. Frye marveled at the sight of people floating in such a massive zero-g environment without the need of a pressure suit.

"Wolf tells me the fabricator screwed up the capacitor plates," Frye said to Quinn, the bulk of his attention still on the equipment maneuvers taking place in the hangar. He and Regis were wearing electromag shoes, which allowed them to stand fixed to the hangar's floor while the gravity was off.

"It happens," Quinn replied. "A less credible manufacturer would have shipped them as-is, and there would probably have never been a problem. These guys found a very minor flaw in the plates during a post-fabrication scan and did the right thing. Everyone makes mistakes, Volya – the key is finding people who will admit when they have done so and attempt to correct it. Those are the people you hang on to."

Probably. That was a hell of a qualifier when discussing the primary power system aboard a vessel designed to travel the billions of kilometers between star systems, and all the more so considering that this would be one of less than a dozen known vessels currently capable of traversing the interstellar void. Frye decided that he wouldn't press the issue. After all, Regis was right about mistakes – Frye himself had made more than his fair share. Instead, he watched the rest of the installation procedure in silence.

The volume of the hangar was truly staggering. The

False Flag 23

Veritas wasn't a large vessel; as a courier craft, it was designed to accommodate a crew of two — a pilot and a navigator/engineer. The *Marco Polo*, Cosmocor's prototype zero point vessel, had been assembled in this bay, and it was nearly three times the size of the *Veritas*.

Given the cost of the facility, Frye was standing in some of the most valuable real estate in the galaxy, and it was currently being occupied by his ship. The engineers and technicians doing the work were some of the best alive, and none of the work was costing Frye a penny — Regis had insisted that the retrofit would be a wedding present. Frye had no idea what the cost was, but he knew it was millions of dollars, at least. He also knew that to Alainn's uncle, the cost was trivial. Once again, he found himself awed not only by the technological marvel he was standing in, but by the man standing next to him who had built it all.

A tone in his ear interrupted Frye's thoughts. Alainn was calling.

"We're about an hour from pre-flight," Alainn said as soon as Frye had answered, "and Wolfie is here with the new kid."

"OK, I think we're done here," Frye responded. "Where should I meet you?"

"I had Stewart take them to the briefing room on the flight deck," Alainn answered. "I'm on my way over there now."

"I'll be right up," Frye replied before terminating the connection. Turning to Quinn, he held out his hand. "Once again, Regis, I can't begin to express how much I appreciate what you've done for us."

24   *The Union Chronicles*

Quinn, who was only slightly taller, but significantly more broad-shouldered than Frye, grasped the offered hand in his own, then pulled Frye in and clapped him on the back with his other arm. "You're family," he said genuinely. "Good luck and safe travels."

"Thank you," Frye replied, and then turned to leave the hangar.

"Volya?"

"Yes?"

"Take care of my niece."

"Yes, sir. Just so you know, though, it usually goes the other way 'round."

***

The briefing room, like every room aboard the station, was well-appointed, spacious, and comfortable. During previous trips to the station, Frye had met with Quinn in the executive conference room, which was smaller than the room he currently found himself in, although more luxuriously furnished. The briefing room, while comfortable, was clearly designed with functionality, rather than elegance, in mind. It consisted of six rows of forward-facing titanium-alloy tables and plush captain's chairs. At the front of the room was a lectern, and a large viewscreen took up the majority of the front wall. A beverage station was along the back wall which served water, coffee, tea, and soft drinks from the station's stores.

Hartmann was seated at one of the front tables, and he rose to greet his friend when the door opened.

"Volya! About time, you sonofabitch!" He crossed the

False Flag 25

front of the room and slapped his friend and former captain on the back. "Here, I want to introduce you to Halwyn Pryce."

Frye looked over to where Hartmann had been sitting. In the next seat over was a kid that Frye figured couldn't be a day over twenty-five. The young man stood up hesitantly and made his way around the table.

In the moments it took for the young man to make his way over, Frye gave him a quick appraisal. He was of medium height and skinny, with shaggy, dirty blonde hair. He was wearing cargo pants and a t-shirt; the default uniform of pilots everywhere.

Halwyn extended his hand as he approached. "It's a pleasure to meet you, sir. Mr. Hartmann has told me a lot about you."

Frye took the offered hand, and was pleased with the young man's firm grip. "What exactly has he told you?"

"That you're one of the best pilots in the galaxy," Halwyn replied. "And that you're a nice guy, but mistaking that for weakness would be a magnificent error."

Frye looked over at Hartmann. "'Magnificent error?' Doesn't sound like you."

Hartmann grinned. "I'm working on my vocabulary. Tryin'a sound cultured'n shit."

At this, Alainn, who had been leaning quietly up against the back wall, drinking coffee, let out a snort. "Stick with the misanthropic bastard act, Wolfie. It suits you better."

"Are you going to let her talk to me like that?" Hartmann addressed the question to Frye with mock offense.

"I let her do whatever she wants," Frye replied. "Crossing her would be a 'magnificent error'."

Halwyn seemed lost in the banter, and Frye decided to shift the attention to business matters. "Regis tells me that the *Veritas* should be ready in a few hours."

"Sounds about right," Hartmann concurred, also moving on to the business at hand. "Once the final testing is done, we'll be ready to head out."

"Good." Frye then turned back to Halwyn. "How's it going with Commander Riker?"

The young pilot grimaced involuntarily. "I don't think I've ever been this sore, or thrown up this much."

"The life of a cockpit jockey doesn't really lend itself to physical activity." Frye replied. "Have you learned anything?"

"Yes, sir – I just hope that none of it is necessary."

"That makes two of us," Frye replied. If everything goes well, your skills as a pilot will be all that is required. How long have you been flying?"

"My father is an interstellar freighter pilot," Halwyn answered. "My mother died when I was young, and we have no other family, so I was forced to go with him. I literally cut my teeth on a ship's bridge, and could conduct port maneuvers before most people learn how to drive." The young pilot's visage had shifted from deferential to confident as he discussed flying – a shift that Frye interpreted as genuine confidence, and not false bravado.

"And you've been flying with your father this whole time?"

False Flag   27

"Yes, sir. We do a lot of mining runs throughout this part of the galaxy."

"So why are you leaving your father's employ?"

Halwyn hesitated before answering. "Have you ever worked for your father, Mr. Frye?"

Frye nodded. "I worked the family farm when I was younger."

"Then you know what it's like to want to strike out on your own," the young pilot said. "I have no problem with my dad, but it's time for me to make my own way in the world."

Again, Frye nodded. He understood the desire completely. He had stayed on the family farm much longer than he wanted to. "Fair enough," he responded. "You're confident that the modified systems on the *Veritas* won't be a problem?"

"I think I'll be fine. I've spent a few dozen hours in the holosim, and it doesn't feel much different from a normal ship."

"It isn't," Frye concurred. "I didn't even get any simulator time before I tried it, and I lived to tell about it."

"And from what I hear, it's a hell of a story to tell," Halwyn replied, with admiration in his voice. "Stealing a starship from Union custody has to be one of the ballsiest things I've ever heard of. You've gotta have big brass ones." Halwyn's face suddenly reddened, and he turned sheepishly to Alainn. "Pardon the language, ma'am," he said quickly.

Alainn smiled. "How sweet of you." Then she raised an

eyebrow. "Naïve as shit, but sweet."

Hartmann let out a chuckle, and Frye shook his head and rolled his eyes. Halwyn turned an even brighter shade of red, and for a moment it looked like he might bolt out of the room, never to return.

"I'm just giving you a hard time," Alainn said. "It really is a nice gesture, and not one that I'm used to, given the shady company I keep." Turning to Frye, she continued. "Is there anything we need to go over, or was this just a meet and greet to see if we could get the kid to run away?"

"How much have you told him?" Frye asked Hartmann.

"Just that we were headed to the Union to pick someone up," Hartmann replied. "I figured I'd let you do the explaining."

"Fair enough," Frye said. A few minutes' worth of discussion wasn't going to be enough to trust the young man completely, but Hartmann was satisfied, and he'd learned long ago to trust his former navigator's instincts.

Frye pulled his tablet comp from a pocket in his flight suit and synced it to the large viewscreen on the briefing room wall.

"A week ago, I was contacted by a man named Roland Kendrick, whom Alainn and I met several months ago while taking care of some... unfinished business in the Union," Frye began. "When I say contacted, I mean that he initiated a voice comm with me from within the Planetary Union, at a distance of approximately eight parsecs." To emphasize the point, Frye pulled up a chart on the viewscreen which showed the relative positions of

False Flag   29

Neirin and Saiorse.

"That's impossible," Halwyn interjected.

"Call it what you want, but it's reality," Frye responded. "A year ago, it was common knowledge that a Casimir-powered ship was impossible. A thousand years ago, we were sure that subspace tunneling was a fantasy. Hell, as far as I know, the tech runs on witchcraft and the blood of virgins, but it works."

"And naturally, someone wants to steal it," Hartmann chimed in.

"Naturally," Frye replied. "This time, however, our job doesn't involve figuring out who is after the tech. We've been hired to get Kendrick and his brother, Wallis Aeron, the inventor of the communications system, off of Wallis' home planet of Neirin, out of the Union, and to safety here in Saiorse." Frye waited for someone to jump in, but the faces in front of him were silent, so he continued.

"According to Roland, six standard weeks ago, Wallis Aeron's apartment was broken into by people whom Wallis assumes were after his comm tech. Wallis was able to barricade himself inside of a safe room in his apartment and contact the authorities, but the intruders bolted before the cops arrived.

"Fortunately, and by complete coincidence, Kendrick arrived at around the same time, and was able to get his brother away from the house. They are currently holed up in Tionscal, one of a half-dozen large cities on Neirin." The image on the viewscreen zoomed in on one of Neirin's continents, highlighting the location of Tionscal. "Aeron is also in possession of the only copies of the engineering schematics for his tech.

"Our job is to make our way to Tionscal, rendezvous with Kendrick and Aeron, and get both of them, along with Aeron's data, back to Saiorse."

"Why doesn't he just go to the authorities?" Halwyn asked.

"From our experience, the authorities in the Union aren't always exactly trustworthy," Frye replied. "Wallis has reason to believe that the intruders were tipped off by someone when the cops were called, and there's no telling who is involved. We have to assume that the authorities may be involved in the theft attempt."

"What exactly will happen when we get him back here? Won't people still be after him?" Halwyn was asking all of the questions that Frye had asked of Kendrick when they first spoke.

"Unlikely," Alainn interjected. "We're a significant distance from the Union, and therefore from those who are pursuing our client. "Furthermore, it's a big Universe, and once we've left the Union, it will be nearly impossible to track us," she continued. "We travel with counterfeit paperwork, in vessels that have no official registration. Once we leave the Neirin system, finding us becomes a near statistical impossibility.

"And finally, the simplest answer is that it's not our problem. We're being hired to bring Wallis Aeron here to Saiorse. What he does when he gets here is his own issue. My guess is that my uncle will probably have a proposition for him that will include very competent security, along with a very hefty salary, but that is up to Mr. Aeron."

"Now, back to the task at hand," Frye said, trying to get things tracked back to the mission briefing, "In a few

False Flag   31

hours, Alainn and I will depart for Neirin in the *Seguir*. We will make port above Luka, Neirin's primary spaceport and Wallis Aeron's home city, shuttle to the surface, and make our way to Tionscal. There, we will rendezvous with Kendrick and Aeron, and escort the two of them to Pristav, a smaller port city on the other side of the planet.

"Halwyn, you will pilot the *Veritas* to Pristav and make port. Wolf will descend to the surface to meet up with us. From there, Wolf will take Aeron and Kendrick spaceside, and the four of you will return to Saiorse.

"Aeron will leave an encrypted copy of his schematics with Alainn and me. The two of us will return to the *Seguir* and make our way home along a different route. That way, if either one of us is compromised, the other still has an opportunity to return home with the tech. Ideally, everyone gets through and reassembles here in six weeks or so, but splitting up gives us some insurance. Any questions?"

"You said the schematics you'll have will be encrypted," Hartmann responded. "Who has the key?"

Frye smiled. "Regis. Roland transmitted it directly to him. If Alainn and I are captured, the schematics in our possession will be completely useless, and the key can't even be tortured out of us, because we won't have it. Until the data drive gets here, it's a useless hunk of silicon and graphite."

"That might be of little comfort to you," Hartmann observed wryly.

"I don't know," Alainn replied. "The encryption key could always be used as a bargaining chip to get us back, I suppose. Of course, if anyone decides that we're a good target for abduction, they may regret that choice." At this, she broke into an evil grin.

"What do you mean?" Halwyn asked.

"We had some... issues the last time we were in the Union," Frye replied. "Since then, Alainn, Wolf and I have put an emphasis on counter-abduction and escape and evasion training."

"Sounds like fun. What exactly is our cover?" the young pilot continued.

"In this case, we're going with something simple: the truth, or at least a rough approximation of it." Frye explained. "Cosmocor is supplying a courier contract to Alainn and me authorizing us to pick up a communications array and to you and Hartmann for the transport of an engineering consultant. As usual, we will be traveling under assumed identities, but the details of our trip are commonplace enough that they don't need to be altered. We will make a pit stop in Haos to obtain identity documents, and then we will continue on to Neirin."

"If there's nothing else," Alainn interjected, "We need to get going." With that, she headed up to the front of the briefing room and shook hands with Halwyn. "Good luck, and welcome to the team."

"Thank you, ma'am," the young pilot replied.

"I like him. He's polite," Alainn said, turning to Hartmann. "Try not to turn him into an asshole." From the corner of her eye, she could see Halwyn's face redden again.

"I'll miss you, too," Hartmann said with a grin. "Try to keep my friend here out of trouble."

Chapter Two

As he and Alainn headed down the gangway to board the *Seguir*, Volya Frye felt a familiar surge of adrenaline hit his system. As a pilot, departing on a voyage had always given him a rush; he loved traveling through the immeasurable expanse of space, and though he'd been happy planetside for the past few months, now that he was headed back into the black, he knew that it was where he would always belong.

The adrenaline rush was amplified by the fact that they were headed into what could become a very dangerous situation. Frye had seen first-hand the lengths that people would go to when paradigm-shifting technology, and the fortunes it offered, was discovered. And while Kendrick was a friend, and someone he'd gladly stick his neck out for, this was a paid gig – the first time he'd ever agreed to take what was effectively a mercenary job.

For her part, Alainn was undaunted. This was her life, tracking down people and desired objects, providing protection, and transporting things in and out of areas that they didn't necessarily belong. For her, it was just another day at the office. As they headed down the gangway, she checked items off on the list on her tablet, which was connected to the *Seguir's* central systems.

33

"Food stocks, oxygen, and water are full," she said absently, more to herself than her husband. Going over the checklist was mostly just habit at this point – the ship's systems were self-monitoring, and would have instantly set off an alarm if there had been anything amiss.

"Ion fuel for the short-range thrusters is at one hundred percent, and the Casimir generator is reading nominal," she continued as they crossed through the outer hull and into the *Seguir's* airlock.

"Fuel cell backups are fully charged and reading five-by-five..." Alainn's methodical pre-flight continued, but now the *Seguir* had Frye's undivided attention. The smell of silicone-based lubricants, titanium alloy, and the slightly metallic tang of filtered air wrapped around his head. The ship's cramped but clean prep room awaited him on the other side of the airlock. He crossed the few steps inside, and then opened his locker to inspect his EVA suit. Like the ship itself, the suit would have alerted him to any abnormal condition, but conducting a visual examination was like going over the pre-flight checklist – a comforting, if completely anachronistic, habit passed down from the early days of space flight. His hands ran along the folds of high-tensile nano-fabric before tucking it back into the locker.

Satisfied with his suit, Frye headed towards the small storage and maintenance area at the ship's stern. Setting his bag at his feet, he opened a cabinet against the port bulkhead. The cabinet lit up to reveal a stock of spare parts, but Frye reached his hand under one of the shelves and his index finger found a small biometric reader, which verified his DNA signature, and the shelves slid into the floor with a hydraulic hiss, revealing the *Seguir's* armory.

False Flag 35

Frye quickly verified the selection of compact autorifles, long-range rail rifles, and flak guns. Most of the small arms were always kept aboard, and ordnance had been replenished by Cosmocor dock workers the previous day. This equipment wasn't listed in the *Seguir*'s database, however, so checking it over visually was a necessity, rather than a ceremonial habit. Frye counted ammunition, checked the charge levels on the weapons' electromagnetic accelerators, and worked the action on each weapon, verifying that they were mechanically functional. Once satisfied, he raised the false-wall shelving unit and closed the storage cabinet.

The next stop was the cabin he would share with his wife. He had gotten to know the *Seguir* well over the past several months, but sharing the cramped captain's quarters with Alainn would be a first. The last time he had piloted the ship, he had avoided this cabin – at first, because in Alainn's absence, it made him feel like an interloper, and after her rescue because he didn't want to rush things.

In the cabin, he stowed his clothing and other personal effects, and then headed up to the bridge. Alainn had seated herself at the co-pilot's station, leaving the pilot's seat for Frye. He settled into the chair, swiping his hand over the panel to bring the ship's control systems to life.

The Casimir generator that powered the ship took its power from the quantum vacuum's zero point energy state, exploiting spontaneous pair production to harness virtually unlimited stores of energy. Since the energy was effectively free, the generator was left active at all times, making for a much easier startup process when initiating flight operations.

Frye brought up the *Seguir*'s heads-up holodisplay and once again verified that all systems were operating at nominal. Once finished, he brought the short-range ion thrusters online. When the magnetic containment field reached capacity, he contacted the flight control center for departure approval.

"Flight comm, this is *Seguir*, requesting cast-off acknowledgement," he said through his commlink.

"*Seguir*, this is flight command," the voice on the other side answered. "You are free to cast off moorings and depart. Godspeed and good travels."

Frye tapped a command sequence on the control panel and the mooring lines, which tethered the vessel to the station and supplied the ship with oxygen, water, and other life support systems, released from the ship's hull with a barely perceptible shudder.

With the ties to the station gone, Frye directed the *Seguir*'s short-range thruster system to inject a stream of argon gas into the magnetic containment field. The magnetic field pressurized the gas until it compressed into high temperature plasma, which was then directed through the nozzle and into the void of space. The resulting thrust pushed the *Seguir* away from the station, slowly at first, but with a constant acceleration.

Frye keyed the commlink again. "Wolf, we are underway. How are things aboard the *Veritas*?"

"Five-by-five, Volya. We're right behind you. See you in Haos." The commlink went dead.

"Navigation calculations?" Frye asked, turning his attention to his wife.

"Complete," Alainn replied.

False Flag 37

Frye killed the short-range thrusters and slowly scaled the gravity well generator up, engaging the drive that would allow long-distance travel. With the course plotted in the navcomp, Frye instructed the ship's autopilot systems to proceed to the next jump point.

There was a barely perceptible jolt as the *Seguir* began skipping across the folds in the space-time manifold that the gravity well created, and then the inertial dampener kicked in and compensated for the shift in velocity, and everything was eerily quiet and still. Barring something unexpected, the ship would not require any pilot intervention for thirty-six hours.

From a pocket on his flight suit, Frye produced a small comm chip and plugged it into the console. The prototype commlink that Roland had sent him wasn't compatible with regular models, but was easily integrated with the ship's systems. He pulled up the control interface and keyed in an address. A few moments later, a familiar voice was heard over the ship's comm system, slightly distorted by whatever technological wizardry was allowing him to speak instantly over such a vast distance.

"Volya?"

"Yeah, Roland. We're en route. The navcomp has travel time at just over three hundred seventy-two hours to Neirin, standard time."

There was a brief pause while Kendrick checked the figures. "Just over sixteen days," he said resignedly.

"Are you in trouble?"

"No," Kendrick sighed. "It's been quiet. I'm just sick of these shit hotel rooms."

"Just sit tight," Frye replied. "We'll be there as soon as

we can."

Once the call was terminated, there was very little to do but wait. Unless something went wrong, or a course correction had to be made, the ship only needed a pilot for jump and docking maneuvers. The next two weeks would be spent prepping for the mission to come and attempting to fight off boredom and cabin fever.

***

Ten thousand kilometers behind the *Seguir,* Hartmann's comm channel buzzed. He brought the call up on the bridge comm system so that Halwyn wouldn't feel left out.

"What's up, Volya? Don't tell me – you forgot to pack clean underwear and we need to turn back."

"I should probably double-check, but that's not why I'm calling. I just got off the comm with Roland, and everything is set. He hasn't seen anything odd, so hopefully we're just going on a quick milk run."

"Right," Hartmann replied. "I give it even odds that we get arrested at the border before we even get things started. And even if we do get into the Union, if this gets messy like it did last time, we're going to earn every dollar Roland's brother is paying."

Halwyn was silent for a few moments after the comm went dead, but Hartmann could tell he was troubled. "What did I get myself into?" the young pilot finally asked. "You guys made it sound like we were going to pick up a VIP and that there might be some static planetside. But it sounds like we're talking about something on a much

False Flag   39

bigger level."

It was Hartmann's turn to be silent. He debated with himself about how much to tell the pilot before answering. "It has the potential to be considerably more complicated than a simple pickup," he began.

"That much is obvious," Halwyn shot back. "Now tell me what you've gotten me into."

"Watch your tone," Hartmann growled. "I told you this could be dangerous, and you made the decision to come aboard. Like everyone else, you're here for the money, so don't act like you're being taken somewhere against your will."

Hartmann stood and headed aft towards the galley, returning a few moments later with a bottle and two glasses. "Here," he said, pouring a considerable amount into one of the tankards and handing it to Halwyn.

"I don't drink whiskey," the younger man said in refusal. It was true – he never drank anything harder than the occasional beer, and especially not when he was in control of something as complex as a starship. His father would be mortified to see an open bottle of liquor anywhere near a ship's bridge.

"A man who doesn't drink whiskey is a man who can't be trusted," Hartmann said in response. "But suit yourself. When I'm done telling you our story, you'll beg for a drink." He drained the glass he had poured for Halwyn and refilled it, then sat back in the co-pilot's station, putting his feet up on the control panel.

"Nine months ago, Volya and I were working salvage in the Union. It was the two of us and a mechanic burnout named Stroj Benik." Hartmann's head tilted back against the headrest as his mind drifted to the events that had taken place over the last few months.

"While conducting a sweep through a mostly uninhabited system, we began having reactor trouble — the kind of trouble that is usually fatal. We were hours from a meltdown when we found a derelict craft adrift but under power near the border.

"We boarded the craft, intending to use it as a lifeboat and then claim it for salvage, when we discovered that it was full of tech that didn't exist - the same tech that today powers the *Seguir* and the *Veritas*. It was very strange, but we didn't have any time for the oddity of it to really sink in. We had barely gotten settled, and were just going over the systems when the Marshal's service showed up and arrested us for piracy."

"But that would never stick," Halwyn said. "You were salvage pilots. You had a legitimate reason to be there."

Hartmann took a long pull from his glass. "You'd think so, but it was a setup. Turns out some people had approached Stroj, our mechanic, and offered him a deal to confess to the piracy and agree to testify against Volya and me."

"But why? Sounds awfully convoluted."

Hartmann smiled before taking another pull from the glass. "That's what I thought, but it was actually pretty smart. The people responsible wanted the tech, but wanted to be able to pin the theft on some lower-class pirates. Then, they could take legitimate legal possession of the vessel without too much suspicion and reverse engineer the systems."

False Flag 41

"So who set you up?"

"A Union Navy Admiral and the CEO of an energy megacorp. Their mistake, though, was thinking we'd go quietly. Volya and I managed to escape, steal the ship back, and return it to its rightful owners."

"Cosmocor."

"Exactly. Along the way we met Alainn. She was contracted to find the ship, and without her we probably would have never made it to Saiorse."

"So where does this Kendrick guy come in?"

Hartmann's visage clouded. "I was happy to be out of the Union, and would have gladly just walked away, but Volya couldn't let it go. At this point, we didn't know who all of the players were, or what had happened to the ship's crew, and Volya wasn't going to stop until he got to the bottom of things. He wanted justice, both for us and for the crew of the stolen ship. I chickened out, Alainn went with him, and they went back to the Union to get the answers Volya needed. Volya killed a naval intel operative, and Kendrick was the cop that took the initial homicide call. The feds shut him out, and he went off the reservation trying to find out what was going on. He tracked down Volya and Alainn, but ended up on their side.

"Eventually, they figured out the whole story, and the people behind the conspiracy were dealt with. In the process, a bunch of people ended up kidnapped, injured, or dead, including more than one Union official, a mob boss, and a wealthy CEO. As you might imagine, there are a lot of people in the Union, and even some surrounding systems, that would like nothing more than to see all of us dead."

"And with all of that, you're willing to head back into it, just because this Kendrick guy calls?"

Hartmann chuckled grimly and drained his glass. He refilled it and then continued. "Roland saved Alainn's life, and things never would have gotten wrapped up without him — at least that's what Volya tells me. Volya feels like he owes Roland, so off we go."

"But why are you coming?"

"Because I should have been with Volya all along," Hartmann said ruefully. "I never should have let him take the Union on by himself. I owe Volya my life, so I go. Besides," at this point Hartmann's mood lightened, and Halwyn caught a glint in the navigator's eye, "There's a lot of fucking money at stake."

Halwyn was overwhelmed. He'd left his father's employ to find an adventure, and it appeared as though he wasn't going to be disappointed. He suddenly felt very small, and wasn't sure that he was up to the task. "I think I'll take that drink now," he finally said weakly.

Hartmann grinned. "That's my boy."

***

Haos' reputation as a sort of smuggler's base of operations was well-deserved. The laws were no looser than in Saiorse, but Haos attracted the kind of people who were willing to break Union laws in order to make their fortunes transporting contraband into the increasingly prohibitionist state.

The purpose of the visit was to procure identification

False Flag 43

documents for the crews of the *Seguir* and the *Veritas*, and there was no better place to buy a new, clean identity than Haos. Counterfeiters there were experts at crafting detailed character profiles that could fool Union border security, local cops planetside, and even the Marshal's Service.

Halwyn had wanted to accompany Hartmann and Alainn to make the deal, but the grizzled old navigator had been adamant. "These assholes will eat you alive," he had said, without offering any room for argument. "Don't stray far from the ship, either. We need to be ready to go as soon as I'm back." Frye stayed aboard the *Seguir*, keeping the ship prepped for a quick departure, should one be needed.

Halwyn, however, wasn't planning on staying cooped up. After days aboard the *Veritas*, the orbital station where they were docked seemed massive. Desperate to stretch his legs, Halwyn made his way to the station's hub and found a bar. His commlink was active, as always, and he could be back aboard the *Veritas* in less than five minutes if Wolfgang called.

"So, what brings you to this shithole?" The question came from the next barstool over. Turning to see the source of the voice, Halwyn found himself face-to-face with someone who looked remarkably similar to himself – early twenties, close cropped blonde hair, and nondescript flight suit.

"Refueling and picking up some provisions," Halwyn replied. "You?"

"Same. Where you headed?" The stranger took a pull from his beer.

"Union," Halwyn said. "Some system called Neirin."

"Never heard of it," the stranger said, "But who can keep track of all of 'em, you know?" He shrugged his shoulders.

"I hear ya," Halwyn said, taking a pull from his own beer. "Lot of space out there."

His remark was met with a grunt of agreement. "Tell me about it. You haulin' freight?"

"Nah, picking up a contractor. Some engineering guru."

"And they sent a private ship? Must be a hell of an engineer."

"I guess so," Halwyn replied. "All I know is that they sent us to get him, and the trip has been boring as hell so far."

"Ain't that just the way it works? You think that being a rocket jockey is going to be some kind of adventure, but it turns out to be boring as a fuckin' physics lecture. You have any idea why this guy is such a hotshot?"

"He works on comms," Halwyn said with a shrug. "That's all I know."

The young pilot's commlink interrupted the conversation. It was Wolfgang. Halwyn keyed the link open. "What's up, boss?"

"You aboard?"

"Close by, and she's ready to sail as soon as you are. Everything OK?"

"Five by five," Hartmann replied. "I'll be aboard in ten. If you're not there, I'm going to figure out how to fly the damn thing myself, and I'll leave you here, understand?"

False Flag 45

"I'll be aboard in five," Halwyn said without missing a beat. He'd spent enough time with the former naval officer to just ignore the gruffness. He paid his tab and headed towards the berth where the *Veritas* was moored. He didn't look back, and never noticed the stranger in the next barstool key his commlink when he was gone.

Three

"The purpose of your visit to the Union?" the customs agent asked. The Seguir had been hailed within an hour of making the subspace jump into Union territory. This was no surprise, and thus far, the customs inspection had been cursory.

"We're picking up engineering schematics from a contractor," Frye replied, offering his tablet to the inspector. "As you can see here, we have a contract issued by Cosmocor, a shipbuilder in the Saiorse system."

The inspector took the tablet and gave the document an inspection more thorough than Frye remembered getting during his previous border crossings. For a moment, the inspector's demeanor gave Frye concern, but he appeared to be satisfied, and handed the tablet back.

"Very well, Captain," the inspector said with the insincere smile of a bureaucrat, "everything appears to be in order. Now, if you and your co-pilot will submit to a facial scan, we'll be finished."

"Excuse me?" Alainn interjected. "We've never had to do that before."

"New regulation," the inspector stated impatiently. "We have to verify that you're not on our 'no entry' list,

46   *The Union Chronicles*

and this will serve as a record of your entry."

Alainn wanted to protest, but she knew that it would be futile. She and Frye would be denied entry if they objected. She wasn't completely convinced that the results would be clean, however — they'd crossed too many powerful people to be sure that things had been properly covered up. If they wanted to continue, they would have to accept the intrusion, and if things went sideways, they'd just have to improvise. She could tell that her husband had the same idea — while his body language remained calm, there were subtle signs that he was preparing for a fight. Muscles almost imperceptibly tensed, and his right foot dropped back slightly, ready to assume a combative stance, should the need arise. The movement was so slight, however, that only a well-trained eye would catch it, and the bureaucrat in front of them was clearly not a fighter. If things went bad, though, there would be a small contingent of marshal's service deputies aboard the inspection vessel that could complicate matters.

The inspector pulled the facial recognition scanner from a loop on his belt and waved it across Frye's face. A moment later, he repeated the process with Alainn, and then consulted his tablet.

"OK, you're all set," he finally said. "Enjoy your stay." With that, he headed through the airlock and down the gangway to his own ship.

"That was... intrusive," Alainn remarked as soon as the outer hull door had closed.

"What do you expect?" Frye asked. "They don't even trust their own citizens, so why would they trust a couple of foreigners? At least the scan came up clean; for a

False Flag   47

second I was worried that there was going to be an incident."

Alainn wasn't sure that things were going to be so simple, but she let it go. *Nothing to be done about it now*, she thought to herself. "Alright, let's get the hell out of here," she said aloud to Frye.

"On it," he replied, heading down the corridor to the bridge. A few minutes later, they were once again speeding on their way to Neirin.

"Thirty-two hours to our destination," Alainn said once the navcomp calculations were complete.

***

On approach, Frye could tell that the station orbiting above Luka was sparsely occupied. Neirin was a relatively busy world, so Frye assumed that there would be more traffic. That didn't appear to be the case, however.

"*Seguir*, you are cleared for arrival at berth C-47," The control room operator intoned over the ship's commlink. "I am sending the approach vector to your navcomp."

Moments later, the navigation system had a docking solution plotted, and Frye eased the *Seguir* toward the assigned berth.

"Something seem odd to you?" Alainn asked as they made their final approach.

"Yeah," Frye replied. "This whole deck seems empty." While the station was relatively busy, the berth that they had been directed to was on a deck that appeared to be completely devoid of other vessels. "I don't like it," he said.

"I'm with you," Alainn replied. "Let's bug out and try to figure out what's going on."

Frye was about to kill the approach, but found the control panel unresponsive. Something had taken control of the *Seguir*, and the ship settled into the mooring with a jolt.

"Shit!" Frye exclaimed. "They must have placed a control bot in with the navset they transmitted." He attempted to override using the manual control panel, but gave up after a few attempts. It was useless — the *Seguir* was under someone else's control.

A few seconds later, a thump was felt against the outer hull as the gangway was moved into place.

There was silence for a few moments, and then the ship's commlink chirped. Before Frye could respond, a voice came over the *Seguir's* address system. Whatever malware had been used to hijack the nav systems obviously was giving the person on the other end full control of the ship's comm systems.

"Crew of the merchant vessel *Seguir*," a nondescript female voice said, "This is deputy Linn of the Planetary Union Marshal's Service. We have your ship on lockdown. Please prepare to be boarded."

"What is this about?" Alainn shot back. "You have no right to disable a lawfully-operated private vessel."

"Let's cut the innocent act, Ms. Marwol," the deputy said. "I assume that this *is* Ms. Alainn Marwol, yes? You and Mr. Volya Frye are wanted for a number of serious offenses, including hijacking, kidnapping, possession of illegal weaponry, and using false documents to obtain entry into Union space.

False Flag 49

"Your vessel has been disabled, and there is a team of armed deputies at the gangway. I suggest that you surrender quietly, or we will be forced to breach your craft and take you into custody by force. You have two minutes to comply." With that, the commlink went dead.

"What the hell?" Frye asked.

"No time for that," Alainn responded. "We've got to act. There's no fucking way that I'm surrendering to a squad of Union thugs. Come on." She darted from the bridge and moved quickly into the prep room.

"Put your EVA suit on, and hurry," Alain commanded as she opened her own locker. Frye didn't question her. He opened the locker and hurried to get the suit on.

As soon as his helmet was on and the oxygen supply was working, Alainn held the safety switch that kept the airlock from depressurizing when the door to the ship was open and hit the button to dump the atmosphere from the airlock. With the door into the rest of the ship open, the entire vessel began to rapidly depressurize. The feature was designed to quickly extinguish a fire in the event that one ignited aboard, but it could also be employed to make the vessel a very dangerous place.

Before the atmosphere completely left the Seguir, there was a commotion on the other side of the outer bulkhead door. This noise gradually quieted as the atmosphere left, taking with it the propagation medium for the sounds. Still, it was clear that the breach was imminent.

"Stand back," Alainn said over the suit radio loop. "This is probably going to be a little... explosive."

She and Frye moved against the wall perpendicular to the airlock door and waited. Before long there was an explosive rush of air, and three bodies flew through the airlock and into the prep room. Two of them clipped their heads on the doorway between the airlock and the prep room, and were unconscious, or possibly worse. The third landed in a heap on the floor, dazed but still awake.

"Move! Now!" Alainn yelled as she headed into the airlock. Frye caught his bearings and followed right on her heels.

The vacuum aboard the Seguir had caused air from the gangway to rush violently aboard the ship as soon as the door was opened. Even the three deputies who were not pulled aboard had been knocked to their feet like someone hit by a large wave while playing at the beach. They were still slightly dazed, and both Frye and Alainn used the opportunity to dash past them down the gangway.

As they passed, Frye saw that one of the deputies had dropped his autorifle on the metal walkway as he fell. Without losing his forward momentum, he scooped the weapon up off of the deck and followed his wife aboard the station. As he ran, he spun around and fired a few rounds in the general direction of the deputies to ensure that they kept their heads down and did not pursue.

The corridor was empty – an eerie sight for a commercial station. Frye checked his bearings against the visual assessment of the station he had done on their approach.

"This way," he said, pointing to his left and taking the lead.

They sprinted down the corridor toward the station hub, removing their EVA helmets and tossing them aside as they did so. As they neared the end of the corridor, they could see that a barricade had been erected to keep the

False Flag   51

public out. Two deputies stood with their backs to the corridor, keeping bystanders away.

"Someone went to a lot of trouble to give us a proper welcome," Alainn observed wryly.

"I feel so loved," Frye replied. "I'll take the one on the right; you get the one on the left."

Frye slammed the butt of the autorifle into the base of the deputy on the right's skull. The man crumpled into a heap on the floor as Alainn placed the second deputy into a choke hold, clamping onto the carotid area and putting him to sleep in a few seconds. It was over just as some of the public bystanders took notice of what was going on.

Frye and Alainn hurtled the barricade as a voice called out from behind them. "Stop! Marshal's Service! You are under arrest!"

A small crowd had gathered on the other side of the barricade, and the call from the deputy grabbed the attention of a few more, but Frye and Alainn shoved their way into the hub's interior. Frye knocked down several people in the scramble, and had to fight the urge to stop and help them back up.

"Not exactly original," Alainn said of the deputy's command.

Suddenly, a shot rang out, causing most of the crowd to drop, leaving Frye and Alainn exposed.

"I'll give it low marks for originality," Frye responded, "But I'll admit that he's making a real effort to sell it. Right," he said, ducking down a service corridor to avoid any follow-up gunfire.

"We have to get off of this station," Alainn said.

"The *Seguir* is locked down," Frye answered.

"And we'd never get another ship prepped in time, assuming we could find one unoccupied that we could steal," Alainn continued. "Where's the shuttle bay?"

"That won't work," Frye said, taking a quick left down yet another service corridor, "They'll have them locked out."

"That only leaves one option," Alainn said with a scowl.

"Yeah, the pods," Frye replied unenthusiastically.

"Fuck."

False Flag

Chapter Three

"Here," Frye said as they rounded another corner. The pod entrance was clearly marked, and both he and Alainn slipped in quickly. As they did so, a tungsten slug from a gauss pistol embedded itself in the wall next to the door. The marshal's deputies were right behind them.

Without even strapping in, Frye slammed the large red 'eject' button on the sparse control panel. The door slid closed, there was a slight jolt, and then the pod accelerated rapidly down the track and jettisoned itself from the station. The rapid acceleration caused Frye to slam up against the inner hull.

"You OK?" Alainn asked with concern. She'd seen Frye strike his head, and was worried that he would have a concussion, or possibly even lose consciousness.

"Ungh, I think so," Frye replied. He reached back to rub his head where it had struck. It was wet. He checked his hand, and sure enough, it was covered with blood. "Shit."

The pod had stopped accelerating, so Frye took the opportunity to float over to one of the empty seats and strap in.

"Are you sure you're alright?" Now Alainn was really

False Flag   55

concerned. As soon as they landed, they would have to create as much distance between themselves and the pod as possible. It was equipped with a tracking system that would lead the authorities right to it.

"I'll be fine," Frye said, not completely convincingly. "You know that head wounds always look worse than they are."

"You're sure?"

"Yes, Alainn, I am sure," Frye replied a little testily. "We don't have time for this."

"Fine. Since you're in such good shape, why don't you try Roland and let him know what's going on."

"What exactly is going on?"

"Hell if I know, Volya, but something tells me we've all been had."

Frye unzipped his EVA suit and reached into a pocket on his flight suit, retrieving the special comm chip. He slipped it into his tablet and keyed Kendrick's address, but there was no response. "No answer," he told Alainn. "Maybe we're too close to reentry."

"You think that matters with this new tech?" she asked.

"I have no idea," Frye responded. "I still don't have a clue how the damn thing works. Wolf tried explaining it to me, but I ended up daydreaming about space dinosaurs. We'll try again after touchdown."

The pod began to shake, indicating that they had made contact with Neirin's atmosphere. As the tremors intensified, Frye put the majority of his focus on not vomiting. The blow to his head had left him dazed, and the shaking as they slammed through the planet's atmosphere at thousands of kilometers per hour wasn't helping.

After a few minutes, however, the ride smoothed, and shortly after that, the parachutes deployed, slowing their descent in preparation for landing.

"Still nothing," Frye said after trying Kendrick a second time.

"Dammit," Alainn responded. "What about Wolf?"

In their rush to flee from the Marshal's Service, Frye had completely forgotten that Hartmann was inbound, and would be arriving at the Pristav station, on the other side of the planet, in just a few hours. He changed to his primary comm chip, entered the address and established a connection with the navigator.

"Wolf, we've run into some deep shit, and we're headed planetside. What's your ETA?"

The signal took a few seconds to traverse the empty space between them before Hartmann's response came through. "We'll be at Pristav in three hours, seventeen minutes. What happened?"

"Marshal's Service was waiting for us at the station. They took control of the *Seguir* and we barely made it out. We're headed planetside in one of the station pods. Wolf, they knew who we were – they called us by name, and seemed to know about our history here." Frye wanted to continue, but his head was starting to throb, and he was getting slightly dizzy.

"Alright. I'm changing course for Luka. With any luck, they won't know me. Maybe I can figure out what's going on, and we can come up with a plan to get you two off planet."

False Flag   57

"What about Roland?"

"We'll figure that out later. Right now, we need to get you and Alainn sorted out. Find somewhere to lie low and I'll call when we dock."

"Alright, Wolf. Stay safe, and be careful when you make port. Be ready in case they know you're coming."

There was a chuckle at the other end of the comm. "At the very least, I'll give them something to think about." The comm went dead.

"OK," Alainn said after a few moments, "What have we got?"

"I've got my tablet, Roland's comm chip, and this," Frye replied, holding up the autorifle he had taken from the deputy on the gangway. "And also, possibly, a concussion."

"That's better than what I've got," Alainn answered, removing her tablet from its mount on the wrist panel of her EVA suit. "This is all I got away with."

A few moments later, the pod touched down with a jolt. The impact wasn't particularly harsh, but the sudden stop made Frye dizzy and caused another wave of nausea to wash over his body. With a spasm, he vomited on the floor of the capsule.

"I'd say that's a for sure on the concussion," he said weakly.

Alainn had already unfastened her harness and hit the button to open the capsule door. "No time for that now," she said. "We have to move, and fast."

"I'm right behind you," Frye said shakily, unfastening his own harness with more effort than should have been necessary.

The capsule had been programmed to avoid heavily-populated areas and had touched down in a cornfield, flattening a two meter circle in the tall stalks. The rest of the crop, however, rose above the top of the capsule, shielding it from anything but an aerial view.

Frye and Alainn quickly doffed their EVA suits and headed into the field, wanting to put as much distance between themselves and the capsule as possible.

"I think we have company," Frye said, pointing to the horizon. A second pod was floating towards the ground a few hundred meters away. That put at least one, but as many as four deputies on their tail.

Alainn said nothing in response, but quickened her pace. Frye tried to keep up, but he was growing increasingly dizzy, and was having a hard time putting one foot in front of the other. Suddenly, he stumbled and fell face first into the dirt.

Alainn heard the cornstalks rustle and Frye's body hit the ground and she turned, just as Frye was attempting to pick himself up.

"Don't give up now," she said, helping him to his feet and throwing his arm over her shoulder. With assistance, Frye was able to continue forward, although at a much slower pace than Alainn was comfortable with. The leaves from the stalks seemed to reach out in a deliberate attempt to slice at her face, and with only one arm available, it was difficult to keep them at bay. She glanced over her shoulder in time to see the parachute from their pursuers' pod settle atop the corn. The pod was down, and in moments they would have marshal's deputies on their trail. Fortunately, the cornfield was an ideal concealment location. As long as they kept moving

False Flag 59

without making too much noise, the deputies would have an almost impossible time tracking them down.

Alainn wanted to stop and check her tablet to see where they were, and what was nearby, but she and Frye needed to put as much distance between them and their pursuers as possible first. They couldn't move for too much longer, however; if Frye really did have a concussion, he would need some rest in order to recover. Extended movement would only prolong the nausea and dizziness, and increase the chances of neural damage, which couldn't be repaired until they were out of danger and could find decent, and anonymous, medical care.

"I haffa stop an rest," Frye slurred, as though reading Alainn's mind. "Jus for a minnit." Alainn could also tell that he was increasingly relying on her for support; at this point she was almost dragging him along.

"We have to keep moving," she responded. "Just for a few more minutes, Volya. Stay with me."

"Okay. I love you Alainn. I wounnit go anywhere without you."

"I love you too, Volya. Just try and stay awake for a few more minutes."

Off to her left, Alainn could make out the roof of a structure over the tops of the corn. It was probably an equipment shed, Alainn reasoned. It was an obvious place to hide, and their pursuers would no doubt check for them there, but Volya needed to get off of his feet. If nothing else, it was a better defensive position than the cornfield. They could make a stand there, and maybe take out whoever was on their tail before they could call for reinforcements.

Alainn shifted course and headed toward the

60   *The Union Chronicles*

structure. It took several minutes to cover the five hundred meters, and Frye was obviously losing strength with every step.

Finally, they broke through into a clearing. The building was an equipment shed, just as Alainn had assumed. There were no doors on the side facing them, so she dragged Frye around to the other side, wondering what kind of security mechanism the door would have.

As they rounded the corner, she realized that would not be an issue: the door was open, revealing a huge harvester bot in one of the equipment bays. Unfortunately that wasn't the only thing that caught her eye — there was someone standing in the doorway, and he had already seen them.

Alainn's eyes met the stranger's, and for a brief moment she contemplated running back into the corn, but Frye was just too heavy.

The stranger broke the silence. "Bring him in. Here, let me help." He rushed up and supported Frye on the other side. "What happened?" he asked.

"He hit his head," Alainn answered.

"In my cornfield?"

"Not exactly. It's a long story."

"I hit my head inna spaceship," Frye slurred, clearly on the verge of unconsciousness.

They took Frye inside of the shed and to a small sitting room in a back corner. Dark wood paneling covered the two exterior walls, while the two walls separating the room from the equipment were made of floor-to-ceiling acrylic windows. A dark leather sofa and two easy chairs sat opposite each other, with a wood and titanium coffee table between them. A bar, constructed out of what appeared to be mahogany, sat against one of the back walls, and a massive viewscreen adorned the other. In addition to the bar, there was a small kitchen. It was furnished remarkably nicely for a room in a farming equipment shed, or even for many residences, Alainn reflected.

The stranger helped Alainn recline Frye on the sofa as she took in the space.

"Nice place you have here," Alainn observed.

The stranger smiled. "I don't really have a lot to do out here; the bots take care of almost everything. But I have learned that my wife and I get along a lot better if we spend the day apart, so I spend a lot of time out here. 'Absence makes the heart grow fonder' as the old saying goes."

"Fair enough," Alainn responded. The man appeared to be in his early sixties. She was sure he had more marital experience than she did.

"I am Siorus," the stranger said, extending a hand.

"Alainn, and this is my husband, Volya." Alainn took the proffered hand and shook it. "Do you have a first aid kit handy? This head wound is going to need sealed up."

"Of course, hang on." Siorus headed to the kitchen area and pulled a satchel from one of the cabinets. He crossed the room and handed it to Alainn.

"Thank you," she said, opening the case and finding a tube of nanopaste. She popped the sterile seal on the tube and squeezed the paste into Frye's still bleeding head wound. The nanites in the paste were activated by hemoglobin in the blood, and immediately went to work, stopping the bleeding and beginning the process of sealing the laceration in the scalp. In a few hours, he would be good as new.

"Let's see if we can get his head cleaned up a little bit," the stranger said, heading back into the kitchen and wetting a towel in the sink. "Please, make yourself comfortable," Siorus said, indicating one of the easy chairs opposite the sofa. Alainn unstrapped the autorifle from her back and set it on the floor, then took her seat. Her host didn't seem the least bit taken aback by the fact that she was armed; he had made no comment regarding the weapon, and had given it no more than a brief glance. Instead, his eyes bored into hers with a relaxed intensity – a paradox which Alainn found rather unsettling.

Siorus returned with the towel and began wiping the blood from Frye's head and neck. "So, Alainn, how exactly did you end up in my cornfield?"

"It's a long story."

"Well, as I may have mentioned, I've got nothing but time," Siorus replied with a smile.

A buzzing sound cut in as Alainn was contemplating her answer, and her host raised an eyebrow.

"No one ever comes out here," he said, "And now I have yet another unexpected visitor." He stopped wiping Frye's head and turned to Alainn. "Friends of yours, perhaps?" From his tone, it was clear that while he said 'friends,' his meaning was the opposite.

"Doubtful," Alainn said. Her muscles began to tighten, and a surge of adrenaline hit her bloodstream as her autonomic system prepped her body for a fight.

As Siorus headed through the warehouse to the open bay door, Alainn contemplated her options. Running was out – Volya had fallen asleep almost immediately upon

False Flag   63

laying on the couch. That left fighting – something that Alainn was more than capable of.

She picked up the autorifle and popped the magazine from the receiver. It was full, giving her seventy-five high-velocity 5mm tungsten rounds. It should be more than enough. *It will have to be*, Alainn told herself as she slipped out of the sitting room and into the robotics bay. The massive harvester blocked her view of the door, but fortunately that also meant that whoever was at the door couldn't see her, either.

The room was dimly lit by an LED bank on the ceiling, but it had been turned down, and the harvester bot cast a deep shadow all over the room. The floor was bare plasticrete, and Alainn was thankful that she was wearing her soft-soled flight boots, giving her the ability to move noiselessly across the floor.

By creeping along the back wall, Alainn made her way to the far side of the harvester bot, rifle at a low ready. As she moved up the side of the bot, muffled voices could be heard, which resolved into intelligible speech as she got closer. Alainn checked once again to make sure that the weapon was energized and chambered. She wouldn't kill Siorus, but she would put a tungsten slug through the head of a Union thug without a second thought. Satisfied that the weapon was ready, she tucked herself up against the corner of the harvester bot, ready to engage.

"So you've seen nothing out of the ordinary?" The voice was unknown to Alainn, but that didn't make its owner any less obvious. *Marshal's Service*, Alainn thought, steeling herself for a confrontation.

"Nope," she heard Siorus reply. "It's just been me and my nephew here all day. You can ask him, but I'll have to wake the lazy son of a bitch up. He puts in a few hours' work programming the equipment, and he thinks that entitles him to a nap." A moment later, Siorus continued. "Tell you what, let's go wake him up and you can grill him all you want. The look on his face when he gets woken up by a Marshal's deputy will be priceless."

"That won't be necessary, sir," the voice replied. "Just keep your eyes open and report anything suspicious. And lock the doors; we have reason to believe that the fugitives are armed and dangerous. We will be combing the area; we will make every effort to preserve your crops."

"Of course. Thank you, deputy. You sure you don't want to come in for something to drink? The couch is occupied, but I've got some fine whiskey and a comfortable chair."

"I'm on duty, sir. Thank you anyway."

"Alright, suit yourself."

A moment later, the large bay door began to close silently on a hydraulic track that was clearly well-maintained. Alainn knew she needed to get back to the sitting room, but her mind was reeling. Why had this stranger covered for her and Volya?

"You can come out now, Alainn - he's gone."

Siorus' words hit her as she was trying to come to terms with his actions. What the hell was going on?

With the gig up, Alainn decided to see what she could learn about the circumstances. She rounded the corner of the harvester, weapon at her side.

"Why did you cover for us?"

Sirous smiled. "How about we have this conversation in a more comfortable setting?"

"Fine by me," Alainn responded. "But one more

False Flag   65

question."

"Yes?"

"How good is the whiskey you've got?"

***

The whiskey was fantastic. Siorus had wasted no time pouring two glasses, neat, once they returned to the sitting room. It was real oakwood-aged stuff, not the cheap chemical imitation that most people drank. Alainn savored the aroma and the flavor as she settled back into the leather chair.

"How much do you know about corn, Alainn?"

The question came out of left field, and Alainn had no idea what Siorus was getting at. "I know it goes good with butter," she replied wryly. "Of course, what doesn't?"

Siorus smiled in a knowing way that made Alainn slightly uncomfortable. He didn't seem to be a simple farmer, but so far she couldn't figure him out. "You have a point there," he said charitably, "but I'm talking on a botanical rather than gastronomical level."

"Then absolutely nothing," Alainn replied, trying not to get irritated by the coy game.

"Corn, like any other agricultural product, is historically prone to parasites," Sirous explained. "A few thousand years ago, before we had figured out how to bioengineer our ecosystems, corn was plagued by parasitic activity. Cutworms, flea beetles, corn borers, armyworms – the list is quite extensive, and every one of these creatures feeds off of the crop, ruining it and in some cases spreading devastating disease.

"Nowadays, it's a lot easier," Siorus continued. "We have genetically engineered corn to be resistant to disease, and the parasites have been bioengineered out of the food chain, so they were never introduced to planets like this when they were terraformed. But in the old days, they were a real problem."

"I'm sorry, but I don't follow," Alainn replied.

"A parasite takes and takes, but doesn't contribute to the system," Siorus said. "It's not a symbiotic relationship, because the parasite doesn't bring anything to the table. All it does is consume, and in the process, it destroys that which it takes from. The only way to survive is to take more. Eventually, it kills the host, and has to move on. Do you pay taxes, Alainn?"

Now the point was obvious. "No," Alainn responded. "Where I come from, we don't pay taxes. We pay fees for services rendered."

Siorus seemed genuinely surprised. "So it's a symbiotic relationship?"

"Exactly."

"Amazing. Of course, you understand the concept of confiscatory taxation?"

"The concept? Yes. The justification? Never."

Siorus chuckled. "You ever steal from someone that actually owned what you were taking?"

"No sir. That would be wrong."

"Good girl. You want to tell me anything else about what you're doing?"

"It would probably be better for you if I didn't."

Siorus smiled again. It was the same expression, but

now Alainn found it far less unnerving. "Nowadays, we engineer the parasites out of the system, agriculturally speaking. Societally speaking, they still tend to crop up now and then, and when they do, they consume until there is nothing left. What's worse is that they have such a sense of superiority about it, as though being non-productive and merely taking from others were some kind of higher state of being. If something or someone were to show up and give them a hard time, that would be a crying shame. You know what I mean?"

"I think I do."

"Good. My wife will be expecting me for supper soon, so I'll be heading back to the house. If someone were to avail themselves of my sitting room, and some of the food I've got, well, I probably wouldn't notice. I'm getting a little bit old and senile."

Now it was Alainn's turn to smile.

***

With the immediate threat contained, and Volya sleeping peacefully on the couch, Alainn's mind was free to drift to the events of the day. The Marshal's Service had known their identities, and had time to prepare the orbital station for their apprehension. That this had something to do with Kendrick's brother was undeniable. The idea that they had been summoned to the Union only to be coincidentally waylaid by the Marshal's Service was too far-fetched.

Shit, Alainn said to herself, realizing that in the rush to escape, the *Seguir* had been left unsecured and under the

The Union Chronicles

control of Union operatives. She grabbed her tablet and attempted to connect to the server aboard the ship, but with no success. Whatever malware had been used to take control of the ship was preventing her from accessing the systems remotely. Is that what this was about? Another play for the ship's technology?

With the ship unsecure and in Union hands, and no way to verify what was going on in orbit above, Alainn had only one choice. She activated a separate application on her tablet and keyed a command into the interface.

Chapter Four

Alainn dozed in one of the leather chairs, autorifle laid out across her lap. She wanted to make sure that Volya got the rest he needed, but she also wanted to be on the move early, before Siorus came back in the morning. After the previous day's events, they needed to get to Roland quickly to let him know what was going on. There was, however, a nagging part of her mind that told her he already knew – he wasn't answering his commlink, which Alainn was sure meant that he and Wallis had been compromised in some fashion, if they hadn't always been.

A buzzing noise pulled her from her fitful sleep. At first she thought it was her commlink, that perhaps Hartmann was calling to let them know he'd made port, but the tone wasn't quite right. It took Alainn a few moments to realize that it was the shed's proximity alarm; the same noise that had alerted Siorus to the deputy's arrival a few hours earlier, and had no doubt notified him of she and Volya's approach before that.

It was three o'clock local time, Alainn's tablet told her. Too early for Siorus, she figured. Farmers got up early, but not *that* early. Alainn double-checked the rifle and activated the viewscreen on the wall, which was tied to the security feeds from around the perimeter.

"What's going on?" Volya sat up on the sofa and reached to the back of his head where the nanogel had done its job, leaving his scalp completely repaired. He still had a headache, but was no longer dizzy. He glanced around at his surroundings in confusion. "And where the hell are we?"

"A barn, if you can believe it," Alainn responded without turning around. "And we have company. You good to go?"

Frye stood to his feet and walked over to the kitchenette, where he splashed some cold water on his face and ran his fingers through his hair. There was still some blood matting his hair to the back of his head, but that would have to wait. "Yeah, I think I'm OK. What kind of company are we talking about?"

"The uninvited kind." Alainn pointed to the viewscreen, where three black-clad figures could barely be made out in front of the large equipment bay door. "Marshal's deputies, most likely."

"Options?"

"We don't have many," Alainn replied. "We're kind of cornered in here. I think that we're going to have to shoot our way out."

"Three guns against one?"

"I don't like the odds either, but unless you have a better suggestion –"

"Actually, I might," Frye replied, looking through the windows into the equipment bay.

False Flag 71

Alainn followed his gaze through the window. "You aren't really thinking..."

"Yes," Frye said with a grin, "yes I am." He headed out of the sitting room and into the equipment bay, Alainn close at his heels.

"You need to hurry," Alainn whispered, leveling the autorifle in the direction of the bay door. "They'll breach the door any second."

Frye said nothing. Instead, he worked furiously at the control panel. The controls weren't much different from those he had become familiar with working on his father's farm, and in moments, the harvester came to life.

The massive robot was powered by its own fusion source, and the electromagnetic motors that drove the wheels hummed to life quickly. At the same time, the bay doors began to slide open.

"Quick, against the front wall," Frye hissed, moving around the harvester's side opposite the door's opening. Alainn followed, and soon they were pressed up against the wall. Moments later, the harvester headed out towards the rows of corn.

Initially, Alainn assumed that Volya's plan was to ride the bot away from the building, but now she understood. As the gigantic piece of machinery cleared the door, the attention of the three intruders was on the bot, not the interior of the equipment bay. They had made the same assumption Alainn had.

There was a split second of confusion, which was enough time for Frye and Alainn to scurry along the barn and around the corner.

"Where are we going?" Frye asked.

"We need to go by the farmer's house. He hid us when the patrol came by the first time, and I want to at least let him know what happened. Maybe if we rough him and his wife up a little bit and restrain them, they'll be able to convince the authorities that they were victims."

"Oh, good; I've always wanted to pistol-whip a farmer's wife," Frye said with a grin.

"Shut up and follow me," Alainn said, sighing.

There was a clear path from the shed, and Alainn could see the silhouette of a house in the distance, perhaps two kilometers away.

"We need to hustle," Frye said. "Those guys won't be far behind."

The rest of the distance was covered at a flat out run. The house was dark, but as they approached, it was obvious that the front door was ajar. Alainn held up a hand and Frye halted a meter behind her and off to one side, able to cover the door while she approached.

They cleared the house quickly. Before they entered, Alainn knew what they would find, but she did it anyway, hoping against hope that she was wrong. She wasn't. In the bedroom upstairs, she found the bodies of Siorus and his wife. They had both been shot in the head. Nothing else looked out of place until Alainn looked at Siorus' fingers. Four of them on his left hand had been broken. She brushed past Frye, back down the stairs, and headed back towards the front door.

"Alainn?"

"We need to go. Now."

Frye caught up to his wife, who was now jogging into the cornfield. "What was up there?"

False Flag 73

"They tortured the farmer and his wife, and then killed them," Alainn said. "Those aren't the actions of law enforcement, that's how a hit squad operates."

"So you're saying these guys aren't Marshal's Service?"

"I'm saying there's no difference anymore. Let's get out of here."

***

The cornfield seemed to go on forever. "Are you sure the road is this way?" Alainn asked, brushing a cornstalk from her face for what seemed like the thousandth time. It was still dark, making navigation through the crop difficult. Fortunately, however, there had been no sign of the men from the barn.

Frye double-checked his tablet. "Yeah, this is the right direction. We're about four kilometers from the road."

"And does the corn go all the way?"

"I hope so. It's a pain in the ass, but it will help hide us from satellites and drones."

"Shit, I hadn't thought about that. I'll deal with the leaves."

A few kilometers through the field, and Frye's commlink chirped. It was Hartmann.

"Hey brother, we're on our final approach to the Luka station. I'll be planetside in a couple of hours."

"Anything suspicious show up on your approach?"

"I don't think so," Hartmann replied. "We're headed into a berth near a few commercial ships, so it doesn't look like we're being isolated. I did see something interesting, though."

"What's that?"

"There's a government ship in one of the upper berths, and it's non-military. Looks like an *Opinbera*-class, the kind they use to ferry VIP's around in. Seems a little out of place in a system like Neirin."

"OK, thanks, Wolf. Get down here as quick as you can. We're going to find a place to lie low until we hear from you."

"Stay safe, brother." The commlink went dead.

"Try Roland again," Alainn said, for what seemed to be the hundredth time.

Once again, Frye obliged, and once again, there was no response. Frye took the chip out of his tablet. It appeared fine, but a closer inspection revealed a missing pin.

"Shit," he said.

"Broken?"

"Yeah. It was loose in my pocket when we bolted from the *Seguir*. It must have gotten damaged in the scuffle."

"Well, at least that explains why Roland isn't answering."

The mention of the *Seguir* reminded Alainn once again that she needed to fill Frye in on the full extent of their situation. She had been trying to avoid this conversation, but he needed to know. "I had to scuttle the *Seguir*."

"Obviously."

"I'm sorry, Volya, but we just can't - wait, what?" Alainn had been ready to defend her decision, and was dumbfounded that Frye had brushed it off so easily.

False Flag 75

"You can't let that tech fall into Union hands," Frye said, shrugging his shoulders. "We'll just have to hitch a ride home with Wolf and the new kid."

"Well, that was anti-climactic. I was getting ready for a fight. Isn't this the point in the story where something is supposed to come between us?"

"And then one of us learns a valuable lesson about love and/or forgiveness?" Frye smiled.

Alainn laughed. "Nothing fazes you, does it?"

"I've been framed, arrested, shot at, beaten, and seen the worst humanity has to offer. Before that, I was broke, and on more than one occasion had to choose between spending what little money I had left on food or reactor fuel. I was shaken down by petty bureaucrats and betrayed by someone I thought was a friend, so you're going to have to try a little harder than that."

"OK, but just remember that you asked for it. Something else has been bothering me. I don't know if there's anything to it, but something just doesn't feel right."

"What do you mean?"

"Why are we here, Volya?"

"To help Roland."

"Exactly. He called, and we came running. Right into a trap."

"You're not suggesting he's somehow involved, are you?"

"I'm suggesting that it's a possibility. It's just a little odd that a few short weeks after he gets back to the Union, we get a call for help, and as soon as we show up, we find ourselves in a gunfight."

"Come on, Alainn; Roland can't be in on this, especially after what he did to help us."

"Maybe that's why he *is* in on this, Volya. Maybe he's doing it under duress."

Frye had to concede the point. It was possible that Kendrick was being used against his will. "Okay, say he called us in under false pretenses. What exactly do we do?"

"Well, the simple answer is that we meet up with Wolf, get off of this damn planet, and get the hell home."

"Sure, but we don't know that Roland is involved, and if he is, what his reasons are. What if he really is in trouble? If that's the case, we can't just leave him."

Alainn sighed. Part of her wanted to argue for selfish self-preservation, but it was an argument that she would never win with her husband, and she wasn't sure she wanted to. He was a good man, someone who would do the right thing, even if it came at great personal risk, and that was one thing about him that she would never want to change.

"Fine," she said after a moment. "We meet up with Wolf and try to figure out what is going on. But if we find out that Roland is playing us, then we're gone."

"Agreed."

"Good. Where exactly are we headed?"

Frye pulled out his tablet and consulted the navigation program again. "We're only a few kilometers from Luka. I'm hoping that we can find a place to get something to eat, and maybe some less conspicuous clothes. Then we

False Flag   77

find somewhere to lie low until Wolf gets here."

"Did it occur to you that that puts us in more or less the exact same position that Roland was supposedly in?"

"The irony isn't lost on me."

They continued on in silence, and thirty minutes later, the cornfield abruptly ended at the side of a maglev roadway, leaving them exposed. There wasn't any traffic on the road, but the sun had risen, and that would likely change soon.

"We're going to have to ditch the gun," Frye said.

"Yeah," Alainn agreed, dropping the autorifle into the dusty ground at the edge of the cornfield.

"We're getting close," Alainn said twenty minutes later as they continued along the roadway. In the distance, she could see the silhouette of buildings against the breaking sun. She quickened her pace, and Frye followed suit. Thirty minutes later, and they were at the outskirts of the city. Low-slung housing complexes dominated the landscape.

"We need to find somewhere to lie low," Alainn said. "Look for a place that seems to be vacant."

"Like that one?" Frye asked, pointing to a small house across the road. He gestured to his tablet screen. "It's posted on a local board as being for rent."

Alainn looked at the small bungalow. "That will work. Hopefully we can get inside without any trouble."

The lock proved to be simple enough, and in a few minutes, they were in the living room of the empty house.

"Too bad it isn't furnished," Alainn said, surveying the vacant sitting room.

"At this point, I don't really care," Frye replied,

collapsing on the floor and leaning against one of the walls. "I'm just glad to be out of that damn corn field."

"Weren't your parents farmers?"

"Soybeans," Frye replied with a grin. "Totally different. You can sleep first, if you like. I'll take first watch."

"I doubt I'll be able to sleep," Alainn replied, lying back on the floor, "but it would feel good to close my eyes for a few minutes."

Moments later, she was quietly snoring.

False Flag

Chapter Five

"Stay with the ship," Hartmann said as he headed through the prep room. He didn't wait for a response before heading through the airlock and down the gangway toward the shuttle station, rolling a titanium case behind him. He made his way down the corridor, through the hub, and to the shuttle station. He purchased a ticket, and in less than an hour was on his way planetside.

The navigator rented a car from the terminal stack on the surface and loaded the case into the cargo compartment. Before he did so, however, he opened it and removed one of the Gauss pistols, securing it in a holster inside of his waistband. Once settled into the driver's seat, he activated his comm and placed a call to Frye.

"Volya, I'm planetside," he said once the commlink was established. "Where should I pick you up?"

"We're in a house at the edge of town," Frye replied. He gave the address, and then terminated the link. "Wolf will be here in thirty," he told Alainn, who was rolling her neck back and forth.

"Glad to hear he didn't get the same welcome we

False Flag 81

did," she replied, wincing in pain as she manipulated her shoulder with her hand. "You know, I'm getting too damn old to sleep on the floor."

A half hour later, the high-pitched whine of an electric turbine indicated the arrival of a vehicle. Frye peered carefully through a front window to verify that it was his former navigator before unlocking the door.

"I don't think that I've ever been so happy to see you," he said in greeting, clapping his arms around Hartmann's shoulders. He looked down at the bag Hartmann was carrying.

"Please tell me that's what I think it is," he said.

"All kinds of goodies," Hartmann replied with a smile.

"Dibs on the shower," Alainn said, reaching around Frye and grabbing the case.

"Before you get too comfortable, and this probably goes without saying, but you know you guys are in hot water, right?" Hartmann asked.

"What's the official story?" Alainn asked.

"You're wanted by the Marshal's Service for suspicion of trafficking in contraband," Hartmann answered. "UMS agents attempted to apprehend you when you docked over Luka, but you were able to escape to the surface in a pod. Citizens are urged to report any sightings to local law enforcement or to the UMS outpost aboard Luka station."

"Super. We need to figure out what's going on and then get the hell off of this planet," Alainn said.

"First, I'd suggest that you make some changes to your appearance," Hartmann said. "Your images are up everywhere. I stopped on the way here and bought some stuff that might help."

Alainn opened the bag and sorted through the

contents. "This should work. Good thinking, Wolf"

Hartmann looked uncomfortably at Alainn. "There's one more thing, and it involves the *Seguir*…"

"You mean the useless piece of slag formerly known as the *Seguir*?" Alainn asked.

Hartmann did a double-take. "So *you* did that? You made a hell of a mess."

Alainn shrugged. "They had control of her, and I can't let that tech fall into Union hands. I had a stand-alone self-destruct system built into the ship before we left Saiorse. I wasn't going to have a repeat of the *Marco Polo*."

"And the *Veritas*?"

"Same thing," Frye replied. If the Union captures her, she gets melted – or at least all of the important parts of her do."

"And were you going to tell me that I've been flying around in an explosive-rigged spaceship?"

"Relax," Frye said. "It's not the whole ship – just the reactor and the servers."

"Which control the life support systems," Hartmann said.

"Look, we can discuss this later," Alainn interjected. "Bottom line was that I had to scrap the *Seguir* to keep it out of Union hands, and now we've all got to get home on the *Veritas*. But before that, we need to figure out what is going on here. And to do that, we need to find Roland."

"Do you know where they were staying?" Hartmann asked.

"No, he just said that they were at a hotel in Tionscal, and from the way he talked, it was a dive," Frye replied.

"Basically, we're at square one," Alainn said.

"And we have no idea who was after them?" Hartmann knew the answer before he asked, but he asked it anyway.

False Flag   83

"No," Frye replied.

"We're not even positive that anyone actually is," Alainn interjected.

"What exactly is that supposed to mean?" Hartmann asked.

Frye shot his wife a mildly frustrated look. "Alainn thinks that maybe Roland is compromised," he said. "She thinks that maybe he was forced to call us in under duress so that we could be captured."

"Don't be so dismissive, Volya," Alainn shot back. "It certainly fits what happened to us spaceside, and it's not like you haven't been stabbed in the back before."

Frye was about to protest, but Hartmann chimed in first. "She has a point, brother. We've been down this road before."

"Look, I don't want to fight about it," Alainn said, "You're a very trusting man, and I love you for it, but it opens you up to being used."

"So I'm a sucker, is that it?" Frye responded defensively. "You know, if it wasn't for Roland's help, I may never have gotten you back, and now you can't wait to declare him the enemy so that we can bail on the job."

"That's not it and you know it. I don't want to believe that Roland is the reason we're in this mess, but I'm not going to dismiss the possibility, either. You aren't the only one who's been burned by a supposed ally." Turning her attention to Hartmann, she changed the subject. "Since we're at square one, then that's where we start. We go to Wallis Aeron's apartment. Maybe we'll find a trail there. If not, we head to Tionscal to see if we can pick up a trail." With that, she turned and headed to the bathroom.

    ***

Thirty minutes later, Alainn's shoulder-length hair was three inches shorter, and the natural black had been replaced with a bright copper red. She had applied dark eye makeup to her normally unadorned face and changed her eye color to green. The only things that remained from her previous appearance were a t-shirt and cargo pants. Frye gave a low whistle as Alainn stepped out of the bathroom.

"You know, I could take that as an insult," Alainn said. "If I look so good as a completely different person, what did you think of me before?"

Frye kept his mouth shut, knowing that Alainn was still irritated with him over their disagreement about Roland. Anything he said would be the wrong thing, so he decided not to say anything at all.

For his part, Frye had shortened his already close-cropped hair, and his natural dark brown was now blonde. His perpetual stubble was gone, replaced by a well-groomed goatee, and his brown eyes were now blue. It wouldn't fool facial recognition software, but to the human eye, he and Alainn were two completely different people than they had been a few hours before.

"That should work fine," Hartmann said, eyeing them both. "Now let's get out of here."

In the car, Hartmann activated the navsat system and ran a search for Wallis Aeron. Aeron's address was listed, and in a few moments, the vehicle had plotted a course, and the autopilot took over.

In the front passenger seat, Frye tried to focus on the task at hand, but with nothing to do until they arrived at Aeron's house, it was difficult. Why was Alainn so quick to blame Roland for their run-in at the station? And worse,

False Flag 85

what if she was right? After all, Roland was the only one who knew that they were coming, at his request. The truth was that there were plenty of people in the Union that had a reason to want them in custody or worse, and many of them would go to great lengths to make it happen. Something else was bothering him as well.

"What about the ship?" he asked aloud.

"What ship?" Hartmann asked, completely lost.

"The VIP ferry that you said you saw on approach," Frye answered. "You said it was unusual. Why?"

"Neirin isn't exactly the kind of place that Union VIP's visit on a regular basis," Hartmann replied. "If you hadn't noticed, it's a bit...anti-establishment."

Frye hadn't noticed. Looking out the window, he didn't see anything that stuck out.

"It's not so much what you'll see," Hartmann explained, "As what you won't." Realizing that his friend was lost, he gave a more explicit explanation. "See any cameras?"

Frye didn't, and he shook his head, although he still looked confused.

"He's a rocket jockey, Wolf," Alainn said. "He's not used to being planetside, so nothing looks abnormal to him."

"Think about the orbital stations that we've spent time on," Hartmann said. "Remember all of the surveillance?"

"Sure," Frye replied.

"Well, most Union cities are the same. There are cameras everywhere. But Luka is different. You won't see them anywhere, because every time they've been installed, they get vandalized. Eventually the authorities just gave up."

"Well that should be an easy crime to solve," Frye said.

"If you vandalize a camera, it should be recorded, right?"

"It's electronic vandalism," Hartmann explained. "It's done over the networks, or with targeted EMP's, and no one is ever able to trace it. At least that's the story I've heard. Neirin is actually somewhat infamous. When I was in the Navy, there were a few stories that got passed around about this place, especially amongst the tech savvy sailors. This place is home to some of the best signals and tech people in the galaxy, but they're an independent bunch.

"The Union more or less turns a blind eye, as long as things stay planetside," Hartmann continued. "A lot of the interstellar signals originating here are scrubbed, though, because a lot of it contains subversive messages and malicious code designed to cause problems for the authorities."

"You mean there's an active effort to supress dissenting viewpoints? Color me not surprised," Alainn observed.

"Yeah, the cruisers at the jump points monitor communications," Hartmann answered. "Everything gets pretty heavily edited."

"And nothing gets done about it, because the stories can't leave the system," Alainn observed.

"More or less. Obviously, the authorities can't censor everything, but when news does get out, the media outlets tend to downplay what's going on. To the extent that anyone thinks of Neirin, they see it as a collection of nutty political extremists.

"And that's why the shuttle is odd," Hartmann continued, steering the conversation back to Frye's original question. "Government bigwigs don't make this a regular destination. They've decided that it's better to

False Flag   87

focus on containment rather than active engagement. You won't find many surveillance cameras, and there aren't likely to be too many Marshal's Service deputies planetside, either."

"Good news for us," Alainn chimed in. "We'll be able to operate with some degree of anonymity."

"And it gives us a clue," Frye said. "I doubt that the arrival of a government official at the same time as us is a coincidence. That means that whoever is on that ship is probably involved in the attempt to arrest us."

A few minutes later, the car stopped in front of a skyrise apartment building. Hartmann double-checked the navcomp, and then turned to his companions.

"Apparently, this is the home address of one Wallis Aeron," he said, opening the driver's side door and exiting the vehicle.

The door to the building was secured with a DNA scanner. "How are we going to get in?" Frye asked.

"Leave that to me," Hartmann replied. "Just keep your eyes open, and block the view from the street." He reached into a satchel and pulled out a small cable, one end of which he plugged into a maintenance port on the scanner. The other he connected to the dataport on the tablet attached to his sleeve. A few keystrokes later, and the door clicked and slid open. Hartmann disconnected the cable, and then motioned towards the door with a flourish, inviting his companions to enter first.

"Always the gentleman," Frye chided.

"Nice," Alainn said as they slipped inside. "How does it work? Aren't there an almost infinite number of possible DNA combinations?"

"Yeah, hacking a DNA profile would be impossible,"

Hartmann replied. "This code, however, works like a simple worm. It hacks into the database the locking mechanism is attached to and inserts a DNA profile, then sends that profile command to the lock. DNA is an amazing encryption mechanism, but the network security is usually much less impressive. This little piece of code just attacks the weak point in the system. Now as far as the building is concerned, I'm Wallis Aeron. Should make things a little easier."

"Brilliant," Frye replied, "And scary."

"Invent a lock, and someone will come up with a way to break it," Hartmann said with a shrug.

They rode the elevator to the thirtieth floor and found apartment number 3076, which was listed as Aeron's home address. Hartmann was the first to the door, which was locked. Hartman placed his hand against the DNA reader and the door opened silently.

"What exactly are we looking for?" Frye asked as they entered the sparsely-furnished living room.

"I'm not really sure," Alainn answered, "But this is where things started, and we've got nothing else. If we can't find Wallis and Roland, maybe we can figure out what happened here, or maybe where they went. Heading to Tionscal and checking out every dive hotel isn't going to be very effective."

The only interesting room in the apartment was the den, which was outfitted as a workshop, with racks of electronic equipment along one wall, and a worktable running the full length of the opposite wall.

"Nice gear," Hartmann observed.

Frye approached the terminal on the worktable and

False Flag   89

activated it. The screen displayed a symbol of some kind, but was otherwise blank.

"Good luck," Hartmann chuckled. "Given your technical skills, and the reputation of Wallis, I'm guessing we'll both die of old age before you get in."

"You want to give it a go?" Frye asked defensively.

"Hell no," Hartmann answered. "I'm way out of my league here – I just have the good sense to recognize that fact."

"Anything?" Alainn asked, peeking her head into the den.

"Nada," Hartmann replied.

"The rest of the house is the same," Alainn said. "Other than the door, there's no evidence that anything happened here."

"So what now?" Frye asked.

"Come with me. I'm going to check with the neighbors," Alainn replied. "Wolf, access public police reports on the datanet and see if you can find a reference to the break-in here. And take another look around to see if we missed anything."

***

"According to the official police report, a unit was dispatched to this apartment five weeks ago in response to an emergency call placed by Wallis Aeron," Hartmann said, "So that part of the story stacks up. They arrived and found a man, later identified as Roland Kendrick, a former homicide detective, acting suspiciously at the front door.

He was arrested, but released when his credentials and relationship to Mr. Aeron were confirmed. No sign of Wallis was found in the apartment. Officially, he never turned up, but since there were no signs of foul play, the case seems to have been back-burnered."

"So Roland's story is legit," Frye said.

"Seems to be," Hartmann replied. "What did you guys find?"

"Not a damn thing," Alainn responded. "Wallis was a bit of a recluse. He didn't really interact with the other tenants, and he had groceries delivered by an autoserv system. They only knew he was missing because the cops did a canvass of the floor when he went missing."

"Alright," Frye said to his wife. "You're the expert. What's our next move?"

"We split up. You and I are going to head to Tionscal to see if we can pick up a trail there. Wolf, I want you to see what you can find out about our VIP friend spaceside. Find out who it is and what they're doing here. But be discreet - I don't think that whoever it is is on to you. They know about Frye and me, but maybe the fact that we have backup and another ship has escaped them."

"Consider it done. 'Discreet' is my middle name, after all," Hartmann said with a grin. "Comm me if you need anything." A few minutes later, he was gone.

"OK, for the time being, we assume that Roland is on the level," Alainn said as she and Frye walked the few blocks to the nearest tram station. "If he and Wallis did head to Tionscal, then they were there two weeks ago when we checked in. Between then and the time that we arrived, something happened. Hopefully we can find figure out what that something was."

False Flag   91

"And even if he has been compromised in some fashion," Frye continued, "At the very least we know that he was here, so we aren't completely grasping at straws."

"At least some of the story is true," Alainn agreed. "Right now, our task is to find out how much."

"While avoiding whoever it is that is out to get us," Frye reminded her.

"I've been thinking about that," Alainn replied. "The guys on the station were Marshal's Service, without a doubt, but I'm not so sure about the hit squad at the farm. They may be government, but I don't think that they were with the Service."

"Why's that?"

"They weren't using standard gear, for starters. And while I don't put murder past the Union, Service grunts wouldn't be put up to something like that. It's more likely that they were operators with one of the black ops groups. My guess is that a deputy followed us planetside and lost our trail at the farm. He reported in, and whoever is running things sent some specialists to lean on Siorus." At the mention of the farmer's name, Alainn was quiet for a moment.

Frye understood the silence. "Don't worry, Alainn. We'll find out who did this, and we'll deal with it."

The moment passed, and Alainn continued. "What I don't get is why the government would try and take the tech this way. I get why they did what they did to the *Marco Polo* - we weren't under their jurisdiction. But why do that with a Union citizen? There have to be less convoluted ways of getting what they want."

"It's one of a thousand," Frye said, almost to himself.

"What?"

"Something Roland said. He told me that in a corrupt

government, the crime isn't that there is a single massive conspiracy, it's that there are a thousand minor ones. The buraucracy is so over-inflated, so fractured, that separate factions form, and those factions compete for control. 'The government' isn't out to get us, because 'the government' isn't a cohesive thing - it's just a conglomeration of warring agencies."

"Perceptive," Alainn observed.

"He had some first-hand experience," Frye said. "Kind of like what happened to Wolf, but in his case, it worked out better for them to give him a medal than send him to prison."

"And to the people in charge, either option is morally neutral," Alainn said, shaking her head. "Kill, praise, or imprison - it doesn't matter, so long as it furthers the narrative."

They rode the inner city tram to Luka's transit hub, and then purchased tickets on an express train to Teorann. Although Alainn was on the lookout for a tail, none of the other passengers stood out, and the trip passed uneventfully.

Teorann was a thoroughly unremarkable city stretched out in a plains region of Neirin. The train had passed through what seemed to be an unending sea of cornfields, wheat, and other staple crops. The cornfield that Frye and Alainn's pod had landed in just outside of Luka was apparently a small representation of the continent as a whole.

"I didn't realize that this was a farming planet," Alainn remarked as wheat gave way to soybeans outside of the train's window.

"It's the water supply," a fellow traveler, seated across the aisle, said in response. As Alainn and Frye turned to look at him, his face reddened. "Sorry, I wasn't

False Flag 93

eavesdropping, I promise," he said sheepishly.

"What about the water supply?" Frye asked.

"The oceans on Neirin are freshwater," the traveler replied. "It's an anomaly that makes irrigation much easier."

"And all of the tech in Luka?" Alainn asked.

"A happy coincidence," the man said. "The planet's crust is extremely metal rich, so Neirin is also a perfect place to manufacture elemental superconductors and other tech components. The two things are actually connected; the high metal content in the crust means that there are fewer water-soluble salts to be deposited into the water supply."

"Farming and high technology," Frye mused. "Never would have drawn that connection."

"Most people don't," The man said with a shrug. "High tech industry and one of humankind's oldest professions – it's counter-intuitive. Name's Brannon, by the way," he continued, offering his hand.

"Vals," Frye replied, giving the false name on his current identity documents, "and this is my wife, Sahte."

"What brings you to Neirin?" Brannon asked. "You're obviously from off-world."

"Looking for work," Frye said. "I'm a robotics technician, and there seemed to be a lot of openings available in Teorann."

"Harvesting equipment," Brannon said. "There are a couple of large equipment manufacturers out there that are always looking for technicians."

"You know the city well?" Frye asked.

"Born and raised. I work in Luka now, but go home a few times a year to see my parents."

"Any recommendations on where to stay? We don't want to spend much on a room until I find work."

The Union Chronicles

"Check the Bedryf district," Brannon replied. "That's where most of the factory guys live. It's cheap enough, but not too shady."

"Thanks for the tip," Frye said.

"No problem," Brennan replied.

"I suppose Bedryf is as good a place to start looking as any," Alainn said, after Brannon had excused himself to go to the dining car. "Maybe we'll get lucky."

Chapter Six

As far as Frye could tell, Tionscal was all plasticrete, titanium, and carbon-ceramic composites – highly functional, but dull and uninspiring. The buildings in Luka had been works of art - gleaming monuments to architectural and engineering prowess. The sheer mass of gleaming alloys, composites, and acrylics was nearly blinding. Here in Tionscal, all of the factories looked roughly the same: a dull grey, rectangular plasticrete exterior, distinguishable from each other only by the signs that provided the company name. None of these were megacorps, although it was likely that many, if not all of them were subsidiaries in one form or another. It seemed that no one owned a business anymore; everyone had a boss, until you reached the top, and there were very few people that occupied those positions.

Mixed amongst the assembly facilities were tenement buildings that were as neat, efficient, and uninspiring as the factories themselves. Frye had seen far more run-down accommodations in his travels – these were well-kept, just boring.

Frye and Alainn had disembarked the train at the Tionscal station and taken a tram to the Bedryf district. They had just emerged from the subterranean tram station and were heading down the sidewalk, which was crowded with people going about their daily business.

Alainn had pulled up a list of efficiency hotels on her tablet. There were more than a dozen of them in the industrial district, which covered an area a little more than twelve square kilometers. Unless they got lucky early on, it was going to take a while to check them all.

"The first place is just up here on the left," Alainn said as they headed away from the tram station. Twenty meters down the sidewalk, there was a sign advertising rooms for rent.

The entryway was an unadorned recess in the plain plasticrete wall, and a flaw in their plan immediately became apparent.

"It's an autoserv," Alainn said as they entered the entry alcove. On the wall, next to the door, a terminal invited them to rent a room through a secure credit transfer.

"Good luck asking it if it's seen Roland," Frye chuckled.

"Excuse me," Alainn turned around and called out to a passing pedestrian. A man in coveralls turned and walked up.

"Do any of the hotels around here have human attendants?" Alainn asked.

"None that I'm aware of," the man said with a shrug. Alainn thanked him, and the man headed back down the sidewalk.

"Damn," she said, shaking her head. "I can't believe I was so stupid. Of course the hotels are unattended."

"What now?" Frye asked.

Instead of replying, Alainn keyed her commlink. "Wolf," she said when Hartmann answered the comm, "That police report you pulled up about Wallis – were there pictures of him attached?"

False Flag 97

"Yeah," Hartmann responded. "The cops put out a 'Be on Lookout' alert as part of the investigation. It included an image pack."

"Great," Alainn replied. "I want you to put out a notice on every local net board you can find in Luka and Tionscal. Two thousand credits for any information on Wallis or Roland's whereabouts. I've got a few images of Roland on my tablet. I'll upload them to you – put those on the post as well. If anyone calls and sounds legit, set up a meeting."

"Will do. Anything else?"

"How are you coming on the identity of our VIP?"

"Nothing yet. The entire deck that the ship is docked at is blocked off. I'm working on tapping into the station's manifests, but security is pretty good. I'll get it, but it might be a couple of days."

"Alright. Let Volya and I know the second you have something." Alainn killed the comm and turned to Frye. "Sometimes you have to cast a big, low-tech net. Hopefully someone saw something and will come forward for the cash."

"And in the meantime?"

"We find somewhere to set up shop. Not here, though; call me old-fashioned, but autoserv hotels give me the creeps. Too cold and impersonal."

The city center was only marginally more upscale than the industrial district, but Alainn was able to locate a decent hotel that was staffed by humans. After getting settled into the room, she and Frye headed downstairs to the lobby bar and settled into a corner booth.

"So we just hang out until we get a call?" Frye asked, after taking a sip of whiskey.

"Pretty much," Alainn said, knocking back her own glass. "We checked Wallis' house and found nothing, which was no surprise. We have no idea where he and

Roland went when they got here, so basically, the trail is cold. Someone saw them, though. We just have to hope that they see the posting on the local net and decide that they want the reward money."

"I guess I just figured that tracking people would be more... complex," Frye said.

Alainn shrugged. "Sorry to disappoint. The simple methods are always the best. I've found more people through bribery, half-truths, and outright bullshit than I've ever gotten as a result of high-tech detective work. Someone will come forward, and it'll give us a lead. From there, maybe you'll get to see something more exciting."

Alainn's commlink buzzed. It was Hartmann. "Give me some good news, Wolf."

"I got a hit on the post I put up. A girl that works at a coffee shop in the industrial district says that Roland came in nearly every morning for a month. She wants to meet."

"Set it up. Somewhere public near the tram station in Bedryf, an hour from now."

Hartmann was silent for a moment. "There's a bar a block from the station. I'll send the details to your tablet."

"Good. Tell the girl she's meeting Volya. Send her his picture."

***

Frye sat at a table facing the bar's entrance, sipping on a beer. It was a typical working-class pub, with men and women in coveralls sitting at the bar and around the few tables scattered across the floor drinking away the day's frustrations. A style of music that Frye was unfamiliar with competed with the increasingly drunken conversations for prominence. It was a good location for a meet – public, but the alcohol consumption and the noise would make a

False Flag 99

private conversation easy to have without being overheard.

At one corner of the bar, Alainn had struck up a conversation with a man and woman, and was doing a convincing job of playing the part of a mildly intoxicated robotics technician. Frye knew otherwise – he could tell that she was nursing her drink and keeping a careful eye on both Frye and the door without being obvious about it.

A few minutes after ten o'clock, a young woman entered and glanced around the bar furtively, clearly looking for someone, but apparently unsure exactly who she was expecting to see. As her eyes swept the establishment, Frye caught her gaze and gave a slight nod. The girl made her way to the table, casting glances left and right as she did so, as though she expected someone to dart out at her. As she sat at the table, Frye could tell that she was trying, and failing, to keep from trembling.

"You the one looking for those two guys?" she asked quietly.

"I am," Frye replied. "You said that you had some information?"

"You have money, right? Two thousand?"

"I do, provided that you have something useful to tell me." Frye glanced up and saw Alainn move from the bar and out the front door.

"Um, okay," the young woman said a little more confidently. "I work at a coffee shop a few blocks from here, and the guy you're looking for - the older one - he started coming in a couple of months ago, almost every morning. He was a nice guy, as far as I could tell. He would come in, buy a cup of coffee, and then just sit at one of the tables near the window. I thought it was kind of weird, you know, just sitting there. He didn't read or work on anything. Just sat there and drank coffee and looked out the window. After a while, he'd leave, but he'd always be back the next day."

"And you never saw the younger man?"

"No."

"When was the last time you saw the older man?"

"A couple of weeks ago. He's not in trouble, is he?"

"Why would he be in trouble?"

"The last day I saw him, something made him leave in a hurry. He was sitting where he always did, and then all of a sudden he jumped up and ran out the door."

"Any idea what had him spooked?"

"Not a clue. Like I said, he jumped up, ran out the door, and that's the last I saw of him."

"What's the name of the coffee shop?"

"Orismis," the girl said with a funny look on her face. Frye understood why - he'd seen at least a dozen of the shops in Luka and Tionscal since arriving on Neirin. He wasn't familiar with the chain, but they were obviously big on-planet.

"Of course," Frye said with a grin. "Can you tell me where the shop you work at is located?" The girl gave the address, and Frye produced an envelope, which he passed across the table. "Thanks. You've been a big help."

The young woman looked wide-eyed at the envelope. "I don't see any reason to worry about paperwork, do you?" Frye asked. Technically, a transfer of that much cash was illegal, but he figured the girl wouldn't mind avoiding the taxes.

As expected, she shook her head and quickly pocketed the envelope. "Is that all?" she asked.

"That's it," Frye replied. "Thanks again for the information." The girl nodded as she stood up, and then headed out the door. Frye waited two minutes, and then activated his commlink.

False Flag   101

"Well?" he asked as soon as Alainn answered.

"I think she's clean," Alainn answered. "It doesn't look like there was anyone outside waiting for her, and she headed straight for the tram station when she left."

"OK; if she was on the up and up, then Roland was at the same coffee shop every morning, meaning that he was probably staying nearby. Feel like taking a walk?"

"How romantic," Alainn said. "A moonlit stroll through factories and low-rent motels."

"Just trying to keep the flames of passion burning, my dear. And hey, if we get really lucky, maybe you'll get to shoot someone."

"Just meet me out front, you silver-tongued devil."

***

"He was obviously here keeping an eye on something," Alainn said. They were standing in front of the Orismis shop that the girl had indicated. It was one of a few businesses that appeared to cater to tenants in the industrial neighborhood, and was constructed of the same drab grey plasticrete that made up the rest of the area.

Frye stood in front of the window, trying to get a feel for what Roland would have seen sitting at one of the tables inside.

"He was watching the front door of his hotel," Frye said. Across the street and three doors down was one of the autoserv hotels that had come up on the list they had generated. "He probably just needed to get out of the room for a little while every day, but wanted to keep an eye on things. From here, he can watch the front door, but he also gets a little bit of fresh air."

"And the day that he disappeared, he saw something," Alainn continued. "Someone showed up at the hotel that alarmed him, and he ran across the street to confront whoever it was."

Frye keyed his commlink, and a few moments later, Hartmann answered. "Wolf, I need you to track down the owner of an autoserv hotel in the Bedryf district."

"No problem. I'll get on it as soon as I'm back aboard the *Veritas*," Hartmann replied. "But I've got some other news that you may find interesting. I've been out making friends this afternoon, and I think that I have something on the identity of our VIP."

"Go on," Frye said.

"Well, the official word is that it's a delegation from the Ministry of Communications, here recruiting for engineers and compliance officers. You know, interviewing the best and the brightest signals and communications people in one of the Union's tech hotspots."

"But you're not buying the story?"

"It's too convenient. Our guy Wallis is working on revolutionary communications tech, and the government just happens to send in a delegation right when he gets it worked out? And now they're talking to everyone in the system who may have worked with him?"

"Yeah, seems a little too coincidental."

"And that's not all. Maybe I'm just being paranoid, but I swear that this place is crawling with spooks. Honestly, I know you want to get off of Neirin, but for now, it's probably safer for you planetside."

"Interesting. Thanks, Wolf."

"Well, I think we've got all we can for now," Alainn said. "It's getting late – let's call it a day and head back to the hotel."

The tram station platform was nearly empty when they arrived. A few people in work clothes – technicians just getting off of second shift at the factories - were scattered

False Flag   103

about, but the crowds that had been on the streets when Frye and Alainn first arrived in the afternoon were gone. They stepped aboard the tram and found seats as far from the other passengers as possible.

"OK," Alainn said once they were seated, "Let's go over what we know. Roland calls us for help because someone is after his brother, because he's come up with gear that will revolutionize the way we communicate. We know that the gear is legit, because we've seen it. We also know, based on the police report, that Wallis placed a call to the authorities about a break-in, and that Roland was there when it happened. He tells us that he's headed to another city with Wallis in order to lie low until we get here and extract him.

"Then, Roland goes dark sometime between our departure from Saiorse and the time we get to Neirin. From the story we got from the coffee shop girl tonight, Roland was in fact here, and we have a pretty good idea where he was staying."

"And based on her story," Frye continued, "something spooked Roland a couple of weeks ago and she never saw him again. The timing puts it just after we talked to him when we left Saiorse.

"We also know that somehow, the Marshal's Service was tipped off to our arrival, and that they know who we are."

"They knew we were coming because they have Roland."

"So they grab him at the hotel, and then lean on him until he gives us up?"

"Maybe. Or maybe he had something on him that gave us away," Alainn said. "Or maybe Wallis gave us up."

"It does make sense," Frye conceded. "So what do we do?"

"Well, there will be time to ponder those things later," Alainn replied. "Right now, there are more pressing issues. I think that we're being followed."

Two men had boarded the car moments after she and Frye had gotten on, and they had sat on the opposite side of the car and towards the front, but Alainn had caught them looking in their direction several times. It wasn't definitive, but it was enough to justify some kind of action.

"We get off at the next station," Alainn told Frye quietly. "Just stick by me."

Frye nodded his understanding, and Alainn could see his muscles tighten and his eyes dilate, ready to act.

Alainn tried to remain calm, and made a point not to look over at their suspected pursuers. At the next stop, she waited until the doors were just about to close, and then quickly stood up and darted out onto the platform as the doors slid shut, Frye close on her heels. As they made their way to the escalator that would take them to street level, she chanced a look over her shoulder. The two men were nowhere to be seen, but she couldn't be sure that they had gotten stuck on the tram car.

"We've got to move," Alainn said as she quickened her pace towards the station exit.

Back at street level, Frye followed her around a corner into an alley that was draped in shadow. The darkness allowed them to view the entrance to the tram station without being easily spotted.

Frye's commlink buzzed, followed by Hartmann's voice. "Volya, what the hell is going on down there? I managed to tap into local UMS comms about an hour ago, and a call just went out saying you've been spotted."

"Dammit," Frye said, turning to Alainn. "We've been made. We need to get out of here, and fast. Wolf, give us some options."

False Flag   105

"OK, I have an idea, but I don't know if you're going to like it."

"I bet I'll like it better than prison," Frye responded impatiently.

Hartmann didn't have time to reply. Before Frye could even finish his sentence, a black van pulled up. The door was halfway open before the vehicle stopped at the curb. As soon as it did, the door opened all of the way and head popped out.

Alainn's gun was in her hand before the vehicle stopped, and Frye was just clearing his holster when the head spoke. "Don't shoot! We're here to help! Get in the van, quick!"

Frye looked at Alainn. She shrugged, and lowered her weapon, although she didn't holster it. "Can't be worse than trying to outrun the Marshal's Service on foot," she said, heading towards the vehicle.

Frye and Alainn had hardly sat down before the van was off again. The driver made a series of quick turns before making a left onto what appeared to be a busy thoroughfare. Even at almost midnight, there were plenty of cars on the road, and the van quickly blended in, slowing down to match the pace of the traffic.

Frye glanced around at the interior of the vehicle. It wasn't a newer model, but along one of the walls, opposite of the bench he found himself on, were racks of what appeared to be expensive electronics equipment. Next to him, Alainn was also trying to get her bearings, her Gauss pistol still in her right hand, resting on her lap.

The head that had appeared in the van's doorway belonged to a petite young woman, who had moved to the front of the vehicle and sat in the passenger seat. From where Frye sat, he could see that she had a pale complexion and shoulder-length blonde hair, but not much else.

"Sorry if we startled you," the woman said, turning to look over her shoulder, "But the pigs were on their way. We needed to get out of there, and fast. I assume that you are Mr. and Mrs. Frye?"

Volya was struck speechless by the question, but Alainn clearly didn't have the same problem. "Who the hell are you? Don't get me wrong, I appreciate the lift, but how do you know who we are?"

"My name is Lyt," the woman replied, "and this is Agera. We heard that you were coming. I'm just glad we tracked you down when we did."

"Heard we were coming? From who?"

"Wallis Aeron."

***

"So Wallis is with you?" Frye asked.

"No," Lyt replied, shaking her head. "We're not exactly sure where Wallis is, but we believe that he may be off-world."

"And Roland?"

Lyt looked confused for a moment. "Oh, the brother. I'm afraid that we don't know that, either. Agera thinks that he's dead, but I'm not so sure."

Frye was about to ask what they did know, but Alainn broke into the conversation before he could speak.

"OK, back up for a second," Alainn said. "You didn't really answer my question: who the hell are you, and how do you know who we are?"

"My apologies," Lyt said. "Agera and I are members of a loose network that calls itself Samizdat. We scour the nets for evidence of government malfeasance and corruption, and pass the information that we gather to our

False Flag 107

fellow members. Our goal is to get as much information out about the Union's crimes as possible."

As Lyt spoke, the van exited the thoroughfare and pulled onto a side road, which led into a residential neighborhood. Like everything else in Tionscal, the homes were plain; single-story steel and acrylic bungalows clearly built with function, not aesthetics, in mind. The van pulled into a small attached garage, and Agera killed the ignition.

"Let's talk inside," Lyt said, opening the passenger-side door, and activating the cargo door through which Frye and Alainn had entered the vehicle.

The house was tastefully, if inexpensively, furnished, and seemed utterly… *normal*, Frye reflected to himself as they made their way to the sitting room. He noticed that Alainn had slid the Gauss pistol back into its holster inside of her waistband, but was keeping a watchful eye on their hosts.

For the first time, Frye got a decent look at Agera. He was average height and a bit on the scrawny side, with shaggy hair that hung limply over his ears. It looked like he hadn't shaved in a while, but the stubble was thin and patchy. All in all, a thoroughly unimpressive specimen, and a sharp contrast to Lyt, who seemed well put together.

"Can I offer you a drink?" the young woman asked as they seated themselves in the living room.

"Whatever you've got, make it stiff. And a double," Alainn said.

"And make it two," Frye added.

"I'm afraid that there isn't any alcohol in the house," Lyt said. "I believe that there's some tea, or pineapple juice."

Alainn looked at the girl as though she'd offered her a baby bottle. "What is this, grade school?"

Lyt looked hurt. "I'm sorry, but this isn't my place."

"How about water?" Frye asked.

"I can manage that," the young woman replied, returning a moment later with two glasses.

"So," Alainn said, "are you going to finish answering my question?"

This time, it was Agera who answered. "After the break-in attempt at Wallis' house, he went into hiding, but not until he made contact with us. He told us that his brother, Roland, knew some people who would help them get off-world and somewhere safe. He asked us to check you out."

"Once he gave us your names, we dug up what we could," Lyt continued. "You've been scrubbed from most of the official narratives, but we were able to piece a few things together about you."

"We know that you're a former salvage pilot, Mr. Frye," Agera picked up, "and that's almost all that exists officially. Unofficially, you're known to be behind the destruction of a UMS patrol vessel and the kidnapping of a high-ranking UMS official, among other crimes.

"You, on the other hand, are an almost complete mystery," Agera said, turning to Alainn. "As far as the Union authorities know, you are a foreigner who has entered the Union using false documentation, and you escaped federal custody several months ago.

"More recently, a UMS warrant has been issued for your arrest, and although the charges are similar to the crimes you're actually known to have committed, the story has clearly been modified to hide some of the more embarrassing aspects. Suffice it to say that while your past misdeeds have been largely covered up, you are once again very much on the official radar."

"I'm impressed," Alainn replied. "How did you find so much out so quickly?"

False Flag 109

"As I said," Lyt said, "We have a small but active network, which includes individuals from all walks of life. Agera is an electrical engineer, and I am a lawyer. The only thing that ties us all together is a conviction that a change is needed, and a commitment to that cause."

"Tell us about Wallis," Alainn said, changing the subject.

"Wallis Aeron is a brilliant physicist and communications engineer," Agera replied. "He's also an anarchist, an eccentric, and a bit of an asshole."

The final comment drew a look of rebuke from Lyt. "He's not an asshole. He has Asperger's Syndrome."

"Which as a simple genetic malady is easily corrected," Agera countered, "which means that he's an asshole because he chooses to be."

"Look, I don't really care about his disposition," Alainn interjected, "According to the story that we got, someone tried to break into Wallis' apartment to steal some tech that he was working on. Roland told us that he showed up right after it happened, and that he brought Wallis to Tionscal. Now they're both missing. What happened?"

"Not a clue," Agera answered. "Wallis never checked in with us after his initial contact. We sent him what we'd found about the two of you, but we didn't hear back."

"That's not uncommon with our group," Lyt chimed in. "We aren't a tight-knit organization. We pass along information, but we're deliberately decentralized. It wasn't until the warrant for you hit the nets that we realized something was wrong."

"You keep talking about this organization," Frye said. "What was it again?"

"Samizdat," Lyt answered.

"Samizdat, right. What exactly is your purpose?"

"In a nutshell, we attempt to gather and disseminate

information regarding the Union's abuses of power and promote alternative concepts of governance," Agera said.

"With what purpose?" Alainn asked.

Agera laughed. "That is a fantastic question, and the answers vary, depending on who you talk to. Some of us just like to bitch about the injustices we see, and to know that there are others out there who see the same thing. Others believe that maybe, just maybe, if we get enough information out, and are deliberate and meaningful about putting forward better alternatives, that enough people will join us to actually change things."

"And which are you?" Frye asked.

"Let me ask you a question first," Agera said to Frye. "From what I've been able to piece together, you've done enough to earn yourself a half dozen life sentences on Fangelsi. What did you hope to accomplish?"

"I was trying to get justice," Frye said simply.

"And how did that go for you?" Agera asked.

The question made Frye uncomfortable. He'd asked himself the same thing a thousand times. "The people who wronged me paid," he finally answered, but it rang hollow even as he said it.

"And what are you doing now?" Agera continued.

"My friend asked for my help," Frye said with a shrug.

"From what I gather, your friend Roland asked you to help in a situation not too unlike that which started your original vendetta, no? Someone comes up with a revolutionary idea, and others try to steal it, right?"

Frye reached for his water. His mouth was suddenly dry, and he knew why – Agera was voicing the things that were eating at him about this job. Finally he answered. "I suppose you could see it that way," he replied.

"And how do you see it?" Agera asked, turning his attention to Alainn.

False Flag   111

"More or less like you do," Alainn replied with a shrug, "but I'm here to get paid. You can deal with your own fucked up government."

"And that is precisely what we plan to do," Agera said with a grin. "You see, the problem with just taking care of those who wronged you is that the Union is like the mythical Hydra – if you cut one head off, two more will grow in its place. I guarantee you that whoever you 'dealt with' has been replaced with someone else who is just as cravenly ambitious. Furthermore, as you can see from the current case, you're not the only one who is victimized in the name of progress or political ambition.

"The truth is that we live in a dictatorship. To be sure, it's not a dictatorship headed by an iron-fisted tyrant, but it's a dictatorship all the same. It's a dictatorship of bureaucracy, and that's far, far worse, because it is the machinery that is dictatorial, not the individual. If we were ruled by a despot, it would be a simple matter of assassination to remove the oppression. As it is now, you could kill a thousand petty tyrants, and they would be replaced by tomorrow morning, with all of the structure held firmly in place.

"To truly be free, we have to bring the whole thing crashing down, and that's where Wallis Aeron comes in."

"Because your attempts at communicating and organizing are constantly being thwarted by Union authorities," Frye said.

"Exactly. It's not enough that the government controls the megacorps, and the megacorps in turn control all mass media – they have to actively work to oppress any opposing viewpoints. Of the flood of information that we could disseminate, only a trickle gets anywhere. But with Wallis' new communications tech-"

"Nothing gets intercepted," Alainn concluded.

112   *The Union Chronicles*

"It's better than that," Agera said. "It can't even be listened in on, because there's no transmission."

"But do you really think that getting the message out will convince enough people to revolt?" Frye asked.

"Who knows?" Agera answered, his excitement calming, "Wallis didn't think so – he was in it more for the challenge of figuring out the technology – but I'm hopeful."

"I don't know if it will work," Lyt said, "but I know that it's the only possibility. The key is in getting people to know that they have the power; that if we all stand up, nothing can stop us. In order to do that, we have to be able to communicate with each other."

"The hydra can't be killed alone," Alainn said. "Even Hercules needed help." She looked at Frye, who nodded.

"We're in," he said.

***

"So tell me why you think Wallis is off-world," Frye asked. "Why wouldn't they just kill him?"

"They can't kill him, because they can't replicate the technology," Agera answered. "Wallis told us that he had a prototype unit with him, along with a set of heavily-encrypted schematics. Other than those two physical items, all of the information is in Wallis' head. The schematics can't be cracked, at least by conventional means, so killing Wallis would effectively kill the tech. And as much as they don't want it getting into the hands of the filthy masses, they want that tech for themselves. Ergo, they must be keeping Wallis alive.

"As to why I believe that he's off world, call it a hunch. Wallis doesn't have many friends, but those he does have are here. It simply makes sense for them to take him

False Flag   113

somewhere out of the way."

"And Roland?" Frye asked.

"Like Lyt said, I think that they probably killed him. But if he is alive, most likely he's with Wallis."

"Or he wasn't with Wallis when he was taken," Alainn said.

"Going back to the theory that he's in on it?" Frye asked, although with less irritation than he had previously shown.

"Not necessarily. We know that he was probably across the street when Wallis was taken, or at least I assume that that is what startled him. Maybe he was just too late."

"Then why hasn't he contacted us?"

"No idea. Like I said, it's just a possibility."

"So you know where Wallis was staying?" Lyt asked.

"We figured it out last night," Alainn answered. "We found someone who had seen Roland. We have someone working on tracking down the hotel's owner so that maybe we can get a look at the surveillance footage. Then maybe we can figure out who took them."

"You know, if Wallis was taken off-world, then maybe there's a record somewhere. That's how I tracked you down," Frye said to Alainn. "But Roland had someone with credentials who was able to access transit records. I don't suppose you two have someone on the inside?"

Lyt shook her head. "Probably, but I don't personally know anyone. Like I said, our organization is fairly loose. I could put some feelers out, though."

"It could take a few days," Agera said. "Of course, if I had access to the right equipment, I could probably sneak into whatever datanet we needed."

"You don't have the right gear?" Frye asked. "I thought you were an electrical engineer?"

114   *The Union Chronicles*

"I am, and a damn capable one," Agera said. "Unfortunately, all of my gear is at work. I've written some minor comm anonymizers, but any real hacking would instantly be traced back to me."

"But if you had access to anonymous state-of-the art equipment..."

"Then with a little time, I could get whatever we needed."

"Then we need to get you to Luka Station," Frye said. "My ship is moored there, and I guarantee that you will find the equipment aboard more than up to the task."

Agera looked surprised. "OK, then. I guess we should get going."

"Not we – you," Alainn said. "We'll go back to the hotel and see if we can find anything there. Our friend Wolfgang will meet you spaceside, and he'll help you any way he can. Just don't piss him off, or he might shoot you in the face."

Frye keyed his commlink, and waited a moment for Hartmann to answer. "Wolf, I've got someone headed your way. An electrical engineer named Agera. I need the two of you to try and work some magic; see if you can find any evidence that Wallis was taken off-world."

"You've got it," Hartmann replied. "Any chance this Agera is an attractive young lady?"

Frye laughed. "Afraid not. I don't think he's your type." Agera gave Frye a concerned look, which just made the pilot laugh again.

"Damn. You know that we've already got an excess of testosterone aboard, right?"

"Sorry, buddy. Hey, speaking of testosterone, is Halwyn at least keeping out of your way?"

"I think that he's going stir crazy," Hartmann said. "I sent him out to wander the station for a little while."

False Flag 115

"Alright. We need to figure out if we can give him something productive to do," Frye replied. "If not, we can cut him loose and send him home."

"OK, anything else?"

"Yeah, do you have any info on the owner of that hotel?"

"Hang on." There was a brief pause, and Frye could hear Hartmann working at the *Veritas'* control terminal. "There's nothing in public records. It appears to be locally-owned. I'll do some more digging, but right now, I've got nothing."

"Alright, thanks, Wolf." Frye killed the comm.

"How fast can you get spaceside?" Alainn asked Agera.

"I'll leave now," the engineer replied. "Where do I go when I get there?"

"I'll give Wolf your description. Let Lyt know when you're headed up, and I'll have him meet you at the shuttle terminal."

"So you don't trust me." It wasn't a question.

"Let's just say it's better for everyone if I don't send you up with our berth number and comm addresses. We're wanted, and you can't give up what you don't know."

"Fine." Agera stood to leave.

"Be careful," Lyt said. Agera nodded and headed back to the garage.

"You know, you should have given him a little bit more trust than that," Lyt said after Agera left.

"Like I said, it's best for everyone," Frye said. "I'm not trying to be insulting, and I appreciate you sticking your necks out to save us from the Marshal's Service, but the last thing I need is for the info about our ship getting into the wrong hands. Consider it an extension of trust that I even offered to let him aboard."

116   *The Union Chronicles*

"Look, it's late," Lyt said, letting the issue go. "There's a guest room that the two of you can use. Let's get a couple of hours' sleep and then head back into town. By that time, Agera will be headed spaceside and maybe your friend will have some more information."

"Sounds good," Alainn said. She was exhausted, and could tell that Frye was, as well.

As soon as they were shown to the guest room, Frye collapsed on the small bed. He was just about to go to sleep when he realized that Alainn was still just sitting on the edge of the bed.

"What's up?" he asked.

Alainn shook her head and put her finger to her lips, indicating that she didn't want to talk. Frye glanced around the room, as though he would find a listening device sitting on the nightstand. He looked over at Alainn, who was regarding him with a cocked eyebrow. Frye smiled, realizing how silly he must look.

Alainn motioned to the door and stood. Frye followed suit, and soon they were standing outside in the bungalow's small front yard.

"You think someone's listening?" Frye asked.

"I don't know. It just seems a little odd," Alainn said. "These guys show up just as the Marshal's Service is coming down on us, and if you didn't notice, they still didn't answer my question about how they found us. They're probably legit, but we need to be careful – at least until we have a better idea what is going on. This whole business has been a clusterfuck from the beginning, and I don't know what to believe."

"Agreed. I'll let Wolf know to be on his guard."

"Good. Now let's get back inside before Lyt realizes we're gone."

False Flag

Chapter Seven

In his dream, Frye was running through a field. He knew that he was being chased, but he couldn't see his pursuer. The field seemed to go on forever, and he kept running, knowing that sooner or later, he would have to stop. If he didn't find somewhere to hide, he would be caught.

A building appeared in the distance, and Frye changed his course, aiming for the small structure. In the doorway, he could see Alainn motioning for him to hurry. He ran through the door and Alainn slammed it shut behind him. No sooner had the door closed than someone began pounding on it.

"Don't open it," Alainn commanded as the pounding became more frantic. She turned and began walking into the interior of the building, which appeared to consist of a single dark room. Alainn was quickly engulfed in shadow.

"Where are the lights?" Frye asked, following her into the building.

Alainn didn't answer, and Frye couldn't see her anymore. He turned around and the door was shrouded in darkness. He looked around and realized that only blackness surrounded him.

"Alainn?" he called out, but there was no answer.

"Where did she go?" a voice asked next to him. Frye jumped and spun around, looking for the source of the voice. It was Roland, who was suddenly standing next to him.

"You scared me," Frye gasped, struggling to regain his composure. "Where are we?"

Roland shrugged his shoulders. "Come on, we have to help my brother." He turned and started walking. Frye followed, but Roland was quickly shrouded in darkness, and Frye could no longer see him. He called out repeatedly, but there was no answer.

Frye began to walk, his hands out in front of him to avoid running into anything. The building wasn't that big, so he assumed that he would find a wall momentarily, and then he could follow it until he found a door or a light switch.

His foot struck something sitting low to the floor. Frye moved his foot and jumped. There, jutting out of the plasticrete floor was a man's face. Frye leaned over and tentatively touched the cheek. It was a mask. As he picked it up, the mask turned to ash and crumbled in his hands.

"Volya?" Alainn called out to him.

"Where are you?" Frye called back.

"What do you mean 'where am I'? I'm lying next to you."

Frye's eyes snapped open. He was in the guest room; Alainn lying next to him, propped up on her elbow.

"Sorry, I was dreaming," Frye said, shaking the cobwebs from his head. "What time is it?"

"Four."

Frye groaned. They'd been in bed for a little over three hours. "I suppose we'd better get going," he said unenthusiastically.

As Frye was dressing, Lyt knocked on the door. "Agera

False Flag   121

just called," she said through the door. "He'll be at the station in an hour."

"I'll have our friend meet him at the shuttle terminal," Frye responded.

As soon as he'd finished getting dressed, he keyed his commlink. It took a few moments for his friend to answer, and when he did, he did not sound happy.

"Sumbitch, Volya. You have any idea what time it is?"

"Yeah, it's too damn early. And something tells me that it's gonna be a long one," Frye replied. "You've got company inbound, and he's gotten about as much sleep as the rest of us."

"Super. What does he look like?"

"Young kid. Mid-twenties, maybe. Long dark hair that probably wasn't washed as recently as it should have been. Skinny and pale, like he doesn't spend much time outside. He's wearing jeans and a black shirt. Name's Agera."

"Got it. You know what, Volya?"

"What's that?"

"Hearing you call someone in their twenties a 'kid' makes me feel really damn old."

"Calling someone in their twenties a kid makes me feel old, too, Wolf. Guess we'll just have to get used to getting old."

"Well, I suppose it beats the alternative."

Frye let out a dark chuckle. "You never know. The way this is going for us, we might not have to worry about it. Oh, and while we're on the topic of how sideways this seems to be going, keep an eye on the kid."

"And why is that?"

"Nothing specific. We just don't know these people, so keep your guard up."

"Will do. Anything else?"

"That covers it for now. Comm me when your new roommate shows up."

* * *

"So how do you know Agera?" Alainn asked as she, Frye, and Lyt walked toward the nearest tram station an hour later. "The two of you don't exactly seem cut from the same cloth."

"The truth is, we don't really know each other much at all," Lyt replied. "Samizdat is made up of all kinds of people, from different walks of life. Our only link is a desire to see things change."

"If you don't know each other, then how did you end up together in this mess?" Frye asked.

"It just sort of happened. Agera knows Wallis a little bit - I think that they've had some professional contact before. They don't like each other much, or so I gather from Agera, but they share common ideals, so they mostly put their personal differences aside.

"I work for the law firm that represents Wallis in his patent and royalty matters. I've never worked with him directly, but I did meet him at our offices once. Very quickly, we each recognized that the other was a part of the movement, and so we maintained infrequent contact with one another. When Wallis asked Agera to check into the two of you, he also asked for my help. As an attorney, I have access to information that isn't available to the general public. So I helped Agera where I could. Then, when Wallis went missing a couple of weeks ago, we decided to track the two of you down."

"How exactly did you manage that?" Alainn asked. As she had mentioned to her husband the night before, Lyt seemed to have a habit of dodging the question. Alainn

False Flag 123

wanted to see if she would try and avoid it again.

"We've been watching Wallis' place," Lyt answered. "When you showed up, we followed."

"Makes sense," Alainn answered.

"How are we going to avoid a repeat of last night?" Frye asked. "We had marshals on us, and we know that they're looking."

"I've got that covered," Lyt replied as they headed aboard the tram.

***

A fifteen minute tram ride led them to a part of the city that Frye and Alainn hadn't seen before. Lyt led them out of the station and down a side street. She ducked into a beauty salon and Alainn and Frye followed.

They walked through the main floor of the salon, past rows of booths, about half of them occupied by customers and stylists, and into a back room.

"Desteen?" Lyt called.

A woman emerged from a corridor that appeared to lead to a back door. "That's me. What do you want?"

"I'm Lyt."

Desteen's severe gaze didn't lose its intensity, and she remained silent.

Lyt held her left arm out with the underside of her forearm up. She pressed her index and middle fingertips into the flesh of her forearm and then released the pressure. The image of a stylized 'S' appeared briefly on her arm, and then dissipated just as quickly.

Desteen nodded and then did the same with her own forearm. The 'S' appeared just as it had on Lyt's arm and disappeared.

The woman appeared to be satisfied by the ritual. "I

124   *The Union Chronicles*

assume they're them?" she asked, nodding towards Frye and Alainn. Lyt nodded in assent.

"Follow me." With that, Desteen turned and headed down the corridor. Before they reached the back door, she turned and opened a door that led to a storage closet.

"In here," she said, motioning for the three to enter the cramped room.

Already on alert after being taken to an unknown location, Alainn entered the room carefully, eying her husband and allowing her right arm to brush against the small of her back, where her Gauss pistol was stowed. Frye gave an almost imperceptible nod and dropped his left hand casually into his pocket, where Alainn knew he kept a collapsible shock baton. He left his right hand free in case he also needed to go for his sidearm.

As soon as the door closed, Desteen reached across to the far wall and hit a hidden switch. With a click, a hidden door recessed itself into the wall, revealing a small room with a chair not unlike the ones that they had passed in the front room.

"Sit," Desteen commanded, looking at Frye.

"Wait just a minute," Alainn interrupted. "How about you tell us what is going on first?"

"We need to change your appearance," Lyt said. "The Marshal's Service was on to you last night."

"We tried that already," Frye said. "The haircut and color method apparently didn't work."

"That's why we're going with something a little more... in depth," Desteen said.

"Facial reconstruction? Not a fucking chance," Alainn said.

"No, nothing quite that drastic," Lyt said.

"Or that obvious," Desteen continued. "We'll redo your hair length and color, of course. We can look at a new

False Flag 125

eye color, as well. But the real trick is to make you invisible to facial recognition, and to do that, we'll need to inject you with a small dose of nanites."

"And you don't consider that drastic?" Frye asked sarcastically.

"Well, they won't alter your appearance," Desteen said. "What they'll do is make it impossible for any facial recognition algorithm to pick up on your key facial indicators. Basically, you'll be invisible to any kind of AI facial identification. Besides, it's a fairly small dose, on the order of what would be applied to close a large surgical incision or a bad injury."

"And how exactly did you come up with this? It sounds like something that the authorities would be highly interested in keeping from the general public," Alainn observed.

"Which is why we're doing it in a hidden back room in a beauty salon," Desteen answered. "I'm not a beautician – I'm a nanobiologist, and I came up with the idea myself. Very few people know that the technology exists."

"Is that how the symbol on your arm works as well?" Frye asked.

"More or less," Desteen said. "The nanites embed themselves in your skin tissue, and have the ability to modify pigment. In theory, if you injected enough of them, you could change the skin tone throughout your entire body, but that's something I haven't tried yet."

Alainn wasn't sure what to do. She didn't know Lyt or the organization that she belonged to very well yet, but the prospect of not having to worry about facial scanners was enticing. Since the scanning technology relied on skull shape, rather than outward appearance, it was impossible to fool them with a dye job and a haircut. The only other option that she'd ever heard of involved radical reconstructive surgery that would actually alter bone structure.

Frye appeared to have fewer reservations. "Alright, nothing ventured, nothing gained, I suppose," he said, and seated himself in the chair.

Alainn was about to try and stop him, but she realized that he was right. With the Marshal's Service on their tails, it was going to be tricky getting back into orbit and out of the Union. She'd managed it once with Frye and Hartmann, but even over the last six months, she could see that security was growing ever tighter. She wondered how much her own exploits had influenced this development, and how much was being motivated by groups like Samizdat. She'd always heard rumblings – rumors that systems were planning to secede from the Union, or that dissidents were plotting revolution – but she'd always dismissed them as far-fetched. Now, however, it seemed much more plausible that the Union was on the verge of fracturing, and that she may well be playing a part in its demise.

Desteen took an injector from the table by the chair. From her pocket, she produced a small vial and loaded it into the device.

"This will sting," Desteen told Frye, who simply nodded. She placed the tip of the injector where his jaw bone met his neck and pulled the trigger. Frye winced, then moved his jaw side to side and rubbed the injection site.

"You weren't kidding," he said.

"Sorry," Desteen replied. "I'm working on a topical gel that can simply be rubbed into the skin, but I don't have it worked out yet."

Frye got out of the chair and Alainn took his place. Desteen repeated the procedure.

False Flag 127

"OK," she said when Alainn's injection was complete. "You're all set. Lyt will take you back out front and you can take care of hair, eyes – whatever you need."

"You aren't going to do that here?" Frye asked.

"Like I said, I'm not a beautician," Desteen said.

***

A little over an hour later, both Frye and Alainn looked far different than they had when they walked in. Frye's hair was back to its natural dark brown, but it was longer than he was used to keeping it. His eyes were now hazel, and he was sporting a thick but well-trimmed beard.

For her part, Alainn had kept her hair red, but it was a more natural auburn than the bright copper it had been just an hour earlier, and it now hung several inches past her shoulders. Her eyes were a bright green.

"We should get you both a change of clothes, as well," Lyt said as they exited the salon. "There are a few clothing stores nearby."

Frye and Alainn both purchased new clothing and wore it out of the store. They walked the short distance to the tram station and were about to head for the neighborhood that Frye and Alainn had been in the previous evening when Frye's commlink buzzed. It was Hartmann.

"He's here," Hartmann said, as soon as the pleasantries were exchanged.

"Good," Frye replied. "Anything on the hotel?"

"Yeah, it's owned by a management company that's based in Luka," Hartmann said. "I'll send you the info."

"Great, thanks," Frye replied. "Go ahead and shift focus to finding out if Wallis was taken off-world."

"Already on it. Hopefully this new kid will be of some assistance."

Frye killed the link.

"Did Wolf get anything?" Alainn asked.

"Yeah. The hotel's ownership is in Luka. Looks like we're headed back to the big city."

***

"So, how are you planning to get your hands on the hotel surveillance footage?" Lyt asked as they approached the building where Gastamo Hospitality had its corporate offices. The office building was located away from the glamorous downtown area, and Frye assumed that their offices would reflect the same no-frills ambiance that the hotel they'd seen earlier had.

"I'm going to ask nicely," Alainn replied as they entered the lobby. "Stay here," she continued, pointing to a small seating area near the front windows.

Lyt looked like she was about to argue, but Frye cut her off. "We don't need the three of us barging into the office, demanding to see surveillance footage," he explained. "It'll make people nervous. Alainn can take care of this herself." With that, he headed over to an uncomfortable-looking couch and sat down. Lyt followed.

Alainn boarded the lift and rode to the sixteenth floor. She hadn't been entirely up front with Lyt; her plan was to ask nicely for the security footage, but if that didn't work, she was prepared to ask less nicely — a possibility that made her uncomfortable. Whoever was in charge here legitimately owned the security footage, and had no obligation to show it to her — in fact, an argument could be made that tenant privacy required them *not* to allow her to view it. What made Alainn uncomfortable was the fact that she agreed in principle, but was prepared to violate those principles in order to find out what was going on.

False Flag 129

The lift opened into a clean, but dated-looking lobby. A young man sat at a reception desk, slouching in his chair and looking bored. As Alainn approached, he straightened his posture in a belated attempt to look professional.

"Can I help you?" he asked.

"I certainly hope so," Alainn replied. "I'm hoping to speak with your chief of security about one of your properties in Tionscal."

The receptionist gave her a concerned look. "Is there a problem?"

"I hope not," Alainn replied, "but I really need to speak with someone in charge of site security."

"OK, please just give me a moment," the receptionist replied. "If you'll have a seat over there, I'll be right back with you."

Alainn walked over to the seating area that the young man had motioned to and sat down. While she waited, she listened in as the receptionist called to someone behind the doors that separated the reception area from the rest of the office.

"Mr. Bürge? There's someone in the lobby asking to speak to our head of security," the receptionist said quietly into the commlink, clearly trying to keep the conversation private from Alainn. "No, she says it's about a property in Tionscal. Yes, sir," he said, nodding his head as though the other person could see him. He killed the link and looked up at Alainn.

"Ma'am?"

"Yes?" Alainn replied, standing and approaching the desk.

"I'm sorry, but our head of security isn't in right now," the receptionist said. "Perhaps you'd like to make an appointment?"

Alainn smiled. "What is your name?"

130   *The Union Chronicles*

"Mikel," the receptionist replied.

"You're lying to me, Mikel," Alainn said, still smiling. "I don't like being lied to, especially since I've been so polite, and my request is not an unreasonable one. Now, get back on that comm and get whoever it was that told you to blow me off out here, or else I'm going through those doors, and if you get in my way, I'll go through you, as well. Understood?"

Mikel rolled his eyes and keyed his commlink again. "Sir, it's me again. She insists on speaking with someone, or she's threatened to make some kind of a scene. Yes, sir."

He turned back to Alainn and smiled insincerely. "Someone will be right with you. Please have a seat."

Alainn returned to the seating area and keyed her own commlink. Instead of speaking, however, she typed a message to Frye: *Things are about to get ugly.*

A few moments later, the doors to the back office opened and a barrel-chested man strutted out into the waiting room and up to Alainn.

"Ma'am, I'm afraid that we have a problem," he began.

"You're certainly right about that," Alainn said in response, "and your next words will determine exactly how big that problem gets. A friend of mine disappeared from one of your hotels approximately two weeks ago, and I'm looking for some help tracking them down. I get that help, and I go away quietly."

"I certainly don't appreciate your implication that something happened to one of our tenants," the man replied, "and I can assure you that we've had no incidents at any of our fine properties. Now, I'm afraid that we are all quite busy-"

"Wrong answer," Alainn said, her voice still quiet, but threatening. "You're lying to me, and as I told your lackey

False Flag   131

over there, I don't like being lied to. I'm willing to bet that you know exactly what I'm talking about."

Alainn could tell that the man in front of her was getting nervous. While he maintained his smug demeanor, his eyes had begun to twitch, and there was a subtle, but noticeable, pallor spreading across his face.

The man swallowed. "Mikel, call the police." He turned his attention back to Alainn. "You've overstayed your welcome. I suggest that you find your way out before the authorities arrive."

Alainn composed herself. "Bad move," she said, turning and heading back towards the lift. Without another word, she headed back down to the lobby.

Downstairs, Frye greeted her with a raised eyebrow. "Well?" he asked.

"Smug son of a bitch," Alainn seethed through her teeth.

"So I'm guessing you didn't make a new friend today?"

"Quite the contrary," Alainn said as they headed towards the front door, "We've got a date tonight. He just doesn't know it yet."

***

Karl Bürge left the office in time to catch the 7pm tram from the station located two blocks away. It had taken him nearly an hour to calm down after his run-in with the woman earlier that day, and something told him that his threat earlier would only keep her at bay for so long...

Caught up in thought, he didn't notice the man behind him until it was too late. Suddenly, his knees buckled, and he was forced into an alleyway.

"We could have done this in the comfort of your office," a familiar voice said from the shadows, "But this works just as well, as far as I'm concerned." The owner of the voice stepped out into the small ray of evening sunlight that was able to penetrate into the narrow alley. It was the woman from earlier.

"You're out of your mind," Bürge hissed.

"Listen," Alainn replied, "I don't really have time for this. I need some information. You have that information, but for some reason insist on lying to me."

"I have no idea what in the hell you're talking about, you crazy bitch," Bürge shot back, his voice increasing in both pitch and volume.

"Keep it down," Alainn commanded, "And if you call me 'bitch' one more time, I will hurt you. If you lie to me again, I will hurt you. Call for help, I will hurt you. Basically, if you do anything other than tell me what I want to know, I will hurt you. Do I make myself clear?"

"Perfectly. Now let me make myself clear," Bürge responded. "I don't know who the fuck you think you are, but you can't drag me into an alley and threaten me."

Alainn looked over Bürge's shoulder and nodded. Almost immediately, an electrical pulse shot through his body. Bürge crumpled to the alley floor.

"I'm not threatening," Alainn said, crouching down to Bürge's level, "I'm telling you what will happen if you continue to refuse to help me." She stood back up. "Believe it or not, I don't like doing this. I find it distasteful – immoral, even. That being said, something happened at your hotel. I can tell that you know, and that you are trying to cover it up. That makes you a liar, and for that, I will make you pay. Alainn nodded again, and another electrical pulse rocked Bürge's body, this one causing him to lose control of his bladder.

"Okay!" he hissed through clenched teeth. "I'll tell you what I know, but it isn't much. About two weeks ago, our

False Flag

control system went down at one of our properties in Tionscal. Diagnostics showed that power was out to the entire building for about four minutes. Not long after, I got a call from Tionscal PD about a disturbance at the same property. Some tenants heard what sounded like an argument coming from one of the rooms while the power was out. When the lights came back on, nothing seemed amiss, but the room that the fight was reportedly coming from was empty."

"And who was the room registered to?" Alainn asked.

"The last name was Kendrick," Bürge replied.

"The power was out, but the cameras should have been on a backup," Alainn said. "What did they show?"

"Nothing," Bürge answered. "They're on a backup, but everything went down. Primary, backup systems – all of it."

"EMP," Frye said from behind Bürge. Alainn nodded in agreement.

"I told the cops that the room was vacant, and that the noise must have had something to do with the air handlers shutting down because of the outage," Bürge said. "It was bullshit, but they bought it because the room was clean – no personal items, no signs of a struggle, nothing. It was like this Kendrick guy just disappeared. I told them the room was vacant, and they just wrote it off."

"And you swept it under the rug, because a break-in and kidnapping would be bad for business," Alainn observed.

"Look, I've got a business to run," Bürge said.

"Sure, you couldn't let a little something like two people disappearing get in the way of profits, right?"

"Two people? Who was the other one?" Bürge asked.

"Kendrick was travelling with his brother," Alainn replied.

134 *The Union Chronicles*

"Well, they weren't both staying in that room," Bürge said. It was a single."

"Worried that they were cheating you on the extra person charge?" Alainn asked sarcastically.

"Well I don't like it," Bürge replied. "It's basically theft. And that's why we have security measures in place to prevent it. Trust me, there's no way that two people were staying in that room."

***

"Sounds like you've had quite a day," Hartmann said over the commlink.

"And yet we're nowhere," Alainn replied. She was pacing back and forth across the sitting room floor in the suite she and Frye had rented, glass in hand. She and Frye had called to fill Wolfgang in on the events of the day.

"How's the kid doing?" Frye asked.

"Which kid?" Hartmann asked. "You've practically got me running a fucking daycare center up here."

"Funny," Frye replied. "I'm talking about Agera. He getting anywhere with the transit records?"

"He was able to break in to the commercial transit database a couple of hours ago," Hartmann replied. "So far, we haven't seen anything suspicious. He's trying to hack into the more restricted government manifests now. I'll let you know as soon as that happens."

"All right," Frye responded. "I'm not sure what else we can do down here. We're at a total dead end. Nothing we've found out makes any sense at all."

An unfamiliar voice chimed in. "Actually, it might."

"Halwyn?" Frye had forgotten all about the young pilot, and was surprised to hear his voice.

"Sorry to butt in, but I had an idea."

False Flag 135

"Well?" Frye prompted.

"You said that you couldn't figure out why Roland would be staying somewhere away from his brother, but you're making the assumption that he was actually staying there. What if he wasn't?"

"Shit," Alainn said, stopping in her tracks. "It was bait."

"Exactly," Halwyn replied. "You assumed that Roland was staying at the hotel, and went to the coffee shop every day just to get out of the room."

"But he was there looking to see if anyone showed up," Frye chimed in.

"And someone did," Alainn continued. "Which is why he left in such a hurry."

"But he already knew someone was after him," Frye countered. "Why set a trap? All he needed to do was lie low until help showed up."

"Because something unexpected happened," Alainn said. "For some reason, he suspected that someone close to Wallis was involved, and he needed to make sure. So he set a trap, and when they showed up, his suspicions were confirmed."

"But I thought you guys said this Wallis guy was a recluse," Hartmann said. "He probably wasn't out advertising what he was working on to his small social circle."

Alainn's eyes suddenly went wide as things clicked into place. "Wolf, where's Agera?"

"Down in Engineering," the navigator replied. "He said it was easier to work at the terminal down there where it was quiet."

"Listen," Alainn said. "It's Agera. He knew Wallis had a working comm unit. He knew that we were coming. He's got the technical know-how to rig an EMP that would take down a hotel's primary and backup systems. Wolf, you need to get down to Engineering and secure him, understand? Wolf?"

The comm was dead.

Chapter Eight

Kendrick didn't like it. Breaking into the freight yard and sneaking aboard a freight transport car alone would have been tricky enough, but doing it with a physically awkward and tactically clueless thirty-something was an exercise in mental torment. Several times, Kendrick was tempted to leave his brother to whatever fate his pursuers had in store.

The reward for his perseverance was a cramped hiding place inside of an irrigation pipe being sent from a fabricator in Tionscal to one of the coastal pumping stations that supplied irrigation water to the inland agricultural operations. Wallis had apparently fallen asleep, much to Kendrick's relief, giving the former detective a couple of hours of silence in which to rest and recharge.

Unfortunately, rest wasn't forthcoming. He desperately needed to get in touch with Volya, to let him know what had happened, but for some reason, his pilot friend wasn't answering his comm.

Roland had been furious when he found out that Wallis had asked a couple of friends to look into Volya and Alainn. He wasn't offended that Wallis wanted to make sure that his friends were legitimate – he hadn't seen or

138   *The Union Chronicles*

spoken to his brother in a decade, so he didn't expect the younger man to simply take his word for it. The problem was that Roland didn't know Wallis' friends, either, and he didn't approve of letting anyone know that they had help on the way. Now it appeared that his suspicions were well-warranted.

That bastard Agera, Kendrick thought to himself as he listened to rain begin to beat down on the pipe that served as his shelter. Once Roland had learned of Wallis' research into their rescuers, he had decided to put a plan into place to test the loyalty of Wallis' friends. He had rented a room at an autoserv hotel across town from where he and Wallis were staying, and had contacted the engineer from the room, asking him to go back by Wallis' apartment and make sure that everything was secure. It was a thin excuse for contact, but it was the best that he could come up with on short notice.

Then he waited. Every day, he went to the hotel across town. He would have a cup of coffee at the shop across the street, watching foot traffic, making sure the coast was clear. Then, he would go inside and check the door for the room that he had rented, which he had rigged. If anyone had gone in or out, he would be able to tell.

After a couple of weeks, he decided that he'd been too suspicious. Wallis' friends, just like his own, were trying to help. He kept up the routine, however, because it gave him an opportunity to get out of the hotel for a couple of hours each day, and if he were being honest with himself, the stakeout made him feel just a little bit like a cop again, which was silly, but comforting.

Then it happened. As he was sitting in the coffee shop, a black van pulled up to the curb and three men got out. A few minutes later, they disappeared into the building. Kendrick stood, tossed his half-empty cup into the

False Flag 139

receptacle by the door, and raced across the street.

The autoserv terminal by the front door was blank, and the door itself was open. Somehow, the power to the building was out. Kendrick didn't wait around to get any more information. He grabbed the registration number from the van and quickly made his way to the tram station.

He had given the number to Wallis, who was able to quickly track the number to his colleague Agera, whom he had enlisted in his attempt to verify Mr. and Mrs. Frye's credentials.

When the local nets had blown up with wanted notices for Frye and Alainn, Kendrick knew it was no coincidence. He grabbed Wallis and they fled. The freight train had been Kendrick's only method for getting out of town without being spotted. Now Frye wasn't answering his comm and he had no idea how he was going to get Wallis off planet and to relative safety.

The freight train arrived in Marineiro shortly before daybreak. Kendrick had finally settled into a fitful sleep an hour before they arrived, but had come to as the train slowed into the freight yard.

"Wallis, get up. We've got to go." The younger man stirred, then groaned as his body protested the cramped, chilly condition it had been subjected to overnight. Grabbing his bag, he followed Kendrick out of the end of the irrigation pipe.

The morning was cold and wet; a slight, constant drizzle was coming down from a starless pre-dawn sky. The two men's shoes squished through the muddy train yard as Kendrick led the way toward a grove of trees at the edge of the yard.

The rain was light enough that the tree canopy kept the two men mostly dry while they decided what to do next.

"How far are we from a local tram station?" Kendrick asked.

Aeron took out his tablet and called up a local map. "Maybe a half kilometer," he answered a moment later.

"OK, then let's get going," Kendrick said, hoisting his bag onto his shoulder again. Looking at the map, he got his bearings and headed off with Aeron beside him.

The grove of trees quickly gave way to roads and buildings, and in less than ten minutes, Kendrick and Aeron were on the tram platform. A quick ride downtown, and they had found a place to stay that could have been substituted for any of the hovels that they had stayed at in Tionscal.

Before going inside, Kendrick counted out three hundred credits in various denominations, then stuffed them in his front pocket.

"I need a room for four nights," Kendrick said to the desk clerk.

The clerk, who seemed as tired and worn as the building he was supervising, seemed to regard the intrusion as more of an inconvenience than a source of income. "Three seventy-five," he said.

Kendrick pulled the wad of cash from his pocket and made a show of counting it. "Shit. Make it three nights," he said absently. It was a show – he knew the published rate for the room – he'd had Wallis look it up before they went inside - and knew that he'd be short. He hoped that the desk clerk would assume that he was a down-on-his-luck day laborer. After the past eight weeks without a haircut, almost a week without a shave, and a morning spent walking through the drizzling rain, he knew he looked the part.

"There's a five percent surcharge for cash," the clerk

False Flag 141

said disdainfully. Kendrick had also anticipated this. Paying in cash was seen as a sign that the tenant was working under the table, so requiring a surcharge was an easy score. An illegal worker wasn't likely to go to the cops and complain about the extortion. It also meant that the hotel would be keen to avoid any kind of activity that might draw the attention of the authorities.

"You're fucking killing me," Kendrick said in mock protest.

"Then go somewhere else."

Kendrick pretended to ponder his options for a moment, and then tossed the cash across the counter. In exchange, he received a keycard. The clerk offered no change – no surprise there.

"Room four twelve," the clerk said. "And no funny business. If you're gonna have women up, there's an hourly charge."

"Thanks," Kendrick mumbled, but the clerk had already turned his back and returned to whatever it was that slum supervisors did to pass the time.

The room, as expected, contained a couple of beds, a single dingy chair in a corner, an outdated viewscreen on the wall opposite the beds, a bathroom that may or may not harbor infectious disease, and a kitchenette that may or may not have been more hygienic than the bathroom. The drizzle had turned into a light rain, which tapped against the acrylic windows, adding to the melancholy atmosphere. Kendrick took an almost lustful look at one of the beds, but managed to tear himself away and headed towards the door.

"Stay here," he told Wallis. "No comms. Don't talk to anyone, and don't leave the room."

"How am I supposed to eat?" Wallis asked.

"Order takeout."

"That would require using a comm *and* talking to someone," the younger man observed.

Kendrick massaged his temples with his hands. "Fine. You can use your comm to order food. Nothing else. Understood?"

"Yes. Thank you for clarifying," Wallis replied. "Where are you going?"

"To find our ride off of this planet," Kendrick said. "I'm headed back to Luka."

***

The drizzle turned into a full, driving rain as Kendrick made his way back to the tram station. *At least it's a warm rain*, he thought to himself as he quickened his pace. Once inside the dry station, he bought a ticket to the city's transit hub, where he could catch a train back to Luka.

Aboard the tram, Kendrick inconspicuously scanned the other passengers, but was satisfied that he hadn't been followed. His quick escape to Marineiro would have been nearly impossible to follow, especially since the people following him had been at a dead end at the hotel in Tionscal. Kendrick wondered if Agera knew he'd been the victim of a counter-surveillance trap, or if he assumed that he had bad information. Ultimately, it didn't matter – if he ever came face-to-face with the electrical engineer again, he planned on killing him either way.

At the transit terminal, Kendrick made his way to the ticket booth and bought a one-way fare to Luka. The train wouldn't depart for another couple of hours, so he made his way to the shopping mall that was connected to the terminal. He purchased a new set of clothes, complete with shoes, and then took them into one of the public restrooms to change out of the soaking wet garments he

False Flag   143

was wearing.

In the restroom, Kendrick changed into the dry clothes, and then leaving his old clothes in the trash, he headed into an electronics store and purchased a small fusion battery pack, and then headed to the bar adjacent to the train terminal for a drink. He grabbed a stool and ordered a beer, glad to be dry for the first time in hours.

He took his first sip, and nearly spit it out. Staring back at him from the viewscreen mounted behind the bar were the faces of Volya and Alainn. After overcoming his initial shock, Kendrick realized that the viewscreen was playing a feed from a local newsnet.

"What's the story with them?" Kendrick asked the bartender, nodding towards the screen.

The bartender shrugged. "Marshals are after 'em. They made some kind of scene last night spaceside, then escaped to the surface."

"Can you replay it?" Kendrick asked. The bartender nodded, and then started the news story from the beginning.

> *The Planetary Union Marshal's Service has released additional details on the suspects being sought in last night's incident aboard Luka Station.*
>
> *Authorities say that arrest warrants have now been issued for Volya Frye and Alainn Marwol in connection with the murder of Siorus and Réimse Arbhar. The bodies of Mr. and Mrs. Arbhar, who operated a large-scale farm near Luka, were found this morning by Marshal's deputies near where the pod that Frye and Marwol used to escape Luka station touched down.*
>
> *Frye and Marwol fled Luka station yesterday as Marshal's deputies attempted to board their ship to*

serve warrants on a number of smuggling and other charges. One deputy was killed and two others wounded in the confrontation.

The Planetary Union Marshal's Service has enlisted the help of Neirin's planetside law enforcement community in the attempt to locate Mr. Frye and Ms. Marwol. Any citizens with information regarding the pair's whereabouts are urged to contact their local law enforcement agency. The Marshal's Service warns that the pair are armed and considered extremely dangerous. Do not approach them if spotted. Instead, contact law enforcement.

The news story continued, showing the exterior of the Arbhar home, as well as a shot of the pod used by Frye and Alainn to escape to the surface, but no new information was given.

Kendrick drank his beer and tried to stay calm. Now it made sense why Agera had waited so long to take the hotel room bait: he was waiting for Frye and Alainn to make it in-system before he put his plans into action. The fact that he showed up at the hotel the same day that Frye and Alainn made it to Luka Station couldn't be a coincidence.

Kendrick checked the time. His train would board in forty-five minutes. He quickly finished his beer, left the bar, and found a secluded corner in the terminal. Sure that there was no one within earshot, he activated his commlink. Wallis didn't answer.

For a moment, Kendrick started to panic, but then he remembered the instructions he'd given his younger brother just a few hours earlier, and composed a quick message. *You can use the comm to order food and to*

False Flag   145

answer a call from me. After the message was sent, he tried again. Wallis answered almost immediately.

"I'm not comfortable with all of these changes in the rules," the younger man said before Kendrick could even say anything in greeting. "As a police officer, I would have thought that you had respect for rules. Weren't you any good at your job?"

Kendrick stifled the urge to swear. "I'm not a cop anymore, Wallis," he sighed, "and since when do you care about the rules? Aren't you an anarchist?"

Wallis was silent for a moment. "Point taken," he finally said. "What do you need?"

Kendrick scanned the area to make sure he was still out of earshot of anyone. "I need a gun," he said. "Do you know anyone who could help me out?"

There was another moment of silence before Wallis answered. "Possibly," he said.

"Look, I need a yes or no answer here," Kendrick replied.

"I'm not sure," Wallis said. "I believe that I know someone, but given our current communication protocols-"

"Wallis?" Kendrick interrupted.

"Yes?"

"Can you make the call without giving away your location?"

"Of course. It's a simple matter of writing a disposable anonomyzing algorithm. I can-"

"Wallis?"

"Yes?"

"Is that a yes?"

"Yes, that's what I said."

"Then just fucking do it. I don't need all of the fucking details."

146   *The Union Chronicles*

"There's no need for profanity, Roland."

"Whatever. I'll be in Luka in about four hours. Send me the details before I get there."

***

An hour before Kendrick arrived in Luka, his comm buzzed. It was Aeron.

"What do you have for me?" he asked without a greeting.

"I'm sending you an address," Wallis replied. "Ask for Delo. He'll be able to give you what you need. It'll cost two thousand, cash."

"Thanks, Wallis."

"Don't thank me yet," the younger man replied. "I do not know Delo personally, and the address is in a very undesirable part of town. I suggest that you be very careful."

"Thanks for the warning, but I've dealt with bad neighborhoods and dangerous people before."

Before the train arrived in Luka, Kendrick went into the train's bathroom and opened the small backpack that held his remaining cash, along with a change of socks and underwear and a few other necessities. He took one of the socks out and slipped the fusion battery he had purchased into the spare sock. He then concealed the improvised weapon in the interior pocket of his jacket.

The train arrived on time, and Kendrick made his way to the city trams. He boarded the line that would take him to the neighborhood that Wallis had indicated and immediately understood why his younger brother had been so nervous. The car had been repeatedly vandalized, with graffiti covering walls, windows, and seats. The car that Kendrick sat in was almost empty initially, but as he

False Flag 147

neared his destination, it began to fill up with increasingly destitute individuals. The older ones had a look of resignation, as though they knew their station in life and while they didn't like it, had simply given up hope of making it any better. The younger ones had a different look - anger. Life and circumstance hadn't beaten the fight out of them yet. Kendrick knew that many of them would become predators, preying on others in order to get by. Others would use their anger as a motivation to claw their way out of the slums. Still others, the minority, would recognize the causes of their poverty and would channel their anger as a catalyst for change. There were so few of those, though, Kendrick reflected. The vast majority would either become part of the faceless defeated masses or the local criminal element that preyed on them.

Kendrick's stop was announced, interrupting his reflection. He exited onto the platform and made his way up to street level. The streets themselves were spotless - the cleaning bots scrubbed the streets clean, even while the society that walked them rotted away.

The address that Wallis had provided belonged to a run-down tenement building. Kendrick made his way inside and to the unit that Wallis had indicated. He buzzed, and a few moments later, he heard footsteps shuffling up to the door.

"Whozit?" the voice on the other side demanded.

"Roland Kendrick. Wallis sent me."

The door opened, and Kendrick found himself face-to-face with a small mountain of a man. Delo was a head taller than Kendrick, and considerably wider. He wasn't fat or fit – simply a massive human being, the kind of specimen that most people would find instantly intimidating. Kendrick, however, had dealt with plenty of big men before, and knew that all too often, they took it for granted that their size would do all of the work for them.

"You look like a fuckin' cop," Delo growled.

"That's probably because I used to be one," Kendrick replied. "Do you really want to do this out here?"

The large man seemed taken aback by Kendrick's lack of regard for the differences in the two men's stature. For a moment, he seemed to contemplate something, and then he motioned the former detective inside with his head. Kendrick made his way into the cramped sitting room, and Delo closed the door to the hallway.

"Money," Delo said, holding out his hand. Kendrick reached into his pocket and pulled out twenty hundred-credit notes. He had left the remainder of his cash, along with his backpack, in a locker at the transit station.

Delo counted the cash, moving each bill from one giant paw to the other. "It was twenty-five hundred," he said, his eyes boring a hole into Kendrick's forehead.

"Like hell it was," Kendrick said, staring back. "The deal was two grand. That's all I've got, so if you don't want to deal, I'll just take it back and go elsewhere."

"You're free to go elsewhere," Delo said, holding up the handful of cash, "But I'll go ahead and hold onto this. Now get the fuck out."

Kendrick turned as though he was about to head back to the front door. Instead, he slipped his hand into his jacket pocket and grabbed the improvised flail. He swung quickly around, making the weapon an extension of his outstretched right arm and catching Delo square in the temple with the two-kilo battery pack. The man crumpled into a heap as he lost consciousness. Kendrick bent down and collected the cash from Delo's fist.

His instincts told him to get out of the apartment quickly, before the larger man regained consciousness, but

False Flag 149

he didn't want to leave without what he had come for. The apartment was a one bedroom, so there were limited places to store illicit weaponry. Kendrick headed directly for the bedroom closet.

He found two inexpensive and worn Gauss pistols hidden in a box in the back of the closet. He checked the magazines, finding both loaded with thirty 5mm rounds and fully-charged power supplies. He tucked them both into his waistband at the small of his back and made his way back through the sitting room. Delo was conscious, but having trouble getting to his feet. He was also between Kendrick and the door.

"Ima fugyou up," he mumbled in Kendrick's direction.

"Are you familiar with the story of David and Goliath?" Kendrick asked.

Delo gave him a blank stare. "You know what? Never mind," Kendrick said. "I'm not really in the mood for witty repartee anyway." He pulled one of the pistols out and pointed it at the massive man's head. "I'm leaving, and I'm taking these and the cash with me. On the ground, face down, feet crossed, hands on the back of your head."

Delo glared at him. Kendrick assumed that he was trying to look threatening, but given the man's dazed state, it was not having the intended effect.

"I'll give you until the count of three," Kendrick said. "After that, I paint the wall behind you with what is undoubtedly a disappointing quantity of brain matter. One..." Kendrick didn't have to continue. Delo slowly dropped to his knees, and then prostrated himself on the floor, crossing his feet and placing his hands on the back of his head. Kendrick made his way around the man and slipped out the front door, concealing the pistol as he did so.

As soon as he was clear of the apartment building, he

keyed his commlink. Wallis answered almost immediately.

"What the fuck, Wallis?"

"Could you be more specific? And again, Roland, I find the profanity completely unnecessary."

"Specifically, you sent me to buy a gun from a guy roughly the size of an interstellar freighter, only dumber. Which is fortunate for me, because if he was smart *and* gargantuan, I'd be out two grand, or possibly worse."

"He tried to rob you?"

"He took my cash, and then tried to up the price. When I told him it didn't work that way, he tried to keep the money."

"Since you said 'tried,' I assume that he was unsuccessful."

"I hit him in the head with a battery pack, took the guns and the cash, and left."

"So you got the gun?"

"Yes, I got the gun, Wallis."

"Then I don't see what the problem is. Besides, I warned you that this might happen."

"Yes, thank you, Wallis. You were amazingly helpful."

"Don't mention it."

***

Kendrick returned to the transit terminal and retrieved his backpack. He went into the nearest restroom, secured himself in one of the stalls, and then removed one of the pistols from his waistband and stowed it in the backpack.

The former detective had no idea how he was going to find his friends. He knew that they were on-planet, and that they were likely trying to find him, but Luka was a city of ten million, and he couldn't be sure that they were even in the city. During their last conversation, he had told

Volya that he was in Tionscal, so it was just as likely that they were making their way there in an attempt to track him down.

There was one option, but it was a long shot. Volya and Alainn had brought backup with them – a man named Wolfgang that Kendrick had never met. Even though his friends were compromised, there was a possibility that there was at least one potential friendly still off of the official radar. Kendrick keyed his commlink again.

"Wallis, I need you to check on something for me," Kendrick said.

"What do you need?"

"I'm looking for a ship, but I don't know what name it is registered under. It would have docked either at Luka Station or Pristav, and it would have been within twelve hours or so of the *Seguir*. The craft would be small – it has to be crewed by two people, and would have been registered as a courier vessel. How long will it take you to put together a list?"

"Not long – give me a half hour or so. But it's likely to be a pretty long list. I would say at least a dozen vessels."

"Don't worry about that, just get me the list."

"Of course. I'll call when it's ready."

***

Fifteen minutes later, Kendrick's commlink buzzed. It was Wallis.

"I have your list."

"Give it to me."

"There are a total of fifteen vessels that match your description. Eleven of them docked at Luka, and four at Pristav. All fifteen are of a class that could be sailed with a two-person crew, and arrived within twenty hours of your friends."

"Great. Do you have details on the vessels?"

"Of course."

"How many of them are domestic?"

"Eleven of them have Union registry. Three of the four at Pristav, and eight of the vessels at Luka."

"What's the story on the one foreign vessel that docked at Pristav?"

"The *Prokureur.* It's registered to the Väärennös system. Manifest states that it is carrying confidential legal documents for a Väärennösian citizen currently imprisoned on Neirin on suspicion of intellectual property theft."

"Well, that rules Pristav out."

"Why do you say that?"

"If you have the opportunity to pick your own cover, you don't ever choose anything to do with the legal system. Way too much scrutiny. The good news is that I'm in the right place. What about the three foreign vessels at Luka station?"

"Hang on." There was a brief pause. "Got it. You're looking for the *Confoi.* Registry says it's out of Forfalsket, but that's easy enough to fake. According to customs, it declared a destination of Pristav when it cleared the border checkpoint, but now she's moored at Luka."

"Good catch, Wallis. Looks like I'm headed to Luka Station."

***

In the shuttle terminal, Kendrick purchased a ticket for the next trip to Luka Station, and made his way to the gate. A half hour later and he was aboard the shuttle, pushing through Neirin's atmosphere and into the black.

False Flag 153

There was a slight shudder as the craft punched through Neirin's exosphere and crossed into the vacuum of space, and then the craft went completely still. The inertial dampeners had been activated at takeoff to negate the effects of the shuttle's rapid acceleration. Now the craft felt completely stationary, although Kendrick knew that they were actually hurtling through space at nearly twenty thousand kilometers per hour towards Luka Station, which was in geosynchronous orbit 37,000 kilometers above the city.

On approach, Kendrick could tell that things aboard the station were far from business as usual. One entire deck of the station was nearly empty, with a lone civilian craft flanked by a pair of patrol cruisers. Even at a distance, Kendrick knew that he was looking at the *Seguir*. As the shuttle got closer to the station, he was able to make out a jagged, gaping hole in the ship's lower deck, which Kendrick knew housed the revolutionary reactor system. The work was far too sloppy to have been done as part of a recovery effort, and Kendrick realized that Alainn had probably scuttled the ship as she and Frye fled their Union pursuers in an attempt to keep the technology from being stolen.

As he disembarked the shuttle, Kendrick could feel tension in the air. There was a pronounced increase in Marshal's Service presence above and beyond what had been in place when Kendrick arrived a few weeks ago, and a cold sweat broke out on the former detective's brow when he realized that he was carrying two handguns on his person – a violation that could get him ten years on Zatvor. He quietly cursed himself for not stowing his bag in a locker at the terminal planetside.

Kendrick left the shuttle terminal and headed to the station's hub. Luka station was composed of eight decks, and was capable of mooring anything from small private craft to large freighters, although most of the bulky agricultural material that was moved off-planet shipped out of Pristav. The hub was open from Level 1 to Level 8, creating a massive, forty-meter tall central room that helped alleviate any feelings of claustrophobia that may arise from being in what amounted to a steel can hurtling through the vacuum of space at a staggering velocity.

None of those things were of particular interest to Kendrick, however. He didn't get claustrophobic in space, and had too much on his mind to contemplate his position in the cosmos, either physically or philosophically. Wallis had told him that the ship he was looking for was moored on deck F, berth seventy-two. In the hub, he hopped into a lift and headed six floors up. Exiting the lift, he passed a bar and several stores carrying various provisions before finding a corridor that would take him out to the ring where the ships were moored.

Except that the corridor was blocked by marshal's deputies manning a makeshift checkpoint. Kendrick stopped in his tracks, unsure of what to do. His hands gripped the straps on his knapsack, his palms beginning to sweat, the gun inside now feeling like it weighed a ton.

Without making contact with the uniformed deputies, he walked past the corridor and attempted to blend in with the other people on the hub's F-level mezzanine. He made his way back around to the bar that he'd seen across from the bank of lifts. He went in, found a stool at the counter, and ordered a beer.

"What's with all of the uniforms?" Kendrick asked as the bartender set the glass in front of him.

"Haven't you heard?" the young man asked. "A couple of smugglers tore through here yesterday. Made it planetside – now the Marshal's service is trying to make

False Flag 155

sure that they don't make it back off-world before they're caught. No one gets to the gangways without going through the checkpoints."

"So who gets through?"

"If you've got a ship docked, or work on one, or have a passenger ticket, you get through," the bartender replied. "Or if you're station crew. And that's it."

Kendrick decided to let the issue drop. Continuing to ask questions about the security situation would be suspicious. Instead, he decided to change the subject.

"I heard about the smugglers on the news. I wonder what they were carrying."

The bartender shrugged. "No idea, but they swarmed that ship, that's for sure."

"I assume their ship is the one on the deck all by itself?"

"That's the one. The whole deck is closed off. I imagine they'll be moving it to the Marshal's Service station soon."

"I saw a big hole below decks on our approach. What happened?"

Another shrug. "Got no clue. They're keeping a pretty tight lid on the whole thing. We only know what's been released, and what we saw when the escape happened."

"You were here?"

"Yeah. Damndest thing. I heard a commotion and went out to look over the railing. Made it just in time to see everyone hit the floor while two people made a break for one of the corridors with a couple of deputies on their tails."

Another patron caught the bartender's attention and he made his way to the other end of the counter, leaving Kendrick with his thoughts.

Kendrick was almost certain that he knew the berth that Frye's ship was in, but that was it. He'd never met

Wolfgang Hartmann and had no way to contact him. He couldn't even wait around for the guy to make a trip outside of the checkpoints, because he didn't know what he looked like. He had to figure out a way through the checkpoint.

The easiest method would be to purchase a fare on a commercial ship, but they were berthed on different decks than private craft, and it was unlikely that he could make it through the F deck checkpoint with a ticket for a ship moored on a different deck. It wouldn't be quite so simple.

Kendrick motioned for the bartender and ordered another beer. If he was going to sit and plot, he might as well be comfortable.

Posing as a member of a ship's crew seemed the best way through. Marshal's deputies posted to the station would know most of the station crew, and their identification documents would be almost impossible to duplicate, at least without the proper equipment. With hundreds of ship crewmembers milling about the station, coming and going regularly, it would be almost impossible for the Marshal's Service to properly verify everyone's identity. That was the weak point. Now, he just needed the name of a ship, and for his name to be put on the crew manifest. Fortunately, he knew someone who could do just that. Kendrick keyed his commlink, and Wallis answered a few moments later.

"I need to be a crew member on a ship moored on F deck," Kendrick said as soon as his brother answered.

"Now may not be the best time to think about a career change, Roland," Wallis answered. "We're kind of in the middle of something."

Kendrick was silent for a moment. "Was that a joke, Wallis?" he finally asked.

"Yes," Wallis responded. "I'm quite proud of it. See,

False Flag 157

what I did was pretend to take your request literally, even though it was obvious that, given our current situation, you were clearly working on some kind of elaborate ruse."

"Yeah, I got it," Kendrick said.

"But you didn't laugh."

"I'm laughing on the inside. Now, are you going to help me out?"

"Of course. You need to be listed on the station manifest as a crew member for a vessel on F deck."

"Exactly. The Marshal's Service has set up checkpoints at the corridors to the ship berths. I need to be listed as crew to get past. Pick a ship and list me as the navigator or something."

"I hardly think that you're qualified to be a ship navigator, Roland. That kind of specialty requires a significant amount of training, otherwise-"

"Are you joking again?"

"No, Roland, navigation is a serious responsibility."

"Wallis, I'm not going to be doing the fucking job, I just need to get past the checkpoint," Kendrick hissed.

"But what if the deputies manning the checkpoint ask you questions to make sure that you know the job?"

"It's a document checkpoint, not a quiz show, Wallis. Just put me on the damn manifest."

"Of course. But Roland?"

"What, Wallis?"

"The profanity really is unnecessary."

"I disagree, Wallis."

***

"Identification, please," the marshal's deputy said, his monotone delivery making it clear that he felt the assignment was not a proper use of his talents.

Kendrick handed over his government identification card, hoping that the slight tremor in his hand wouldn't make the deputy suspicious. He had moved the second handgun from his waistband to his backpack, and the two Gauss pistols, while lightweight, felt like a pile of stone on his back.

The guard swiped the card through a reader attached to his tablet. The seconds seemed to stretch into an eternity while Kendrick waited to be cleared. He knew that Wallis' skills were unmatched, but his rational recognition of his brother's abilities had little effect on his nerves.

Finally, the deputy nodded and handed the card back. He motioned for Kendrick to pass through the temporary barricade. The former detective slipped past without another word, sure that at any second the deputy would realize his mistake and stop him.

Once he was halfway down the corridor, Kendrick realized that he had been holding his breath and was beginning to get dizzy. With an audible sigh, he released the air from his lungs and took a few deep breaths in an attempt to relax.

Berth seventy-two was along the outer ring, midway between the corridor that Kendrick had walked down and the one next to it. Through the windows along the outer ring, Kendrick could see the ship docked outside. Through the ship's forward bridge windows, he could see two men; one a young man in his early to mid-twenties, and another who appeared to be around thirty-five or so. Kendrick assumed that the older one would be Wolfgang Hartmann, and the younger would be the pilot that had been hired to fly the ship. The two men appeared to be having a conversation, although they weren't looking at each other, so Kendrick assumed that they were talking over the ship's comm system.

False Flag 159

Suddenly, the older man's countenance changed, and he leaned over the control station on the bridge. Although Kendrick couldn't hear him, the man appeared to be shouting. He slammed a fist down on the panel, and then his face went ashen. The younger man's face also took on a sickly pallor. Then, nearly simultaneously, the two men collapsed onto the floor.

Kendrick bolted toward the gangway and hit the button next to the sliding door. It opened with a hiss, and he ran down the short gangway to the ship's entry door. It was locked. Kendrick pounded on the hull with his fist, but was rewarded with nothing more than the echo of his strikes reverberating through the ship's hull.

A few moments later, another sound caused Kendrick to panic. It was the sound of metal scraping against metal, followed by the hiss of air escaping into the vacuum of space. The ship was moving away from the gangway.

Kendrick took a few steps back from the ship's hull, and could see it moving against the collar that connected it to the gangway. The hiss grew into a dull roar, and somewhere behind him, an alarm began to sound. Something was causing the ship to back out of the mooring while it was still tethered to the station, and in a few moments, Kendrick was going to get sucked out into the vacuum of space.

He turned to run back towards the gangway door, but he knew it was too late. The alarm he had heard was a breach alarm, and as he turned around, the gangway door slid shut, sealing both the breach and Kendrick's only exit.

Air was escaping the gangway quickly now, and already, Kendrick was finding it hard to breathe. The ship was using its thrusters to break away from its moorings, and already the gangway collar had broken loose, leaving a widening gap between the collar and the ship's hull. The rush of air slowed as the atmosphere in the gangway dissipated and the amount of space available to facilitate its escape grew. In seconds, there would be no air in the gangway, and Kendrick knew that he would have only a few moments before he lost consciousness, and a minute or so more before his heart would lose the battle against the increasing pressure in his veins and he would die.

With only seconds of consciousness left to spare, there was only one thing to do. Kendrick dove towards the retreating ship's hull, crossing what was now nearly a meter of open space, and grabbed the manual airlock release. The vacuum was causing the air in his lungs to expand painfully, so he expelled everything from his lungs in an attempt to avoid pulmonary trauma. The door to the ship's airlock slid open and Kendrick tried to pull himself inside. Already, he could feel the saliva in his mouth begin to boil, and his ears began to pound as the air trapped in his skull fought to escape.

Something wasn't letting him in the door. *Backpack*, he realized. It was caught on the outside handle. He shrugged the bag off of his shoulders and in a final struggle, slipped inside the airlock and closed the door.

As his vision began to cloud, Kendrick reached up with the last of his strength and hit the 'pressurize' button inside the airlock. As he lost consciousness, he wondered if the air would arrive in time.

Chapter Nine

Lyt Nevin stood up from her sofa and paced the floor of her small sitting room for what felt like the thousandth time. After the incident at the Gastamo offices, she had been unceremoniously dropped at her apartment by her new acquaintances with no indication what they were planning to do or when she would hear from them again.

She had tried to catch up on some case work, but had been unable to focus on anything other than Wallis' predicament and the events of the past twenty-four hours. When she had begun associating with the Samizdat network, everything had seemed extremely abstract. It was a way to voice her frustrations with the status quo, and to feel like she was speaking truth to power, without really sticking her neck out.

Now, however, it felt all too real. Wallis Aeron was the target of some shadowy conspiracy. Twenty-four hours ago, she had helped two foreign fugitives escape from the Marshal's Service, had made arrangements to make them anonymous, and had gone with them to shake down a Union business for information. What she had done would get her charged with aiding and abetting fugitives, but if her involvement with a subversive organization, even one as non-violent as Samizdat was discovered, those charges would get elevated to conspiracy and treason. She would spend the rest of her life on the prison planet Abis, if the authorities didn't simply make her disappear.

And the couple she had been asked to assist treated it all with casual indifference. She had committed a handful of felonies, and they just dropped her off at her front door as though it was nothing.

Lyt sat back on the sofa, activated her viewscreen, and pulled up a local newsnet, half expecting to see a story about the arrest of her new acquaintances.

Instead, splashed across the screen was the headline NEAR DISASTER AT LUKA STATION AS SHIP BREAKS MOORINGS. Lyt activated the link, and the story began to play.

Authorities are investigating an incident at Luka Station that caused a brief depressurization and nearly triggered an evacuation of the station. A spokesman for the Transportation Ministry has issued the following statement:

"Earlier today, a vessel tore loose from its moorings while docked at Luka Station. We have reason to believe that the incident was intentional and the result of the theft of a small civilian spacecraft, as the craft in question ignored hailing requests from the Marshal's Service and moved quickly away from the station in the direction of the nearest jump point. A Marshal's Service patrol craft was dispatched to pursue the vessel, and a blockade has been set up at the jump point."

The Marshal's Service has declined to comment on the incident, saying it will issue a statement

False Flag

once the vessel has been recovered. This marks the second crisis event on the station in as many days. Yesterday, two individuals fled the Marshal's Service during a fumbled attempt to serve a warrant and escaped to Neirin's surface. The Marshal's Service will not comment on whether or not it believes that the two incidents are related, but there is some speculation that the two fugitives managed to gain access to Luka Station in spite of increased station security and stole the ship in an attempt to escape the system.

Lyt stared at the screen, unable to believe what she was seeing. It couldn't be Volya and Alainn – they had a second ship docked, and would therefore have no need to steal a craft. It couldn't be a coincidence, though; somehow, the events had to be related. She just couldn't figure out how. Caught up in the news story, she didn't hear the door to her apartment slide open.

She did, however, hear the footfalls behind her, and she turned around just in time to stare down the barrel of a Gauss pistol.

"Evening, Lyt," Alainn said from behind the weapon. The attorney shifted her focus from the bore of the gun to the person behind it, and then her eyes caught movement in her peripheral vision. She turned her head to see Volya Frye move into a flanking position beside her sofa, his own weapon aimed at her head.

"What the hell?" Lyt said. She had intended to sound indignant, but her voice failed her, and instead it came out as a questioning whisper.

"Cut the shit," Alainn commanded. "Where's he headed?"

"Where's who headed?" Lyt asked, but almost as soon

as the words were out of her mouth, she knew.

"Agera stole your ship," she said, nodding to the viewscreen, which had moved on to a different story.

"And you're going to tell us where he's headed," Alainn said.

"But how should I know?" Lyt almost whimpered. "I barely know the guy."

"Then how'd you know he stole the ship?" Frye asked.

"I- I just figured it out," Lyt stuttered. "I saw the story on the news, and then the two of you barged in."

Alainn lowered her pistol slightly. "So you really don't know where he's headed?"

"I really don't know. But what does it matter? He'll never make it past the blockade. He'll get grabbed before he gets through any of the jump points in the system."

Alainn dropped the gun to her side. "Yeah, that's not going to happen with this ship," she said.

"You're saying that it can run a Union blockade?"

"I'm saying it won't have to."

***

"Give it six hours," Frye said, trying to lighten the mood. "Either Wolf will get the upper hand and kill Agera, or he'll drive him to suicide with his insanity."

Despite the circumstances, Alainn let a smile briefly cross her face. "Ten dollars says he surrenders to the Union in four just to get away from him."

Guns had been holstered, and now Frye and Alainn were seated with Lyt in her living room. Something needed to be done, but no one had any idea where to begin.

"It sounds like your friend is kind of a handful," Lyt said.

Frye chuckled. "That's putting it lightly. He's one of the

False Flag 165

most loyal men I've ever met, and smart as well, despite his attempts to appear otherwise."

"He's just a bit of a misanthropic bastard is all," Alainn said.

"Well, that's not *all*," Frye corrected. "He's more than a little dangerous, as well. A while back, he and I were in a little bit of a jam, and he overpowered two armed Union Marshal's deputies. Your buddy Agera better have him buttoned up tight, or he'll end up regretting it."

"And that would be a bad thing?" Lyt asked.

"Not at all," Frye said darkly. "I for one hope he kills the little shit."

"That would make things easier," Alainn observed. "We've already lost one ship, and I'd like to know we've got a ride home."

"Something tells me we won't be heading home for a while," Frye said.

"But I have promises to keep, and miles to go before I sleep," Alainn muttered.

"What?"

"Never mind. I forget that you aren't an ancient literature buff."

"Tell you what: when we get home, I'll take up reading as a hobby," Frye said. "Until then, let's worry about how we're going to track Wolf down."

"What about Wallis?" Lyt asked.

Alainn frowned. "Shit," she said, "I'd almost forgotten why we were in this God-forsaken place. Not only have we lost two ships, a pilot, and a navigator, but we haven't even found the people we came to exfiltrate."

"You said that you thought Wallis had been taken off-world," Frye said, turning his attention to Lyt.

The woman shook her head. "That was Agera's theory," she said. "I never saw any reason to think that was the case."

"And that theory gave him a perfect excuse to get aboard our ship," Alainn said.

"But we offered," Frye observed.

"Given the circumstances, what else would we do?" Alainn turned to Lyt. "Who did the background investigation on us?"

"I pulled public records," Lyt said, "But Agera did most of the heavy lifting. He said he had some connections that would allow him to break into government databases."

"You mean those same databases that he needed our comm tech to get into?" Alainn said.

Alainn's implication wasn't lost on her husband. "So Agera has the ability to dig into government records," Frye said. "He finds out about our previous run-ins with the Union, and somehow finds out about the tech we'll be bringing with us.

"Then, when we get here, he meets up with us, but tells us he needs access to advanced comm gear to dig into government records, knowing that it will get him access to one of our ships," Frye continued, his voice growing more excited.

"And of course we oblige," Alainn said, taking over. "He gets spaceside, and then sequesters himself on the engineering deck, claiming that he needs some peace and quiet. He manages to get control of the ship's systems, and from there, he somehow manages to overpower Wolf and Halwyn."

"He's been planning this since Wallis asked him to look into us," Frye said.

"Which means he's the reason that Roland set the trap," Alainn continued.

"All of that is fascinating," Lyt interjected, "but how does it help us? Wallis and his brother are still missing, and

False Flag   167

your ship is still headed God knows where."

This seemed to take the wind out of Frye and Alainn's sails. There was silence for a moment as the pair contemplated their new ally's words.

"She's right," Frye said. "We may know how Agera did it, but it doesn't help us."

"Maybe," Alainn replied, "but it gives me an idea. Lyt, how do you get in contact with Wallis?"

"We've used a secure subnet that Agera set up," she replied.

"And you haven't communicated with him directly?" Alainn asked.

"No," the lawyer replied. "He hasn't answered since we sent the data we'd collected on you."

"Have you tried his comm?"

Lyt looked like she'd just been scolded by a teacher for failing a particularly easy exam. "No. Agera said he'd tried, but there was no answer."

"Of course he did. Give it a try."

Lyt grabbed her tablet off of the table beside the sofa. She keyed an address and waited.

"No answer," she said a few moments later.

"Message him," Alainn directed. "Tell him you're with us, and that we need to arrange to pick him and Roland up."

Lyt keyed a message into the tablet. "Now what?"

"We wait," Alainn said.

***

It wasn't a long wait. Less than a half-hour later, Lyt received a response.

"He wants to know how he can be sure it's us," she said.

"Tell him Roland can verify it as soon as he talks to us on the comm," Frye said impatiently. "And tell him we don't have a lot of time for games."

Lyt send the reply and waited. The reply came back in less than a minute.

"He says that isn't possible at the moment."

"We don't have time for this shit," Alainn snapped. "Tell him that his options are limited. Either we get a call in the next five minutes or we're gone. I'm tired of fucking around."

Lyt started typing the message, but Alainn interrupted. "And make sure you put the part about us not fucking around in there," she said. "I swear I'm not kidding. I want off of this damn rock, and I don't care how it happens, but it's happening soon. I get jerked around one more time, and I'm going to find someone that I can justify killing."

"Done."

Five minutes later, Lyt's comm buzzed. "Wallis?" Lyt answered, sending the call to the viewscreen so that Frye and Alainn could hear.

"It's me," the voice on the other end said. "What's going on? I asked you not to contact me."

"I have a couple of people here who were rather persuasive," Lyt replied.

"Circumstances have changed," Alainn said. "Where's Roland?"

There was a brief silence. "He's not here," Wallis finally said.

"I didn't ask where he isn't," Alainn responded impatiently.

"He's aboard Luka Station," Wallis replied. "He couldn't reach you, so he went looking for your partner Wolfgang."

"Can you reach him?" Alainn asked.

False Flag 169

"I haven't tried," Wallis answered. "I talked to him a couple of hours ago, but he told me to stay here and keep off of the comm. I shouldn't even be talking to you."

"Get him on the comm," Frye said. "We need to wrap this up and get off-world before anything else falls apart."

There was another brief silence as Wallis attempted to raise his brother. "He's not answering," he said a few moments later.

"Shit," Frye muttered.

"Where are you?" Alainn asked.

"Marineiro," Wallis replied.

Alainn turned to Lyt. "How far away is that?"

"It's out on the coast," she replied. "A couple thousand kilometers, I'd say."

"Less than two hours by air," Frye said. "We could charter a private flight and be back in four hours or so."

"Go," Alainn said. "I'm going to stay here and make arrangements to get off-planet, and try to figure out how we're going to track the *Veritas*."

"I'm on my way, Wallis," Frye said. "Sit tight, and stay quiet until I get there."

***

Frye was tense throughout the ten minute tram ride to the transit station. The facility would be full of surveillance equipment and the Marshal's Service would be well-represented, especially given the events on Luka Station over the past two days. He was also exhausted – the four hours of sleep he'd gotten in the past forty-eight hours were barely keeping him upright.

He exited the tram and silently prayed that the nano injection he'd had nearly twenty-four hours ago worked. As he expected, there were more uniformed deputies than usual, and he had to make a conscious effort not to look nervous.

Frye hopped on a moving walkway and rode out to the private craft satellite terminal, where he was dropped in a darkened lobby. He checked his tablet. Three o'clock – not exactly a good time to try and charter a flight.

None of the charter desks were staffed, but Frye could see a light on in a back room at one end of the lobby. He made his way across the tiled floor and to the counter of a small charter service. The light was coming through a slightly opened door. Frye maneuvered around the counter and knocked on the door, opening it far enough to slip his head inside.

The door led to a short corridor. Frye slipped through the door and walked down the hallway. There were a couple of offices, but both were dark and empty. At the end of the corridor was another door. Frye tried it, and found it to be unlocked. It led to a small hangar, which housed an air shuttle that Frye estimated would seat five or six passengers.

"This is a private area," a voice to Frye's right said. He turned to find a woman in a flight suit eyeing him. "What the hell are you doing here?"

"Looking for a ride," Frye said. "I need to get to Marineiro, fast, and I'm willing to make it worth your while."

"At three in the morning?"

"I'm willing to make it even more worth your while if there are no questions, and you let me get some shut-eye on the flight out," Frye said.

The woman raised an eyebrow.

"I will tell you that it's nothing illegal," Frye said, smiling. "I need to pick someone up, and it's quite urgent. I need you to fly me out, wait a half hour or so while I go get

False Flag 171

him, and fly us back. I'll pay you twenty thousand for a half-day's work."

The pilot's eyes grew wide. "Deal," she replied. "But I want half up front."

"No problem," Frye said. "Let's get going. I'm on a tight schedule."

Ten minutes later, Frye was strapped into one of the passenger seats. The shuttle was comfortable, but not opulent – Frye speculated that it mostly got used by small businesses that had need of a private craft but couldn't justify the expense of owning and maintaining their own.

The pilot, who had introduced herself as Jarat, completed her pre-flight checklist and transmitted a flight plan to the control tower. For his part, Frye transferred ten thousand credits to her account, using an untraceable dummy account that he had tied to his false identity. Once Jarat verified the payment, the hangar roof retracted, the takeoff fans whirred to life, and the small craft was airborne. Moments later, they were at cruising altitude and speeding towards Marineiro. Frye missed all of it – he had fallen asleep minutes after collapsing into the seat.

Ninety minutes later, the slight jolt of the aircraft making contact with the ground roused Frye from his much-needed rest. Through the windows, he could see that the Marineiro airfield was right at the edge of the water. They had landed on a small pad outside of the private craft terminal building.

Jarat turned around in the pilot's seat. "We're here," she said.

"I'll be back in about thirty minutes," Frye said, getting up and hitting the button to open the passenger door.

The humid summer air hit Frye as the door slid open. It was a little over an hour until sunup, but the air was already warm and sticky. Frye remembered what he'd been told about Neirin's fresh water oceans, and wondered if the lack of salt in the nearby body of water was a contributor to the high humidity.

He walked quickly to the terminal. Marineiro did not have a spaceport, so the transit terminal was small and nearly deserted. A few ground crew members milled about, but it was nothing like the bustle of Luka.

Fortunately, there was a car rental stack, and Frye ordered a small sedan, which was delivered moments later. He gave the address of the hotel that Wallis had provided him to the navcomp, and moments later he was headed into town.

Marineiro wasn't a large city; it appeared to Frye that there wasn't much beyond the massive pump facility that dominated the modest skyline, which was barely visible in the early pre-dawn hour.

Frye pulled up at the hotel and activated his commlink. There was a brief wait, and for a moment Frye was convinced that Wallis wouldn't answer, that something *else* had gone wrong, and that he and Alainn were doomed to an eternity of slowly-spiraling calamities that would keep them forever searching for their friends on this planet that they had quickly come to hate, but never finding them.

"Mr. Frye?" Wallis' voice cut into Volya's fantasy of doom and snapped him to attention.

"I'm outside," Frye replied. "Get out here so we can get going."

Two minutes later, an awkward, rangy-looking man exited the hotel and approached the car. Frye slid the passenger compartment door open, and the young man slipped inside. He was carrying a small duffel bag which he tossed into the back seat. As soon as he sat down, Frye was back on the road, speeding back towards the airfield.

False Flag 173

"What happened to the commlink Roland sent you?" Wallis asked.

"It got damaged when we had to run from the Marshal's Service," Frye explained. "Ever since then, we've been running in circles trying to track you and Roland down."

"Roland wasn't answering his comm," Wallis replied, "So I ran a trace on it. He's not aboard Luka Station. It appears that he is on a ship."

"Shit," Frye muttered under his breath.

"I assume that the profanity, which I find thoroughly unhelpful, by the way, means that you are upset, and as such I can only assume that you know what his departure is about."

"He's aboard my ship," Frye said.

"Your ship? And may I ask why your ship is headed away from Neirin at a high velocity without you or me aboard?"

"Your buddy Agera stole it, and took the navigator and pilot along with him for the ride."

"I would like to point out that Agera is not my 'buddy'," Wallis protested. "In fact, I find him quite unpleasant."

"Then why did you get him to dig up dirt on my wife and I?"

"Despite our disparate personalities, I assumed that he could be trusted," Wallis answered. "He holds membership in a group which I trust, and which holds political views similar to my own."

"Samizdat," Frye interjected.

Wallis seemed surprised that Frye knew the name. "Yes," he replied hesitantly.

"Lyt filled us in," Frye explained.

Wallis nodded. "Given your particular background, and

the mission you accepted to provide for my extradition, I'm sure she decided that it was safe to assume that you would be sympathetic to the cause."

"She would be correct," Frye said. "I'm in no hurry to assist the Union."

The car exited the motorway, and the autopilot navigated the vehicle back to the rental stack. Frye and Aeron exited the vehicle, and Frye returned the car. The two men headed through the terminal, which was now host to a few passengers and a full complement of ground crew, and out onto the platforms. Frye directed the younger man to Jarat's craft, and they boarded.

"You're late," the pilot said. Frye gave her a questioning glance. "Thirty-two minutes," she said in response.

Frye couldn't tell if she was serious or kidding, so he didn't respond. Instead, he fastened himself into his seat's harness and got ready for takeoff. Jarat shifted her focus to getting the aircraft off of the ground.

"Can you fix my commlink?" Frye asked Wallis as the shuttle rose into the air.

"I built it, didn't I?" Wallis replied. "I'll need to get into my workshop."

"We can make that happen," Frye said. He activated his commlink, and Alainn answered a moment later.

"I've got Wallis," Frye said without greeting. "We're airborne and headed your way."

"Well, at least something is going right," Alainn replied.

"And I think we have a way to find out what's happening on the *Veritas*."

"And are you going to share with the rest of the class?"

"Of course. Meet us at Wallis' place in two hours."

Chapter Ten

"You think Roland is aboard the *Veritas*?" As promised, Alainn had been waiting at Wallis' apartment when the cab had dropped Wallis and Frye off. The three were now in the physicist's workshop, with Wallis hunched over the commlink that Roland had sent Frye.

"It makes sense, doesn't it? He went to Luka Station to find Wolf, and now he's dropped off of the radar."

"You're right," Alainn replied. "But if he's aboard, wouldn't Agera have taken the comm from him?"

"Probably," Frye conceded, "But it may not matter. Wallis thinks he can open the comm channel remotely, and then use it to track the ship's movements."

"So you two really have a Casimir drive powered ship?" Wallis asked, his attention still fixed to the comm chip in front of him.

"We had two," Alainn said.

"And now, technically, we have none," Frye interjected.

"So this may be our only hope of tracking Agera down," Alainn said. "Nothing else in the galaxy is going to catch up to that ship, so we need to know where they're headed."

"That should do it," Wallis said, sliding the comm into a

port on his desktop terminal and opening a diagnostic program. A series of characters that neither Frye nor Alainn could make any sense of ran across the screen.

"It's working," Wallis said. "Now to modify the programming to allow us to open the comm channel to Roland remotely." He opened another program on the terminal and began typing furiously.

"Good to go," the physicist said in a few minutes, taking the comm chip back out and sliding it into his tablet.

"Great, now what?" Frye asked.

"I link up to Roland's tablet through the comm," Wallis answered. "From there, I should be able to tap into the ship's systems and get current position and destination from the navcomp."

"And then we get the hell off of this rock," Alainn concluded.

"Assuming we can make it through the security at the terminal and aboard Luka Station," Frye mused.

"That reminds me, Wallis," Alainn said. "Lyt subjected us to a rather intrusive treatment that is supposed to defeat facial recognition. Do you know if it works?"

"The nanites?"

"Yes."

"They work. Desteen Orvos is a talented nanobiologist, who, like me, has let her dislike for politics impede what should be a stellar career."

"You seem to have done alright," Frye replied.

Wallis chuckled. "I've made quite a bit of money because I create things that people don't want to live without. I have little to no influence professionally, however, because my views on society are considered rather crude and lacking in nuance."

"Agera said that you're an anarchist."

"And in that case, Agera is partly correct. I do not

believe in our current form of government, nor am I particularly interested in participating in a society which submits to its whims."

"And yet you live in the Union," Alainn said.

Wallis shrugged. "I follow my own moral compass. Where it intersects with the law, I suppose that I am law-abiding. Where those two paths diverge, I simply ignore the laws that others would impose upon me. I am creative enough that I never pay taxes, and am not worried that I'll be caught. My other legal failures are in no way unique – the Union has so many laws that everyone violates at least a dozen a week – I'm just aware of it."

"Some people would say that your attitude implies that you think that you're better than they are."

"And those people would be correct. I am better than allowing a cadre of corrupt, megalomaniacal philosopher kings dictate my life to me. To the extent that others allow such a thing to be done to them, I am better than they are."

He's gotta be a blast at parties, Alainn thought to herself. She decided that his political views probably took a back seat to his ego and lack of social grace when colleagues thought of reasons to avoid him.

"Not to interrupt the philosophy class," Frye interjected, "but perhaps we should focus on the task at hand. You know, friends to save, villains to kill, spacecraft to recover."

"I can continue working on the hack in transit," Wallis said.

"Good, then let's head out," Alainn replied. "Hopefully by the time we get spaceside, you can tell us where we're going.

***

Roland Kendrick knew nothing but the headache. For the first few moments of consciousness, it was all he could focus on – he had no past, no identity, and certainly no future. It was only the headache. It was all that there was and all that there ever would be.

It wasn't just the headache, either, he slowly realized. Every single joint ached. He tried moving an arm, only to be paralyzed by the pain. He wanted to cry out, but realized that his mouth was too dry to make any noise. As a matter of fact, everything was dry – eyes, skin, nasal passages – every membrane felt as though it had been baked and then rubbed in sand.

Decompression sickness, he thought to himself. There was a flash of a training session in a class full of young men and women in uniform. *Navy. I was in the Navy.*

Slowly, his mind began to clear, and he started to remember. He was Roland Kendrick, erstwhile homicide detective and apparently the current victim of an angry God's wrath – it was the only thing that explained the pain.

No, not God; God doesn't fly spacecraft. It was a good thing it wasn't God, Kendrick mused, because he wasn't going to be able to kick God's ass, and he planned on getting revenge against whoever had done this to him.

But first he needed to get his legs to work, and that was easier said than done. Ignoring the pain in his arms, he began to rub his legs, attempting to stimulate blood flow and return some of the feeling.

Footsteps echoed through the hull, but they sounded dull and far off. He realized what the problem was – he was deaf in his left ear, no doubt the result of a ruptured eardrum.

Kendrick knew that he needed to get up, get out of the

airlock, and figure out what was going on with the ship and its crew, but the minor exertion of remaining conscious was taking its toll. He just needed to rest for a moment, and then he could get up. Just a moment...

When he awoke, Kendrick had no idea how much time had passed. The headache had calmed, however, and his body seemed at least partially functional. With some effort, he was able to sit upright with his back against one of the bulkheads.

Kendrick looked up at the airlock's doors. One led to the ship's prep room and into the ship proper, and one led outside. Both had windows – the one that led into the prep room provided the only light in the airlock, and the other provided nothing but a view into the inky blackness of space.

Wallis. In the panicked attempt to save his own life, Kendrick had climbed aboard a starship that was departing Luka Station, and quite violently. Now he was headed away from Neirin, away from his brother, and towards somewhere he could only guess at.

Kendrick keyed his commlink, but there was no audio signal. It dawned on him that he wore his earpiece in his left ear, which had been damaged during his sojourn in the vacuum of space. A quick check, however, revealed that the earpiece was completely gone, likely dislodged by the air rushing out of his ear canal after the drum ruptured.

With voice communication out of the question, he composed a quick written message, letting Wallis know his current situation. Since he had no idea how fast the craft was travelling, or how long he'd been out, he wasn't sure how long it would take for the message to reach his brother, or what good it would do.

There weren't many options. Staying in the airlock was the safest bet in the short-term, but the exposure to vacuum had left Kendrick dangerously dehydrated, so he was going to have to move into the ship proper, if he had the strength to stand. The number of people involved in taking the ship was unknown, as was their motive, so getting caught could very well mean a swift death. *Better than dehydration*, Kendrick mused. The EVA suits in the prep room were equipped with hydration bladders, so he wouldn't have to venture very far into the ship. Perhaps he could get into the prep room, grab a suit, and get back out into the airlock without being seen. That option also gave him a slight hope for retaking the ship, but that would have to wait.

Slowly, Kendrick made his way to his feet, using the bulkhead to support himself. His legs were shaky, but they held his weight, as long as he had the wall for reinforcement. He worked his way around to the prep room door and forced himself to take a quick glance through the window.

Empty. A second, longer look confirmed his initial assessment. The prep room was completely empty, and the door into the ship's main corridor was closed. He opened the door and stepped inside.

The suits were stored in lockers along the wall to his right. He opened the locker closest to the airlock door and grabbed the hydration hose. The suits were plugged into the ship's central system, so he was careful not to unplug it from the locker, lest he trigger an alarm on the bridge.

He drank his fill from the hose greedily, water spilling down his chin and wetting the front of his shirt. He knew that he was thirsty, but the water hitting his tongue made him realize exactly how dehydrated the short stay in vacuum had made him.

Finally, his thirst was slaked, and he could shift his focus to other matters. A few minutes upright had sapped

False Flag 181

what little strength he had, but the movement had loosened his joints somewhat.

From previous experience, Kendrick knew that there would be a well-equipped arsenal on board. If he could reach it without being caught, then perhaps he could confront whoever it was that had taken the ship.

Feeling emboldened by the combination of hydration and the barest skeleton of a plan, he crossed the prep room and cracked open the door into the ship's corridor. He was greeted by silence. Poking his head into the hallway, he saw that it was empty.

Now for the hard part, Kendrick said to himself. He'd never been aboard the *Veritas*, and could only hope that the ship's armory was aft, just as it was aboard the *Seguir*. He slipped into the corridor and headed to his left.

As he hoped, the hallway opened up into a small storage room at the ship's stern. On the port side bulkhead were several storage cabinets, which, when opened, revealed a selection of spare parts and maintenance equipment.

"Shit," Kendrick muttered to himself, unsure of how to gain access to the weapons cache that he knew was stored just behind the more mundane gear.

"Problem?" The voice came from behind him without warning, and before he could turn to address the owner of the voice, for the second time that day Roland Kendrick's world went black.

***

"I can't believe that this is the best we could do," Alainn sighed.

The cabin was cramped and musty, and reflected the nature of the ship on which it was located. Commercial flights to Haos by Union-registered vessels were few and far between, since the return trip usually involved meticulous security checks at the border. Union residents of all stripes used to visit Haos in order to indulge of all manner of vices, and frequently attempted to smuggle contraband back home. It was still a popular activity, but travellers paid a premium in order to convince a pilot to go to the trouble.

Alainn had managed to secure two berths on an old retrofitted freighter, but the cabins retained more of their cargo-hauling past than Alainn would have liked.

Frye didn't care. In a way, it reminded him of the *Edrych*. In those days he was poor, but there had been a lot less shooting, which had its own colloquial charm. He dropped his pack on the bed and slumped into one of the cabin's chairs.

"It's not a slab at the morgue, so I'm happy," he said.

"We're not finished yet," his wife replied.

"I guess it wouldn't be all bad," Frye mused. "At least then I could get a full night's sleep."

"You've got six days to sleep," Alainn said.

A knock at the door interrupted the conversation. Frye stood and crossed the short distance to the bulkhead door. Wallis was out in the corridor.

"What's up?" Frye asked.

"I think I know where they're headed," Wallis replied.

There was a brief moment of silence, which Alainn finally broke. "And are you going to tell us?"

Wallis' eyes widened. "Y-yes, of course, obviously," he stuttered. He pulled out his tablet and called up a chart. "Here," he said, pointing to a blank area on the map.

Alainn scowled. "That makes no sense."

"There's nothing there," Frye observed.

Alainn took the tablet from Wallis. "The system isn't

False Flag 183

even named."

"I won't argue with you," Wallis replied, "but that's where they're headed."

Frye shrugged. "Then that's where we're going as well. See if you can find anything out about that system. Is it in Union territory?"

"Nominally," Wallis said. "It lies within what they call their 'border protection zone'."

"So it's territory that they don't really want, but they don't want anyone else to use it, either."

"Exactly," Wallis replied. "I'll find out what is there, but if it isn't even named, it probably means that it's uninhabited."

"Or someone wants us to think it's uninhabited," Alainn observed.

"Yeah, it sounds like more cloak-and-dagger bullshit," Frye replied. "We'll need to gear up for a number of possibilities. Is the guy we're meeting in Haos trustworthy?"

"Hell no," Alainn replied, "But he likes money, so he'll do."

***

The port at Haos was the hedonistic and marginally criminal free-for-all that Frye had come to know and love. For the right price, anything was available here. The hub of the station wasn't fancy - in fact, it had the feel of a run-down industrial warehouse - but the selection of items was unparalleled. On the base level, he passed two weapons merchants, an opium dealer, and someone offering the services of a brothel located down a side corridor.

"I'll pass," Frye said as the pimp called out to him from

his booth.

"You don't wanna miss out on these girls," the pimp replied.

Frye nodded towards Alainn, who was a few steps ahead of him, talking on her commlink. "I go home to that every night," he said. He noted the sex merchant's approving gaze. "Like I said, I think I'll pass."

He picked up the pace to catch his wife. "Didn't see anything you liked?" she quipped.

Frye was tongue tied for a second. "I-uh, he, I mean I didn't -"

"Relax," Alainn chuckled. "Sounds like I hit a nerve. Should I be worried?"

"Not about me," Frye replied, "but the guy at the booth gave you a long, hard look."

Alainn turned up her nose. "I'm all for letting people make their own choices, but I just can't imagine selling my body for money."

"Well, that's nice to hear." Suddenly, a thought struck Frye. "You *do* think that it's their choice, right?"

Alainn understood. "A place like Haos isn't safe," she replied. Sex trafficking isn't unheard of, but it tends to be dealt with violently by the locals if it's discovered.

"I've done a few recovery jobs," she continued. "A daughter or girlfriend will go missing, and I get hired to track her down. Usually, the girl has just run away, but sometimes, they get sold."

"What happens then?"

"I find them and kill everyone involved," Alainn replied with a shrug. "And I'm not the only one. If you're found to have taken someone against their will, whether it's for sex or something else, there are plenty of people around here willing to toss you out of an airlock." She looked back towards the pimp Frye had talked to. "As a matter of fact,

False Flag

legitimate merchants will usually pay you a bounty for doing it."

Frye nodded. "Keeps the profession honest, right?"

"Exactly. There's a financial component as well. Slavery means cheap labor, and if it isn't dealt with, it drives prices down. Dealing with the problem violently makes security an issue for the perpetrators, and guards have to be hired. Keeps prices equitable."

"Seems a little crass."

Alainn shrugged. "Who cares, as long as it means that the right thing gets done?"

"Fair enough."

"And as you well know, it's not like the Union is any better. If anything, making prostitution illegal only makes the industry more violent and prone to abusive conditions, because it moves the whole thing into the criminal underground."

Imogen's face immediately sprang to Frye's mind. He felt his body tighten and his hands curled into fists. He also became acutely aware that if he didn't find Wolfgang and bring him home, the girl would be without her adopted father. *Focus on the task at hand*, he told himself.

They headed to the lifts and Alainn hit the button on the pad for the fifth level. They exited onto yet another crowded mezzanine and around to the other side. There, a large storefront advertised weapons and other tactical equipment. They made their way inside, and a large, barrel-chested man, his massive black beard streaked with grey, greeted Alainn with a warm hug.

"Alainn Marwol! It's been quite a while!" He released the embrace and held her by her shoulders at arm's length. "Just as beautiful as ever, though."

Alainn smiled. "Just remember how happy you are to see me when we start negotiating prices." She turned to

Frye. "Yousef, I'd like you to meet my husband, Volya Frye."

"Husband!" the large man exclaimed. "And all of this time I thought you were saving yourself for me. You know my wife will die sooner or later."

Alainn noticed the look of shock on Frye's face and laughed. "He's all talk," she said. "Agnieska would smack you around if she heard you talk like that," she said, turning back to Yousef.

It was the big man's turn to laugh. "And I would enjoy every minute of it." He turned his attention to Frye and clasped the younger man's right hand in both of his massive paws. "Congratulations, my young friend. You are a lucky man."

"I'm well aware," Frye replied with a smile.

"So, enough chit-chat," Yousef said, switching to a business-like tone. I assume that you're not here on a social call."

"You would be correct," Alainn replied. "We need guns, ammo, and some other equipment."

"Then you've come to the right place. Are you looking for something in particular?"

"We both need full kits. Sidearms, compact autorifles, body armor - the whole package. Good stuff, too. You have Brestov equipment, right?"

Yousef feigned insult. "You know I only carry the best."

"Save it for people who don't know you better. I'm also going to want a long-range rifle; something good out to three kilometers, at least. Throw in some plasmacord, a field trauma kit, and a couple of those Ishikowa ceramic blades I like. Am I missing anything, Volya?"

Frye glanced around. "Yeah, I'll take one of those flak rifles and a stun baton. EMP grenades?"

Alainn nodded. "EMP, frag, flashbang – give us a case

False Flag 187

of each."

Yousef let out a low whistle. "If I didn't know any better, I'd say that the two of you are up to no good."

"Why else would we come to you?" Alainn asked with a sly smile. "Throw in ten thousand rounds of 5mm, six hundred for the rifle, and a thousand ceramic shells for the flak gun. That should cover us."

Yousef had been entering items on his tablet while they talked. "You're paying cash?"

"You know I don't carry that kind of paper around this place. Wire transfer, untraceable."

"Fair enough. Since I'm a nice guy, we'll call it twenty five thousand even."

"We'll call it twenty-two even," Alainn replied with a smile.

Yousef looked like he was about to argue, but changed his mind. He simply shook his head in defeat. "No sense arguing with you. Twenty-three it is."

"Twenty-one, and you crate it up and deliver it," Alainn replied.

The big man opened his mouth to protest, but Alainn cut him off. "Do you want to make it twenty for wasting my time?"

"Fine, you've got a deal," Yousef pouted. "But you know I'm losing money."

"I'm certain you aren't. Like I said, sell the bullshit to someone who doesn't know you like I do."

"Where do you want it delivered?"

"Bay 37C."

Yousef cocked his eyebrow. "You're not-"

"Yes, we are, and it's none of your business," Alainn interrupted.

"You mean he doesn't know?" Yousef asked, nodding his head towards Frye.

"Don't know what?" Frye didn't have any idea what they were talking about, but he didn't think he liked where it was headed.

"It's none of your business," Alainn reiterated to Yousef.

For a moment, it looked as if the weapons merchant was about to argue. Suddenly, however, his countenance changed. He grinned wide and a bottle of vodka materialized out of nowhere.

"Fair enough," he said cheerfully. He took a swig from the bottle and handed it to Alainn. "To another successful deal."

Alainn took a swig from the bottle and handed it to Frye, who did likewise. He had to struggle to suppress a cough – the vodka was the synthesized stuff, and tasted terrible. He handed the bottle back to Yousef while praying that the rotgut liquor didn't eat through his stomach and spill out onto the shop floor.

Yousef promised that the equipment would be crated up and delivered the following morning, and Frye and Alainn took their leave.

"What was that about?" Frye asked as soon as they were out of earshot.

They walked in silence for a few moments. Frye had decided that Alainn was hoping to ignore the question, and was just about to push the issue when his wife beat him to it.

"Kellan Odaran is a smuggler and a world-class asshole," Alainn began. "He's also extremely competent and willing to do almost anything for the right price, which makes him both invaluable and impossible to trust.

"Unfortunately, he's also relentlessly charming, which makes the stuff about him being a two-faced mercenary asshole difficult to figure out."

False Flag 189

Frye had an uneasy feeling in his gut, and it wasn't the vodka. "So you two have a... history."

Alainn nodded and bowed her head slightly in shame. It was a countenance that Frye had rarely seen in his self-confident wife.

"It was a youthful indiscretion," she said carefully. I was twenty and just starting out on my own. I met Kellan at a bar in a system called Luba a few parsecs from here. I was green, he was charming, experienced, and so helpful-"

"I get the picture," Frye interrupted. "Everyone's got a few 'youthful indiscretions' in their past. But why on earth are we using him?"

"Because word has gotten around that I've started taking the Union on face to face," Alainn replied. "All of these folks are willing to break Union law smuggling, but shooting at government agents and kidnapping officials brings the kind of attention that smugglers want to avoid.

"These folks will sell to us because our money is good," she continued, "but make no mistakes, we don't have many friends in Haos, and a few Union Marshal raids will put an end to any goodwill I've built here. Kellan is the only one nearby who will do what we need done. Like I said, he'll do just about anything for money."

Frye didn't like it, but he understood. These folks made their living off of Union prohibitionism. Few if any of them were idealistic, and most of them would be sad to see the regime loosen its draconian ways, since it would be bad for business.

Suddenly, it became clear. Haos wasn't a libertarian free-for-all, it was Union Dynamics. Just like one of the corrupt megacorps, the smugglers and merchants who inhabited Haos made their living off of a corrupt government. They were criminal corporatists, making fortunes off of subjugation, and Frye couldn't wait to leave, even if it was on a ship piloted by Alainn's former lover.

Follow-up stops were made to purchase additional clothing, food, and other necessities, all of which Alainn arranged to have delivered to Kellan's ship.

The final stop was one of the station's hotels, which provided surprisingly decent accommodations, given the generally disheveled nature of the station, and the fact that there was very little tourist traffic.

"It's the first time I've stayed on-station," Alainn observed as they rode the lift up to their fifth-level suite. "Not having a ship makes these tin cans feel so much more…"

"Claustrophobic?" Frye offered.

"Yeah."

"Don't worry; if anything happens, we can always bug out in one of the pods." Frye smiled.

Alainn chuckled darkly. "You'd be better off throwing yourself out of an airlock. I've never been to the surface, but from what I hear, it's a wasteland."

The hotel restaurant turned out to be fairly decent as well. Wallis was waiting for them and, as usual, had his considerable brain power focused intently on his tablet.

"You know," Frye said, after he and Alainn managed to get within a few centimeters of Wallis' back, "for someone on the run, you don't seem very aware of your surroundings."

"On the contrary, Mr. Frye," Wallis responded without taking his gaze from the tablet screen, "I tapped into the hotel's security system an hour ago. I've watched your approach since you got off of the lift."

Deflated, Frye dropped into a seat opposite the physicist. *At least he left us chairs facing the door,* he thought to himself. Alainn took her seat next to him

False Flag   191

somewhat more gracefully.

"So, what've you got?" Alainn said, after she had ordered a bottle of wine for the meal.

"Not much, I'm afraid," Wallis replied. "The system's official Union designation is BZ-3942. There was a mining permit issued a decade ago, but it doesn't appear that anything was ever done with it. As of now, the system is uninhabited, and there are no records of any terraforming or hermetic construction ever taking place. It's a dead zone."

"And the *Veritas* is still heading in that direction?"

"Yes. According to the navcomp, they'll be there in two days."

"How long will it take us to get there?" Alainn asked Frye.

"I'd say at least four," Frye responded. He'd looked at the navigation charts earlier that day. "We need to make four jumps. It's just fortunate that it's such a long straight-line shot from Neirin, or else the *Veritas* would have beat us by even longer."

"And you're sure that your link to the ship can't be traced?" Alainn asked Wallis.

"We've gone over this," the young man replied. "Since there's no electromagnetic transmission, there's no way for the communication to be detected. And your doubt that I could install an untraceable trojan on the ship's servers is simply insulting."

"Yeah, you're a fucking genius, Wallis; we all get it," an exasperated Alainn replied. "The thing is, I don't give a flying fuck how smart you are. Just remember, I could break you in half and not even think twice about it."

Wallis swallowed. "I'll never understand the preoccupation that you people have with profanity and violence."

The wine arrived, interrupting the dispute. Frye was relieved - given the look on her face, he was afraid that his wife might make good on her threat. Instead, she took a sample of the wine that the waiter offered and, apparently satisfied, nodded her approval. He filled her glass and then turned to Frye.

"Please," he said, offering his glass, which the waiter filled.

The waiter turned to Wallis, who shook his head.

"He'll take a glass of warm milk," Alainn said.

"Alcohol impairs the higher-level cognitive abilities," Wallis said condescendingly.

"False," Frye said, taking a sip from his glass. "Nearly every epiphany I've ever had was when I was drunk off of my ass."

"Besides," Alainn said, "The more I drink, the harder I punch." She smiled at Frye, then turned to Wallis. "Alcohol, profanity, and violence, all in less than thirty seconds." She tapped her glass against Frye's and took a swig. Wallis seemed ready to offer a retort, but instead rolled his eyes and turned his attention back to his tablet.

The food was as excellent as the wine, and by the time they left the table to head back to the room, Frye was stuffed and more than a little buzzed. From the way his wife leaned against him in the lift, he could tell that she was feeling the effects of the two bottles they'd drained as well.

Yet again, Frye was struck by how lucky he was. The woman next to him was beautiful, intelligent, and could hold her liquor better than most men he'd met. She knew how to order a bottle of wine in an elegant restaurant, but seemed just as at home draining a beer in a seedy bar. She was confident, it seemed, no matter the situation, and it was sexy as hell, at least to the former salvage pilot.

False Flag 193

"What?" Alainn's question made Frye realize that he'd been staring.

He smiled. "I'm just a lucky guy; that's all."

"You know, tonight's the last night we'll have alone for a while. We should probably make the most of it."

***

Frye arose early the next morning and made his way into the suite's sitting room. He put on his running shoes and slipped out the front door.

The hotel had a well-equipped gym, and at the early hour it was uninhabited. He grabbed a treadmill and started a warmup program, and then turned on the machine's viewscreen. Although he tended to stay away from the news as a general rule, he decided to see what was happening around the Universe.

One story, titled "Union Authorities to Crack Down on Anti-Government Activity," caught Frye's eye and he called up the vidcast. A pretty blonde newscaster showed up on the screen.

"Tiran Heerser, Director of the Planetary Union Marshal's Service, issued a warning to anti-government agitators earlier this week, referring to them as 'anarchists' and saying that any attempts to destabilize the status quo will be met with swift and severe ramifications."

The screen switched to a recording of a man in a suit that was identified as Heerser.

"Over the past few years, the Marshal's Service has become aware of a concerning increase in anti-government and anarchist sentiment in some of the more... bucolic sectors of the Union. This sentiment stems from a misplaced belief that the stability and security provided by our federation are somehow an oppressive force.

"Such an extremist view, coupled with a tendency to live in isolation, has driven a number of members of our society to see government as an oppressive force, rather than the method by which health and security are provided. Unfortunately, intelligence suggests that there are individuals amongst us that are prepared to turn these misguided notions into violent action.

"I am here today to tell the law-abiding public that we will address these issues by any means necessary-"

"Sounds like someone is getting ready to expand the Union's police state," Alainn said from over Frye's shoulder, startling the pilot and causing him to nearly fall off of the treadmill.

"Yeah," Frye said, regaining his balance and continuing his cardio workout while he spoke. "'By any means necessary' doesn't sound good. Something else is bothering me about it, though."

"What's that?" Alainn asked, taking the machine next to Frye.

"I'm not sure," Frye replied. "I just, I mean, I know it sounds silly, having met up with these Samizdat folks, but I don't see all that much anti-government activity, do you? The way they're talking, it's some kind of epidemic."

"Well, it's rumored that they've turned spying on internal electronic communications into an art form," Alainn replied, "So it's likely that they know things that we

False Flag 195

don't. Or, you know, it could just all be bullshit; an excuse for them to increase executive power in the name of security. Either way, let's just get this done and get out of here, so that it's not our problem anymore."

"Works for me," Frye replied. He watched the remainder of the report, but there was nothing new or particularly interesting. The government claims of imminent threats seemed to be accepted without question by the news network – hardly surprising, given that the network was owned by one of the megacorps that benefitted from government regulation and largesse.

Following his workout, Frye returned to the room to shower and dress. He donned a pair of cargo pants and a t-shirt – standard pilot garb – and laced up his leather jump boots. Into his waistband, he tucked his holstered Gauss pistol, and two spare magazines were secured in the left-side cargo pocket of his pants. He slipped a ceramic combat knife into his right boot.

As he was dressing, Alainn returned from the gym and slipped into the bathroom. A few minutes later, she exited wearing clothing nearly identical to Frye's. She readied her own weapons and packed up her belongings, which consisted of the few items that they had purchased recently that hadn't been delivered directly to Kellan Odaran's ship.

Frye donned his jacket and threw his bag over his shoulder. "I don't have anything to worry about, right?"

Alainn looked at him for a moment. "There's plenty to worry about," she finally responded. "We're headed into God knows what kind of a situation, our friends have been captured and possibly killed, and we've taken responsibility for a twenty-something man-child.

"But I assume that you're talking about Kellan. If so, then yes again. He's an opportunistic asshole who is only on our side so long as the money is good. The fact that he's our only option doesn't make it a good option, but it's the only way to possibly salvage this complete clusterfuck of an operation. Honestly, I give him about a fifty/fifty chance of screwing us over, and that's being charitable.

"What I hope you *aren't* talking about is some kind of latent feelings that I might have for him. If so, then you are way out of line, and I hope you enjoyed last night, because it's going to have to last you for a long, long time."

"Well then, I'm going to go with anything but door number three," Frye said, trying to lighten the mood. "But seriously, I'm more worried that he's not over you, and he's going to bust my balls over it."

"Then man up," Alainn said dismissively. "You're ten times the person that he is. Who gives a shit if he's got a problem?"

"It'll just make for an uncomfortable ride, that's all."

Alainn laughed. "As though things have been smooth sailing up until now."

"Point taken."

"Look," Alainn said, touching Frye's arm affectionately, "There's still a lot about each other that we don't know. Kellan is one of those things that I'd have been happy to leave buried. Unfortunately, God has a twisted sense of humor. All I can say is that my past is just that – my past. You are my present and my future."

"OK," Frye said "Then what are we waiting for? Let's go get our friends back."

***

Kellan Odaran's ship, the *Janus*, was larger than the *Seguir* or the *Veritas*. It was closer in size to the *Marco Polo*, and as they boarded the vessel, Frye noted that

False Flag

Odaran had a crew of at least two men. The fact that they wouldn't be stuck on the vessel alone with Alainn's former lover eased the pilot's nerves considerably.

The relief was short-lived, however. One of the crew members had met them at the gangway and led them aboard, but Odaran met them in the prep room.

"Alainn Marwol! It's been what, a decade?" Kellan Oderan was a tall man, standing just a few centimeters shy of two meters. He was built like an athlete, and had an unnervingly strong jawline. Frye was immediately intimidated, and the nervous feeling that he'd been harboring since the revelation that they'd be traveling with Alainn's onetime paramour returned with a vengeance.

Alainn, for her part, seemed completely unruffled. "It's good to see you, Kellan," she replied with the detached disinterest one usually reserved for casual acquaintances. "And it's Alainn Frye now."

Odaran turned his attention to Frye. "Of course! How rude of me. You must be Volya." He held out his hand in greeting.

Frye was nonplussed. Alainn hadn't officially taken his name. As a matter of fact, she'd never referred to herself as 'Alainn Frye' at all – at least not in his presence. They had never talked about it, and up to this moment, he had never really thought much about it.

He pushed the thoughts to the back of his mind and took Odaran's proffered hand. The man's grip was firm, his eye contact was deliberate but not unsettling, and his smile seemed genuine. Either his wife was completely over-stating Kellan Odaran's unseemly nature – or she was exactly right, and he was simply good at hiding it, just as she had said.

"Thanks for the lift," Frye said.

"Well," Odaran replied with a smile, "Alainn is a tough

woman to say no to, and her bank account even more so."

The statement seemed suggestive and crass to Frye, but the man's demeanor was so engaging that Frye felt himself getting over the resentment even though in his mind, he realized it was just what Alainn had warned him about. He was going to have to be very careful around this man.

"When are we getting underway?" Alainn asked, ignoring Odaran's brusqueness.

"Two hours. The station crew is topping off the argon tanks, and my crew is finishing the pre-flight inspection and preparations."

"And all of our gear is aboard?"

"The last of it delivered this morning. You're bringing quite an arsenal. I thought we were going after a simple ship thief."

"Nothing's ever simple, Kellan. You know that. I'll be in my cabin." With that, she turned and departed.

Frye started to follow, but Odaran stopped him. "Volya, I hear that you're quite the accomplished pilot. Perhaps you'd like to accompany me to the bridge for flight prep?"

"Of course," Frye replied, catching himself before he stuttered.

"Excellent. Follow me."

The *Janus* was approximately the same size as the *Marco Polo*, but it was nowhere near as luxuriously appointed. It reminded him of his former salvage ship, the *Edrych* – all utility and no flash.

They walked down a corridor crowded with electrical conduit and plumbing fittings and through a bulkhead door small enough that Frye had to crouch to avoid hitting his head. Odaran nearly had to fold himself in half to pass through.

"Not exactly designed with the vertically-gifted in mind," the taller man said with a self-effacing grin.

"I'm surprised that I don't have a permanent dent in my forehead, as many times as I've misjudged the height on these things," Frye replied. "It must be even worse for you."

"I used to be a genius," Odaran said. "I knocked my IQ down to average a long time ago."

I doubt that very much, Frye thought to himself. A man who understood the value of self-deprecation and humility, even fake humility, was still far above average.

The bridge was, if anything, less grandiose than the rest of the ship. Everything was in its place, but on the shabby side of well-worn. Frye noted the quantity of permatape holding the pilot chair's upholstery together with a grin.

"Obviously I'm no seamstress," Odaran observed.

"It looks almost exactly like the pilot's chair aboard my old ship," Frye replied. "Except you can still see a little bit of the leather on yours."

"I'm a smuggler," Odaran said with a shrug. "I haul a considerable amount of contraband into the Union, and to avoid detection, it's important to look the part. I'm registered as a recovery vessel; an occupation that provides a rather meager income..."

"Tell me about it," Frye interjected. "I ran a salvage rig for years."

"Which explains the permatape chair," Odaran said with a grin. "Good to know that my set dressing is on the mark.

"Anyway, I could travel in much a much more lavish vessel, but what patrol deputy would possibly believe that a steel vulture operating on the straight and narrow could afford a salvage rig decked out like a *Moethus* class cruiser?

"So you run Union registration?"

"Of course. I'm a Union citizen, and as long as you don't look too closely, I'm completely legit. Hell, I even pay taxes – on the meager income that I choose to report."

"And your salvage license allows you to travel without arousing suspicion."

"As long as I'm careful," Odaran replied. "That's what gets most people in trouble – they get careless."

"Why didn't I think of that when I was running salvage?"

"Probably because you're not a criminal."

"I didn't used to be," Frye replied. "Now it seems that I break the law all the time."

"There's a difference between being a lawbreaker and a criminal. A lawbreaker ignores the law in the pursuit of his normal, day-to-day life, whereas a criminal exploits the law for profit."

"Sounds like a distinction without a difference."

"Not true. In the Union, guns are illegal. You ignore that law and carry one for self-defense. I use the fact that they're illegal to charge a huge mark-up when I sell them. You'll kill a man to exact justice, even if the law forbids it. I'll kill a man if I'm paid enough money. You break the law – I exploit it."

"And without rationalization, apparently."

"I'm a sociopath, Volya, but at least I'm self-aware."

"Is that supposed to be comforting?"

"Well, my diagnosable mental disorder, coupled with greed and a poorly-functioning survival instinct means that you've got a ride, so there's that."

Chapter Eleven

Even with a criminal sociopath at the helm, Frye felt the familiar rush of adrenaline as he eased into the co-pilot's seat of the *Janus*. He didn't need to ask where the regular occupant of the seat was – she had been unceremoniously and publicly bumped from her departure detail and sent to see if there was anything she could do to 'make herself useful' in Engineering. Frye had protested the crew shakeup, being more concerned with keeping the peace than getting a chance to fly, but Odaran wouldn't hear of it, and while Frye was unsure of the smuggler's motives, he was happy to have the honor of overseeing the voyage's departure.

"Haos Station, this is the *Janus*, requesting departure vector from berth 37C."

"Copy that, *Janus*, stand by." A few moments later, the traffic controller came back online. "*Janus,* this is Haos Station, you are clear for departure on station vector thirty-eight latitude, one hundred twenty-four longitude. Maximum velocity is eleven thousand kilometers per hour until you reach the signal markers.

"And *Janus*," the controller added, almost as an afterthought, "keep an eye on your collision radar. Some jackass bought a crate of high explosive yesterday and didn't secure it properly. What's left of his ship is creating a bit of a hazard out there this morning."

"Roger that, Haos Station," Frye replied. "Have fun cleaning up." With that, he broke mooring and fired the short-range thrusters.

Once the *Janus* was clear of the speed-control markers, Frye scaled the ship's hydrogen-fuelled arcjet engines to sixty percent. They would run that way for several hours to ensure safe operating parameters before scaling up to ninety. He made a slight course correction to take advantage of a gravity assist from one of the system's gas giant planets on the way to the jump point and then set the ship's autopilot.

"All systems nominal, Captain," he said, turning to Odaran. "We'll be at the jump point in eighteen hours and twenty-two minutes."

"Does it make you uncomfortable to call someone else captain?" Odaran's question seemed genuine.

"I've got enough shit on my plate. If I was worried about that, I'd have no room to worry about the things that matter."

"Some people would say that it's a sign of weakness. That you're too willing to place yourself under someone else's authority."

"I gave up caring what other people thought or said a long time ago. I've killed men for things that matter – I see no reason to get bent out of shape over things that I can't control or don't particularly care about. I have no time for ego or ambition, and if 'some people' don't like it, then they can get fucked."

Odaran laughed out loud. He reached into a cabinet on the bulkhead and pulled out a bottle and two glasses. He poured one and handed it to Frye, and then poured one for himself and raised it in Frye's direction. "I like you,

False Flag 203

Volya. I don't say this very often, but I genuinely hope that you don't die." With that, he tossed the drink back.

"We're all going to die, Kellan. I'm starting to think that at this point all I can hope for is to take a few others with me." Frye drained his glass as well.

"Poignant, but I'm sure it's not entirely true," Odaran said, refilling the glasses. "You're still practically a newlywed, so you can't be ready to throw in the towel yet. You could just go home, you know."

Frye shook his head. "If it was just the ship, I'd already be home. But my friends are on that ship. Besides, someone's been fucking with my life... again. I really hate it when that happens, and the only way I've been able to come up with to discourage it involves a body count."

"Well then," Odaran said, refilling the glasses a third time, "to homicide – justifiable and otherwise."

***

"You two seem awful chummy," Alainn observed when Frye made his way to the cabin. She had her new pistol disassembled, and was oiling and wiping down the moving parts – a completely unnecessary activity for a new gun.

"He's a decent guy, for a sociopath," Frye replied, drawing an irritated glare from his wife. "Look, he is most *definitely* a sociopath, but like you said, he's our only option, and we're stuck with him for a few days, so I figure I might as well make the best of it."

"I'm telling you he's no good," Alainn said.

Frye bristled at her pedantic tone. "I'm well aware of your opinion of him," he acknowledged, "and for what it's worth, I think that you're probably correct, but it doesn't mean that I can't have a drink with the guy – especially when he's providing the booze. Besides, you're the one who set us up with him, remember?"

Alainn deflated somewhat. "Yes, I remember."

Frye sat in one of the chairs against the cabin's bulkhead. "Let's just make the most of it."

"Fair enough," Alainn replied, reassembling the pistol and setting it on the nightstand beside the bed. "Grab Wallis and meet me in the common room. We have a lot to go over between now and when we catch up to the *Veritas*.

The common room aboard the *Janus* was a haphazard collection of furniture and fixtures that would have been more at home in a seedy planetside bar than aboard an interstellar ship. The table that Frye, Alainn and Wallis found themselves around was made of roughly-finished wood – an anachronism aboard a craft that was currently doing $0.4c$. The erratic nature of the room wasn't only visual, either – Frye was almost certain that he could smell hydraulic fluid leaking from one of the hundreds of lines that wound their way along the walls and ceiling. Odaran's commitment to looking the part of a destitute salvager was commendable, but Frye wondered if it bordered on hazardous.

"The motivation is irrelevant," Wallis stated. "I've got a track on your ship and the destination coordinates from the navcomp. You are obviously well armed and properly trained, so retaking the ship should be simple. Then you fulfill our agreement to get me out of here, with my tech, and you get paid."

"And what if Agera is meeting up with mercenaries or foreign agents in order to sell the ship to them?" Alainn countered. "We run up against a squad of well-armed professionals, and our gear and training suddenly becomes a lot less of an advantage. No, we need to know what he's up to so that we know what we're going to be going up

False Flag

against. You're sure that he hasn't attempted to communicate with anyone?"

Wallis looked at Alainn derisively. "I have full access to all of the ship's systems, so yes, I'm sure that he hasn't made contact with anyone."

I could snap you like a twig, you smug little prick, Alainn said to herself. Aloud, she said nothing.

Frye sensed Alainn's irritation and attempted to intervene on her behalf. "Alainn is right. We'll be better prepared if we have an idea what Agera is planning to do. My guess is that he plans on selling the ship. The real question is how long he's been planning the heist." Frye looked at Wallis. "How long ago did he find out about us?"

"Shortly after Roland told me you were coming," Wallis replied. "However, I didn't give him any information about the nature of your ship. Roland was very clear that it was not to be discussed."

"Did you do any research into us?" Alainn asked.

"No," Wallis replied. "Roland was very clear on that point as well. Once we left my apartment, he was very paranoid about my communications, even after I explained to him that I was more than capable of doing whatever I wanted to anonymously. That's why I had Agera check on you."

"And nothing that he produced provided any information about the technology that we were bringing?"

"No, at least nothing that he shared with me. But I assume that he would have kept that kind of information private if he was planning on using it for nefarious purposes."

"Ok, so let's say that he finds out about the zero point drive six weeks ago, more or less. He decides to steal both it and your comm tech..."

"Which means that he was probably behind the break-in at your apartment," Frye interjected. "He was going to steal your invention, and when his initial attempt failed, he saw an opportunity to increase his score by taking both it and our ship..."

"But Roland foiled his plans when he set up the trap at the hotel," Alainn continued, "so he decides to cut his losses and steal the ship and at least get half of what he wanted."

"So is there a way to figure out who he's been in contact with?"

Wallis shook his head. "Not from here. Maybe if we were still on Neirin, we could access his personal communications, but at light speed, the lag would be days long from here."

"The buyer's got to be someone connected to the Union," Frye said, "Otherwise; he'd be headed out of Union space. It wouldn't make sense to do an exchange inside the border if it was with a foreign buyer. My money is on Union Dynamics."

"It would make sense that they would want it," Alainn agreed, "But if they're the buyers, why not just take the ship to Upam and drop it off at their headquarters?"

"A little bold to just park a stolen spacecraft on their front lawn, don't you think?" Frye asked.

Alainn scoffed. "They're a megacorp. Who's going to do a damn thing about it?"

"Then why didn't they do that six months ago when they had the chance with the *Marco Polo*?"

"Because those guys weren't connected to Union Dynamics at all, remember?"

"Right; different head."

"What?" Wallis seemed confused.

Frye turned to the physicist. "When we were trying to figure out who took the *Marco Polo*, we made the mistake

False Flag 207

of initially blaming the whole thing on 'the government.' It was only later, with Roland's help, that I came to see that 'the government' doesn't do anything. The Union is a hydra – a beast with countless heads, none of which necessarily know what the other is doing. In fact, it's likely that whoever is behind this heist had no knowledge of the *Marco Polo* incident at all."

"Which leaves us precisely nowhere," Alainn said, exasperation evident in her voice. "I'm starting to think we should have brought more guns."

"Nonsense," Wallis replied. "The nature of the destination indicates that Agera intends to keep the rendezvous clandestine. I have no idea who he is meeting, but I can assure you that they will be focused more on stealth than on addressing a forceful interdiction. I believe that it is safe to proceed as planned."

"You seem pretty eager to push forward, considering that you were ready to abandon everyone a little while ago."

"I'm a pragmatic man, Alainn. Quite frankly, I do not care what you do, provided it gets me what I want as quickly and safely as possible. Since you and your husband seem hell-bent on recovering your ship and your friends, I am merely suggesting that such a course of action seems logical and unlikely to be met with significant armed resistance."

"Your selfish motivations are noted," Alainn observed with sarcasm. Turning to Frye, she continued. "What he says isn't completely without merit."

"I agree," Frye replied. "Something shady is going on, and I'd like to know what it is before we get there, but Wallis is right – this smells like subterfuge."

"I'd still like to have more guns," Alainn said.

"And that's why I married you," Frye responded with a

smile.

Kellan Odaran chose that moment to make an appearance in the common room. "Are we planning an attack strategy?" he asked.

"Something like that," Frye replied. "We're actually trying to figure out if an attack will be necessary."

"Honestly, I hope so," Odaran replied. "I haven't shot anyone in ages."

"And are gunfights included in our rate?" Alainn asked, a note of hostility in her voice.

"I charge per corpse," Odaran replied lightly. It was hard to believe that he hadn't caught on to her enmity, but if he had, he was playing it cool.

"I'm guessing that whoever said chivalry was dead was familiar with your work."

"You do realize that I'm helping you, right?" Odaran seemed genuinely hurt.

"I also realize that you're being paid handsomely to do so," Alainn sneered.

"I'm a fucking businessman, Alainn." The smuggler had gone from hurt to angry quickly. "Did you expect me to drag your ass out here out of the goodness of my heart? I've got fuel to burn, a crew to feed, and quite frankly, I expect to take something away for my efforts. I don't know if you remember, but you made it perfectly clear the last time that we met that we aren't exactly friends."

"Listen," Frye interjected, "Let's just stick to the task at hand, alright?"

Alainn looked at him crossly, but held her tongue.

"I think that's best," Odaran replied. "So, what do we know about the system we're headed to?"

Wallis had witnessed the brief spat in detached silence, but was the first to speak when facts were asked for. "It's a dead system. There are four planets orbiting the binary

False Flag   209

stellar pair, but the tidal forces created by the stellar coupling make their orbits erratic. Terraforming was never attempted."

"Any navigational issues we should be worried about?" Odaran asked.

"There's a minimum safe distance from the stellar pair, but it's published," Wallis replied. "Other than that, we should be fine."

"Jump points?"

"Two. We'll be using one, and the other ties the system to Tuaithe, a sparsely-populated farming system."

"Why the hell did the Union bother to claim this place? Uninhabitable, and the only jump point that leads into another Union system is farmland."

"Because no one wants their food messed with," Frye replied. "People tend to shrug off farming systems, but keep in mind that without them, no one eats."

"You grew up on a farm, didn't you?" Odaran asked.

"I did."

"Well, no offense meant. And your point is a good one. So, am I to assume that this uninhabited system will be monitored by the Union in some way?"

"Patrol craft, I assume," Frye replied. "According to our information, there's no station anywhere in-system."

Odaran's brow furrowed. "OK, so there's no station, and the planets are uninhabitable. How exactly do you plan on getting aboard the ship, since they won't be docked anywhere?"

"We board it as she's adrift," Frye replied matter-of-factly.

"And you don't think they'll see that coming?"

"It won't matter," Wallis interjected. "I've got full control of the ship's systems. When the time comes, I will simply shut the drive system down, and we will board her much like a derelict." He looked up at Frye and Odaran. "I mean that you will. I have no interest in such brazen displays of brute force."

"So it's basically a salvage operation, but with people onboard?" Odaran asked.

"That's pretty much it," Frye replied.

"And how many bad guys are we expecting?"

"As far as we know, only one."

"Shit, my 'I get paid by the body' joke kinda seems lame now, doesn't it?"

"Just hope that Wallis is right, and he isn't meeting with any naval vessels," Alainn said. "Anything with exterior armament shows up, and we're toast."

"Once we get in-system, I can monitor the official traffic channels to see if anyone is nearby," Wallis offered.

"Sure, but if you were buying stolen technology, would you be using the official comm channels?"

"It doesn't matter," Wallis replied. "I can hack into the transponder grid. Those can't be turned off."

Alainn nodded her approval. "At least that will give us some warning."

"And if we decide that the area is too hot, this is a salvage rig, after all," Odaran interjected. "It would be perfectly legitimate for us to be doing a sweep of an outlier system looking for scrap."

"How long until we arrive in-system?" Alainn asked.

"We're about thirty-six hours from the jump point," Frye replied.

"Well, I guess there's nothing to do but wait," Alainn said with a shrug.

***

"We're being hailed," Frye said over the comm. They

False Flag   211

were approaching the jump point that would lead them to
BZ-3942.

"By who?"

Frye had expected the question. The system they were
in was uninhabited and as far as the charts were
concerned, unclaimed.

"Union patrol cruiser."

"But we aren't even in Union space yet."

"I'm sure that they'll just go away if you remind them
of that."

"Shit – OK, patch it through."

Frye routed the call to Odaran's cabin, but kept the
bridge connection active. He sent the call to his headset,
so that no one could hear him listening in.

"This is Captain Kellan Odaran of the *Janus*."

"*Janus*, this is Union patrol vessel *Orszem*. Course
projections indicate that you are headed to a Union jump
point. Please state your intentions."

"*Orszem*, I am a bonded and licensed salvage operator.
I intend to enter BZ-3942 and conduct a sweep for derelict
vessels."

"Your registration beacon has been read and
confirmed," the voice on the other end replied. "However,
your flight manifest indicates that you are en route from a
system flagged for frequent illicit activity. Please prepare
for boarding and inspection."

"*Orszem*, we are in international space. You do not
have the authority to conduct a search outside of the
Union's borders."

The response was immediate. "*Janus*, you will prepare
for boarding and inspection. If you do not comply, you will
be refused entry to Union space and your registration will
be flagged."

"Very well," Odaran replied. "Stand by; I will let you

know when we are ready for boarding."

"You have five minutes," the disembodied voice at the other end replied. "If you don't have anything to hide, that should be more than sufficient." The comm went dead.

Almost immediately, Frye could hear heavy footfalls on the metal walkway to the bridge.

"Mother*fuckers*," Odaran spat as he crossed through the doorway onto the bridge.

"Problem?" Frye asked, as innocently as he could.

"Damn right there's a problem," Odaran shot back. "But don't give me that confused act. You know exactly what I'm talking about."

Frye looked at him quizzically. "How?"

"Because I'd sure as hell be listening in if I was in your position. Let's not waste time on bullshit – we've gotta get ready for a Union glove up our collective asses."

"Relax," Frye said. "It's just a routine border crossing inspection."

"Routine? Is it routine for the Union Navy to conduct inspections? Have you ever seen an inspection done on the wrong side of the border? No, this isn't routine."

"You don't have anything that they'll find, right?"

Odaran was beside himself. "I'm a fucking smuggler, Volya! Of course I have something to hide! I've got close to a hundred kilos of synthetic opiates in the hold.

"That's not the problem, though. I've also got three people aboard who aren't part of my crew manifest. That's going to be more than a little hard to explain."

"I don't think that will be a problem," Frye said.

***

"Your paperwork seems to be in order," the lieutenant said to Odaran. They were in the common room aboard

False Flag   213

the *Janus*. "What exactly was your business in Haos?"

"We refueled and re-provisioned," Odaran replied. "I've also had some luck getting word about potential wrecks there in the past."

"You are aware that Haos is a major hub for the transport of contraband into the Union?"

"Yes, sir. That's one of the reasons that it is so good for picking up on potential wreck sites – there's a lot of traffic, and travelers tend to talk."

"But you can see why we might find it suspicious that you are attempting to cross into the Union using a lightly-trafficked system, after visiting an outpost known for smuggling?"

"I also know that your men have searched my ship and come up with nothing."

"You seem quite confident."

"I know that they've found nothing, because there's nothing here to hide. Lieutenant, I am a citizen of the Planetary Union. I have committed no crime, and yet I have the distinct impression that you are determined to delay my entry."

The lieutenant clearly resented Odaran's refusal to be cowed. "There's still the matter of your guests," he sniffed.

"As I told you, they were looking for a ride to Tuaithe," Odaran offered.

"I've been told that there's farming work there," Frye interjected. "I have experience running agri-transport shuttles, and my brother-in-law is a robotics technician."

"And what caused you to leave your last post?"

It's none of your fucking business, you bureaucratic prig, Frye said to himself. He couldn't believe that he'd once tolerated living in a system where government officials presumed to have the authority to detain and question citizens with impunity. And once again he recognized the irony that he was, in actuality, engaging in criminal activity while simultaneously bristling at the questions posed by law enforcement officials.

"Environmental catastrophe," he said, swallowing his anger in pursuit of the bigger picture. "We were on Anialwch. Local authorities decided to try and tweak the terraforming; you know, warm it up a little to try and lengthen the growing season. Problem is, they went too far. Now the whole damn world's a desert. See, the thing about terraforming is that..."

The lieutenant held his hand up to silence Frye. "I'm not interested in planetary engineering," he said dismissively. He turned his attention back to Odaran. "Your operating license does not have passenger transport endorsement. Accepting fare for transporting passengers is a violation of the conditions of your license."

"What fare?" Odaran asked. "I was headed near Tuaithe anyway, so I offered to give these folks a lift."

"Out of the goodness of your heart, I'm sure," the lieutenant replied sardonically.

"It's true," Frye said. "We wouldn't have had money to pay him if he'd asked – which he didn't. See, when we left Anialwch, we were completely broke. I had to sell my father's prized..."

"Enough!" the lieutenant spat, his anger palpable. "You think that I haven't heard all of this before? That I haven't heard every possible rationalization to explain away lawlessness? You peasants think that you're so clever..."

The lieutenant's life nearly ended right there. Alainn, who had spent the past thirty minutes struggling to play the part of deferential farmhand's wife, reached for the knife that she had concealed at the small of her back. *Enough is right, you son of a bitch*, she seethed to herself.

Before she could act on her anger, however, an alarm

False Flag   215

sounded in the distance.

"What the?" the lieutenant looked over his shoulder towards the corridor that led to the ready room and the airlock. His right hand shot to the commlink in his ear. "I'm on my way," he said tersely.

"You will stay put," he told the passengers and crew of the *Janus*, and then he turned on his heel and walked rapidly out of the room.

"What crawled up his ass?" Odaran asked.

"I suggest that you take this opportunity to make a hasty departure, Captain," Wallis said. Everyone turned in his direction. Up to this point, he had been completely silent.

"You want me to break mooring with a docked Union vessel?" Odaran asked incredulously.

"I doubt that they will take much notice, as they are otherwise occupied," Wallis replied. "They believe that their reactor is about to go critical."

"And why would they believe that, Wallis?" Alainn's question implied that she already knew the answer.

"Because I rigged their reactor to go critical," Wallis replied nonchalantly.

"Shit!" Odaran interjected. "If we're anywhere nearby when it blows..."

"That is why I suggested that we proceed with haste," Wallis said matter-of-factly. "Honestly, sometimes I believe that I'm surrounded by monkeys. Profanity-spewing monkeys."

Frye and Odaran made a break for the bridge, and Alainn was close at their heels. Frye got there first and dropped into the pilot's seat out of habit.

Odaran didn't seem to mind. "Make for the jump point, full power!" he commanded.

"On it," Frye replied, his hands flying across the control

panel. The ship's short-range thrusters flared to life, and moments later, there was a jolt as the *Janus* tore the moorings loose from the *Orszem*. There was another jolt as the primary boosters lit, and then the inertial dampeners kicked in and the ship was eerily still.

"Velocity?" Odaran asked tersely.

"Four thousand six hundred kilometers per second and climbing," Frye replied. The ship shuddered. "The *Orszem* is no longer on radar. Or, you know, in existence, apparently."

Odaran keyed his comm and buzzed the engine room. "Status report." A moment later, he nodded, apparently satisfied that the ship wasn't damaged. "Good." He killed the link and turned to Alainn. "What the hell was that? Who did you bring aboard my ship?"

"What, you don't have room for more than one psychopath aboard?" Alainn asked.

The smuggler ignored the barb. "Get him up here."

Alainn turned and grabbed the microphone for the ship's public address system. "Wallis Aeron, you are cordially invited to the bridge." She killed the PA and turned back to Odaran with a sarcastic smile.

A few moments later, the young physicist arrived, eyes raised expectantly. "Is there a problem?"

Odaran's face grew red. "You're damn right there's a problem. What the hell did you do?"

"I tapped into the ship's systems as soon as they hailed us," Wallis replied. "Then I made a slight modification to the fusion reactor's containment programming – small enough that it would go unnoticed for thirty minutes or so. I figured if they were aboard for that long, we needed a way to get them off."

"And if they were gone by then?"

"Then we would not have had to get away from the

False Flag   217

detonation so quickly."

"So you were going to kill them no matter what?" Frye
was aghast.

"I suppose I could have returned the containment to
nominal parameters once they left," Wallis replied. "If I
thought about it."

"You could have killed us all," Odaran seethed.

"Nonsense," Wallis replied. "The calculations were
quite simple. I knew to within fifteen seconds when the
reactor would go critical."

"So you're a damn rocket scientist. What happens
when the ship's data recorder transmission synchs with
the local Marshal's service database and they find out that
they were docked with us when the ship blew?"

"First off, we aren't in Union space, so there's nowhere
for that transmission to go," Wallis replied. "Secondly, I
disabled the data recorder's transmission capability when I
made the reactor adjustment. Really, what do you think I
am, an idiot?"

Odaran looked at Alainn, who shrugged. "He's an
annoying prick and a braggart, but as irritating as it is, his
high opinion of himself isn't without merit."

Odaran's countenance shifted. "Good work," he said
with a malevolent grin. "I could use a man like you on my
crew."

"You couldn't afford me," Wallis replied.

"It's too bad, because the two of you are a perfect pair.
Bloody psychopaths," she muttered as she headed off of
the bridge.

***

"Why do you care that Wallis blew the ship up?" Frye
asked. He and Alainn had retired to their cabin for the

evening, and Frye could tell that his wife was still agitated. She was lying on her back on the bed, and he had taken a perch on the cramped cabin's lone chair. "You know, we've both killed our share of Union officials."

Alainn shook her head. "I don't really care about that," she said with a sigh. "Truth is, I was about to cut that lieutenant's throat myself – Wallis just beat me to it."

"My problem is that he had no motivation to do so, other than the fact that they were inconveniencing us. I'll kill someone for what I believe in, or in self-defense, or even out of revenge. But blowing up an entire ship full of people because they delayed my flight is completely sociopathic."

"It was a little more serious than that," Frye replied. "That lieutenant seemed completely bent on finding a reason to arrest us."

"Absolutely," Alainn agreed. "And like I said, one way or another that Union bootlicker was headed for an early grave. But Wallis did what he did before they even docked. He set a time bomb to make sure we weren't hassled, and didn't seem the least bit concerned with disarming it if it turned out to be unnecessary. Lyt said that he had Asperger's, but I don't think that even begins to cover it."

"Nothing's been right since we left Saiorse," Frye said. "We don't even get off of the ship and we have the Marshal's Service on our backs. The incident at the farm, Roland's disappearance, the *Veritas* getting stolen with Hartmann and Pryce aboard – we've been on the defensive from the second we arrived at Neirin, and now the guy we're supposed to be rescuing is looking more and more like a maniac."

"And it feels like we're being played, somehow," Alainn said. "I don't know exactly how to put it, but it's like you said the other morning about the so-called anti-

False Flag 219

government activity: it just doesn't smell right."

"You think that we're headed into some kind of trap?"

"I don't know," Alainn replied, her eyes aimed at the ceiling. "I can't make the pieces fit together that way. There's no way that Agera would have anticipated Roland stowing away on the *Veritas* with one of Wallis' comm chips. He couldn't have foreseen us being able to follow him. So no, I guess I don't think that we're headed into a trap. More than anything, it just feels like everything that's happened in the last two weeks is complete bullshit."

A slight shudder interrupted the conversation. "We're through the jump," Frye observed.

"Well, I guess no matter what, we're about to find out what's really going on."

Chapter Twelve

"And you're sure that there's no one else there?"

"I'm sorry, Alainn, but I only know the one language. 'The ship is alone' is the only way I know to say it, and that's not going to change, no matter how many times you ask."

"So what's he doing?"

"As far as I can tell, the ship is at all-stop," Odaran said impatiently. "Again, not going to change."

"Sorry; it just doesn't make sense."

"He's probably waiting for the buyer to show up," Frye said. "With any luck, he'll think that's who we are."

The *Veritas* was still well out of visual range, but it had shown up on the *Janus'* sensor array two hours earlier. It was just sitting there, looking eerily like a derelict.

"Shut down everything but life support," Alainn told Wallis.

"He'll know we're coming," Frye cautioned. "He may kill the others if we get too aggressive."

"He's going to see us coming soon anyway – assuming he hasn't already," Alainn countered.

"I believe that I have a better idea," Wallis said. "If I lower the oxygen concentration in your ship's support systems, everyone aboard will pass out and we can take the vessel without incident."

"Assuming Agera doesn't don one of the EVA suits," Frye said.

"Look, at some point we're going to have to make a move," Alainn replied. "I don't like it any more than you do, but this is a shitty situation, and there's the possibility that it will have a shitty outcome. The oxygen play seems like as good a plan as we're likely to get. Besides, we don't even know for sure that Agera hasn't killed them already."

They hadn't talked about the possibility that Hartmann, Pryce, and Kendrick were already dead, but Frye knew that it was a likely scenario. "I know," he said to Alainn quietly. He nodded to Wallis. "Do it."

Wallis went to work on his tablet. "Done," he said a few minutes later. "Anyone aboard the ship will be out in about thirty minutes. I also installed a virtual kill switch on the drive, so if he attempts to run, I can neutralize the ship's propulsion."

"I guess it's time to get ready to board," Alainn said, heading aft toward the *Janus'* hold, Frye following close behind.

"Kind of a letdown that we brought all of this gear and we probably won't get to use it," Frye said, trying to lighten the mood.

"You know, I could go for a good face-to-face gunfight right now," Alainn replied, opening one of the *Janus'* hidden compartments and pulling out a large equipment crate. "We've been on the defensive and in the dark since we got here. At least gunfights are relatively straightforward."

Frye stripped off his t-shirt and donned a long-sleeve nanofiber pullover. On top of the armor, he strapped on a tactical vest with pockets for extra magazines, gear, and weaponry.

False Flag 223

Alainn followed suit, and Frye's concentration faltered as she removed her shirt. "Later, big guy," his wife teased, noticing that his attentions had strayed from their preparation.

"I'm going to hold you to that," Frye replied with a grin, slipping a carbon-ceramic knife into its sheath on his vest. He added six magazines for his autorifle and four for his gauss pistol alongside the knife. His collapsible shock baton and a tube of first aid nanopaste also found a home.

"Help me with this," Alainn said, handing Frye a small air tank. Frye grabbed the tank and fastened it to Alainn's vest, and then handed her the mouthpiece and regulator. He turned his back to her and she did the same for him. With low oxygen levels aboard the *Veritas*, they would have to bring their own.

Frye double-checked the batteries and magazines on his pistol and autorifle, and then slipped the pistol into a holster on his thigh. He clipped the rifle to a retractable sling mounted to his vest. Gloves and a balaclava made of the same nanofiber armor as his pullover were donned, and a ballistic facemask connected to the air tank completed the ensemble.

"Good to go?" Alainn asked, her voice muffled by her own face mask.

"Five-by-five," Frye replied.

The pair returned to the bridge, where the *Veritas* was now clearly visible. Odaran's co-pilot had the helm, and the captain was leaning against the bulkhead, looking through the front window at the ship, which was growing larger by the minute.

"We'll be in range in about ten minutes," the co-pilot said.

"I have the breaching equipment set up in the prep room," Odaran told Frye. "I assume that you'll be familiar with its operation."

"I've done this a few times," Frye replied. He motioned to Alainn, and then headed off of the bridge and towards the prep room midship. On one of the benches was a coil of cable. When connected to the *Veritas'* airlock door, it would send an electromagnetic pulse that would disrupt the door's electronic lock long enough to breach and enter the vessel. Frye grabbed the coiled cable and looped it over his arm, and then entered the airlock. Alainn followed and closed the door behind her. Frye plugged the cable into a receptacle on the airlock bulkhead and handed the coil to Alainn.

Through the porthole window in the airlock's exterior door, the hull of the *Veritas* was clearly visible. As Frye watched, the pilot leveled off with the airlock door of the other ship and closed to within a dozen meters.

"Docking collar deployed," the co-pilot's voice said across the ship's PA system.

Metal scaffolding surrounded by an airtight polymer sheet unfolded around the airlock door and spanned the void between the two ships. There was a slight shudder as the collar made contact with the *Veritas'* hull, and the polymer material billowed out and then stretched taut as the gangway was pressurized.

"You're all clear," Odaran's voice said over the PA. "Good luck."

Frye didn't reply, knowing that the PA was one-way. Instead, he nodded to his wife and hit the button to open the airlock's outer hull door. The door hissed as it recessed into the hull, and Frye took point, stepping out onto the gangway, autorifle at a low ready. Alainn followed, unspooling the disruptor cable behind them.

The distance between the two vessels was covered in moments, and Frye found himself at the airlock door of his

False Flag 225

ship. He grabbed the manual release and pulled – just as expected, it was locked. Turning to Alainn, he grabbed the cable leads and attached them to the door.

There was a buzz, followed by a metallic click as the electromagnetic pulse overrode the door lock. Frye grabbed the manual release again, and this time the door hissed and he was able to push it open.

Alainn placed her hand on his shoulder, indicating that she was ready for entry. Without turning around, Frye nodded and headed into the airlock.

As soon as Alainn closed the outer door, Frye opened the door into the prep room. The lights were on, and everything appeared normal. Frye crossed the small room and opened the door to the corridor, motioning with his hand towards the bridge. He moved into the corridor, autorifle at the ready, and Alainn swung out behind him, turning the other direction to clear the hallway behind them. Satisfied that it was empty, she shuffled backwards to keep up with Frye as he made his way forward, keeping her weapon ready should Agera appear from one of the cabins.

Like the ready room, the bridge was empty, but everything appeared to be in place. Frye cleared the room and then rejoined his wife in the corridor. He tapped her shoulder and she took the lead, heading aft towards the cabins and the hold.

The *Veritas* had two small cabins and a cramped galley and common room, all of which were empty. There were no signs of struggle, nor were there any signs that anyone was aboard. Frye began to get a gnawing feeling in his gut. *Just like everything else on this job*, he said to himself, *we're one step behind, and nothing quite makes sense.*

The hold, which wasn't much more than a storage space for maintenance parts, food, and other supplies, was likewise empty.

"He must have been down in engineering when he passed out," Alainn said, motioning towards the stairs that would take them to the lower deck.

"I guess," Frye replied, but his voice lacked conviction. He was certain of it now; they were being played somehow, and nothing good was going to come of their trip below deck.

With each footfall on the metal staircase, a new, gruesome image appeared in Frye's mind. He saw the bodies of Hartmann, Pryce, and Kendrick slumped in the corner, their blood comingling in a pool below their lifeless bodies. He hit the bottom stair and his eyes immediately scanned the corridor. Nothing. They were as clean as they had been weeks ago when he and the others had departed from Saiorse.

Alainn reached the door that led to the water and air reclamation systems. She turned to Frye, who nodded. A moment later, Alainn had the door open and the lights flickered to life.

Without seeing the room, Frye could tell by his wife's expression that she had found their friends. The rifle dropped from her hands and swung limply on its sling as she rushed into the cramped room, Frye close behind her.

"They're alive," Alainn said, her hand already on Hartmann's neck, checking his pulse.

The three men were slumped against the wastewater reclamation tank. Hartmann and Halwyn Pryce were unconscious but appeared untouched, while Kendrick had matted blood on the side of his head and a nasty black eye. Frye moved to the former detective and checked his pulse. It was strong. He reached into one of the pockets on his vest and pulled out the tube of nanogel, which he opened and applied directly to Kendrick's scalp.

False Flag

227

Alainn snapped up and grasped her rifle in one fluid movement, and then moved back to the door. The sudden motion startled Frye.

"See something?"

Alainn shook her head. "No, but Agera has to be here somewhere," she replied.

"The reactor room is the only place left," Frye said.

"You stay here," Alainn responded. "Try and wake Wolfie. I'll go find Agera."

Frye nodded and Alainn slipped out the door. Frye turned back to his navigator friend and gave his shoulders a shake, but there was no response. He needed to get the oxygen levels on the ship turned back up. Frye keyed his commlink. "Kellan?" he said, but there was no answer. He switched addresses. "Wallis?" Again, there was nothing on the other end. He was about to try again when Alainn came back through the door.

"He's not there," she said.

"That's impossible," Frye replied. "We checked the rest of the ship. We have to wake up Wolf. Maybe he can tell us something." Frye stood and ran up the stairs. He stopped in the storage room and grabbed an oxygen mask and opened the trauma kit. Grabbing a syringe of dextroamphetamine, he headed back down the stairs.

"If this doesn't wake him up, nothing will," he said, stepping around Alainn and plunging the syringe into Hartmann's thigh.

The effects were almost instantaneous. Hartmann shuddered, and then his unfocused eyes shot open and he gasped. "What the hell?"

"That's what we'd like to know, Wolfie," Alainn responded. "Here," she added, handing him the oxygen mask. "The air mix isn't conducive to consciousness. Put this on."

The navigator slipped the mask on clumsily and blinked as his eyes began to focus. "Alainn? Volya?"

"Where's Agera, Wolf?" Frye asked.

The navigator shook his head to try and clear the cobwebs. "OK, the last thing I remember was you telling me to get down to engineering because Agera was dirty," he said. Noticing the look on Frye's face, he raised his eyebrows. "What?"

"That was two weeks ago, Wolf."

Hartmann's jaw dropped. "What the hell happened?"

"That's what we'd like to know. Agera stole the ship and apparently left it out here in the middle of nowhere. So you've been out this whole time?"

Hartman nodded.

"Must be some kind of chemical-induced coma," Alainn said.

"How'd he get here?" Hartmann asked, nodding in Kendrick's direction.

"Not sure exactly," Frye replied. "We think that he managed to stow away right before Agera bolted. Obviously he was found, though." The pilot stood up and headed to the bulkhead door. "Let's wake him up and find out."

"How'd you find us?" Hartmann asked after Frye had left the room.

Alainn nodded towards Kendrick. "We used Wallis' comm. Kendrick had one on him."

Hartmann cocked an eyebrow. "That thing uses quantum entanglement, right?"

"That or wizard magic," Alainn said with a shrug.

"Well, I may have just come out of a two week coma, but that doesn't sound right. You can't determine position based on quantum communication, because there's no transmission." Noting Alainn's questioning look, he added,

False Flag   229

"The tech may be new, but the theory behind it isn't."

"Well, Wallis used the commlink to connect to the *Veritas'* navcomp," Alainn replied.

Hartmann appeared to be unconvinced, and was about to respond, but Frye came through the door with two syringes and oxygen masks, interrupting the conversation. He handed one set to Alainn, who used the needle to amp Halwyn. Frye did the same to Kendrick.

Hartmann's young apprentice came to first. He gasped, eyes darting back and forth before focusing on Alainn.

"Hey babe," he said, sounding like a drunken sailor.

"That had better be the drugs talking, kid," Alainn said wryly, handing him the mask.

Halwyn blushed. "Sorry, ma'am. Um, how'd you get here?"

"Kid, if your parents didn't fill you in on that one, maybe you should buy a book or something. The more important question is why this ship is out in the middle of nowhere, and the asshole who stole it is nowhere to be found."

The young pilot was clearly confused. "Apparently, we've been out for a couple of weeks," Hartmann explained.

Halwyn rubbed his temples. "I really should have stayed on the milk runs with my dad."

"Problem is, after you meet these two, things have a tendency to go off the tracks." The voice belonged to a groggy Roland Kendrick, who had come to while the others were tending to Halwyn.

"You called us, Detective," Frye pointed out.

"Fair enough," Kendrick replied, slipping on the mask that Frye offered. "Just out of curiosity, exactly how fucked are we?"

"Well, I don't exactly have any warm, fuzzy feelings,

given the state we found you all in, but now that we have you back, my ship back, and your brother close at hand, it looks like we can head home."

"You found Wallis?" Kendrick asked. "Is he OK?"

"He's fine," Frye replied. "He's aboard the ship that brought us out here."

"How exactly did you end up on board?" Alainn asked.

"I couldn't contact you, but I was able to track down your backup," Kendrick replied, nodding in Hartmann's direction. "I was on the gangway when the ship suddenly broke mooring. Barely managed to get myself inside. Once I did, someone got the drop on me. That's the last thing I remember."

"We're just lucky you managed to get yourself aboard," Frye said. "Your commlink was the only thing that allowed us to track you down. Wallis was able to tap into it to give us your position."

Kendrick looked confused. "What are you talking about, Volya?"

"The comm you sent me got damaged, which is why we couldn't contact you when we made planetfall at Neirin. Wallis repaired it after we met up with him. He used it to establish a connection with your tablet, and from there tied into the *Veritas'* systems. We tracked the navcomp here."

Kendrick was ashen. "Volya, I lost my tablet in the scramble to get aboard. It's floating around Neirin station somewhere."

The knot in Frye's gut, which had abated since finding his friends, returned with a vengeance. He bolted upright and ran out into the corridor.

He was halfway up the steps when a jolt shook the *Veritas*. He quickened his pace, racing through the upper deck corridor towards the prep room and airlock.

False Flag

"Volya?" Alainn called from behind him. Frye didn't slow down. He entered the prep room and crossed through to the airlock, hoping against hope that he was wrong. He reached the airlock porthole and looked into the void of space.

He wasn't wrong. The *Janus* was retreating into the distance, the short-range thrusters firing and positioning the craft for a burn into deep space. He and Alainn had been played again.

Chapter Thirteen

"What do you mean they're gone?" Frye had called Alainn on his commlink rather than go back downstairs. Instead, he had gone to the bridge to check on the ship's systems.

"I mean that just like everything else on this god-forsaken job, this was some kind of setup," Frye replied. He pulled up the *Veritas'* life support systems. "Just as I thought. Ship diagnostics show that life support is nominal." He slipped his face mask off and took a deep breath.

"Wallis led us all the way out here, just to dump us on our ship?" Alainn asked, joining Frye on the bridge. "It doesn't make sense."

"Nothing about this entire job has," Frye said. "It sure didn't take Kellan long to sell us out."

"I'm sure Wallis offered him more money," Alainn said with a shrug. "I told you Kellan was unreliable."

"You seem awfully serene about it."

"Nothing to be done about it now. Don't get me wrong, if I ever come within a parsec of Kellan Odaran again, I'm going to kill him with a smile on my face, but it's probably in our best interests at this point to cut our losses and head home."

233

"You think it will be that simple? I'm sure we didn't get led all the way out here just so that Agera could give us our ship back. Whatever is going on, something tells me we haven't seen the worst of it yet."

"Well, there is one person on this ship who might know." Alainn turned and left the bridge, Frye following close behind.

"You don't honestly still think that he had something to do with this, do you?" Frye asked.

Alainn spun around. "I don't know, Volya, but it's pretty damn clear that his brother was playing us, so at the moment I'm not really in a mood to give anyone the benefit of the doubt."

"What's going on?" Hartmann asked as Frye and Alainn entered the common room.

"I don't know, but let's see if we can't figure it out," Alainn replied, standing in front of Kendrick with an icy stare.

The detective looked from Alainn to Frye and then back again. "What?"

"You know what," Alainn said. "Why was your brother so keen to get us on board, and why did he bolt as soon as we were?"

Kendrick was indignant. "How the fuck should I know?"

"It's awfully convenient that you brought us into this mess, and then disappeared as soon as we made it to Neirin," Alainn replied. "Did you tip the feds off, too, or was that just a happy coincidence?"

Kendrick looked to Frye. "You don't honestly believe this shit, do you?"

Alainn didn't give her husband time to answer. "You seem awfully defensive, Roland. What do you have to hide?"

"Not a damn thing, Alainn. Maybe I'm defensive

False Flag 235

because I've been in hiding trying to protect someone who has been lying to me for weeks, and now you're accusing me of being part of some kind of crazy-ass conspiracy. In case you didn't notice, I'm still on board."

"It would make sense that someone involved would have to be left aboard. After all, they didn't just drop us here so that we could go home."

"And if I had gone with Wallis that would make me guilty, too. Either way, you want me to be the bad guy, so you make the facts fit the narrative. Fuck that, Alainn – I'm not playing your game. If you want to shoot me, fine. I have nothing to prove to you – I would have hoped that you knew me better." Kendrick thought for a moment. "We haven't been properly introduced, but I'm assuming that the gruff gentleman to my left is Wolfgang Hartmann, right?"

"Pleased to meet you, Detective. I've heard a lot about you – and until a few minutes ago, none of it had to do with you being part of a nefarious, if ill-conceived, plot."

"The pleasure is all mine, Mr. Hartmann, but I'm more concerned with the gentleman to your left."

"Me?" Halwyn had been mostly silent since he had awoken, and the sound of his voice caused everyone to look in his direction.

"Yes, you," Kendrick replied. "Wolfgang's reputation precedes him, but I'm afraid that I have no idea who you are."

"Halwyn Pryce," the young pilot replied.

"And have you been part of this crew for long?" Kendrick asked.

"It's my first time out," Halwyn replied with a dark chuckle. "I think I should have stuck with hauling ore with my old man."

Kendrick glared at Alainn. "So, you have a complete

unknown on your crew, but you decided that I'm the bad guy." His eyes bored into her. "I saved your fucking life," he seethed, "and you think that I'd roll on you in favor of a brother that I haven't seen in a decade."

Halwyn grew wide-eyed. "I-I didn't, I mean I don't... look, I didn't do anything."

"Relax, Junior," Kendrick said, "no one thinks that you did. They'd rather blame the burned-out old cop who has actually been in the line of fire with them."

Volya Frye had seen his wife angry; homicidal, even. He had seen her happy, confused, passionate, and recalcitrant... very frequently recalcitrant; but he had never seen her look guilty until now. The look on her face told him that she was struggling with the fact that she had very likely accused an ally of a despicable act.

"Fine," she replied quietly. "If you didn't have anything to do with this, at least you can help us figure out what your brother and his little friend are up to."

"I'd be happy to, but I don't have a damn clue," Kendrick replied, shaking his head. Frye was taken aback by how quickly his friend seemed to dismiss Alainn's accusations, but he realized that as a detective, Kendrick had probably leveled serious accusations at hundreds of suspects who had turned out to be completely innocent. It was all part of the process.

"Tell us about Agera," Frye said, breaking into the conversation for the first time.

"I never trusted that little bastard," Kendrick spat.

"You set a trap for him," Frye prompted.

Kendrick smiled. "Figured out my ruse, huh? You two would have made good detectives."

"But if Wallis and Agera are working together, why didn't Agera know about the trap?"

"Son of a bitch," Kendrick said, deflated.

False Flag 237

"Yeah," Alainn interjected.

"Did I miss something?" Frye asked.

"It was a false flag op," Alainn replied. Seeing her husband's confused look, she elaborated. "Wallis' goal was to get us to Neirin, so he fakes a break-in at his apartment, knowing that his brother will call us in. Roland sequesters Wallis in a hotel and sets a trap for anyone looking for them."

"At some point, Wallis has to modify his plan," Kendrick said, continuing where Alainn stopped. "It probably happened when your comm broke and you didn't make contact. At that point, Wallis needs to get us on the move, so he has Agera spring the trap in order to put things in motion again."

"Seems unnecessarily complex," Halwyn interrupted.

"To you, maybe," Alainn responded, "But keep in mind that these guys are geniuses, and they specialize in system theory. They're trying to program an outcome, and they see us as variables to be manipulated."

"And we've done a pretty damn good job playing our part so far," Kendrick added.

"Well, I for one am tired of the game," Frye said. He turned to Hartmann. "Join me on the bridge."

"Where are we headed, Captain?"

"Home, if the *Veritas* will take us there."

***

"So the systems are functional?"

"Five by five," Frye replied to his wife's question.

"It doesn't make sense," she replied.

"I've been thinking," Frye said, "What if Wallis and Agera just wanted the tech? Wallis lures us here, Agera steals the ship and bolts, giving him enough time to hack into the engineering systems and download the info that they need to recreate everything."

Alainn appeared unconvinced. "Then why was Wallis so hell-bent on getting us back aboard? He nuked a Union patrol ship because they got in our way, Volya. He wanted to make sure that we were here, and that makes me very much want to be somewhere else."

"I'll admit, it's not a perfect theory, but I haven't been able to come up with anything better."

"Well, I think that we should be ready, because it's not going to be that simple."

Frye nodded. "Agreed. Call everyone to the common room."

Alainn cocked her eyebrow. "Are you giving me an order?"

Frye grinned. "This is my ship. You melted yours, remember?"

"Careful, hotshot." Alainn activated the *Veritas'* PA system. "Ladies and gentlemen, this is your first officer. We are approaching cruising speed, and beverage service will begin momentarily. In the meantime, the captain has requested your presence in the common room immediately."

Frye opened the locker next to the pilot's seat and grabbed a bottle. "Can't fail to deliver," he said with a smile as he headed for the corridor, Alainn close behind.

The ship's passengers were in the common room by the time Frye arrived. He went into the galley, retrieved five glasses, and joined the rest of the *Veritas'* current residents.

"What's up?" Hartmann asked, as Frye set the glasses down on the dining table and began pouring.

"As far as I can tell, we're headed home," Frye replied, handing the navigator a glass. "But as my lovely wife has

False Flag

pointed out, nothing has exactly worked out as it seems.

"So, until we're all safely back home, we need to be ready for anything. To that end, the bridge is to be manned at all times. Wolf, you and Halwyn will take one watch, Alainn and I will take the other. We will switch every ten hours. At least one person is to be on the bridge at all times. Understood?"

Both Hartmann and Pryce nodded. "Good."

"And me?" Kendrick asked.

"You won't be of much use on the bridge, Roland, but you know your way around a ship. I want to know what's been tampered with. Check everything – life support systems, EVA suits, the armory – I want to know why Agera was aboard. If you need help with ship diagnostics, ask Wolfgang or myself."

"Got it."

"Alainn and I will take the first shift. You guys get some rest."

***

Frye sat in the pilot seat, finishing his dinner. Beside him, in the co-pilot's station, Alainn did the same. This shift, just like the eight that had preceded it, had been completely uneventful. The closest star system was nearly a parsec away, and the only way that they would run into anyone out here in the interstellar void was if someone had made a very wrong turn. According to the navcomp, they had crossed out of the Union into international space five days ago and were well on their way to Saiorse.

The first few days had been stressful; Frye had spent his shifts on the bridge sure that at any moment they would be hailed by a patrol vessel and arrested for something that Wallis had orchestrated, and he spent his off time sleeping fitfully. In his dreams, they had all been arrested or killed a half-dozen times. It had made him jumpy and irritable.

The rest of the crew seemed to fare no better. Alainn had taken to wearing a sidearm around the ship, and there was an autorifle propped against the rear bulkhead in the bridge. Another was situated similarly in the cabin that they shared. Hartmann, who had done his best to sell Halwyn Pryce's abilities to Frye and Alainn now constantly berated the young pilot over an array of perceived deficiencies. "The Kid," as Hartmann had begun referring to him, had become a nervous wreck as a result, second-guessing nearly everything that he did.

Kendrick, who had spent the last few months in the constant belief that he and his brother were under the threat of attack from some mysterious group, took to the stressful new situation with an almost cold indifference. He spent the first few days conducting a painstaking search of the ship. "At least I have something to do," he had replied when Frye asked him about his serene acceptance of their current situation.

Every piece of equipment, every suit, every gun, and every tool had been accounted for, and none of it appeared to have been tampered with in any way. Likewise, nothing had been found aboard that didn't belong. Other than the arsenal, which they knew about and had taken efforts to conceal, no contraband was aboard that could be used to implicate them in a crime.

The only suspicious thing that had been discovered was found during a check of the engineering room, which Hartmann had assisted with. According to the access logs, no one had used the Engineering terminal at any point since the *Veritas* had departed Saiorse. Since Agera had been using the terminal when he took the ship, it was

False Flag   241

obvious that the logs had been falsified.

In Frye's mind, that settled things – Agera and Wallis had been after the zero point technology, and had orchestrated the whole thing in order to get it. Alainn, however, remained unconvinced, pointing out that they still had no idea why Wallis had gone to such great lengths to get them back aboard the ship.

As the days crawled by with nothing happening, paranoia had given way to boredom and cabin fever. The cramped conditions, limited hygiene facilities, and lack of privacy ensured that while the specter of imminent arrest or death was fading, the irritability remained intact.

"We'll pass by Gwerddon in a few days," Frye said, setting his dinner plate down on the console. "We're far enough from the Union that it should be safe to stop and get some provisions."

Alainn sighed. "Normally, I might be inclined to disagree," she replied. "I'd prefer to get home before assuming that we're out of danger.

"But it would be nice to replenish the water tanks so I could take more than a two-minute shower. Besides, if I don't get off of this ship for at least a few hours, I'm going to kill someone," she continued. "Let's do it."

Frye nodded and pulled up the navcomp. He entered in the new destination and received confirmation from the navigation system that the course correction had been made. "Fifty-one hours," he told his wife.

A few hours later, Halwyn Pryce arrived on the bridge for his shift.

"Where's Wolf?" Alainn asked.

"Galley," the young pilot replied. "Making coffee, I think. Anything happening?"

"Yeah, we've decided to make a pit stop," Frye said. "We're going to resupply in Gwerddon in about forty-eight hours."

"Yes, sir. Anything else?"

"Nope, quiet as usual. You have the helm."

"OK, see you in ten hours."

Frye and Alainn left the bridge and headed aft. As they passed through the common room, a curse could be heard from the galley."

"Problem?" Frye asked, peeking his head in.

"Damn right there's a problem," Hartmann growled. "We're out of coffee."

"Well, I've got some good news. Alainn and I talked, and we think that we're far enough out that it's safe to make a stop. We'll resupply in Gwerddon in a couple of days."

"But what am I supposed to do right now?"

"You'll just have to deal with it," Frye said with a shrug. "With everything that's happened, is running out of coffee really that big a deal?"

"Don't make me kill you in your sleep, Volya."

"I feel bad for the kid," Frye said after he and Alainn had made their way down the corridor to the cabins. "If he thought that Wolf was a bastard before, just wait until the caffeine withdrawal kicks in."

Just as they made it to their cabin, Kendrick appeared from the aft storage room.

"Evening, Roland," Frye said.

"Is it?" Kendrick asked.

"Somewhere, I suppose," Frye said with a smile. "Just so you know, we're out of coffee, so you might want to avoid Wolfgang."

"No offense, Volya, but given our current situation, avoiding anyone isn't exactly an option."

***

False Flag   243

The promise of some time off of the ship, even if it was only a few hours, and even if it was only an escape to the slightly larger confines of an orbital station, was enough to raise everyone's spirits briefly, but as the hours ticked closer to arrival, the cabin fever returned, worse than before. Frye was certain that the walls were literally closing in and the ship had shrunk. Hartmann was drinking too much when he was off-shift, and even the normally unflappable Roland Kendrick, tempered by years of soul-crushingly boring stakeouts, was showing signs of cracking.

"I hired you, you little prick; I'm not your servant!" Hartmann left the bridge in a huff and ran into Frye in the common room.

"Problem, Wolf?"

"You're damn right there's a problem," the navigator growled. "I've gotta fetch that kid's meals like he's a helpless little baby and I'm sick of it."

"Wolf, you know the deal. Halwyn's qualified to fly this ship, and you aren't. He can't leave the bridge while the two of you are on shift."

"What are you saying, Volya? You taking his side? Rocket jockeys gotta stick together, right? And the rest of us can all get fucked."

"What I'm saying," Frye responded as calmly as possible, "is that right now, someone who is qualified to fly the craft must be on the bridge at all times. It's been over a week – this isn't some kind of surprise."

"Well it's bullshit," Hartmann countered. "And it's easy for you – you've got Alainn on your shift. Either one of you can fly, so no one has to play second-class citizen. Why don't you trade me her for the kid – give me something nice to look at for a while."

Frye took a deep breath. "That's my wife you're talking

about, Wolf. Since I know you're stressed, I'm going to let that one go, but..."

"But what, Volya? You gonna kick my ass?"

"I won't have to. You talk about Alainn as though she's a piece of meat again, and I'll tell her." He raised an eyebrow at Hartmann, looking for a response, but the navigator was silent.

"And do you realize what being on the bridge for ten hours means for your young protégée? The poor kid can't even take a shit – he's been downing anti-diarrheal caps for days, and he has to piss in a can he keeps under the pilot's console. He sends you off of the bridge so that he can do what little business he can't medicate away in privacy.

"In twelve hours, we'll be docking at Gwerddon. You can stretch your legs and cool down a little. Hell, if you want to, you can catch a commercial flight home. Or maybe some of the others will. And once we're back underway, maybe we can loosen things up a bit. Fair enough?"

Hartmann looked down at the floor. "Fair enough. And I'm sorry for that crack about Alainn. That was way out of bounds."

"I understand. We're cool – just try to keep it together, brother."

Frye left Hartmann in the common room and headed to the bridge, where he found Pryce hunched over the pilot's console. He jumped when the bulkhead door creaked open, and Frye could tell that he was hurriedly zipping up his pants.

"I was just, um..."

"Taking a piss?" Frye offered.

"Yes, sir," Halwyn replied.

"I really hope so," Frye replied. "Because you know I

False Flag   245

have to use that console, too."

Halwyns' face grew red. "I, I wouldn't do that on the bridge..."

Frye laughed. "Relax, kid; I'm just busting your balls."

"I get enough of that from Wolfgang, sir."

"You know," Frye said, sitting in the co-pilot's seat, "he's the one who got you on this gig. Alainn and I were... unconvinced that someone with your limited experience would be the right choice for the job."

"Should I thank him or blame him?"

"Look, all that I'm saying is that everyone is stressed. He stuck his neck out for you though, so cut him some slack."

"I suppose you're right."

"Of course I'm right – I'm the captain."

"I just don't think that I have much to offer."

Frye smiled. "You're the one who figured out Roland was setting a trap for Agera, remember?"

"It didn't do much good."

"I'm going to share a secret with you: most of the time it doesn't. You'll have a dozen good ideas before one of them pays off. The others will occur to you too late, or you'll be in a position where you can't act on them, or your adversary will have planned for it. Brains are vital, but they're only one component. You ever hear of a Fashewar?"

Halwyn raised an eyebrow. "You mean the explosive?"

"It's an anti-personnel device. When activated, it detonates, launching metallic spheres in the direction that it is pointed. There's a lot you can learn from it."

"How, exactly?"

"Brains are only part of the equation. You also have to face the enemy, be explosive, and have balls of steel."

Halwyn chuckled, and then was silent for a moment.

"Wolfgang told me you were a farm boy."

"He's right; I was."

"But you talk like a soldier."

Frye shook his head. "I most certainly do not. Soldiers take orders. I make my own way."

"I guess what I mean is that you're a warrior – I'm not."

"Kid, you're a lot more like me than you realize. And I'm no warrior. I've just been in the wrong place at the wrong time enough that I've had to adapt. Now I'm trying to put those skills to use. So far, it hasn't gone so well, but there's an upside."

"What's that?"

"I'm not dead yet," Frye responded with a grin. Standing, he went to the cabinet at the back of the bridge and grabbed a bottle of whiskey.

"You all drink a lot," Halwyn observed.

"Less than some, more than others," Frye replied with a shrug. He motioned to the young pilot with a glass.

Halwyn shook his head. "I'm on shift."

"And I'm the captain. Have one." Frye poured before Pryce could reply.

"So what happens next?"

"We go home."

"But what about the guy who took your ship? Are you just going to let him get away with it?"

Frye hesitated. "We got the ship back," he finally replied, taking a sip of the brown liquid. "And I know a little something about going after revenge. You might tell yourself that you're just out for justice, but it has a way of eating away at you. I'm inclined to just let it go."

"Are you afraid?"

Frye sighed. "I used to be. The truth is that I lived my life in fear. Not so much anymore. See, you assume that I don't go after Wallis because I'm afraid of him. Maybe I let

False Flag 247

it go because I'm not afraid. Fear of inadequacy, of a loss of control, is what drives most revenge. The truth is that I just don't have the energy for that anymore. I want to go home with my wife, maybe have a few kids, and occasionally help someone in need. Men like Wallis and Agera will always exist."

"So this isn't going to end with some epic climax?"

Frye laughed. "Life isn't like that. The stories always end with a battle between good and evil, but they never show the aftermath. Do you know why?"

Halwyn shook his head.

"It's because it's anti-climactic. Someone has to clean up the mess, and everyone has to get back to their lives. If I can skip the face-off and go straight to the part where I'm back at home, I'll take it."

"But you lost an entire ship," Halwyn pointed out.

"And will killing Wallis Aeron get me a new one? We got screwed over," Frye said with a shrug. "Better luck next time, I guess." He drained his glass and stood. "I'll be back in an hour to relieve you."

***

"Something isn't right." Hartmann was in the co-pilot's seat, checking the *Veritas'* trajectory.

"Everything shows nominal," Halwyn replied.

"Look out the window," Hartmann replied. "What do you see?"

"Space?"

Hartmann resisted the urge to belittle the young pilot. Frye had been right – the kid was doing his best, he was just in over his head. "OK, but what shouldn't be there?"

"Son of a..." Pryce's voice trailed off.

"Yeah." He activated his comm. "Volya? You and Alainn

better get up here. Like now."

A few minutes later, a groggy Volya Frye arrived on the bridge, followed by Alainn, who was in much the same condition. "What is it?" Frye asked.

"We're in a binary system," Hartmann said. "Gwerddon is a unitary system."

Frye looked out of the window. Sure enough, straight ahead, two stars were barely visible. "What the hell?"

"According to the navcomp, we're two hours from Gwerddon station," Hartmann said. "But we aren't even in the right system."

"Then where are we?"

"I have no idea."

"What happened?"

"I don't know, Volya. Everything has been reading fine. We're just not where it says that we are."

"I'll tell you what happened," Alainn said. "We just discovered part of Wallis' plan."

"But I thought we decided that there was no way he was able to control the ship remotely," Frye replied.

"He isn't," said Hartmann. "Agera must have uploaded a virus to the navigation system so that it would tell us we were going to one place, while we're actually headed somewhere different."

"Can you fix it?"

"I'm decent with a computer, Volya, but these guys are in a completely different league. I can try to shut everything down and restore it, but it's a long shot."

"Do it."

"We need to be at all stop in order to power everything down."

"You heard him, Halwyn – shut 'er down."

"Yes, sir." The young pilot went to work on the console. A moment later, he leaned back in his seat, a

False Flag 249

puzzled expression on his face. "Nothing's responding, sir."

Alainn chuckled darkly. "Of course it isn't. You remember when we got to Neirin, Volya?"

Frye remembered. "You think that was Wallis, too?"

"I imagine that he had something to do with it. In any case, you remember that we never regained control of the *Seguir*. Wallis is taking us on a ride, and we have no choice but to sit back and enjoy the scenery."

"Well, I guess that means that the bridge duty has been completely unnecessary," Frye noted.

"Does that mean that I'm free to hit the head?" Halwyn asked.

"Knock yourself out, kid," Frye replied. The young pilot stood and headed off of the bridge.

"You think you can figure out where we are?" Alainn asked Hartmann.

The navigator sighed. "Yeah, I can do it with a set of charts. It's been a while, but it was beat into us during training. Give me a few hours and I think I can figure it out."

"Good." Alainn turned to Frye. "We may actually have an edge."

"How do you figure?"

"Wallis and his greasy little friend are sending us on a joyride, but they set things up so that it would seem like we were headed wherever we told the navcomp to go, right?"

"Right..."

"Well, maybe our planned pit stop in Gwerddon caused us to figure out what was going on before they expected us to?"

"Seems pretty thin."

"Maybe, but it's something. I've made do with worse. We've been two steps behind since we took this damn job;

maybe this is a chance to gain some ground."

"At this point, I guess we should take anything we can get." Frye hit the PA button on the control panel. "Roland, your presence is requested on the bridge."

The detective arrived a few minutes later. He had clearly been woken from a deep sleep, and his thinning grey hair gave the impression that there was some kind of windstorm between his makeshift bed in the storage room and the bridge.

"This had better be good," Kendrick said.

"Did we interrupt a pleasant dream?" Hartmann asked suggestively.

"Yeah – I was dreaming that I was somewhere other than this tin can."

"Well, it's something, but I wouldn't call it good," Frye said. He briefly filled the detective in on the situation.

"Sounds like we're fucked," Kendrick deadpanned. "Can I go back to sleep now?"

"We were fucked before we ever showed up in Neirin," Alainn replied. "We knew that the other shoe was going to drop sooner or later – now maybe we've got a chance to figure out what's going on so we can mount a response."

"OK," Kendrick replied. "What do we know?"

"We know that Wallis wants us somewhere," Frye said. It seemed obvious, but he figured that it was as good a place to start as any.

"We know that he wasn't after the ship," Alainn continued. "If he was, Agera could have just taken it."

"I'd agree," Kendrick replied.

"And we know that whatever the plan was, having us alive is important," Hartmann chimed in. "Otherwise, Agera could have just killed us while we were out."

"Morbid, but correct," Kendrick said. "So we're meant to end up somewhere alive."

False Flag   251

"This seem familiar to you?" Hartmann asked, looking at Frye.

"You think it's a frame-up?"

"Can you think of a better explanation?"

"I can't," Alainn interjected.

"I can't either," Kendrick agreed.

"So Wallis Aeron, genius physicist, did all of this for a simple frame job?" Frye was unconvinced.

"No one said it was simple," Alainn said. "Obviously there are details set up that we don't know about. The fact remains, though, that we're either being set up or he plans to hurtle this craft into a star, completing the most convoluted Rube Goldberg homicide in the history of humankind."

"I changed my mind," Hartmann said. "I'm gonna go with that one. Fits the 'crazy psycho' vibe those two creeps give off better. No offense," he added, looking at Kendrick.

"None taken," Kendrick replied, "But I think that maybe we should stick with the line of inquiry that doesn't end with us plunging into a hydrogen fusion-fuelled oblivion."

"OK, so we assume that we aren't about to be the victims of the most complex murder ever conceived. Why are we being set up?"

"We're set to rendezvous with a navy vessel. They arrest us and impound the *Veritas*. While all of the legal issues get worked out, the ship's tech is fair game."

"So it's not similar to the last time we were framed, it's *exactly* like the last time we were framed?"

"You know the Union's motto," Hartmann said with a shrug, "If it doesn't work, try it until it does."

"Too pedestrian," Alainn said dismissively. "Besides, if they wanted to impound the ship, Agera would have just killed you all and alerted the authorities anonymously. A

252 *The Union Chronicles*

ship full of bodies is a really good reason for the Marshal's Service to haul a rig into impound."

"As much fun as contemplating my good fortune in not being murdered yet is," Hartmann interrupted, "how about you all take the brainstorm session somewhere else? We need to figure out our bearings, and I can't really do that while you all are distracting me."

Frye held his hands up in mock surrender. He turned and left the bridge, followed by Alainn and Kendrick. Halwyn met them in the common room.

"Roland, what do you actually know about the break-in at Wallis' place?" Alainn asked.

"Just what he told me, which means jack shit, I imagine."

"But the cops were there, right?" Frye asked.

"Sure," Kendrick replied. "So what? Wallis sets his place up to look like it got busted into, then calls the cops. They take a report, and as far as the official record goes, it happened." Kendrick chuckled. "They arrested me almost as soon as I got there. I wonder if Wallis planned it that way or if it was a coincidence."

"It's an interesting question, but I think we should focus on why he did it, not the details," Alainn replied. "What exactly is he trying to do?"

"Maybe we're being kidnapped," Frye suggested. "Your family has deep pockets – maybe this is about ransom."

"Let's take a step back," Kendrick said. "Forget the specifics; let's focus on motive in general. In general, people commit crimes for one of four reasons: money, power, sex, or revenge. Ransom would fall into the money category, but from everything I know about Wallis, money means very little to him, and he has plenty of it."

"Sex is out, too," Alainn said. "Ten to one the kid's a

virgin, and I don't think that he has much drive to change that status." Noticing Kendrick's look, she chose not to elaborate. "It's a woman thing, detective. Trust me."

"So that leaves power and revenge," Frye said. "You ever do something to him that would cause him to want you and a bunch of people you've only known for a few months dead?"

"We're brothers in the loosest biological sense of the word. I've only met the kid a few times, and those were pleasant enough. Unless there's something that I'm completely unaware of, he has no more reason to hate me than any other random stranger."

"Which leaves power," Alainn said. "He did mention that he doesn't have much status."

"But why would he care?" Halwyn asked. "From the impression I get, he doesn't exactly hold other people in high regard. Why would he care what they think?"

Alainn grinned. "I like you, kid. Your naiveté is charmingly refreshing. You remind me of Volya here when we first met. Something you'll come to understand is that the more contemptuous the individual, the more they care what others think. Someone who looks down on others expects that those others will be compelled to look up. When that doesn't happen, it becomes a problem."

"I would agree with that assessment," Kendrick replied. "Wallis is dismissive of others, but cannot stand to have his capabilities questioned. He considers other people beneath him, but seems to think that he is owed their respect."

"So you think that he's out to dominate the Universe?" Frye was skeptical.

"He would certainly see it as within his capabilities," Kendrick replied. "And it would explain why he and Agera were associating with anti-government types. If you want to destabilize the current system, you might as well use a network that's already in place."

"So you think that we're unwitting accomplices in a plot to overthrow the Union government?" Halwyn asked.

"Could be," Alainn answered with a shrug. "It fits in with his Samizdat associations, and the comments he made about the Union government.

"If that's it, though, he went to a lot of unnecessary work," Frye said. "We probably would have just helped if he'd asked nicely."

"And handed us a big box of cash," Alainn added. "But something tells me that whatever he's doing, we won't like the part he has us playing."

"Well, maybe once Wolf figures out where we're going and where we're headed, we can figure out what is going on. Until then, maybe we should focus our efforts on either getting control of the ship back or getting off of it," Frye suggested.

"We'll never break through whatever security Wallis put on the system," Alainn said.

"What if we reset everything?" Halwyn asked.

"We need systems access to do that."

"Unless we cut the power feeds," Frye said.

"We would have to take everything off-line... including the life support systems," Alainn pointed out.

"True, but the re-boot would only take about an hour. There's more than enough breathable air to last that long."

"I'm OK with it," Alainn answered, "But we need everyone's buy in. Something goes wrong, and we all suffocate."

"Do you think it will work?" Kendrick asked.

"Maybe," Frye replied. "If whatever Wallis embedded in the systems is running in the virtual memory, it will get

False Flag 255

dumped when we power down. If not, it'll come right back up with the rest of the systems."

"I doubt he'd leave something like that to chance," Kendrick said, "But maybe we'll get lucky. I say do it."

Frye looked at Halwyn. The young pilot was pale. "A full reset is risky. I've never seen one done on a ship that wasn't in a maintenance bay."

"I've done it before," Frye said. "My old ship, the *Edrych*, was a tin can, and the systems would lock up from time to time. The only way to get them back up was to disconnect everything from the reactor, then plug it all back in. This one time," Frye continued with a chuckle, "the computers wouldn't reboot when we plugged 'em back in, and we had to do it all over. Twice. Finally, everything came back, but Wolf and I thought that we were goners..." He stopped, noticing that Halwyn was white as a sheet. "Relax, kid – it worked out, didn't it? Besides, that ship's software had more bugs than an entomologist's wet dream. It'll be fine, really."

"I suppose if everyone else is OK with it, then I am, too," Halwyn replied with a tremor in his voice.

Frye headed down the corridor and stuck his head onto the bridge. Hartmann was making calculations on the chart table, occasionally looking up through the windows out into space.

"Any luck?" Frye asked.

"I need to take a few more readings," Hartmann said, touching the table and bringing up a new chart. "The problem with space is that so much of it looks the same. Give me another hour or so and I'll have it."

"I was thinking we'd try a hard reset."

Hartmann looked up from his charts. "You think it'll work? I mean, that Wallis kid doesn't seem to be the type to half-ass code like that."

Frye shrugged. "Can't hurt to try though, right?"

"Depends. You remember that time on the *Edrych* when everything locked up after you plugged it back in?"

"I seem to recall you almost shitting yourself because you were sure we were going to die."

"Right. At least I didn't start crying."

"I was crying because I was laughing at you. For such a tough guy, you sure get worked up easily."

"Go cut the damn power and leave me alone."

Frye made his way back to the common room. "Wolf's in agreement," he said. "Let's see if this works." He crossed the room and headed down the corridor. Before he passed through the bulkhead, he turned and looked over his shoulder. "Make sure anything important is strapped down. We'll lose gravity once the power's off."

Downstairs, he walked to the end of the passageway and opened the door to the engineering deck. The room was spotless, as usual, and the antiseptic white surface coatings reflected the room's already-bright lighting, causing Frye to squint until his eyes adjusted.

The Casimir reactor was in the center of the room. The rectangular, titanium-encased power source was completely silent, and could run indefinitely, at least in theory. If something went wrong, and the systems failed to reboot, the reactor would hum along until the ship was found, or the mechanical components failed. For a fleeting moment, Frye contemplated the fact that if they died, they could be far enough out that the ship may not be found for decades or more, and a future salvage pilot, much like himself, may marvel at the antiquated technology someday.

And now he had to cut it off from the rest of the ship, along with the battery backups. There was a maintenance panel against the starboard bulkhead that would allow him

False Flag 257

to cut the power. He just had to throw a switch, wait a half hour for all of the capacitors to discharge and the ship to go dead; then power everything back up. *Simple as that*, Frye told himself.

He opened the panel and reached for the switch, but right before he cut the power, he noticed a grease smudge on the cover that contained the main electrical feeds. On another ship, grease would be a common sight in the engine room, but Frye made sure that his was spotless, and with the minimal maintenance that the *Veritas'* drive systems required, it was easy to keep it that way. Something had been tampered with.

Frye realized that his fingers were on the switch and yanked his hand away as though the switch itself were electrified. He needed to figure out what had been done before he killed the power.

There was a small maintenance kit against the starboard hull. Frye opened it and grabbed a screwdriver. Returning to the panel, he removed the retaining screws that held the cover in place and pulled it off, revealing the wiring inside.

The panel was simple; there were large leads that came off of the Casimir generator, a second set of leads that led to the battery backups, and a third set that fed power to the main distribution panel. The switch had three positions: in the 'on' position, power was fed from the generator to the ship and kept the battery packs charged. In the 'batt' position, the generator was cut off from the ship, and critical systems, such as gravity and life support, would run on battery power. If the switch was turned to 'off' both the generator and battery pack were isolated from the ship, and all systems would cease to function.

Removing the cover, however, revealed an extra set of

leads, which were connected on the same side as the wiring leading to the main panel. "Wolf," he said, keying his commlink, "I need you down here, now."

"What's up?"

"Now. And bring Alainn." Frye killed the link.

A few moments later, he could hear boots clanking on the metal stairway.

"What is it?" Wolf asked. "Why isn't the power out?"

Frye motioned to the extra set of leads with his finger. "Where do you suppose those go?"

"Let's find out," Hartmann replied. "Hang on a sec." He turned and left the room, returning a few moments later with a satchel that he had retrieved from the storage room. He opened the bag and removed a set of clips, which he attached to the extra wire leads. Next, he pulled a hand-held unit from the bag and turned it on.

"This way," he said, heading back out of the room.

Frye and Alainn followed the navigator down the corridor, but they didn't get far. Hartmann stopped in front of the room that housed the *Veritas'* atmosphere control equipment.

"In here," he said, opening the door.

Inside, the room was dominated by the air scrubber, a massive unit that reprocessed exhaled carbon dioxide, turning it back into breathable oxygen. With it, the *Veritas* could maintain a breathable atmosphere for months at a time.

"Whatever those wires go to, it's in there," Hartmann said.

Frye left the room, returning with the maintenance kit from the reactor room. Using the screwdriver, he removed a maintenance panel from the scrubber and looked inside.

"Hand me a light," he said, reaching behind him. Alainn grabbed a flashlight from a mount on the bulkhead and

False Flag 259

placed it in his palm.

Frye swept the light around inside the duct, which fed processed air back into the ship. In one corner, the beam illuminated a cylinder that had been hastily mounted inside the duct.

"What do we have here?" Frye said.

"See something?" Alainn asked.

"Yeah. Hand me a six millimeter wrench."

Frye took the wrench and placed the flashlight in his mouth. With some effort, he was able to pull the canister from the wall. As he got a closer look, he could tell that the wire leads from the reactor room were indeed hooked to the cylinder, but one of them had come loose. He gave the other one a tug and it also came free, allowing Frye to pull the canister out of the access door.

"What is it?" Hartmann asked.

"Knockout gas," Alainn replied. "It has to be."

"One of the wires was loose," Frye said. "Otherwise, we'd all be unconscious."

"So we're only awake by dumb luck?"

"Seems like."

"Well, we know why the navcomp isn't working," Alainn mused. "We were put on a preprogrammed course. I'll bet that the gas was supposed to go off as soon as we attempted to fly the ship. We go to sleep and the ship heads off on whatever course Agera set up."

"You've got to figure out where we're headed, Wolf," Frye said, urgency in his voice.

"On it," the navigator said, turning and heading back upstairs.

Chapter Fourteen

"So he killed his mother over his curfew?" Halwyn was incredulous.

"Kid, I've seen people kill each other over just about anything," Kendrick replied. "If it's something that you've found the slightest bit annoying, I guarantee you that I know of a case where someone killed over it."

Hartmann crossed through the bulkhead into the common room where Kendrick and Halwyn were sitting.

"What's going on, Wolfgang?" Kendrick asked.

"I think that it's time for us to talk about how *our* lives are going to end, Detective."

Hartmann's words were still hanging over the room as Frye and Alainn entered. "I'm guessing that this isn't good," Frye said, noting the expressions on the people assembled in the room.

"I finished going through the charts," Hartmann replied. "It's possible that I'm off, but it looks pretty grim."

"Well?"

"Based on our bearings, the only destination that I can come up with that makes any sense is Awdurdod."

Frye's hands went to his face and Alainn pursed her lips.

"They aren't fucking around, are they?" Kendrick said.

Halwyn was confused. "I'm sorry, but I don't know what that means."

"Awdurdod is the capital planet of the Planetary Union," Hartmann explained.

"Why is that so bad?" Halwyn asked.

"Because it isn't like back home," Alainn replied. "In Saiorse, we're allowed, even encouraged, to visit our government houses. Our constitution ensures that representatives come from the people and return to their fold when their term is over.

"The Union is different. People who get into the government there never leave. Even after they retire, they become lobbyists for the megacorps or the labor cartels. The people that the Union supposedly represents aren't allowed to visit Awdurdod without special permission."

"Special permission that we don't have," Hartmann added.

"I'm guessing that our arrival won't be welcomed," Frye said.

"It won't be noticed for a while," Hartmann pointed out. "All of the security is focused at the jump points. We'll be crossing over through the void. Unless a patrol ship happens to cross paths with us, we'll be deep inside the system before we're ever discovered."

The gnawing at the back of Frye's mind was gone – everything was clear now. "These guys went to the trouble of stealing a ship capable of penetrating Awdurdod's defenses, and then filled it with some of the Union's least wanted. We have three people on this ship with very legitimate grievances against the Union government, and we're headed to the capital. It's virtually guaranteed that we'll make it through..."

"You're thinking we're about to become unwitting terrorists?" Kendrick asked.

False Flag   263

"That's exactly what I think," Frye replied. "An attack on Awdurdod would serve as justification for whatever kind of response that the Union wanted to mount. Add to that the fact that you, Wolf, and I all have a reason to hate the powers that be, *and* the fact that we have recently associated with anti-government groups..."

"And you have everything that you need for a massive crackdown," Alainn interjected. "Son of a bitch," she said, shaking her head. "They set the whole thing up. Our escape on Neirin station, meeting up with Samizdat, the destruction of a patrol vessel..."

"They created the perfect group of anti-government lunatics," Kendrick said, shaking his head. "Impressive."

"So, you think they were hired by the government?" Hartmann asked.

"A false flag operation? Fake a terrorist attack in order to justify yet more police action? It's possible," Kendrick replied. "I know for a fact that they've taken advantage of similar circumstances in the past. Maybe certain factions have graduated to setting them up."

"But what's the point in heading into such a heavily-guarded system?" Halwyn asked. "Once we show up on radar, they'll shoot us out of the sky. Not exactly a major event."

"They won't be able to get a firing solution," Alainn replied. "The gravity field generator makes it almost impossible."

Hartmann's head snapped up at the mention of the *Veritas'* primary propulsion system. "Exactly how powerful is that thing?"

Alainn hesitated. "I don't know exactly, why?"

"Could it generate a field the size of, say, a medium-sized moon?"

"I suppose so. Where are you going with this?"

"Think about it. If something with that equivalent mass were to collide with a planet..."

"Shit," Alainn spat out. "They're going to use us as a gravity bomb."

***

Alainn's epiphany left the crew reeling. They were going to die, and they were going to take several billion people with them. Even if the ship never made contact with Awdurdod's surface, the gravity field would cause massive tidal and tectonic disruptions planetside. Most of the damage would be done before the *Veritas* ever broke through the capital world's atmosphere.

"We have to figure out a way to scuttle the ship," Frye said.

"You want me to commit suicide, just to save the lives of a bunch of bureaucrats? Like hell," Hartmann countered.

"We die either way," Kendrick observed. "We should do the right thing and make sure that we're the only ones."

"Bullshit," Hartmann said. "I'm not thrilled that your brother set us up to die, but I can't exactly argue with his target. I've got some unfinished business with the brass on Awdurdod. If I'm going to eat it, I might as well take a few of them with me."

"And their spouses? And children? Listen to yourself," Alainn chided. "You're pissed, and rightly so, because people treated you as a faceless commodity. Is your solution really to embrace the deaths of a billion faceless others?"

Hartmann glared, but said nothing. Frye recognized the look – his friend was upset, but he also knew that Alainn

False Flag 265

was right. Once the shock of their situation wore off, Hartmann would be able to think clearly.

Not that it matters, really, Frye thought to himself. They were going to die, and nothing was going to change that. It was something to be accepted...

"How long until we cross into the Awdurdod system?" Halwyn asked, interrupting Frye's thoughts.

"About forty-two hours," Hartmann replied. "After that, it's another sixteen to the planet itself."

"Then we have a little bit of time," Halwyn said.

"Time for what?" Hartmann snapped. "To contemplate our deaths?"

"I'm just saying that maybe we can figure something out," the young pilot replied, deflated.

"Sometimes there's nothing to figure out," Hartmann grumbled. "Sometimes the damage is already done. Face it, kid, at this point; we're nothing more than walking corpses." With that, the navigator shuffled past the others and out of the common room.

"Did you have something in mind?" Frye asked Halwyn.

"It's probably insane."

"At this point, I don't think that much matters," Frye replied.

"What if we bailed out?" Seeing the look on Alainn's face, Halwyn shrugged. "Told you it was crazy."

"Crazy? Sure it is," Alainn replied, "But it might be possible. Where do we bail to?"

"Once we get picked up on approach, we'll be pursued," Halwyn said. "The Marshal's Service may not be able to shoot us down, but you know that they'll try."

"You want to do a ship-to-ship EVA jump?" Alainn asked derisively. "You are insane."

"Your husband has done it," Kendrick interjected.

Alainn's head turned towards Frye. "When was this?"

"When we kidnapped Delmont," Frye replied. "It really isn't as difficult as it sounds."

"If it works, then we're aboard a ship full of Marshals," Alainn pointed out.

"That worry you?"

Alainn chuckled. "Not really. So you figure we take the ship and bug out?"

"Makes sense," Kendrick replied. "Once the *Veritas* is identified as a threat, all of the attention will be on it. Problem is, it will still be a threat, even if we aren't aboard. All of those people you were worried about are still going to die."

"No it won't," Alainn replied. "We can't bail out while the gravity drive is running, so we'll destroy the reactor and the drive system just before we jump. Both the *Veritas* and the *Seguir* are equipped with a self-destruct mechanism that will turn the vital equipment to slag. With the gravity drive offline, the ship will be a sitting duck. I figure we'll have two minutes or so to bail after the drive is offline. After that, the *Veritas* will be vaporized."

"Not much room for error," Kendrick observed.

"It's better than nothing," Alainn replied. "We've just got to make sure we're lined up for the jump and pull the trigger at the last possible second."

"Only one problem," Frye said. "There are five of us, and only four EVA suits. Someone is going to have to stay behind."

The room went quiet. "We'll just have to think of something else," Halwyn offered.

"There is nothing else," Alainn replied. "Any ticket off of this ship involves the use of the EVA suits."

"The Marshal's Service might board us," Halywn offered weakly. "Then we can fight our way aboard their ship."

False Flag 267

"You want to take the chance that they'll board us rather than simply blow us out of the sky?" Frye answered. "Ten to one, if we wait to get boarded, we all die. This is our only shot. Well, yours, I suppose, anyway."

"What are you saying?" Alainn said.

"It's my ship," Frye replied. "As captain, it's my duty to get everyone else to safety."

"Like hell," Kendrick said angrily. "You're only here because of me. I'll stay."

Frye was about to respond, but Kendrick cut him off. "I'm the oldest person here, and the only family that I've got put us on this damn ship," he said. "I'm not going to allow you to make Alainn a widow. I'm staying, and that's final."

***

Frye knocked on the door to the cabin, but there was no answer. After knocking a second time, he opened the door and stepped inside.

Hartmann was sitting in the chair next to the bed, holding a half-empty bottle in one hand and a ratty piece of paper in the other. His eyes lifted to the doorway as Frye stepped inside.

"What will she do when I don't come home?" the navigator asked, showing a rare moment of vulnerability. "I never should have left."

Frye recognized the scrap of paper. On the other side would be the image of an auburn-haired girl, her green eyes betraying a life that held more pain than her short years should allow.

"She's already been orphaned once," Hartmann continued.

Frye motioned for the bottle. For a moment, Hartmann

looked as though he didn't want to let it out of his grasp, but he relented, handing it over. Frye took a pull and coughed.

"I'll never understand why you still drink this shit," he said with a gasp. "You know we have better stuff in the galley, right?"

"This isn't the time for jokes, Volya."

"I disagree. We've laughed in the face of death countless times."

"Things have changed. I've never been responsible for someone else."

"Well, then cut the melodrama and let's get you back home, big guy." Frye turned towards the door. "Come on; we've got a plan."

***

"What do you think?" Frye asked, after detailing the plan to Hartmann.

"It should work," the navigator replied. "If nothing else, it'll make for one hell of a spacewalk."

"And you really think that you can access the ventilation system from the outside?"

"There should be a port on the hull for oxygen replenishment. The couplings are a standard configuration, and we've got a spare in the hold, so it shouldn't be too difficult."

"And you think we'll be in-system in a few hours?"

"It's hard to be positive without the navcomp, but we're close. I'd say we'll be spotted within the next eighteen hours or so."

"OK, I think that we have everything ready. I guess there's nothing to do now but wait."

"How's Roland doing?"

False Flag

"As well as can be expected, I suppose. He insists that he be the one left behind, and he's keeping his head up, but you know it has to be torture, staring down the barrel of eternity, but having to sit and wait for it to be over."

"Well, he doesn't have long to wait now. If we have anything decent left in the galley, might as well make it for dinner – it'll be the last one any of us has aboard."

Chapter Fifteen

As Frye walked the corridor towards the bridge, he reveled in the familiar smells of industrial lubricant and reprocessed air. Without thinking, his hand extended, making contact with the pristine surface of the *Veritas'* hull, the smooth surface cool against the skin of his fingers. The ship was a tool – an unthinking mass of steel and titanium, but to Frye, every ship he had ever piloted was alive. They all had their own personalities to be learned and secrets to be discovered, and Frye hadn't even owned the *Veritas* long enough to learn most of hers. In a few short hours, that personality would be lost; the ship would destroyed, her body shattered and floating through the black.

At the pilot's station, the incoming signal alarm was buzzing, alerting Frye to what he already knew: the *Veritas* was being hailed by the *UMS Sentinel*, a security patrol cruiser. They had been picked up on Awdurdod's defense network an hour ago, and the patrol ship was demanding that they stop and prepare for boarding.

As expected, there was no way to reply. The *Veritas'* comm systems, like everything else on the bridge, weren't functional. They could receive transmissions, but sending anything out wasn't possible. Frye hit a button on the panel to silence the alarm, and then brought the transmission from the *Sentinel* up.

"...restricted space. You are commanded to go to an all-stop condition and prepare for boarding. Anything other than full compliance will result in classification as a hostile vessel, and appropriate action will be taken. You have twenty minutes and thirty-seven seconds to comply. Attention unidentified craft, you have entered restricted space. You are commanded to go to an all-stop condition and prepare for boarding..."

The message continued on a loop; the only thing that changed was the time remaining before the *Sentinel* would resort to using force to stop the ship. Frye listened to the message once more, and then muted the comm system. With one more look around the bridge, he turned and headed aft.

In the common room, the remains of the evening meal were still on the table. Pryce, who was on kitchen duty, had started to police the dining area after the meal was over, but Hartmann had stopped him.

"You know the meaning of the word futility, kid?" he had asked with a chuckle. Halwyn looked at him quizzically, and Hartmann broke out into a full-throated laugh. "You're cleaning dishes that will never be used again. Everything on this ship is going to be vaporized in a few hours. Leave it."

Halwyn had looked sheepish for a brief moment, but then grinned. "Good," he said, "I always hated kitchen duty. This is a much better solution."

"Was that a joke?" Alainn asked, looking at Frye. "Our little guy is growing up."

Frye gave a mock sniffle. "It goes by so fast."

Now, passing through the empty space, the dirty plates and dishes of cold food gave the room an eerie quality.

False Flag   273

The meal had been lighthearted, but now, like the rest of the ship, the common area was gripped by the specter of loneliness.

Down the corridor, however, voices and movement could be heard coming from the prep room. Frye arrived as Alainn, Hartmann, and Pryce were donning their EVA suits. Kendrick hovered over them, making sure that everything was properly fitted and functioning correctly. It was an unnecessary step – the suits would alert the user to any issues – but Frye knew that it was the detective's way of keeping what was about to happen as far from his mind as possible. To their credit, none of the others pointed this fact out.

Frye grabbed his suit and quickly slipped in, the material forming to his skin and putting pressure against his body. It was uncomfortable at standard atmosphere, but once they entered the vacuum of space, it would be more than welcome. He slipped his tablet into the wrist mount and synced the computer to the suit's internal control systems, verifying that the life support systems were all properly functioning. The compressed air thrusters, which would allow him to control his position and velocity, were fully charged and ready to go.

"All set?" Kendrick asked, handing Frye his helmet.

Frye didn't even want to look the detective in the eye. Even though he knew that someone was going to have to stay behind, and even though it was perfectly rational that Kendrick be the one to do so, Frye still couldn't help but feel guilty. He also knew that despite how he felt, he owed it to the man to look him in the face. He looked up, and the older man's steel grey eyes were there.

"Five by five," Frye replied, holding Kendrick's gaze. The detective nodded and clapped Frye on the back without breaking eye contact.

274   *The Union Chronicles*

"It's on me," he said, acknowledging the elephant in the room.

"You didn't know."

Kendrick shook his head. "Doesn't matter. If someone has to make it right, it needs to be me. I wish it weren't this way, but it is."

"Everyone makes mistakes. The good ones make it right," Frye said quietly.

"What's that?"

"Something a wise man told me. You're one of the good ones, Roland, and the Universe will be worse when you've left it."

Kendrick smiled ruefully, but said nothing.

"It's time," Alainn said, laying a hand on Frye's shoulder. He looked back at Kendrick, but the detective had turned away, making a point to busy himself with something else that didn't matter.

Frye turned towards the others. "I'll go out first," he said. "Once the lead is attached, the rest of you can exit. When you're out, we'll tether our suits together. As soon as we're set, Alainn will trigger the kill switch, and the *Veritas* will go black. After that, we've got a couple of minutes at most before the *Sentinel* gets a firing solution. Do we have everything?"

"We're set," Hartmann replied, hefting a duffel bag onto his shoulder.

"Then I guess this is it," Frye replied. He turned to offer Kendrick a farewell, but the detective had disappeared. He started to move towards the corridor, but Alainn stopped him with a hand on his shoulder.

"It's time," she said. "There's nothing else you can say that will make it better."

"Sometimes things just get fucked," Hartmann chimed in, "it's arrogant to think that you can find the words to

False Flag 275

make it all make sense."

Frye nodded sadly. "Wolf," he said, turning to his oldest friend. "If this goes sideways, I just want you to know..."

"I know, brother," Hartmann replied, "it's been a pleasure to have known me. I get that a lot."

"I was going to suggest that you try not to be such a bastard in the afterlife," Frye said.

"Duly noted."

"Well, see you in a few minutes – or on the other side."

"Good luck, brother." Wolf clapped him on the shoulder.

Frye hoisted his helmet, but before slipping it on, he grabbed Alainn around the waist and pulled her in close. Before she could react, his lips found hers.

"God, I hope that's not the last time I get to do that," he said, releasing her.

Alainn smiled. "Well, if it was, it wasn't a bad effort. Actually, it was pretty good; you might want to hope we all die – you know, go out on a high note."

Frye snapped his helmet into place, his smile visible through the glass. The HUD activated, displaying the EVA suit's diagnostics. In a few minutes, the data it was displaying would mean the difference between life and death, but at the moment, it just felt like it was obstructing his view of the most beautiful thing he'd ever seen.

But then Alainn slipped her own helmet on and the moment was over. Behind her, Hartmann and Pryce did the same. Frye took Alainn's hand and they walked into the airlock. Alainn hit the depressurization button and the door into the prep room closed with a hiss. Moments later, the air was evacuated from the airlock, and Frye felt his suit stiffen as the pressure inside fought to escape into the vacuum of the airlock. A second later, the suit's pressure controls won the battle and movement became almost normal.

There was a tremor in Frye's hand as he reached for the release handle. He grabbed it and looked at his wife. Alainn nodded and gripped his hand. Drawing in his breath, Frye pulled the release. With a hiss, the door opened, and Frye was face to face with the infinite expanse of space.

The time for reflection was over, and Frye sprang into action. He clipped a lead onto an eyehole inside of the airlock and swung himself outside of the craft. Once outside, he attached a second lead line to an exterior point and unclipped the first one. "Your turn," he said to Alainn through his commlink.

Shortly thereafter, his wife whipped around the doorway in his direction. After fastening herself to the exterior tether, she unclipped the other and tossed it inside. She hit the button outside of the airlock door and it closed smoothly.

"You're up, Wolf," Frye said into the commlink.

While he waited for Hartmann and Halwyn to repeat the process that he and Alainn had just completed, Frye looked out into the expanse of space. The *Sentinel* was too far away to be visible to the naked eye; all he saw was a smattering of stars against the inky blackness of space. Turning to his right, Awdurdod's sun appeared as a large white ball over Alainn's shoulder. It was breathtaking, but a stark reminder that they were still on the outskirts of the system, and about to hurtle themselves towards an unseen ship full of people that would be happy to kill them on sight.

"We gonna get on with this or what?" Hartmann

False Flag 277

asked, snapping Frye back to reality.

"Took you long enough," Frye retorted. "I fell asleep waiting for you."

"You can sleep when you're dead," Hartmann replied, "Which may or may not be in a couple of minutes."

"Just upload the coordinates," Frye said.

"Done," Hartmann replied a few moments later.

"Everyone belted in?" Frye asked.

"All set," Alainn replied.

"Good to go," Hartmann answered.

"I-um, yeah," Halwyn stuttered.

Frye released the tether from the *Veritas'* hull. "Target burn in three... two... one... engage."

The compressed air thrusters on the three EVA suits fired simultaneously. The compressed air tanks wouldn't provide much in the way of propulsion, but the *Sentinel* was in pursuit of the *Veritas,* so all that they had to do was slow down enough that the Marshal's Service ship could catch up to them. In an hour or so, the ship would close the distance, and they could attach themselves to the hull. Provided that the *Sentinel* didn't change course. Or that a stray bit of debris didn't vaporize them. *Shit there's a lot that I didn't think about*, Frye said to himself. "Burn it, before we get caught in the gravity wake," he said over the commlink, realizing that if they got torn apart by the ship's drive, none of the other myriad scenarios would get a chance to play themselves out.

"Done," Alainn replied. Frye looked back towards the *Veritas* and caught an almost imperceptible ripple as the gravity field dissipated. Unimpeded, the ship would continue on its current trajectory indefinitely, but Frye assumed that the *Sentinel* would take care of that soon.

"Soooo, anybody know any good stories?" Hartmann asked sarcastically. Frye looked over and could see his friend making a show of twiddling his thumbs – an awkward prospect in an EVA suit.

"Y-you guys seem to be taking this a little bit lightly," Halwyn said, the catch in his voice nearly drowning out the content of his speech.

"When your only choices are to laugh or cry, laughing is at least a little more fun," Alainn replied. "At least this way you get to die with a smile on your face."

Hartmann was more direct. "You have a better idea, kid? Either we're dead or we're not, but at this point, there's nothing to do but wait to find out which one it is."

"Cut propulsion in five... four... three... two... now," Frye said, turning off the jets in his suit as he did so.

The short burn had slowed the group just enough that the *Veritas* was now retreating rapidly in the distance. It was now barely visible, the only indication of its presence the light shining through the windows of the common room. Though the view through the vacuum was deceptive, Frye put it at just over a thousand kilometers and gaining distance fast.

"Time's just about up," Frye noted, checking the timer that he had synchronized to the *Sentinel's* warning message.

***

Aboard the *Veritas*, Kendrick had sealed off the aft section of the upper decks after the rest of the crew had abandoned ship. When the self-destruct mechanism had gone off, the lights flickered; then came back to life as the emergency lighting came on. There was a creaking sound as the air evacuated through the hole that the plasmacord in the engine bay had created. Now, the only livable spaces aboard the ship were the bridge and the common

False Flag 279

room. There was enough air for one person to survive on for a few hours, although with the demise of the life support systems, the temperature was dropping fast. Kendrick hadn't ever really contemplated how cold space was; now he was wishing that he had a heavier coat.

He had thought about just waiting in the engine room to be sucked into the vacuum of space, but had ruled it out based on his previous experience in the void. It was silly to fuss over the exact nature of his death, he realized, but that had just been so damn... *unpleasant.*

Now, however, he kind of hoped that the Marshal's Service would get on with it and vaporize the ship. Something told him that freezing to death would be even worse than having his blood boil inside his veins in the vacuum.

He made his way up to the bridge and opened up the storage locker on the back wall. "Only the best," he said to himself, noting the label on the whiskey bottle. He removed the top and took a long swig, savoring the oaky flavor. He briefly considered grabbing a glass, but decided against it. He made his way back to the common room and dropped onto the sofa with a sigh.

It occurred to him that he should be more contemplative; that with his inevitable demise looming, he should take a few moments to reflect on his life, and perhaps consider what would come next. It was funny; he hadn't ever thought about the afterlife with any seriousness, and now here he was, moments away from it, and he had no idea how to begin.

Not that it really matters, he said to himself. There was no way that he was going to be able to balance the scales now. He'd spent his entire adult life attempting to make amends for the sins of his youth; if the scales weren't balanced now, they weren't going to be.

"Here's hoping you grade on a curve, big guy," he said, raising the bottle before taking another healthy pull. Kendrick wasn't sure if he even believed in God, but right now, he didn't have anyone else to talk to. *Hell, why not*, he said to himself.

"Hey, if you're up there, how's about cutting me some slack," he said aloud. "I'm not such a bad guy, you know." Then it hit him: if He did exist, He actually did know. "I mean, sure, there was that business in the Navy, but that wasn't my fault. And I could have been a better husband, but she went and fucked that doctor – that was on her."

Shit, should I say 'fuck' when I'm talking to Him? This isn't going well; I should cut this off quick.

"You know what? Never mind; I'm just going to hang out here by myself if it's all the same to You." He took another pull from the bottle and looked around the room. For years, patience had been a part of the job description, so why, all of a sudden, couldn't he handle having nothing to do but wait?

"You know, if You really are out there, then why do You let all of this shit happen? You know what I'm talking about – I've seen it all. How in the hell do You just allow it?"

Kendrick waited a few moments, but felt compelled to answer his own question. "Alright, fine; we're the ones who fucked up, but what do You want?"

Another moment passed in silence. Then another. Kendrick took another pull. There wasn't much left in the bottle now. *Maybe there's another one in the galley.*

"Not much of a conversationalist, are You?" Kendrick stood up and realized that the alcohol had affected him more than he realized. He made his way uneasily to the galley. As he suspected, there was another bottle in the cabinet.

False Flag   281

If I was Him, would I want to talk to me? Another pull from the bottle. Back to the couch.

"I'm sorry. Is that what you want to hear? Because I am. For everything – every fucked up thing I've ever done, or wanted to do, or thought about wanting to do. Does that make you happy?"

Kendrick wasn't sure if it was just the alcohol, but suddenly he felt warmer.

***

"Goodbye, friend," Frye whispered. In the distance, the *Veritas* disappeared in a ball of flame that vanished quickly, extinguished in the oxygen-free environment. It had happened without warning; the tungsten-cased explosive fired from one of the *Sentinel's* rail guns must have passed by them within a kilometer or so, but was so small and moved so quickly that it couldn't be seen.

"Our ride is here," Hartmann said, pointing a gloved finger out into the inky blackness.

Frye turned and could see flashing lights in the distance. "They'll come by for a sweep," he said. "Alright, everyone. We've got one shot at this. Let's make it count." From the bag on his shoulder, Frye extracted a magnetic grapple that he had fashioned from some of the salvage equipment he had aboard the *Veritas*. Fired by compressed air, it would propel an electromagnet towards the hull of the *Sentinel*, but Frye only had two thousand meters of nanofilament cable, and enough compressed air for one launch.

"One hundred twenty thousand meters and closing," Alainn said, checking the rangefinder built into her HUD.

"Gimme a course solution, Wolf," Frye said, as calmly as if they were on the bridge of their ship, rather than floating through nothingness, with nothing more than a few millimeters of nanoprene keeping them alive.

"Transmitting now. Damn it's going to be a close one, Volya."

The coordinates and propulsion vector appeared on Frye's HUD. "Jets at sixty percent in three... two... now!" The four suits' compressed air jets fired simultaneously, nudging the wearers in a slightly different direction.

The *Sentinel* was now a large figure through Frye's face mask, and it was growing by the second. From its appearance, it was at least a four-deck ship. That meant a crew of at least ten to fifteen Marshal's deputies.

"Seventy-two thousand meters," Alainn said across the comm. "Sixty-eight... they're closing fast."

"Kill the jets," Hartmann interjected. The others complied.

"Fifty-three thousand meters."

Heavy breathing came across the comm. Halwyn had begun to hyperventilate, and his breathing was loud enough to trigger the microphone in his suit.

"Keep it together, kid," Hartmann growled. There was no response. Instead, the heavy breathing continued, intermittently interrupted by a quiet whimper.

"Thirty-nine thousand. Damnit, kid, stifle it."

Frye hoisted the makeshift grapple gun onto his shoulder. If the *Sentinel's* course continued unchanged, it would pass just over the top of them.

"I don't want to die," the whisper was almost imperceptible, but it was there. There was a tug on the tether as Halwyn began to thrash about.

"Shut the fuck up and stay still, kid. We don't have time for this shit," Hartmann barked.

"But..." the interjection was punctuated by another tug on the cable.

False Flag 283

"One more word or movement and I will cut your ass lose, you understand? You will not take the rest of us with you."

The crying continued, but nothing more was said and the tether went slack. Frye re-aligned his aim.

"Twenty-one thousand," Alainn intoned.

A bead of sweat rolled down Frye's face and into his eye, causing him to blink.

"Eighteen thousand."

Another drop. The sweat was beginning to obstruct his vision.

"Fourteen thousand. You waiting for an invitation to fire that thing, Volya?"

The *Sentinel* now filled up most of Frye's field of vision.

"Eight thousand. Do it, damnit!"

Frye waited another split second; then fired the grapple. The cable unfurled into space as the ship approached.

"Shit, it's not gonna reach in time," Hartmann said.

Halwyn was now openly sobbing.

Frye felt Alainn grip his hand.

Suddenly the cable went taut. The grapple had reached the end of its cable.

"Damnit," Frye muttered under his breath. The *Sentinel* was about to pass by, and Frye could see the magnetic grapple stopped a few hundred meters short. He'd messed up the calculation somehow.

Just as he was about to surrender to despair, however, he noticed that the distance between the grapple and the ship was closing. They were still moving towards the intersection point that Hartmann had targeted.

Then, with a snap, the *Sentinel* came into contact with the grapple's magnetic field, and they began to accelerate towards the massive vessel.

There was a reverberation in the cable as the grapple made contact with the hull a full two kilometers away. Immediately, Frye activated the cable retractor and he began to move towards the Marshal's Service vessel with Alainn, Hartmann, and Halwyn close in tow.

"Cut it a little close, don't you think?" Alainn asked over the comm.

"Nonsense. Piece of cake."

"That why you almost wet yourself a minute ago?" Hartmann interjected.

"I was kind of hoping you didn't hear that," Frye replied. "No matter, though; it worked."

"You alright kid?" Hartmann asked Halwyn. There was no response. "Kid?" he asked again.

Frye felt a tug on the tether that held him to the others. Looking back over his shoulder, he could see that Hartmann had the younger man by the shoulders.

"I can't tell if he's conscious," Hartmann said.

"It'll have to wait until we get inside, Wolf," Alainn replied. "When's that going to be?" she asked, turning to Frye.

"Get ready," he replied. "We're coming in pretty fast; we need to slow down a little, so that we don't end up smeared all over the hull. Five second retro burst in five... four... three... two... now!"

Three of the suits' positioning jets fired, but Halwyn continued on, slipping out of Hartmann's grip and floating past Frye towards the *Sentinel*.

"Shit," Frye said. Halwyn's momentum was going to carry them into the hull faster than he wanted, and the kid was going to hit hard. The tether pulled taut, and Frye could feel it tugging against the deceleration of their jets.

The *Sentinel* was now only meters away. Halwyn made contact first, striking the metallic hull like a rag doll thrown

False Flag   285

by an upset toddler. Frye cringed with the impact. He wasn't sure what the young man's condition had been before, but they were probably going to have to add fractures and internal bleeding to the list. All he could hope was that the ship had a decent sick bay and a competent medical officer.

Frye made contact next. He positioned himself so that he would strike feet first with his knees bent. Even so, the impact was jarring. He felt the collision in his spine, and a dull headache erupted at the base of his skull.

Alainn struck a bit more gracefully, her lower mass and lithe frame absorbing the impact and dissipating it with nothing more than a quiet grunt. Hartmann, however, was less fortunate. As Frye watched, the larger man hit feet first, but at an angle, causing his left ankle to roll over in a direction Frye was sure wasn't natural.

"Son of a bitch!" the navigator exclaimed.

"You OK?" Frye asked.

"Think my ankle's broken."

"Well, suck it up. We've got work to do. We need to find the service access."

They had made contact along the *Sentinel's* keel. According to convention, the airlock would be starboard, along with all of the connections for refueling and resupplying the vessel's life support systems.

Without handholds, and towing the unresponsive Halwyn, the short journey was extremely tedious, requiring small spurts from the positioning jets and using what was left of the compressed gas that powered them. Fifteen minutes later, however, they had located their target: the service access that was used to charge the ship's atmosphere.

Hartmann gently removed the gas canister that Frye had retrieved from the *Veritas'* air scrubber. Before they left, he had attached a short length of hose and a coupling, which he connected to the adapter on the *Sentinel*.

"I hope this works," Hartmann said through clenched teeth. "This is a big ass ship."

"If nothing else, it should slow them down," Alainn replied. "Besides, that canister was supposed to keep us down for over a week; I'm sure it's enough to keep the crew out for an hour or two."

"Here's hoping," Frye said, connecting the hose. He nodded to Hartmann, who connected the leads to a small battery pack.

"How long do we wait?" Hartmann asked.

"You were able to remove the restrictor, right?"

"Yeah."

"Then we wait until it's empty, and then give it a half hour to take effect. Anyone still awake after that gets shot."

"I don't think that I'm going to be able to walk on this ankle, Volya."

"Alainn and I will clear the ship. We'll leave you in the airlock until we can carry you to the medical bay."

"How's the kid?" Alainn interjected.

Hartmann shrugged, a difficult proposition in the suit. "He's not moving, and he hit the hull hard. I don't think that it's good."

"We need to hurry. How's the gas?"

"It doesn't have a readout, and right now it's weightless. I have no idea."

Alainn turned towards Frye. "We can't wait long. Halwyn needs medical attention."

"And if everyone on board is still awake, we'll all get gunned down," Frye responded. "Give it another ten minutes."

The time ticked by slowly. It wouldn't be long before

False Flag 287

the *Sentinel* passed close enough to the wreckage of the *Veritas* to conduct a sweep of the area. After that, it would head somewhere else, and they did not want to be outside of the craft when the thrusters fired.

It was also possible that backup would arrive, and that would be disastrous as well. The crew of the *Sentinel* had undoubtedly reported their engagement with an unidentified vessel, and if anyone else was in the area, company could be on the way. They needed to be long gone before that happened.

"Time's up," Hartmann practically grunted.

Frye made his way carefully to the airlock door and grabbed the handle. As expected, it was locked. From his satchel, he retrieved a small rectangular object with two electrical leads, which he placed on either side of the door handle. He affixed the device to the door and pressed a button.

The disruptor did its job, interfering with the electromagnetic lock and allowing him to work the manual release. With the door open, he floated inside.

Immediately across the threshold, the ship's gravity field took over, and his boots hit the ground. His knee protested the sudden application of weight; he must have twisted it when he made contact with the ship.

"Give me a hand, Volya," Alainn said. Frye turned around to see his wife holding Halwyn just outside of the airlock door. Slowly, she passed the limp figure through, and Frye caught him under the arms, setting him gently on the floor of the room.

"Alright, Wolf, come on," Frye said, gesturing with his gloved hand. Hartmann reached through the door and wrapped his arm around Frye's shoulders, and then stepped gingerly aboard, his injured ankle held off of the floor.

"How is it?" Frye asked, lowering the navigator into a sitting position against the hull.

"Not good; I can't feel it, which means I'm going into shock. You've gotta hurry."

"On it. Hang tight."

Alainn was last through the door, closing it behind her. Frye hit the switch, and there was a rush as air filled the room.

Behind him, Alainn had opened the bag she was carrying. She handed an autorifle to Hartmann, and then did the same to Frye. They had already affixed holsters with sidearms to the suits they were wearing, and in moments, she and Frye were stacked up at the door to the *Sentinel's* prep room. Alainn tapped Frye on the shoulder, and he hit the button to open the door.

Like the airlock, the prep room was significantly larger than the one aboard the *Veritas,* designed to allow a full squad of Marshal's deputies to disembark at once. The room was empty, and Frye quickly made his way to the door that would lead to the ship's main corridor.

With a tap from his wife, Frye opened the door and swung out to the right. Behind him, Alainn covered the corridor to the left. As Frye made his way forward, Alainn covered their rear.

The deck that they were on contained a storage room, a briefing room, the brig, the ship's armory, and the sick bay, all of which were empty. At the aft end of the corridor was a stairwell. They now had a choice; go downstairs to Engineering, or up to the next level, which should be home to the crew's quarters. Frye chose the latter, motioning up with the barrel of his gun. Alainn nodded, and covered him as he ascended the stairs.

The stairwell opened up into a large room, and Frye could immediately tell that the gas had been effective. The

False Flag   289

room was laid out like a dormitory, with a half-dozen bunks against one wall, and a long table laid out on the other side of the room.

Several figures were slumped over the table, and Frye could see a few others littering the bunks. He motioned to Alainn, but it was a wasted gesture – she had already seen them.

Quickly, they slipped restraints on the figures and searched each person, removing anything that could be used as a weapon or a tool, should they come to before a more secure solution was found.

Forward of the barracks was another corridor, which led to the officer's quarters. Three more people were found and restrained. At the bow, they found the officer's mess and common room, along with two more people, both sleeping soundly. Frye and Alainn spent the better part of twenty minutes hauling the five bodies into the barracks.

One more level up and they found the bridge. There were four officers lying on the floor, one of them wearing the insignia of Captain.

"Got the big guy," Frye said, securing him. The others were likewise bound, and they moved aft. Behind the bridge was the Captain's quarters, but they were empty, the Captain having been found on the bridge.

With the other levels cleared, it was time to tackle the Engineering deck. Frye and Alainn quickly made their way down the stairs and cleared the rooms containing the life support systems and the reactor room. Two more were added to the ranks of the unconscious.

"I counted sixteen," Frye said over his comm.

"Agreed. Figure two pilots, two navigators, two first officers, the Captain, two engineers, a medical officer, and a six-man squad of deputies."

"We need to get everyone but the captain and the doctor into the barracks."

"Just like Wolfie to figure out a way to get out of the heavy lifting."

"I heard that," Hartmann's voice said over the comm.

The navigator's voice concerned Frye. It was weak and raspy; the shock from his broken ankle was getting worse.

Frye knelt down and hoisted one of the engineers into a fireman's carry, and Alainn did likewise. With effort, they labored up the stairs and into the barracks, where the two men were deposited on bunks.

The same exercise was repeated on the upper level, with the exception of the Captain, who they left on the bridge. By the time that the rest of the crew was secured in the barracks, Frye's legs burned and he was sweating profusely in his suit.

"Which one do you suppose is the Medical Officer?" Alainn asked.

"This one," Frye said, pointing at one of the uniformed officers. "She's got a caduceus pinned to her lapel."

"Grab her and let's go."

Frye fought the urge to groan aloud and hoisted the woman onto his shoulders. *At least she's petite*, he told himself as he passed by a rather bulky deputy.

The medical bay was small, but looked to be well-equipped. Frye deposited the medic, whose name badge identified her as Likita Kirurgi, on one of the cots and headed to the airlock.

Inside, Alainn was standing over Halwyn Pryce, who was still motionless.

"We need to move him carefully," Alainn said.

Frye nodded. "Hang on a sec." He turned and headed back to the medical bay, where there was a stretcher strapped to the bulkhead. Releasing it, he hurried back to

False Flag 291

the airlock. With some effort, he and Alainn were able to gently move the pilot onto the stretcher and carry him into the infirmary, where they deposited him on one of the beds.

Hartmann was significantly easier. Although his left leg was useless, and he was weak, he was able to move with an arm over each of his friends' shoulders.

"How long until the gas dissipates?" Frye asked, as soon as Hartmann was resting on the last of the medical bay's beds.

"You usually get a full air exchange every hour," Hartmann replied. "I'd say that it's probably safe now." Without warning, he popped the clasps on his helmet and removed it.

Alainn gasped, partly surprised, and partly because of Hartmann's ashen visage. His bald pate and stubbled face were nearly white, and sweat beads were rolling down onto the infirmary bed at an alarming rate.

"Relax, sweetheart," he said with a smile that looked more like a grimace, "If I don't pass out, you know the air is OK, and if I do, all the better for me."

"Give him a dose of morphine," Frye directed, turning his attention to the medic.

"How do we wake her?" he asked.

"Amp her," Alainn replied, tossing a syringe in Frye's direction, "it worked on the others. Same gas, right?"

"Right." Frye plunged the needle into the woman's left thigh and emptied the syringe. He then turned his attention to Halwyn. He didn't want to move the young man any more than necessary, but he needed to check the kid's vitals. He started by removing the left glove and attaching an oximeter to Halwyn's middle finger. There was a pulse, but it was weak, and oxygen concentration was low, indicating that the young pilot's breathing was shallow.

Before he could take any further steps, there was a gasp behind him. He turned just in time to see the ship's medic bolt upright on the bed in an apparent panic.

"Relax," Frye said, before realizing that with his helmet on, he couldn't be heard. He swung his head around, taking a quick glance at Hartmann and verifying that the navigator was still conscious. Then he quickly removed his own helmet before he could second-guess himself.

"Relax," he repeated, and the woman turned to face him.

"What happened?" she asked, clearly disoriented.

"Um, I'm afraid that was us," he replied, smiling in what he hoped was a non-threatening manner.

It was at that moment that the officer realized that her hands were bound. She fought against the restraints and moved as far away from Frye as the narrow bed would allow.

"Take it easy," Frye said, lifting a hand towards the young woman, who recoiled, nearly falling off of the bed. "I'm not going to hurt you," he reassured her, "I'm going to remove the restraints. We have two injured here, and we need your help."

"Where is the rest of the crew?"

"Safe upstairs. Look, I'm sorry, but we need medical attention, fast. We have no intentions of hurting you, or anyone else aboard; we just need your help."

Frye's assurances seemed to calm the woman a bit, and she allowed Frye close enough to remove the restraints. Then, without warning, she darted from the bed and towards the door.

Alainn, however, beat her there, rifle held tight to her chest, menacing but not directly threatening the other woman. With her helmet still affixed, she cut an imposing

False Flag   293

figure, even though she was shorter than the other woman.

"Like I said, we need your help," Frye said. "We have no intention of hurting you, but you aren't leaving this infirmary until my people are patched up."

"And if I refuse?"

"You won't, Doctor Kirurgi – it is doctor, correct? Your oath requires you to render medical attention. Quickly, if you don't mind; I think one of them is nearly gone, if he isn't past the point of no return already."

The doctor took one last glance at the door, and then turned purposefully towards the cot that held Halwyn. "What happened?"

"He hit the hull pretty hard on our approach," Frye replied. "Before that, he was having a nasty panic attack."

Kirurgi scrunched up her face. "Where exactly did you come from?"

"We were out for a walk," Frye replied. "What does it matter? The kid had a panic attack, fainted, and then hit the hull. He hasn't woken up since."

While Frye was speaking, Kirurgi busied herself removing Halwyn's helmet. She then lifted each of his closed eyelids in turn, shining a light into the pupils.

"He's got a concussion, for sure" she muttered, "And the right pupil is completely dialated..." he voice trailed off as she probed the vertebrae that she could reach. "Feels fine here..." She turned to Frye. "I can't tell if there's a spinal injury, but we need to get the suit off so that I can conduct a full-body scan."

Frye quickly helped Kirurgi remove Halwyn's suit, and then stepped back as she lowered the scanning unit. She watched the monitor as the device scanned for fractures, organ damage, and internal bleeding.

"Hairline fractures to the T2 and T3 vertibrae, fracture

to the left scapula, ribs four and five are broken... damn."

"What is it?" Frye asked.

"The left lung is punctured and filling with fluid, and there's a lot of internal bleeding. His gallbladder is ruptured... shit."

"What can we do?"

"There isn't much we can do," Kirurgi replied. "With a fully-stocked trauma center, maybe, but with what I have here, the only thing I can do is make him comfortable. I don't even know if that's really necessary; given the extent of the trauma, his body is already shutting down. He probably can't feel anything."

"You have to do something," Frye insisted.

"I'm telling you, it's not going to matter. There's too much damage."

"Volya," Alainn interjected.

Frye didn't seem to hear her. "What can you fix?"

Kirurgi shook her head. "The fractures and the lung are no problem. I might even be able to drain some of the hemorrhaging, but it's a lot of blood, blood that I can't replace, given my limited stock."

"Volya," Alainn tried again.

"Well then start with that," Frye said, still not hearing Alainn.

"You don't understand; it's a waste of time. That ruptured gallbladder is dumping poison into his system. It has to come out, and I don't have the facilities to do that here. Besides, both his liver and pancreas are damaged, and it looks like there may be a rupture to his large intestine. I'm sorry, but he's too far gone."

Frye was about to respond, but Alainn cut him off. "Volya!" she yelled. Frye snapped around to see that she had removed her helmet and was leaning over Hartmann.

"What?"

False Flag 295

"Wolf passed out."

Kirurgi turned her attention to the other bed. "Get me a shot of epi," she directed. Alainn reached into a drawer in the bedside crash cart and grabbed the syringe, handing it to the doctor, who injected it into Hartmann's thigh.

"What's wrong here?"

"Broken ankle, I think."

"Let's get the suit off and get it scanned."

While the two women busied themselves removing Hartmann's EVA suit, Frye stood by Halwyn's pale, motionless body in stunned silence. The readings from the oximeter grew fainter and fainter.

"Lateral malleolus fracture," Frye heard Kirurgi say behind him. "Two of the ligaments are torn. Other than that, everything looks alright. Let's go ahead and patch him up."

As Alainn watched, Doctor Kirurgi went to work on Hartmann, using a small ultrasonic needle to stitch the ligaments back together before injecting a calcium nanopaste along the fibula. When finished, she slid a compression sock over Hartmann's ankle.

"It'll take about twelve hours for everything to set," she said when she was done. I'll keep him on a morphine drip for a few more hours, and then we can wake him up." Turning around, she saw Frye still standing over the other bed. "I can still try and make him comfortable," she offered.

"No need," Frye replied, "He's gone. Slipped away a minute ago." He turned to Alainn. "Keep an eye on things here. I'm going to go have a chat with the captain. The rest of the crew will be waking up soon, I imagine, and we need to get going." With one last rueful glance at the body of Halwyn Pryce, Frye turned and left the infirmary.

Chapter Sixteen

"What the hell happened?" The captain, whose name badge identified him as Cefo, sat against the bulkhead, looking around in a daze as the effects of the gas wore off. "And who the hell are you?"

"My name is Volya Frye."

"Should that mean something to me?"

Frye smiled. "I don't imagine so. I'm nobody, really."

"And how, pray tell, did you find yourself aboard my ship?" Cefo struggled to his feet, and immediately clasped his left temple.

"Drink this," Frye said, offering the captain a glass of water. "I've been told that the gas has a dehydrating effect."

"What gas?" Cefo asked, after downing the water in one long pull.

"I'm afraid that was us. You see, we needed to get aboard without starting a gunfight. It seemed easier if you all were asleep."

"I don't know who the hell you are, or who you think you are, but this is an official Marshal's Service vessel..."

Frye held a hand up to interrupt. "I'm well aware, Captain. I'm also well aware that by incapacitating your crew and boarding your ship, my colleagues and I have violated enough laws to earn a half-dozen life sentences on Vangla, or whatever overpopulated prison planet you send people like us to nowadays.

"You should know, however, that I mean you no harm. If I did, I would have killed you all while you were unconscious. So now that that's out of the way, we need to have a talk."

"Where is my crew?"

"Secured in the barracks, with the exception of Doctor Kirurgi, who is attending to one of my crew." Frye pointed to the security feed monitor. "You should know that we have disarmed everyone, and the armory has been secured. This is in everyone's best interests, I assure you – as I've said, we have no intention of hurting anyone, but we will defend ourselves, should the need arise."

"How kind of you," Cefo sniffed. "Now, I hope that this talk we are about to have includes an explanation as to where the hell you came from, why you have hijacked a government ship, and what you plan to do with it?"

"A few hours ago, you engaged and destroyed an unidentified ship. That ship, the *Veritas*, was mine."

"And it was in a restricted zone. You refused to answer our hail requests. I had no choice."

Frye held his hand up again. "I understand. And, while I mean you no harm, the *Veritas* represented a very real threat. Until you came along, our only other option was to destroy the ship ourselves while still aboard. Fortunately, you showed up and gave us the chance to escape with our lives... most of us, anyway. We were able to abandon the *Veritas*, and we made our way here."

Cefo seemed genuinely impressed. "How?"

"EVA suits. We're very good," Frye said, noting the look of shock on the captain's face. "As I said before, we gassed your crew to avoid an armed confrontation, let

False Flag 299

ourselves aboard, and secured the ship."

"Why was your ship a threat?"

"Software hijack. The men who did it intended to fly the ship into Awdurdod. Billions would have died. The ship contains, or contained, a next-generation gravity drive that would have decimated the planet at full power. As I said, destroying the ship was the right call."

"If what you're saying is true, this needs to be relayed to my command immediately. Now that you are aboard, Mr. Frye, I will make arrangements to have you transferred to the Marshal's station at Awdurdod. If your story checks out, perhaps the charges for entering restricted space and hijacking can be reduced to a lesser charge. They may even see fit to drop the matter altogether, but that's not a call for me to make. I will be sure that the mitigating circumstances are known, so that they can be taken into account."

Frye chuckled. "We're not going to Awdurdod, captain. I've seen the Union's version of justice, and I want none of it. Besides, my friends and I aren't exactly the kind of people that your superiors will want released back into the wild."

"Nevertheless, I have a duty to turn you over."

"Then you and I are going to have a problem, Captain. I've been polite, and as I've already pointed out, I've kept you and your crew alive and well, despite having the upper hand." Frye's hand moved down to his thigh holster and rested atop the grip of his Gauss pistol. "But make no mistake; I am in charge here. So this is my counter-offer: We're leaving Awdurdod. You will take my crew and me where we want to go, and you will drop us off. You will make no attempt to call for help. Is that clear?"

Cefo hesitated for a few moments. "I can see the wheels turning, Captain," Frye said. "You're trying to figure out how to agree to my terms and then double-cross me later. Maybe you'll even manage to do it. All that I will say is that that road is littered with corpses, and I've seen enough death already today. I'm not your enemy, Captain, so let's not change that."

Without a word, Cefo nodded. "Good," Frye said, activating his commlink. "What's the status down there?" he asked Alainn.

"Wolf's awake," she replied.

"Can he move?"

"Not for a couple of hours, at least."

"Damn, OK. How'd he take the news about Halwyn?"

"About like you'd expect. He brought the kid in; he feels like it's his fault. Doesn't help that the last thing he said to him was a death threat."

"Nothing to be done about it now. Look, I need you up on the bridge. Bring the doctor – I don't want Wolf to have to babysit."

"On our way."

"May I ask where we are headed?"

"Somewhere neutral, where we can catch a ride home. Before we leave, Captain, I'm going to tell you our story. Something tells me that the men who planned the attack on Awdurdod won't give up once they realize that this plot failed. Maybe you can use the information."

Alainn arrived on the bridge a moment later with Doctor Kirurgi. "What did you do with the body?" Frye asked.

"We put Halwyn in a cryosack and stored him in the hold," Alainn replied. "I don't like treating him like cargo, but we couldn't leave him in the infirmary with Wolf."

"Agreed."

"So where are we headed?"

"We need to get out of Union space and find someone

False Flag   301

who can take us home."

"Home? What about Wallis and Agera?"

Frye nodded to Cefo. "They're the Union's problem. We need to get Halwyn's body home. Besides, we don't even know where to start looking. It won't take long for them to figure out that their plan failed. Once that happens, they'll be almost impossible to find."

"We could try Kellan. I owe him a visit anyway."

"You really think he knows anything?"

Alainn sighed. "Probably not. But the trail of bodies they left in their wake, and for what? And do you really think that they're done? They were going to kill billions of people, Volya. They'll just try again."

"The trail of bodies..."

"What?"

Frye ignored his wife's question. Instead, he keyed his commlink, but Hartmann didn't answer. His comm had been removed when they took his suit off.

"Keep an eye on them," Frye told Alainn as he turned and ran out the door.

***

Hartmann was staring at the ceiling when Frye ran into the infirmary, but turned to the door as the pilot came through.

"How you feeling?"

"About like you'd expect. But something tells me you didn't haul ass down here to check on me."

"Remember the ship you saw docked at Neirin?"

Hartmann cocked an eyebrow. "Yeah, what about it?"

"You ever figure out what it was doing there?"

"No, Agera was working on the encryption, but..." the navigator's voice trailed off.

"But he wasn't," Frye replied. "And do you remember what you told me about there being a bunch of spooks aboard the station?"

"I do. What are you thinking?"

"I'm thinking that there's no such thing as a coincidence. We've been caught up in the mess that Wallis and Agera left us in, but we were missing something."

"And that something is?"

"The trail of bodies," Frye said. "Well, not so much a trail, but two of them, lying in a farmhouse outside of Luka. Alainn and I assumed that the Marshal's Service sent a hit squad after us, and they killed the couple to get information, but now I don't think that's the case at all. I think they were killed deliberately."

"Why?"

"As part of the plot to make us look like ruthless terrorists. And thinking back, our getaway at the farm was too easy. It didn't seem like it at the time, but if they really wanted us dead, then there's no way we should have gotten out of there in one piece."

"And this relates to the ship how?"

"Someone with the resources to send out a hit squad has to be involved. Wallis and Agera were using the Samizdat network, but that's a political organization. Someone well-connected is involved, and that ship is the only thing that makes sense. I guarantee you, if we find that ship, we'll get some answers."

"Well, we're in the right place. A patrol cruiser like this will have access to the Marshal's Service central database."

"Looks like I'll be asking the captain for more than just a ride." Frye turned and started for the door.

"Volya?"

"Yeah, Wolf?"

False Flag 303

"We catch these guys, they pay."

"That's the idea."

***

"Absolutely not."

"Captain, I'm not sure that you're in any position to refuse."

Cefo set his jaw. "You've already said that you don't plan on hurting us. Either you're being honest, in which case I have nothing to fear, or else you lied, in which case you'll probably kill everyone aboard once you get what you want. Either way, I'm not logging into Central for you."

Frye sighed. "I could torture you. I've done it before."

"Do your worst."

"I could let Alainn here do it. She's got more experience."

The captain swallowed hard. "Eventually, my crew is going to wake up. Once that happens, it will only be a matter of time before they figure out a way out of the barracks. Do you really want to waste what little time you have threatening me?"

"I really don't. What I want is for you to wake up and realize that someone just tried to vaporize your capitol planet, and most of your government with it. I'm just asking for help finding the culprits."

"I'm looking at them."

"Do they teach ignorance as a virtue in the Marshal's academy? If I wanted to hit Awdurdod, I would have."

"You bailed when you realized we were about to vaporize your ship."

"Holy shit," Frye said, rubbing his hands on his face.

"I don't know what you expected, Volya," Alainn said. "These guys are trained to look exactly ten centimeters beyond their nose. Any further might cause problems for the higher ups."

"You think Wolf will know how to get in?"

"Yeah, he'll get it. You know how to fly one of these things, Volya?"

"Simple enough."

"Good. Captain Cefo, you're about to become what we call redundant," Alainn said, shifting her focus to the Marshal. "Here's the thing: my husband is a nice guy. He knows how to take care of himself, and I've even seen him kill before, but he doesn't really like it. It's just his nature – he's a nice guy.

"I, however... well, let's just say that I can be a real bitch. And the bad part for you is that if I were to put together a list of the people I hate the most, the number one position would be awarded to 'badge-toting bureaucrats that ignore what is staring them in the face.'

"Now, you are faced with what could be the simplest decision in the history of decision-making. Someone just attempted a catastrophic act of violence against your government. You have the opportunity to help find the culprits, but it goes against your programming.

"Now, I could threaten you. I could point out that, since you are redundant, we could make you watch as we killed every member of your crew slowly, until you give us what we want. I could point out that there are close to a dozen amputations that I could perform on you before you die, and that the good doctor here would be duty-bound to repair you after each one, leaving you just healthy enough to survive the next.

"But I don't want to do that. I find the idea distasteful on a level you probably can't even comprehend. I would prefer to appeal to your humanity. I would prefer that you volunteer to help out of a sense of civic duty. I don't think

False Flag   305

that will work though, so I'm going to appeal to something else: your ambition.

"I can see that I have your attention. Here's the deal: your ship has been hijacked. No matter what happens from here on, that's a stain that will go on your record. Every time you have an opportunity for a promotion, your superiors will see that mark, and they'll wonder about your competence; your ability to command. You command a ship, but I can guarantee you that you will never command a fleet.

"Your other option is to help us. You find out where that ship is, and you take us there. We find out who on your side is working with the devil, and we hand him to you. You make the bust, and your career gets fast tracked."

"And what exactly do you get?"

"The devil himself. Or themselves, to be more precise."

"And if I refuse?"

Alainn smiled, but it was an unsettling expression. "Then we get to find out just what a bitch I can be."

***

"The ship is called the *Mullistus*," Captain Cefo said, "And it filed a flight plan two weeks ago from Neirin to Kachet."

"When did they arrive?" Frye asked.

"Four days ago."

"How current is the information?"

"This update made it through the relay thirty-six hours ago."

"Who was aboard?"

"According to the manifest, it's a delegation from the Communications Ministry."

306   *The Union Chronicles*

"I suppose it's the best we've got," Frye replied. "We set course for Kachet."

"What about my crew?" Cefo asked. "You surely don't intend for them to be confined to the barracks for a week? You say that you don't want any violence, but I guarantee you that when they wake up, they aren't going to feel the same way."

"You are absolutely correct," Frye replied. "You have a shuttle pod below decks; I noticed it when we were clearing the ship. Once we get close to the jump point and are within range of the sentry craft patrolling the jump zone, we will jettison your crew aboard the shuttle."

"Sir, I request your permission to remain aboard," Doctor Kirurgi said.

"You'll go with the others," Frye replied, "It's safer for you that way."

"I wasn't asking you," the doctor replied curtly, looking at Cefo.

"Permission granted," the captain replied, "Our guests seem to be the kind of people that attract injury; having a doctor aboard couldn't hurt."

Frye briefly considered objecting, but decided against it. Perhaps allowing Captain Cefo this small victory would prevent a larger conflict down the road. He wasn't trying to build a long-term commander/subordinate relationship with the man, after all; he just needed him to be compliant for a week or so. *And he's not wrong about our regular need for medical attention*, Frye thought to himself.

"Fine with me," he replied with a shrug. "Any objections, Alainn?"

"We're just one big, happy family," she replied. "Now can we get the hell out of here?"

        ***

False Flag   307

The *Sentinel* was halfway to the jump point when the crew began to awaken. It was longer than Frye had anticipated, but it still posed a problem.

"What do you want me to tell them?" Cefo asked as Frye handed him the microphone for the ship's public address system.

"Tell them the truth," Frye replied with a shrug, "But if I were you, I would make sure that they understand the consequences of trying to retake the ship. You can also let them know that Dr. Kirurgi will be admitted to the barracks to examine everyone to make sure that there are no ill effects from the gas. We'll also send down some food."

Captain Cefo nodded and composed himself before keying the microphone. "Crew of the *Sentinel*, this is Captain Cefo. Those of you who are awake are no doubt wondering what has happened. Approximately twenty-four hours ago, the ship was overtaken by a group of individuals from the ship that we were pursuing. They claim that their ship was hijacked and that their only means of survival was to board the *Sentinel*. They also claim to have incapacitated the crew to avoid a violent confrontation – an act of goodwill, according to them.

"I have no way to verify their claims, but I can tell you that they have not harmed anyone aboard. They have, however, insisted that they will not submit themselves into our custody, and have instead demanded that we provide safe passage out of the system.

"In order to avoid unnecessary loss of life, I have agreed to their terms, and have negotiated the release of the crew, myself and Doctor Kirurgi notwithstanding. You will be permitted to leave on the shuttle before we make the jump out of the system.

308 The Union Chronicles

"Doctor Kirurgi will be in momentarily to examine everyone and make sure that there have been no ill-effects resulting from your incapacitation. Food will also be provided.

"Do not, under any circumstances, attempt to retake the ship. Our captors have indicated that they have no intention of harming anyone, but will respond with force to any attempt at interfering with their operation. They are armed, appear to be well-trained, and have secured the ship's armory. It is my belief that any attempt at violent confrontation will result in significant loss of life and is not appropriate at this time. I will update you when we approach the time for you to board the shuttle."

"Very good, Captain," Frye said, taking the microphone. "Doctor, you're up. Wolf will accompany you to the galley to procure rations and then down to the barracks. Wolf, we don't want any trouble, but make sure that they know we mean business."

"Got it," Hartmann replied.

"And leave your sidearm here," Alainn added. "The last thing we need is for one of the crew to get ahold of it."

"Like that would happen," Hartmann scoffed, "But I suppose you're right." He unholstered his Gauss pistol and handed it to Frye.

The barracks went silent as Hartmann entered with Doctor Kirurgi, but he could tell that he had interrupted something. He set the food they had brought on the table that ran along one of the walls, and then stood by the door while the doctor performed a cursory exam of each of the conscious crew members. Three people still slept on the beds where Frye and Alainn had deposited them; they were probably the members of the engineering crew and had been closer to the air exchanger when the gas had been introduced. Hartmann wasn't particularly concerned

False Flag   309

with their well-being, but hoped they would wake up soon; it would be easier to keep the crew compliant if they didn't think that their lives were in danger.

Several of the crew members stared at him with open hostility, but no one said anything other than what was absolutely necessary for Kirurgi to finish her examinations. She also checked on the three unconscious crewmembers and, apparently satisfied, joined Hartmann by the door.

"All set?" Hartmann asked. The doctor nodded and they headed out of the barracks and back up to the bridge.

"How is the crew?" Cefo asked as soon as they arrived.

"They're fine, Captain," the Kirurgi replied, "some mild dehydration, but nothing serious. Cole, Gabriel, and Picton are still out, but they were in engineering, so they probably got a larger dose. Vitals are all fine."

"They're going to be looking for an opportunity," Hartmann said to Frye.

"I gave an order," Cefo said.

"And they'll disobey it if they get the chance," Hartmann replied. "They'll think that you've been compromised somehow and aren't able to make the right call. How long until we hit the jump point?"

"Fourteen hours," Frye replied. "Which means that we can move the crew to the shuttle in nine."

"That's probably when they'll make their move."

"Then we'll just have to be ready."

　　　***

Nine hours later, Captain Cefo accompanied Frye and Hartmann down to the barracks. "Ladies and gentlemen," the captain said, getting the crew's attention, "it is time for you to make your way to the shuttle. It is going to be cramped, but the sentry post is only a six hour burn by shuttle. The comms aboard the craft have been disabled, but the beacon is still in operation.

"Again, I must urge you all to conduct yourselves in an orderly and peaceful fashion. With that said, please proceed to the aft bulkhead door."

No one moved. Fourteen sets of eyes stared defiantly at Frye and Hartmann. From the corner of his eye, Frye saw a small grin break out on Captain Cefo's face.

"You expected this, didn't you?" Frye asked.

The Captain's smile grew wider, but he said nothing.

"We're not going anywhere," one of the crew, a petite, blonde-haired woman finally said. "Are you willing to kill a room full of unarmed people?"

"You must be First Officer Varamies," Frye replied. "Most of the crew documentation is sealed, but your name is listed on the command chart on the bridge," he explained, noting the woman's questioning glance. "Ma'am, I applaud your efforts to resist, but trust me when I say that it is futile and unnecessary. If our intention was to kill you, you would be dead already. We really don't want to hurt anyone unless it becomes necessary. That being said, you are leaving this ship. Your only choice is whether or not you do so under your own power.

"The infirmary contains a sufficient stock of Cinolazepam to render everyone in this room either compliant or unconscious. So, you need to decide: either get up and walk to the shuttle on your own, or be injected with a powerful hypnotic and do it anyway. It doesn't matter to me, but I've been told by Doctor Kirurgi that the after-effects are a bitch if it's administered without a painkiller."

"You'll never get away with this," Varamies said, standing, "but I've got no desire to get doped." She looked to Captain Cefo. "You know you'll lose your command for

False Flag 311

this," she said."

"I'm aware," Cefo replied. "But it seems like a small price to pay to avoid a bloodbath here."

First Officer Varamies led the way down the corridor, with the rest of the crew lined up behind her. Hartmann and Frye took up the rear, with Cefo just in front of them.

"How long have you been in love with her?" Frye asked quietly.

"A while," the captain sighed.

"And she doesn't know." Frye said, stating rather than asking.

"She might suspect something, but I've tried to keep things strictly professional."

"She'd have been the first one to fight back. That's why you agreed to our terms."

"Does that make me a coward, Mr. Frye?"

"Of course not. It makes you human. To be honest, from what I've seen, you have good taste." He couldn't be sure, but Frye thought he saw a slight smile cross the Captain's face.

"I guess this means that our offer to hand you a traitor wasn't the irresistible proposition I thought it was."

Cefo chuckled under his breath. "Telling me that you were going to make my career might have been a bit of an oversell, Mr. Frye. You're competent hijackers, but maybe you should steer clear of politics."

"Duly noted," Frye replied off-handedly. "Funny though; it worked out pretty well for the Vice Marshal."

This put a stutter into Cefo's step. "Wait, what?"

"Vice Marshal Delmont."

"You mean Senator Delmont?"

Now it was Frye's turn to chuckle. He lowered his voice. "I kidnapped him in broad daylight and offered him a deal similar to what I'm offering you. Now he's a

Senator."

The color drained from Cefo's face. Before he could recover and reply, Frye moved a few steps ahead. "Ladies and gentlemen," he said with a smile, "It's been a pleasure to play the role of your captor, but I'm afraid that all good things must come to an end. If you'll please board the shuttle in an orderly fashion, we'll have you back to your bureaucratic masters shortly."

Once the crew was safely aboard the shuttle, Frye sealed the door and the three men headed back to the bridge. Cefo was conspicuously silent; it was obvious that he wanted to continue the conversation about Delmont, but seemed unsure of how to proceed. On the way, Frye's comm buzzed. It was Alainn.

"Three hours to jump."

"No contact from the sentry?"

"None."

"They won't bother us," Cefo interjected, "I have regional jurisdiction – it's not uncommon for me to leave the system for a few days at a time. I'm expected to know what's going on at the other end of the jump points."

"Good to know. How far out is the sentry, Alainn?"

"At least four hours. They couldn't make it at this point, even at full burn."

"Alright, jettison the shuttle."

There was a brief pause, and Frye could feel a slight shudder. "Done."

A minute later, and they were back on the bridge. "Go ahead and get the jump calculations going," Frye told Hartmann.

"Already done. Two hours, thirty minutes to jump."

"Good. Do you have an estimate on travel time?"

"Seventy-two hours, if we redline the engines."

"You aren't late on any major engine service, are you

False Flag   313

Captain?"

"She'll handle it," Cefo sniffed, giving the impression that he was insulted that the *Sentinel's* abilities would be questioned.

"You know, in spite of my better judgment, I like you, Captain," Frye said with a smile. "A good captain always has faith in his ship."

Cefo sighed, but remained stoic.

"You want to ask about Delmont, don't you?" Frye teased.

"You're a strange man, Mr. Frye," Cefo replied. "You manage to pull off a ship-to-ship EVA, hijack a patrol vessel, and threaten to torture and kill an entire ship full of law-enforcement personnel, and now you're acting like a child with a secret that he just can't wait to tell."

"And you've bought in to the lie that success is all about position. You have some authority, some pull, so you think that you're on the right track. But here's the secret: no matter what you do, you'll always answer to someone. Me, I don't answer to anybody. I am the ruler of my own life. Mock me all you want, but at the end of the day, which one of us is acting like a child?"

"Fine, so tell me, how does the Union's newest senator owe his political fortunes to you?"

"It's a long story. Let's just say that he was in a situation similar to the one that you find yourself in, and he took advantage."

"And what did you get out of it?"

"Justice."

"Here's the deal," Alainn interjected. "Whoever is aboard that ship has something to do with the planned attack on Awdurdod. You get them; we get the other two. We go our separate ways, and everyone wins."

"Except for the people that we're after."

"Obviously. Those guys are fucked."

"Well, I've already agreed to help you, so there's no backing out now."

Time slowed to a crawl as the jump approached. With the uneasy alliance with Captain Cefo forged, Frye began to move his focus to the ship that they were pursuing. He wasn't sure if Wallis or Agera would be aboard the *Mullistus* when they caught up with it, but he knew that whoever was aboard knew where they could be found. It was just too big a coincidence.

The big question was how much resistance they would encounter aboard the ship. Assuming that the *Mullistus* was docked, getting aboard shouldn't be a problem, but Hartmann's experience aboard Luka station led Frye to believe that a number of intelligence operatives may be aboard. He found himself wishing that they had more knockout gas.

He caught Alainn's eye and motioned towards the door. As he made his way to the corridor, he clapped Hartmann on the back. "Keep an eye on them," he said quietly, tilting his head towards Cefo and Kirurgi. Hartmann simply nodded.

"What's our plan of attack?" Frye asked, once they were down the corridor and out of earshot.

"Anything direct is out of the question," Alainn replied, "but whatever we do needs to be quick. By the time we get there, it will be obvious that the attack has failed, and if the station is half as full of spooks as Hartmann experienced at Luka, we'll be lucky to last ten minutes."

"Bait and switch?"

Alainn raised an eyebrow. "I hope you aren't planning on making me the bait."

"I think we can let our new friends handle that part."

"And the other thing? You think Cefo went through

False Flag   315

with it?"

"I'd bet money on it."

"We've already bet our lives on it if things go sideways. No need to overdo things."

***

The shift to jump space was always unnerving to Frye, even though he'd gone through it a hundred times. It was almost imperceptible, just a slight impression that things were being stretched out. You couldn't focus on it, however; it was merely a feeling, and trying to consciously experience it was like trying to remember a dream – the harder you focused, the less tangible the effect was.

Then, just as the feeling was perceived, it was over – a jump of tens, sometimes hundreds, of light years was completed in seconds.

This had been the third in a series of jumps that the *Sentinel* had made, and after nearly a week, they were in Kachet, the destination reported on the *Mullistus'* last-filed flight manifest.

"Bearings, Wolf," Frye ordered, more out of habit than necessity – the navigator was already at work on determining the *Sentinel's* exact position in the system.

It had been an excruciatingly boring week, and Frye was ready to put their plans into action – provided, of course, that the *Mullistus* was still in port. If it wasn't...

It wasn't something that Frye wanted to contemplate, so he moved on. There was work to do.

"Twenty-six hours," Hartmann said, interrupting Frye's thoughts.

"Excellent." Frye turned to Captain Cefo, who had been given nearly full access to the ship in order to gain his trust, but was nevertheless under constant surveillance.

"You're up, Captain," he said.

The man nodded and activated the pilot's terminal. After a few moments, he looked at Frye and nodded. "She's still in port," he said, "Or at least she was sixteen hours ago."

"Good. Captain, you have the helm." Frye turned and headed off of the bridge, catching Hartmann's eye in the process. The navigator gave a slight nod as Frye headed through the bulkhead.

He found Alainn with Doctor Kirurgi in the common room. Like the captain, the ship's doctor had been allowed to roam mostly unaccompanied about the ship during the past week. The ship's arsenal had been secured, as had anything dangerous in the infirmary, and Frye had decided that providing some degree of autonomy was a relatively safe trade-off in exchange for potential goodwill from their captives.

"Twenty-six hours," he said, noting that the two women had grown suspiciously quiet upon his arrival.

"Finally," his wife said, smiling at him.

Frye checked the impulse to ask what they had been discussing and headed to the beverage station. As a law enforcement vessel, the ship was alcohol-free, so he chose a mild herbal tea and sat in one of the officer's chairs.

"How's Wolf's ankle?" Frye asked Kirurgi, more to make conversation that anything else. He'd already gotten the report from his friend.

"One-hundred percent," the doctor replied, confirming what Hartmann had said.

"That's good," Frye said lamely, taking a sip from his tea. After a few more moments of silence, Frye stood up and left the room, heading towards the First Officer's cabin, which he and Alainn had been sharing. Once inside, he collapsed into the room's single chair, which sat in front

False Flag 317

of an unadorned desk. First Officer Varamies apparently didn't have much back at home that she needed reminded of – *good news for the Captain,* Frye mused to himself, although he wondered if the woman would forever brand Cefo as a coward for allowing his ship to be commandeered. He almost felt bad for the Marshal.

There were, however, matters more pressing than the love life of a Union official. For the thousandth time, Frye went over the plan in his head. As he did so, a familiar feeling once again crept into his head. It was something that he had avoided discussing with Hartmann, and even his wife. Once they had made it aboard the *Sentinel*, all discussions had been about finding Wallis Aeron and his accomplice Agera – what they hadn't discussed was what they would do once they had them.

The fact was that Frye wanted them dead. In his mind, he had raised his pistol and shattered both men's' skulls with a five-millimeter slug a thousand times, and if he was being honest with himself, he had a hard time feeling bad about it.

Then, like always, his thoughts turned to Barrett, the young man who had abandoned his sister's rescue in order to pursue revenge against the man who had victimized her.

But there's no one to rescue this time, Frye said to himself. He had even figured out a way to justify what would amount to cold-blooded murder: he knew that the two men would try again. Somehow, if left alive, they would hatch another plot, and billions of people would die.

Frye drained his mug and shook the thoughts from his mind. There was work to do, and it was possible, even probable, that he would never need to solve his ethical dilemma; something else was bound to go wrong, and he would more than likely be dead by dinnertime tomorrow.

At dinner that night, there was even less conversation than usual. The food aboard the *Sentinel* was surprisingly good, but no one seemed to notice.

"Were you able to hack into the station comms?" Frye asked Hartmann casually.

"Didn't need to," the navigator replied. "Marshal's Service ship, remember? We've got full access. We're close enough now that everything is real-time plus fifty minutes."

"Anything interesting?"

Hartmann shook his head. "Even the secure channels are quiet." He took another bite of his food and chuckled; the first emotion that anyone had exhibited during the meal. "I think that a couple of the tech officers are hooking up on the sly."

"Why do you say that?"

"Two of the techies were talking about a security exercise and one of them mentioned penetration testing. It wasn't long before they started talking about an entirely different kind of penetration."

"That's... probably more information than we needed," Doctor Kirurgi said, blushing.

Hartmann gave Frye a sly glance before continuing. "My apologies, Doctor, but the discussion did lead to something relevant, which is why I brought it up."

"And what is that?" Captain Cefo interjected.

"One of the techs said that she had come across a name in the system's control logs, and thought that she had seen it on a watch list. When she ran it, she told her counterpart that it looked like the information had been tampered with."

"You think it has to do with whatever is going on aboard the *Mullistus*," Cefo said.

False Flag 319

"Either that or someone on the station's staff is getting a payoff from smugglers to alter the logbooks," Hartmann shrugged. "But I figure that it's worth looking in to. Maybe we'll find a smoking gun – whoever is aboard that ship must have a reason for altering official logs, if that's what is going on." Hartmann shrugged, "But chances are, it's nothing."

"There's no way we'll get access," Alainn said dismissively. "The control room is the most secure area on any station."

Hartmann shook his head in frustration. "We've got to try."

"Forget it," Frye said. "Alainn's right; there's no way that's going to work. We'll just have to take our chances going after the ship head-on. We'll have to hope that we can keep the casualties to a minimum."

"I'll do it," Cefo said quietly.

"You know that won't work," Hartmann said to Frye, ignoring the captain. "We'll be outnumbered – it'll be a bloodbath."

"We'll just have to hit 'em hard."

"I'll do it," Cefo said, louder this time.

"What's that?" Alainn asked.

"I'll get the information from the control room. I've got clearance; they have to give it to me."

"You sure you want to get your hands dirty?" Frye asked.

"There's nothing dirty about it," Cefo replied. "There's a security breach in a Union-controlled station. At the very least, I shut down a smuggler's operation and help avoid a body count. I'll take care of it."

"I don't think we should trust him," Hartmann said. "He'll turn on us as soon as we're out of earshot."

"Fine; you'll go with him," Frye said.

The Union Chronicles

"Shit," Hartmann replied with a grimace. "Should've seen that one coming."

***

"That was easier than I thought," Alainn mused as she and Frye lay in bed that night. "I thought we'd have to nudge him a little harder."

Frye smiled. "I don't think that the Captain is a bad guy, and he's more than a little worried that we're telling the truth about someone plotting massive terror attacks in his jurisdiction. Besides, your 'we just aren't good enough' act was perfect. He's got a thing for strong women, but every man wants to rescue the damsel in distress every once in a while."

"I just hope that we don't get him hurt," Alainn said. "For as much as we threatened the guy, I don't really want his blood on my hands."

"That's why Wolf is going with him. Once the alarm is triggered, he'll make sure they get out."

Chapter Seventeen

Kachet was home to a half-dozen shipyards spread across an eleven planet system. Between ore mining, foundries, component manufacturers, and the shipyards themselves, the system was thick with industrial activity, and the traffic was heavy.

Kachet-7, the *Sentinel's* destination, was no less crowded, but the ship's designation as a Marshal's Service patrol vessel resulted in priority docking privileges, which was convenient, but irked Alainn nonetheless. She knew that several ships with legitimate commercial business had probably been bumped to accommodate what the station's control staff assumed was a ship full of law enforcement officers and bureaucrats.

Hartmann had gone through the personal effects of the jettisoned crew and had found a uniform that fit relatively well. Donning the raiment of a Union official had clearly rubbed the navigator the wrong way, but he had nearly lost it when Frye told him that he had to shave his thick stubble.

"You know it's against dress code," Alainn had said, coming to Frye's defense when Hartman looked ready to move from vocal displeasure to physical violence.

"Damnit!" Hartmann said, followed by a string of more

colorful profanity.

"Do you want to look suspicious?" Frye asked.

"You don't understand," Hartmann replied, near panic in his voice, "I look like a fucking twelve-year-old when I shave!"

After finally convincing his friend that a clean-shaven face was the only way to make his costume complete, Frye had to fight against laughter when Hartmann emerged from the head. The grizzled navigator was right: he looked like a newborn without his beard.

"Awww, how cute; he's playing dress-up," Alainn cooed as Hartmann approached the prep room. To his credit, Hartmann held his tongue, although it looked like it required superhuman strength.

"We're just looking for intel," Frye reminded Cefo. "I just want you to run the name Hartmann got from the transmission. Maybe you'll find something that'll put this to rest, and we can all go home."

"Of course. And I'm just trying to avoid a body count."

"Then good luck, Captain." Frye offered his hand, which Cefo shook after a moment's hesitation. Frye grabbed Hartmann and clapped him on the back. "See you in a few," he said.

Captain Cefo led the way through the prep room and the airlock, and moments later he and Hartmann were across the gangway and aboard the station.

"The way you wear that uniform, I can tell it's something you're used to, even though you despise it," Cefo said as they walked down the corridor towards the hub. "Let me guess, Navy?"

Hartmann grunted. "First lieutenant. Certified navigator with signals intelligence training. Did well, too; my career was on the fast track. In fact, there was only one asset that I lacked."

False Flag 323

"Which was?"

"A family with political clout."

"What happened?"

"What is this, biography hour? I got fucked over. Some dipshit with the right last name fucked up, and I got blamed."

Cefo was quiet for a moment. "That's unfortunate."

Hartmann shrugged. "The way I see it, they did me a favor — they showed me their true colors. I'm glad I'm not a part of that shit show anymore."

"I say that it's unfortunate because you're clearly talented. You're wasting your time riding backseat with those other two. With the right connections, you could clear your name, get back in. It's not too late to make a career."

Hartmann laughed, which seemed to take the Marshal by surprise. "Don't even try it," Hartmann said.

"Try what?"

"Turning me. For starters, I've made a small pile of cash since I left the Union; more than I would make in an entire career as an admiral. Second, and more importantly, Volya Frye is not only my friend, but the best man I've ever met. I would put a bullet in your head in the middle of this station, in front of a thousand witnesses, before I'd turn on him, no matter what you offered me."

"Shame," Cefo replied, but said nothing further.

The station's administrative offices were located at the top level of the hub. After Cefo presented his credentials, he and Hartmann were immediately admitted to the station's security office and introduced to Commander Urrus, the head of station security.

"What can I do for you, Captain Cefo?" the commander, a tall, thin man in his mid-fifties, asked.

"I'm investigating a possible smuggling operation,"

Cefo replied. "I have a suspect in custody that has provided information in exchange for leniency in sentencing. I'm here to follow up."

"Of course, Captain. How can I help?"

"I have a name. I believe that he may be aboard the station."

"What's the name? I'll run a search."

"Roland Kendrick."

***

"That didn't take long," Alainn said. From their position, she could see two people exit the *Mullistus'* gangway and head down the corridor towards the station's hub. After a moment, she and Frye exited their hiding place in a nearby maintenance corridor, following the two figures. With the amount of foot traffic aboard the station, keeping inconspicuous wasn't a problem; in fact, it was difficult not to lose their quarry amongst the crowds.

"You've got company incoming," Frye told Hartmann over his commlink.

On the other end, Hartmann nodded. "Understood." He turned to Cefo. "Captain, we're needed back aboard the ship."

Cefo appeared taken aback by Hartmann's statement, but seemed to understand from the navigator's expression that he needed to play along. "Very well, Lieutenant. Commander," he said, turning to Urrus, "I trust that you'll let me know the second something comes up regarding Mr. Kendrick?"

"Of course," the head of security said with a nod.

"What exactly is going on?" Cefo asked, once he and Hartmann had left the security office. "I thought that we needed to find out about this Mr. Kendrick."

False Flag 325

"Roland Kendrick has been dead for over a week," Hartmann said brusquely, "ever since you vaporized him aboard our ship."

Cefo stopped in his tracks. "You used me," he said.

"You're damn right we did, and it appears to have worked," Hartmann said. "A couple of spooks from the *Mullistus* are on the way to the control room to find out who is asking about a dead man."

***

Frye and Alainn took up a post near the entrance to the security office, but their wait was short. As the two men from the *Mullistus* exited, they walked right past their pursuers. Without being too conspicuous, Frye sized the two men up. Average height and build, but with physiques that clearly indicated frequent physical training.

"Operatives, for sure," Alainn commented as they resumed the tail.

"You think we're made?"

"I wouldn't bet against it. Better safe than sorry," she replied, ducking into a bar. Frye followed close behind, activating his commlink as he took a seat next to Alainn at the bar.

"We had to back off," he said as soon as Hartmann opened the channel.

"Were you made?"

"Don't know, but we couldn't take the chance. When they show up, sound the alarm, and we'll come running."

"You get to be the bait next time, Volya."

"I'm kind of hoping that there won't be a next time." Frye paused for a moment. "Wolf?"

"Yeah?"

"It would be best if we could take them both, but if

things go sideways, we can make do with one."

"I can live with that."

Frye killed the link as the bartender was delivering the beers that Alainn had ordered. While it was hardly the time to sit back and enjoy a cold one, Frye understood that there was no way that they could inconspicuously sit at the bar without ordering something. He grabbed the glass and, like his wife, slowly nursed the beverage. They didn't have to wait long.

"We've got company," Hartmann said as soon as Frye answered the call.

"We're inbound," Frye answered, already on his feet. "Take your time opening the door; then take them to the Captain's stateroom."

"Got it." The comm went dead.

The *Sentinel* was two decks down. Frye took the stairs two at a time, Alainn close on his heels. He collided with several people, even causing a particularly rotund man to drop a sandwich, but he paid no heed beyond a rushed and insincere-sounding apology.

On the gangway, Frye finally slowed to a walk. Drawing his Gauss pistol, he keyed open the *Sentinel's* airlock door and slipped inside. The *click* of the door closing behind him confirmed that Alainn had his back.

It had taken them less than three minutes from Hartmann's call to make it aboard the ship. Frye hoped that his friend had taken his time admitting the two men to the vessel; if they were lucky, he and Alainn could catch the two men moments after they were settled in Cefo's private office.

With Alainn steps behind him, Frye raced up to the third deck and to the wardroom. He paused at the door for a moment, waiting for his wife's signal. As soon as her hand clapped against his shoulder, Frye was through the

False Flag 327

door, pistol at the ready.

The two men, who were seated in front of Cefo's desk, seemed genuinely surprised by the intrusion. They recovered quickly, however, and both of their right hands disappeared into their jackets.

"Hands, gentlemen," Alainn said, slipping through the door behind her husband. Both men hesitated.

Hartmann, who had been standing next to the Captain's desk, drew his pistol, a movement that was caught by both operatives' peripheral vision.

"I would do as they say," Captain Cefo advised from his position behind his desk.

The two men looked at each other, and seemed to reach the same conclusion. Slowly, they removed their hands from their jackets and held them up.

"Wise decision," Alainn said. She turned to Captain Cefo. "Get their weapons."

The captain bristled at the command, but he slowly rose from his chair and walked around the small desk.

The move was almost imperceptible. As Cefo reached behind the operative's jacket to retrieve his pistol, there was a quick blur, and before anyone could react, the operative had Cefo in a modified headlock, his weapon trained at the captain's skull. His partner took advantage of the commotion, drawing his own weapon and pointing it at Frye.

"Looks like we have a situat-" the operative holding Cefo began. He did not, however, have a chance to finish the thought before a round from Hartmann's pistol pierced his skull. The body fell limp and the man's weapon clattered to the floor.

The second operative flinched, but before he could react, Alainn sent a five millimeter slug through his shoulder, knocking the pistol away from Frye's direction.

The gun went off; the slug embedding harmlessly in the wall. In a flash, Hartmann closed the distance and disarmed the man.

"Get the doctor," Frye directed Cefo. When the man didn't respond, Frye repeated himself, louder and with more force. "Get Doctor Kirurgi, Captain. Do it now, before this piece of shit bleeds out."

Hartmann grabbed the injured operative and manhandled him towards the door. By the time they reached the infirmary, Doctor Kirurgi was there, prepping a trauma kit. She motioned to one of the beds, and Hartmann deposited the nearly-unconscious man roughly.

In a flash, the doctor had removed the injured man's shirt. She rolled him over gently and saw that there was no exit wound.

"Hollowpoints," Alainn explained, "They keep the round inside the bad guy so no one standing behind him gets hurt."

"They're also illegal and inhumane," the doctor snapped. She eased the man back onto the table and grabbed a laser scalpel and a set of clamps to remove the projectile.

"The gun that fired the round is illegal here, too," Alainn answered, "So you can tell how much I care about your laws. As to its humanity, I'd argue that keeping innocent bystanders safe trumps the comfort of a scumbag."

Kirurgi said nothing. Her focus was on removing the slug, which had mushroomed on impact, creating a round that was now too big for the entrance wound that it had created. Using the scalpel, she made a few careful incisions before reaching into the man's body cavity with the clamp, causing her patient to groan and flinch. A moment later, the clamp was retracted; a small tungsten

False Flag 329

lump held between its jaws. Kirurgi tossed the clamp and the slug into a surgical dish and turned to grab a syringe full of nanogel.

As soon as her eyes were off of the man, he sprang into action, grabbing the scalpel out of Kirurgi's left hand and swiped, slicing through her surgical gown and scrubs, and creating a nasty, but superficial, incision across her abdomen.

Before the man could cause more damage, Alainn was on him. She trapped the man's wrist, wrapping it up in her arm as she delivered a devastating straight punch to his jaw. The man went limp and the scalpel clattered to the floor. Alainn went to work quickly, trapping the man's arms in the restraints used to secure sick or injured prisoners. As she held his left forearm in place, she noticed a dark spot appear on the underside of his forearm, under her hand. Moving her hand aside, Alainn saw a stylized 'S' emblem. Then, as quickly as it had appeared, it vanished. "Son of a bitch," she said to herself, turning around.

Doctor Kirurgi was a mess. Although the cut wasn't deep, it was bleeding profusely, and her entire front was soaked with blood.

Frye acted quickly, grabbing a pair of surgical shears and slicing through the doctor's top, making no effort to conserve her modesty. He threw the ruined garments open and grabbed the nanogel applicator. After applying a generous amount to the wound, he tossed the applicator to Alainn, who used it to seal their prisoner's shoulder.

It was only then that Frye realized he had left the doctor topless, with her arms folded across her chest for coverage. Blushing, he grabbed a surgical gown from a drawer and handed it to her, turning around so that she could don it in privacy.

"I've got something to show you," Alainn said to Frye,

motioning him over to the table. As he walked up, he could tell that their prisoner was beginning to regain consciousness. As Alainn grabbed his forearm, the man jerked, but the restraints held him in place. He looked coldly at the woman touching him, but said nothing.

Alainn put pressure on the man's forearm, revealing the 'S' once again. As before, as soon as she let pressure off, the symbol began to fade, and in a moment, it was imperceptible.

"Our friend here is Samizdat," Frye said.

"Or he wants people to think he is," Alainn replied.

"What is Samizdat?" Doctor Kirurgi asked as she approached the table with a syringe.

"No painkillers until he talks," Alainn instructed, ignoring the doctor's question.

Kirurgi balked at the demand. "That's monstrous."

"It's also the way it is," Alainn said flatly. "He gets his medicine once he's been a good boy and told us what we want to know."

"I won't be a part of this," the doctor said defiantly.

"Then don't be," Alainn said with a shrug. "You patched him up; your work here is done." She nodded to Kirurgi's abdomen. "He obviously wasn't as worried about your well-being as you are about his. Go, get some rest; I'm sure that you could use it."

"So," Alainn began, once the doctor had left the infirmary, "You're a bit of an enigma. The ship you're on has government written all over it, and yet you bear the mark of an insurgent."

From the sweat on his brow and the slight tremor in his face and hands, Alainn could tell that the man was in considerable pain, but was trying not to let it show.

"We need to know who is aboard your ship," Frye chimed in, approaching the table with a syringe in his

False Flag   331

hand. "And you're going to tell us. Unfortunately, we don't have a lot of time, so this is going to ensure your compliance; we just don't have time for anything else." He plunged the needle into the man's arm and depressed the plunger, sending the dose of Cinolazepam into the stranger's bloodstream. "It should hit him in a few moments," he said, tossing the syringe into a waste receptacle.

As they watched, the hypnotic drug began to take effect. It was clear that the man was still in pain, but his eyes began to dilate, and his face took on a placid expression, though it was still pale and covered in sweat.

"What's your name?" Alainn asked, laying her hand gently on the man's arm.

"Weith," the man replied dreamily.

"Are you thirsty, Weith?"

The man nodded. Alainn filled a plastic cup up from the tap and brought it over. Weith gulped it down greedily before handing the empty cup back.

"Weith, we need to know about the people that you are travelling with," Alainn continued, her voice calm and soothing. "Can you tell me who is aboard your ship?"

Weith struggled with the question for a moment. It was clear that he knew he shouldn't answer, but the heavy dose of powerful hypnotic coursing through his bloodstream was too much. "Ami Runai," he replied quietly.

Alainn looked at Frye, who shrugged and shook his head. "I'll check it out," he replied quietly, before heading out of the infirmary. As he left, he could hear Alainn continue her questioning.

"We aren't monsters, Doctor," Frye told Kirurgi as he headed down the corridor. The doctor was leaning against the bulkhead, close enough to the door that she could hear what was going on. "No violence, see?"

"Tell that to his partner," the doctor shot back.

Frye shrugged. "Do you have any idea who Ami Runai is?" he asked, changing the subject.

Kirurgi thought for a moment. "The name sounds familiar, but I can't place it."

"Thanks, anyway," Frye replied, heading upstairs.

He found Cefo and Hartmann in the former's office, and while both men still seemed tense, the animosity that had existed between them appeared to have eased.

"So, Captain, as you can see, we aren't dealing with particularly nice people," Frye said as he entered the office.

"Mr. Hartmann has given me some of the details," Cefo said. "If what he says is true, it makes sense that you were less than eager to surrender yourselves to me."

Frye nodded his head. "I never would have believed the depth of the corruption that grips your government until a few months ago. It isn't easy to come to terms with."

"I can assure you that I had no idea," Cefo said.

"I don't doubt it," Frye replied. "I don't believe that the entire Union is embroiled in some kind of massive conspiracy. A wise man once told me that it's something far more insidious: a thousand minor ones vying for their own little corner of control."

"Sort of like the Hydra," Cefo replied.

Frye smiled. "I knew I liked you, Captain. Now, I'm hoping that you can help me with something. Our new friend, whose name is Weith, by the way, gave us a name: Ami Runai. Do you know it?"

Before he had even asked, he could tell that Cefo recognized the name. The marshal's visage darkened, and when he spoke, his voice was hushed, as though someone

False Flag   333

might be listening.

"Ami Runai is the deputy director of the Union's Signals Intelligence Service," Cefo said, "But it's a poorly-kept secret that it's he, not the director, that actually runs the show. The director is a figurehead; a well-connected but incompetent bureaucrat."

"So we're talking about the guy that runs the Ministry of Communications' spy division," Frye said. "I guess Wallis' involvement makes some sense now."

"And it means that the *Mullistus'* cover story is at least somewhat legit," Hartmann noted.

"So what exactly is going on?" Cefo asked.

"I don't know, but we're going to find out," Frye answered, turning back towards the door.

***

"So one of the highest-ranking spooks in the Union is a traitor?" Alainn asked, after Frye had filled her in on the captain's revelation.

"Looks like," Frye replied. "What else did you get from our friend?"

"Before he passed out, he told me that there are ten other people aboard: A crew of five, Runai, three other operatives, and two civilians."

"Who are the civilians?" Frye was sure he knew the answer, but asked anyway.

"He didn't know," Alainn replied. "Said that they kept to themselves, and no one was given any information about them. I'd say there's little doubt, though."

"Our old pals Wallis and Agera. Three operatives and a ship's crew; that's nothing. How about we go and say hello?"

"I think it would be un-neighborly not to."

Chapter Eighteen

"Of course I'm coming with you," Cefo said. "I need something solid to take back to my superiors."

Frye nodded. "We won't stop you, but realize that our number one priority is Wallis Aeron. He's going to pay us every dime he owes us, and then I'm going to take payment for Roland Kendrick and Halwyn Pryce out of his flesh."

"Understood," Cefo replied. "I do, however, hope that you will permit me the use of a sidearm."

"I think that can be allowed," Frye replied. "Wolf, take the Captain down to the armory and get him outfitted."

Hartmann looked as though he might protest, but instead he nodded. "You got it. Follow me, Captain."

"Good call," Alainn said once the two men were out of earshot. "Four guns is better than three."

"We'd better grab our gear. It's time to finish this."

***

As they walked through the station, Frye felt completely out of place in the Marshal's Service uniform that he had taken from the ship. Although it allowed them to carry their autorifles in the open through the public space, Frye was sure that at any moment, a real Marshal's Service deputy would spot them and there would be an incident before they ever made it to the *Mullistus*.

His fears proved to be unwarranted, however. The throngs of pedestrians parted before them, most of them averting their eyes, lest they draw attention to themselves.

Halfway down the gangway, each of them slipped a hand underneath their coat and withdrew a gas mask, which they slipped over their faces. At the door, Hartmann, Alainn, and Cefo stacked against the door while Frye attached the leads from his disruptor to the locking mechanism. There was a *click* as he pressed the button, and he was able to open the door to the airlock.

Frye slipped inside and hit the button to open the inner door. As soon as it slid open, Hartmann tossed a gas grenade through the two doors and into the prep room. He heard a scrambling of feet just before the grenade went off, and a few rounds whizzed harmlessly by, embedding in the station wall across the corridor from the gangway. A passerby, who was mere meters from taking one of the rounds in the head, jumped back and looked down the gangway. Seeing the three mask-clad figures at the ship's door, she let out an involuntary shriek and ran towards the hub.

"We'll have company any minute," Alainn yelled to be heard through the mask.

Frye reached around the corner and fired a few rounds blindly into the interior of the ship. Taking advantage of the suppressive fire, Hartman slipped through the outer door and leapfrogged Frye, entering the prep room, followed immediately by Alainn. Frye felt a hand clap him on the shoulder, indicating that Cefo was in place behind him.

False Flag 337

"Get the door!" Frye barked. Cefo turned and activated the outer door controls, which slid the barrier into place. Then, as Frye had instructed, he opened the panel next to the door control and reached inside, grabbing a fistful of wires and pulling them loose. Now, the only way to open the door would be manually, from the inside, or by using a breaching charge.

"Clear!" Hartmann called, indicating that the prep room was secure. Frye entered with Cefo hot on his heels, and the two men stacked up on the opposite side of the door from Hartmann and Alainn. Frye nodded to Hartmann, and each man tossed a gas grenade in opposite directions down the hallway. The lack of gunfire or coughing indicated that the corridor was empty. Frye nodded to Hartman, and the two men swung out into the corridor at a low crouch, each of them firing a quick burst down the hallway. As if the ship itself took offense to the fusillade, a klaxon sounded.

The *Mullistus* was comparable in size to the *Sentinel*, and arranged such that the entrance was two levels below the bridge. Above them would be a floor of living quarters, and above that, the bridge. Below them was a floor of engineering and facilities controls.

Hartmann took the lead, heading towards the stairwell at the stern. As he approached, he took one of the remaining grenades and tossed it down towards the Engineering deck. He started up the stairs, autorifle aimed up at the next landing. As Alainn followed him up, a quick burst from Hartmann's weapon indicated that they had company.

"One down!" the navigator called as he continued up the stairs and on to the landing. As Frye made his way up, he could tell that it was a member of the crew; he was wearing a non-descript flight suit instead of a uniform, and a Gauss pistol lay a few meters from the body; Hartmann had kicked it away from the corpse on his way down the corridor.

The remainder of the living quarters were empty; all of the cabins were carefully cleared, but no one was found.

"They're all upstairs," Alainn said at the landing. "We're going to have to go to them. Smart."

"I've got an idea," Frye said, "Follow me."

He took the lead up the next flight, but met with no resistance. "Watch the door to the bridge," he directed Hartmann, and then motioned for Alainn and Cefo to follow him aft.

The upper deck was shorter than the others; it contained the bridge and the Captain's suite, which consisted of an anteroom, a cabin, an office, and a small adjoining conference room. The outer door was closed and blocked; as soon as they attempted to breach it, they would be cut down in a hail of gunfire.

Instead of going to the door, however, Frye made his way as far along the bulkhead as he could. Right next to the outer hull, he found a bare patch of metal that would lead into the Captain's anteroom. He reached into the interior pocket of his uniform jacket and produced a small roll of plasmacord. Using part of it, he formed a small circle in the bulkhead. Using hand signals, he indicated to Alainn that she should do the same around the door. Once she had the material in place, Frye activated the cord he had placed. As soon as it was hot enough to melt through the wall, he used the barrel of his autorifle to punch the piece out.

There was a brief moment between the time the hole was knocked out and the time that the three operatives in the room noticed the breach, but it was enough. Before they could react, Frye had cut all three men down with a

False Flag 339

burst of tungsten slugs. As the last one fell, the bolt on Frye's gun locked back, indicating that his magazine was empty.

"Go!" he yelled at Alainn through his mask. His wife nodded and burned the door frame, kicking it inward and quickly clearing the room. Frye followed, drawing his sidearm.

"They have to be in here," Frye said, nodding towards the door that led into the Captain's office. He was about to repeat the trick when the door opened and a set of hands shot out.

"We are unarmed," a calm voice called out. The door swung open and Wallis Aeron stepped into the room, followed by Agera and a third man, whom Frye assumed was Ami Runai.

"Gentlemen," the third man said, "And lady, if you would call yourself that," he continued with a sneer, looking at Alainn, "please lower your weapons. As you can see, we are unarmed."

Cefo lowered his pistol, but Frye and Alainn held firm in a ready position.

"So, it's going to be that way, is it?" the man said. "Very well, if it makes you feel better. I should point out, however, that in a few minutes, this ship is going to be crawling with station security officers, who will undoubtedly be less forgiving than I am."

Frye took a moment to appraise the man through his gun sight. He was tall and thin, with hair greying around the temples. If Frye had to guess, the man was in his early fifties; young, given his position.

"What's your game, Wallis?" Alainn asked, turning to the younger man. "You don't exactly seem surprised to see us alive."

"It is unfortunate, but not a surprise," the young man

replied. "I learned that our plans failed nearly a week ago; it was only a matter of time before you tracked us down. I must ask, though: how did you escape the ship?"

"The present Agera left for us in the ventilation system had a short in it," Frye replied. "Just dumb luck, really. Fortunately, that's all you need sometimes."

"Son of a bitch," Agera said, shaking his head. "A year of preparation, and we're foiled by a loose wire. Fucking typical."

The robotic technician's statement triggered something in Frye's mind, but he decided to save it for later. "Why'd you leave us alive?" he asked instead.

"We knew that your ship could avoid being fired upon, but it's still susceptible to scanning technology."

"You wanted to make sure that there were life signs aboard," Alainn said.

"It seemed the best way to ensure that our little play felt real. It's the details, you know," Runai replied. "In retrospect, we should have just been satisfied with your corpses."

"So what now? You guys think that you can just wait for station security to show up and arrest us, and that's that?

Runai chuckled. "I don't see why not."

Frye was about to respond, but Alainn cut him off. "You're toying with us. Why?"

"To the point; I like it," Runai replied, stroking his chin. "The simple answer is that I find it amusing. The more complex answer is that, as my young comrade here pointed out, we've had nearly a week to come to terms with the failure of our primary objective and formulate a new strategy."

"And I take it that we're going to play a part in your backup plan?"

False Flag   341

"Naturally."

"There's only one problem," Frye replied, "We've got the guns." A smirk broke out over Runai's face, but he said nothing.

"Something isn't right," Alainn said.

Frye agreed. The three men were far too calm, as though they were certain that the station's security team, which was run by the Marshal's Service, would side with them over Captain Cefo. Frye still had one ace up his sleeve, however.

"So you own station security," he said as casually as possible. "It doesn't matter; any moment now our reinforcements are going to show up."

The smug grin on Runai's face remained unchanged.

Frye looked at Cefo. "They *are* coming, right?"

The captain's face turned red. "How did you know?"

"It's why we let you in to see your crew in the first place. Once you knew where we were headed, we knew that you would pass that information along. Hartmann saw you slip the note to your first officer, so we were sure that help would be coming. We just had to hope that we could convince you that we were telling the truth before they showed up.

"Any minute, this station will be swarming with Marshal's patrols," Frye continued, shifting his focus to Runai. "Until then, perhaps we should retreat to a more comfortable vantage point. To the bridge." He motioned at Runai with his pistol. "Lead the way."

Hartmann looked up as the six figures emerged from the captain's suite. His weapon was up and trained on the first three to emerge, but he relaxed once Frye appeared, his own gun at the ready.

Runai opened the door to the bridge with the biometric keypad and stepped aside. Hartmann swung around the doorway and quickly scanned the room. The three-person flight crew was sitting at their stations, but did not appear to be armed. The crew did not seem surprised at the intrusion, which did little to calm Frye's growing suspicion that once again they were behind the curve.

Come to think of it, none of the three men had appeared remotely surprised when Frye revealed that they had orchestrated the arrival of a Marshal's Service rescue party. In his mind, the plan had been undeniably clever, but the reaction had been...

There was no time for analysis now, Frye reminded himself. He looked at the ship's pilot. "Take us out to two thousand kilometers. Do it now."

The pilot looked at Runai, who nodded. A few moments later, an alarm sounded and there was a jolt as the ship broke free from its moorings. Satisfied that they were now out of the reaches of the station's security team, Frye's mind returned to the bigger picture.

"How did you know that your plan failed a week ago?" Frye asked, turning to Wallis. He knew the answer, but nonetheless he dreaded hearing it from the young physicist.

"I was informed as soon as your ship missed its appointment," Aeron replied.

"How?"

"You know how, Mr. Frye, or else I have given you far too much credit as far as intelligence is concerned."

"How many of those comm units have you produced?"

"Hundreds," Agera interrupted boastfully.

"Seven hundred sixty-three, to be exact," Wallis clarified.

"Mother fucker," Hartmann swore.

Wallis sighed heavily. "Why do you people always

False Flag   343

resort to profanity?"

"Don't worry, it's going to progress to violence in a second," the navigator growled back.

"You said that you'd been planning this for a year," Alainn said to Agera.

"It takes a while to set up a network. Fortunately the Union is good at making domestic enemies, as you well know. Samizdat was a perfect pawn for the game that we were setting up, and they were remarkably easy to infiltrate. Throw in some impressionable young university kids and some general malcontents with nowhere else to channel their rage, and pretty soon you're on the verge of a full-scale rebellion."

"And it's all the easier to control when you have instantaneous communication," Alainn said.

Runai nodded. "All we needed was a catalyst. The attack on Awdurdod was supposed to be it; what was left of the Union government – military brass, mostly – would blame domestic insurgents. We've been very careful to plant the idea that a revolt was brewing, and our communications capabilities made it seem like things were occurring simultaneously but through unrelated channels."

"And how long have we been a part of the picture?" Frye asked, not sure that he wanted the answer.

"There have been rumors surrounding the existence of a Casimir generator for a while," Agera replied, "but when the story got out that a patrol ship had been destroyed by gravitational wake in Trádáil, we knew that it was more than an urban legend."

Frye's stomach fell to his knees. They'd been pawns for months.

"We were wondering how we were going to get close to you," Agera continued, now clearly gloating, "but your little vendetta made that easy. Getting Roland assigned to a case that would lead him to you was simple enough, and given his background, it wasn't a stretch to believe that he would find your cause compelling."

"Stop," Frye said, but his voice faltered, making it sound pleading rather than commanding.

"My part was obvious," Wallis interjected, "but since I'm not sure exactly how much of this you understand, I'll elaborate. I invited Roland to visit, knowing that he had nowhere else to go. When he arrived, I pretended that my comm technology was new and that my life was in danger. Roland's first thought was to call you for help." Wallis paused for a second. "I assume that his absence here means that he did not survive your escape attempt."

"Fuck you," Frye seethed, his had beginning to tremble on the grip of his pistol. Wallis grimaced at the epithet, but said nothing further.

"Are you really going to shoot a room full of unarmed men?" Runai asked. "You've caught us, and as you made clear, you have reinforcements inbound who will, no doubt, arrest us on the good captain's orders."

Frye's heart began to race, and his palm was sweating profusely against the grip of his pistol. He glanced to his right, towards where Alainn was standing. Her weapon was at the ready, but she was expressionless. Glancing to his right, he could tell that Hartmann had murder in his eyes.

"He's right," Captain Cefo said. "These men will be placed in Marshal's Service custody and will be afforded proper due process."

"Bullshit," Frye replied. "He's already admitted that they have some kind of backup plan. He's trying to muddy the waters."

"I won't be a party to murder," Cefo said firmly.

"What murder? He's got something planned, and

False Flag 345

people are going to die."

"And your answer is more bloodshed? Listen to yourself. Lower your weapons – we will wait for reinforcements to arrive and we will handle this properly. If you will recall, that was our deal."

A bead of sweat rolled down Frye's forehead. He'd fantasized about killing Wallis dozens of times over the last week; all it would take was a slight squeeze of the trigger…

"You need my help, Mr. Frye," Cefo said. "If you expect to have it, then this is the requirement."

Frye glanced at Alainn, who gave an almost imperceptible nod. Simultaneously, they lowered their weapons. Hartmann appeared to hesitate for another moment before following suit.

"This is gonna bite us in the ass, Volya," he warned.

"You're probably right, but as the good captain points out, we don't have much of a choice. We need his help."

"Since we've got a little down time," Alainn said, returning her focus to Runai, "I have to ask: what exactly are you hoping to accomplish?"

"I've spent my life in signals intelligence," Runai replied after a brief pause. "What most people don't realize is that every communication, every broadcast, every inane thought posted to a datanet board; all of it is intercepted, analyzed, catalogued, and stored. We have algorithms that check for signs of mental illness, for signs of widespread unrest – hell, we even analyze for signs that a viral epidemic is imminent, so that the Ministry of Health can be properly prepared. It takes an immense amount of data to maintain an empire the size of the Union, and someone has to man the controls; keep the information moving. Right now, that person is me.

"I've learned something during my tenure as the Union's chief information gatekeeper," Runai continued,

"And it's something that I'm sure will not surprise you one bit: the Union is a bureaucratic, inefficient mess. There are countless factions and alliances; ambitious individuals with no real skill save for the ability to build coalitions that give themselves power. The government and the megacorps are, at this point, nearly indistinguishable from each other. The government runs the economy while corporations and organized labor write the legislation. All of the players gain influence and fortune, while the empire itself crumbles."

"I can't say I find anything disagreeable there," Alainn replied.

Runai nodded. "I figured as much. The problem is that while those in government and high-level executive positions are skilled at channeling their greed and ambition, the lower classes, nearly all of whom have the same desires, simply aren't. Whether it is from a lack of intelligence, laziness, or simply bad luck, these people can only advance their station in life by getting those at the top to steal for them."

"Again, you'll get no disagreement from me."

"No, I don't suppose so. Where you and I disagree is in the solution. While you seem to naively believe that leaving people alone to fend for themselves is a viable option, I recognize the truth: people must be ruled. As a group, they are too stupid and lazy to manage on their own."

"My experience says otherwise," Alainn said.

"Give it time," Runai said dismissively. "In any case, the Union is a case study in why people cannot be trusted to govern themselves. The only conclusion is that they must be governed by those more capable. It is the only way to ensure a stable society."

"And there it is," Alainn interjected. "I'm going to assume that you're going to be the one running things?"

False Flag

347

"Why not? Between the three of us," at this point he gestured to Wallis and Agera, "we have an average IQ nearly double that of the average citizen."

"So you're doing this for their own good, of course."

"Of course."

"And the billions you were going to murder? And the billions more who would die in the ensuing war?"

"Unfortunate," Runai replied, with what seemed to be genuine remorse. "But necessary. Our models indicate that the Union is overpopulated. We have to reduce the head count in order to reach the ideal population density. Besides, if history has taught us anything, it's that great strides forward in societal evolution always come at a cost."

"If history has taught us anything," Alainn shot back, "it's that tyrants will always use the promise of utopia for their own personal enrichment."

"You think I'm after fortune?" Runai spat. "I guess I should have known. How could a capitalist like you understand anything but money? How pedestrian, how gauche; I talk about creating a golden age of civilization, led by the greatest living minds in the galaxy, and you think that it's about money."

"I'd rather be a capitalist than a technocrat," Alainn replied. "You talk like people need your brilliance in order to live correctly, but all the while, you plot to steal and murder in order to overthrow a cabal of thieves and killers. I hate to break it to you, but it's all been done before. Your award-winning original screenplay is nothing but a tired and blood-soaked reboot."

"And what about you two," Frye said, indicating Wallis and Agera. "All that talk about being anarchists was just bullshit?"

"More or less," Agera replied.

348   *The Union Chronicles*

"I never claimed to be an anarchist," Wallis corrected. "I told you that I have no use for the Union's government, and believe that I am too intelligent to be ruled. Both of those things are true."

"Sir," one of the flight crew interrupted, "We've got a couple of Marshal's Service patrol craft approaching the station."

"Is it our guests?" Runai asked.

"It's the *UMS Guardian* and the *UMS Protectorate*," the man replied.

"How far out are they?"

"They're docking now."

"I guess it's time to head back in," Frye said.

Runai just smiled.

Frye turned to the pilot. "Take us back." The pilot looked at Runai.

"As you said, there's a backup plan," the intelligence officer told Frye.

Hartmann's rifle shot back up. "Do as he says."

Runai nodded to the pilot. "Do it." The man keyed a command into the console.

Frye relaxed a bit, but after a moment, he realized that the ship wasn't moving. "What's going on?"

Before anyone could reply, the ship shuddered. It was not the kind of motion that Frye associated with controlled flight.

"As I mentioned, we have developed unbelievably accurate algorithms," Runai replied. "The ideal scenario involved a direct act of domestic terrorism against the capital. Had our plan for Awdurdod succeeded, we could have assured the end of the existing Union government and reduced the population to an acceptable level, but without unnecessary casualties. The war would have been brutal, but short.

False Flag 349

"It isn't the only way, however. Once a certain threshold of civil unrest has been achieved, a smaller incident can have the necessary effect. If, for example, a violent confrontation were to occur between the Marshal's Service and a group of terrorists in a commercially-important system, we could reach a tipping point. With most of the command structure intact, the war is bound to be longer and bloodier, but the outcome will be just the same."

"You blew up the station," Alainn said breathlessly.

"And your reinforcements," Runai replied. "The official story will be that there was an attempted attack against Awdurdod, which was foiled by the tireless efforts of the Marshal's service. The perpetrators were tracked here and, when cornered, they, meaning you, chose to blow up the station, taking out the pursuing deputies, several thousand civilians, and billions of credits worth of infrastructure in the process.

"The official story, unfortunately, will contain a number of holes and inconsistencies, which will lead many to believe that some kind of cover-up has occurred. The anti-government elements that we have fostered will insist that the whole thing is some kind of nefarious conspiracy. In the end, the groundwork that we have laid will make armed conflict inevitable."

"Which means that the only way to stop it is to kill you where you stand," Frye said.

Runai held his hand up. "I'm afraid that you are mistaken. At this point, the war will happen even if we are dead. In fact, we are the only ones who can bring things to a satisfactory conclusion. Wallis?"

"That is correct," the physicist said. "The Samizdat network has reached a critical point. The necessary inputs have already been provided, and events will unfold with or without our direction. Our next move will occur when it is time to orchestrate the end of hostilities."

"Agera, what are the projections?"

"Hostilities will persist for approximately four years," the technician replied. "Most of the casualties will be confined to major cities and the spaceports. Our estimates put Union-allied casualties at approximately thirty-six million; rebel deaths will approach 1.2 billion. In the end, logistics will be the Union's downfall; there's a lot of space out there to cover, and really all the rebellion has to do is not lose. Eventually, the costs will be too high for the Union to continue holding on to systems."

"And if we're not around to help coordinate things?"

"It's a little bit less predictable, but without coordination and communication between rebel factions, things get messier. Our models predict six to nine years of fighting, with total casualties on the order of ten billion – two to three billion as the result of combat, and seven due to famine and supply shortages."

"You see, by killing us, you will actually ensure that more people die," Runai said. "Furthermore, as Wallis pointed out, we're done – no one else dies at our hands. Killing us will not save a single life. As a matter of fact, we plan on dropping you off unharmed, so self-defense isn't even justified.

"You have a choice, Mr. Frye: you can walk away, and in so doing bring about the downfall of the Union and the liberation of billions. Or, you can kill us, guaranteeing that billions die unnecessarily."

"And in the end, you come in, take control, and lead your subjects into a golden age," Frye said.

"Your choice," Runai said, smirking.

"We have to let him go," Cefo said quietly.

"What?" Alainn spat.

False Flag 351

"Do you doubt his analysis?" the captain asked.

"Not a bit," Alainn replied. "I'm convinced that these psychopaths are capable of everything that they say."

"Then we go with the option that saves the most lives," Cefo said.

"And condemns the rest to life in a technocracy designed by men with the blood of billions on their hands?"

"We all know the truth," Cefo replied. "We can find a way to bring these men to justice, but killing them now is cold-blooded murder."

"The king is dead, long live the king," Frye said. "I would have expected as much from a Union stooge."

"The choice is yours, Mr. Frye," Runai said. "Are you really willing to let billions die in order to get revenge?"

The muscles in Frye's neck tightened and his hands flexed. He could hear his heartbeat in his ears, and a bead of sweat ran down his temple.

"Fuck it," he said as he raised his Gauss pistol and squeezed the trigger. The five-millimeter slug from his pistol tore through Ami Runai's skull, leaving a red mist on the bulkhead wall. Both Wallis and Agera's eyes went wide, the white contrasting with the blood spatter that peppered their faces.

"Did your models predict that?" Frye asked Agera. The younger man didn't respond. "I guess not," Frye said, squeezing the trigger again and dropping the technician next to his co-conspirator.

"This one lives," he said, motioning to Wallis. "We were hired to take him to Saiorse, so that's where he's going. Something tells me Halwyn Pryce's family will have a few things to discuss with him. Get some restraints."

"What about them?" Hartmann asked, motioning to the crew.

"I think that we're more than capable of flying the ship," Frye replied. "Throw them out of the airlock."

"That's murder!" Cefo cried.

"It's justice," Frye responded calmly.

"You executed those two men, and now you're going to kill the crew? You've already condemned billions of people to death; how is what you are doing any different than what these men were doing?"

"I'm getting tired of the moral equivalence bullshit. If you don't know the difference, then I'm afraid that we have nothing to discuss."

"I can't allow this. These men should be arrested and tried, not murdered."

"Tried? Courts exist to find the truth. Is there any doubt what happened here?"

"No, but..."

"Then there's no need for a trial. Wolf, relieve Captain Cefo of his sidearm. Captain, you will be confined to quarters until we can drop you off somewhere safe. Alainn?"

"You three, with me," Alainn said, motioning to the crew with her rifle. None of the men moved. Before Frye could say anything, Alainn dispatched all three with her weapon.

"You will have to answer for this," Cefo seethed.

"And you know where to find me," Frye replied. "But something tells me that you're going to have your hands full for a while. Let's get this mess cleaned up - I'm ready to go home."

Epilogue

As fighting enters its second year, the Planetary Union is facing a problem that may eclipse even the civil war that has engulfed it: famine. Shipping embargoes imposed by government forces have made the movement of supplies extremely difficult, if not impossible, and planets with limited food production capabilities are reportedly rationing food, while others are reporting shortages of medical equipment and other vital supplies. Union officials hope that this will help break the stalemate that has come to characterize this conflict, with Union forces controlling space, and the rebellion laying claim to nearly every planetary surface.

"I suppose that's where we come in," Alainn said, entering the room just as the newscast ended. Frye was already in his flight suit, having a cup of coffee.

"Are they assembled?" Frye asked. The dark circles under his eyes had gotten worse, Alainn noted. She hadn't seen him in nearly a week – all of his time had been spent on mission prep in orbit.

"They're ready," Alainn replied. "Are you?"

Frye sighed. "I don't know, but we have to try."

"You aren't responsible for this, Volya."

"I know," he replied with a slight smile. "Pulling that trigger didn't cause this, and I'd do it again. I'm not trying to atone; it's just the right thing to do."

It was Alainn's turn to smile. "Then let's do it."

***

The briefing room was packed as Frye approached the lectern. He synched his tablet to the viewscreen on the front wall, and chart appeared. "Ladies and gentlemen," Frye began, "Welcome to Operation Aliman. As you know, the civil war in the Union has turned into a humanitarian crisis the likes of which the galaxy hasn't seen in over a thousand years. In an attempt to force submission, the Planetary Union Navy has blockaded more than a hundred systems, causing desperate shortages in food and medical supplies among many of the Union's poorest systems.

"That's where we come in. Through the generous private funding of millions of citizens throughout Saiorse and other independent systems, we have managed to retrofit eighteen freighters with power and propulsion systems that will allow us to bypass the blockades and deliver the necessary supplies to these systems.

"Additionally, all of the craft have been outfitted with the latest in communications gear, which will allow us to communicate instantaneously with each other, as well as the command organization here in Saiorse..."

Frye's presentation continued, but Alainn wasn't listening. She knew the details inside and out. Instead, she was focused on the faces in the crowd – the seventy-two pilots and crew who had volunteered for the job of running blockades in order to deliver aid to the Union's least wanted.

False Flag 355

Suddenly, she did a double-take as she scanned the back row. *It can't be*, she thought to herself as her eyes went back over the tall figure seated against the far wall.

As the presentation ended and the crews began to file out and to their waiting ships, Alainn slipped out quietly. A few of the captains had approached Frye, looking for more details, or to ask questions that they didn't want to ask in the open forum.

"Did you really think that I wouldn't notice you sitting there?" She had walked up behind the tall figure from the back, waiting until he was nearly at the gangway to his ship, and no one else was around.

Kellan Odaran turned around and smiled. "I'm actually surprised that it took you that long," he said. "Didn't you vet the crews at all?"

"I should kill you where you stand," Alainn replied, ignoring the jab.

"And I wouldn't blame you a bit," Odaran replied seriously. "I'm almost expecting it. But won't that leave you short a pilot?"

"We can find another," Alainn responded.

"Another person willing to volunteer to fly into a war zone without getting paid? You know that the Union will treat us the same way as they're treating the rebels, right?"

"It's the right thing to do," Alainn said, "Which leaves the question: Why are you here?"

"Like you said, it's the right thing," Odaran replied.

"But you don't care about the right thing," Alainn replied.

"Fair enough. Look, it's a little bit complicated. Can I offer you a drink while we catch up?"

***

"Believe it or not, I've always cared for you, Alainn," Odaran said, knocking his glass back. "At least as much as I can care about anyone other than myself."

"You sold me out."

"Without a second thought," Odaran replied, refilling his glass. "That kid offered me so much money that I had trouble keeping a straight face.

"And then I found myself unable to sleep," he continued. "It wasn't so bad at first, but after a while, every time I closed my eyes, I saw your face. It nearly drove me insane. I spent months trying to figure out what happened to you; it became an obsession. I just knew that if I saw that you were OK, I could get some sleep.

"When the war broke out, I should have been thrilled," Odaran said, knocking the second glass back. "Think of the money to be made running guns into a war zone. But I couldn't focus on anything other than finding you.

"Finally, I did. I heard about this project, and somehow I knew that you would be involved. So I used a fake name and credentials to sign up, and finally, an hour ago, my quest ended."

"So now you'll be able to sleep?"

Odaran smiled. "I guess we'll see."

"And our little project?"

"I signed on, and I'll do my part. I'm a hell of a smuggler, Alainn. You'd be a fool to kill me now, when I could help you so much."

"Until you get bored, steal the ship, and start running guns to whichever side pays you more."

Odaran shrugged. "Maybe. It sounds like something I'd do. And maybe I will find a way to make a little cash out of this – would that be such a terrible thing?"

"This is a humanitarian mission."

False Flag 357

"And capitalism and humanitarianism can't coexist?"

"I really should kill you."

"Like I said, I wouldn't blame you a bit. But maybe I'm not quite the sociopath that you remember. Maybe the last year of my life has been a journey. Maybe I'm becoming a decent human being after all."

"I guess we'll see," Alainn replied, draining her glass and standing up to leave. "Thanks for the drink; you've always got the good stuff."

"You don't have to leave, you know," Odaran replied suggestively.

Alainn rolled her eyes. "Maybe you're becoming human, but you've still got a long way to go before you get to decent." Without another word, she took her leave.

"Where have you been?" Frye asked as Alainn joined him on the bridge of the *Mullistus*, which had undergone a retrofit similar to that of the *Veritas*.

Alainn filled him in on her encounter with Odaran, leaving out the sexual proposition the smuggler had worked in.

Frye shook his head in disbelief. "Well, I suppose anything is possible."

"A wise man once told me that everyone makes mistakes; the good ones make it right," Alainn replied.

"And when they don't, it's up to the rest of us to fix the mess," Frye said.

"Everything ready to go?" Alainn asked.

"Five by five," Frye replied.

"Then I guess it's back off into the black."

Made in the USA
San Bernardino, CA
21 November 2014